THE TECHNOLOGY OF GOD
A QUEST FOR THE
SECRET OF CREATION

THE TECHNOLOGY OF GOD
A QUEST FOR THE
SECRET OF CREATION

BY

ALEYA ANNATON

THE TECHNOLOGY OF GOD
A Quest For The Secret Of Creation

By

ALEYA ANNATON

ISBN 978-1-48014-881-9

Printed in the United States of America

FOREWORD

My spiritual journey has spanned over 30 years and many of my profound experiences are detailed in the storyline of this novel. I lived my early life as an atheist, believing only in the world I could see, touch, feel, smell and hear. I have come to learn that nothing could be further from the truth. This is a story of a scientist and a mystic who come together to discover some profound truths about reality that I have discovered.

While the novel stands alone as a thriller and love story, it provides insight into a profound shift in our understanding of creation that is now getting mainstream acceptance as we learn more about how things behave at the quantum level. It expresses some of the theories of Nassim Haramein who has taken quantum physics to another level. I believe civilization is at a point of profound change, both technologically and spiritually, and that this new understanding of reality may be the catalyst for transformations in our civilization that will be as profound as the discovery of fire.

I have been on a journey of intense study to more fully understand quantum physics and ancient wisdom and how they are intertwined. During this journey I have experienced wonders and miracles I would never have believed were possible in my early life. Many of these experiences are expressed in the story.

I want to thank Alan Farrand and Elizabeth Rauscher for their editing. I also want to thank Jamie Martin for her advice and encouragement. I am indebted to Connie Fisher for her work on the cover art and my website www.thetechnologyofgod.com. I would also like to thank Dr. Michael Hyson for his efforts reviewing the scientific information from Nassim Haramein's work, and Holly Ady of The Resonance Project Foundation for all her work on my behalf.

- Aleya Annaton

CHAPTER 1

The resonance chamber burst into flames with a deafening explosion, shattering the lab's contents. The blast sent shards of crystal and viscous fluid hurtling through the air. Alex was thrown across the room by the ferocity of the discharge. He struggled to his feet and raised his arm to shield his eyes from the thick black smoke. He pulled his lab coat over his mouth and gasped for air, trying to breathe through the choking chemicals. The inferno was everywhere and about to engulf him.

Alex closed his eyes. *This is how it ends,* he thought, in both terror and surrender as he braced for the torture of a death by fire.

He knew his brain would register the agonizing pain of his body being cooked alive before succumbing to death. Fire is one of the worst ways to die, as the brain is one of the last organs to shut down. Suddenly there was no heat. He opened his eyes to find himself not in his lab, but somewhere else entirely. Alex looked around in bewilderment. "Where am I? Am I dead? Was that real?"

His body started to singe as the flames reappeared, and he snapped back into the inferno. The alarm began to blare as the sprinkler system rained down clouds of flame retardant, dousing the fire and sending more plumes of smoke into the air. Alex now faced a new form of death as he choked on the noxious fumes, unable to breathe. As terror surged through him, he caught the red glow of the exit sign out of the corner of his stinging, tear soaked eye and staggered to the heavy metal doors. He threw his body against the horizontal bar, allowing his sheer weight to compensate for his lack of strength. The door opened and Alex escaped into the safety of the hallway.

The door slammed shut behind him as he staggered down the hall. He fell back against the wall and slid down into a fetal position on the concrete floor. His lab coat was soaked with blood but he didn't think he had been hurt or that anything had been broken. *No significant wounds,* he thought as he picked some shards of glass out of his forearms.

Jesus! Did I do it? Alex sat, his head spinning, trying to make sense of what had just happened. He started to lose consciousness when the wailing sirens of fire trucks startled him back to reality. The door at the end of the long hallway burst open and two men rushed in carrying hoses and tanks on their backs.

"Hey man, are you all right?" asked one of the men dressed in white HazMat suits. "Joe, take a look at this guy," he said as he waved over a third man who followed in behind them.

"Where's the source of the fire?" the medic asked Alex.

"In there." Alex pointed to the metal doors.

The two men in white HazMat suits pulled open the heavy doors and ventured into the smoke.

"What happened here?" asked Joe, the tall young medic peering into Alex's eyes with a small flashlight.

"The resonance chamber exploded," mumbled Alex. His hands were trembling and his head was pounding with pain. "I'm all right and the sprinkler system stopped the fire, I think."

Alex was bruised and bloodied, but his personal condition was not on his mind. What happened in those brief seconds after the blast was all he could think of. What was it? What did it mean? Had he been right? Had he been correct after all the naysayers and skeptics? The effect certainly was what he had predicted, but feeling it, seeing it … was hard to comprehend. This was an Earth-shaking discovery that would change everything!

The medic wrapped a blood pressure cuff around his arm and slipped an oxygen mask over his face. Another medic, shorter and stocky, appeared wheeling a gurney.

"No!" shouted Alex. "I don't have time to go to the hospital!"

"It doesn't look like anything is broken and your vitals are okay," said Joe. "But you have to get checked out. You might have internal bleeding or a concussion, and you've inhaled some nasty chemicals from what it smells like out here. At any rate, it's also the law."

"No, I can't deal with that now. I have to call Sydney," said Alex, waving off the two men and fumbling around in his pockets for his phone but finding them empty.

"Do you have a phone I could use?"

"Do you want me to call him for you?" asked Joe offering his phone to Alex.

"No, Sydney's a woman."

"Your wife? I can call her for you man."

"No ... well ... yes ... she's my partner er, colleague," blurted Alex, realizing he had just offered too much information. A personal relationship like the one he had with Sydney was not tolerated, and could get them into trouble with the authorities. *Thank God, Sydney was not at the Kona lab with him, but at a conference in Honolulu.* He didn't mind his own injuries, but the thought of something happening to her was unbearable. It was also a stroke of luck that they had hidden the backups in the house the night before, as the dreaded Office of Ethical Behavior police would soon be swarming his lab. It was imperative that the OEB not find out about their work.

"I can call her for you and have her meet you at the hospital," said Joe

"No, let me call her, if you don't mind." Alex wanted to collapse into the comfort of her arms and tell her what had happened in the lab. He thought again what amazing luck that Sydney had made backups the night before and taken them to the house safe. They were the only documentation of the set of frequencies that just produced the most remarkable result.

The two medics lifted Alex onto the gurney.

"Okay, we're going to get you out of here," said the stocky man wheeling him into the cool night air. "Tell the

HazMat guys we're going, Joe."

"Hey, where are they? They should be out of there by now," said Joe as he opened the heavy doors that sealed off the lab. "Holy Christ!" He fell backward letting the doors slam shut. "What the hell is going on in there?" The color in Joe's face had drained to a chalky white as he turned back looking at Alex, his eyes as large as saucers.

Sydney awakened startled from a deep sleep. She was soaked in sweat and her heart was racing. It was a dream … no, a nightmare! She had been in the middle of a room engulfed in flames and felt like she had been about to die! It seemed so real she got up to get a glass of water, when the phone started ringing.

"What time is it?" She glanced at the clock on the hotel nightstand and saw it was after three in the morning. *Oh God, something horrible has happened!* She grabbed the phone. When the holographic image appeared, her heart skipped a beat at the sight of Alex's ashen and bloodied face. Since arriving in Honolulu, Sydney had a feeling she shouldn't have left him to come to this conference, and she hadn't followed her intuition. Now he was in trouble and she wasn't there to help.

Alex's handsome face still excited her. She loved his dark eyes and sculpted features. But now she was filled with dread at the sight of his injuries.

"Alex, my God what's happened to you? Are you all right?"

"I think I'm okay, just a little shaken," he answered. "The resonance chamber exploded at the lab, but I think I did it, Sydney. Something happened. It might have just been a hallucination, but I think I opened a doorway."

As Alex told her more of the explosion and what he had seen, her nightmare flashed through her mind and she realized it had not been a dream at all. Alex had been right. She was altered. She had seen it.

"I just can't know for sure what really happened until I run the experiment again. It won't mean anything to science unless we can document and duplicate the result," said Alex, sighing at the thought.

"When we've got solid scientific proof, we can publish and let the world know," said Sydney, her eyes staring off to the side as she started to contemplate the interest their work would generate from the wrong places. "We'll need to be careful."

Alex sighed. "I know. But now that the lab and the chamber have been destroyed, where will we be able to rerun the experiments?"

"What about Brian Sheppard?" asked Sydney. "He has a lab and most of what we need to rebuild the resonance chamber. He also has a fabricator, so we can manufacture most of the parts right there. We have all the virtual designs in the computer backups that we need to rebuild the chamber. We'll be able to get it up and running quickly. And didn't you tell me that you had made an early prototype and left it with him at U of M?"

"Yes, but it would be better if we could do it on our own. We don't want too many people to know what we're doing here, especially with this kind of outcome!"

"If we can't trust Brian, there's no one we can trust. After all, we've both known him for years, Alex!"

Alex and Brian had met twenty years before at the University of Michigan, when Alex made the first presentation of his theory to the mainstream physics community. That was the beginning of their love-hate relationship. Brian Sheppard was one of the foremost particle physicists leading the team searching for the Higgs boson, and Alex's theory completely negated his work. But they both liked the intellectual sparring and had become close friends. Brian had let Alex use the facilities at the University of Michigan sixteen years before, and Sydney had been Brian's colleague on the faculty many years later.

"His expertise will be extremely helpful to us. Brian will be flabbergasted by what has happened tonight," said Sydney. She was confident Brian would take time out from whatever he was working on to be involved, considering the result that was within their grasp.

"How many new frequencies did you run since I took the last backups?" she asked.

"You should have all but the last twenty or so. I don't think I had gone that far by the time of the explosion, and the specs for the resonator are on the backups," said Alex trying to keep his voice as low as possible so as not to be overheard.

"Thank God!" Sydney let out a sigh of relief.

"The copies at the house are everything that we have left then. Make backups and erase the computer," said Alex.

"There are going to be OEB cops all over the place soon, if they're not there already." Alex glanced at the two medics who were sitting in front of the thick glass that separated him from the driver's area. Now he spoke in a whisper. "Don't come to the hospital until you've secured the work. Remember to do it the way we planned."

"All right, honey. Which hospital are they taking you to?"

"The one off of Queen Kaahumanu Road near Captain Cook."

"Okay. I'll be there as soon as I can. I'll call Brian and arrange everything, and when you're released, we can meet him in Ann Arbor."

"We'd better not talk any longer," said Alex. "For all we know the OEB may be monitoring this conversation, though I'm not using my own phone," he said trying to see if the men upfront were paying any attention to him. They didn't appear to be.

Ever since the United States had become the United Christian States of America, or UCSA, controlled by the ultra fundamentalist right wing of American politics, the Office of Ethical Behavior or *OEB* were the appointed morality police. One had to be careful of any relationship that wasn't a conventional marriage. Out of wedlock sex was an offence that would mean certain expulsion from one's career and even jail time. Alex and Sydney had taken extreme measures to keep their relationship private.

"Yes, we can't be too careful. Take care, Alex. I'll be there as soon as I can." Sydney hung up the phone and fell back onto her bed. She felt completely immobilized with so many questions running through her head. *Had he really succeeded, or did he have a hallucination because of the blast? She knew he was not always prone to adhering to the strictest scientific method, and his unusual encounters could have played a part. We can't reach any definitive conclusions until we duplicate it following a double-blind protocol. If Alex had truly succeeded, the world would not be able to ignore his work any longer and it would change everything currently understood about the fundamental nature of reality,* she thought.

Alex winced at the scream of the siren as he lay on the gurney looking at the mess of tubes and instruments hanging from the ceiling of the ambulance. This was the last thing he wanted to do right now. His mind raced as he tried to reconstruct what he had been doing just before the explosion. *Could he recreate it? Would the backups work? Did they save the frequency that created the effect?* He had run at least twenty different variations today and only backed up some of them. His psyche fought a battle between elation and despair. Was the work he had labored over all his adult life finally yielding the results he sought, or was everything destroyed in the explosion?

As the ambulance skimmed above the maglev rails, the Hawaiian scenery flew by at 150 miles per hour. The blur sent him back to when he and Sydney first began their collaboration and when they fell in love.

    It had been an exciting journey set in motion two years before. The thoughts of how he met Sydney filled his mind's eye with the deep blue of the Polynesian water, and he felt the excitement of their encounter when she arrived in Hawaii for the first time.

CHAPTER 2
TWO YEARS EARLIER

Alex waited in the open-air pavilion that was the Kona airport for Sydney's plane to arrive. He had been waiting months for her to be able to take a leave of absence from the University of Michigan where she had been a Professor of Mathematics with a strong physics background. He had been searching for a long time for a mathematician who could help him publish his theory, without much success, until now. It had been a risky move for an academic to part with the mainstream scientific community. Joining his team to work on a radical theory that challenged much of what was accepted as the nature of reality could potentially end one's career. So he was excited to have found someone of Sydney's caliber to collaborate with him.

It had been actually Sydney who contacted Alex, after reading his article on the infinite nature of matter. She told him she had been working on the conundrum of infinities in mathematics for years, and was so enthusiastic about his theory when they spoke that he hired her on the spot.

As the passengers began to disembark, Alex caught sight of Sydney on the tarmac, her long wavy blond hair blowing in the stream of the jet engine. He waved to her as she made her way through the crowd. Seeing Sydney in person took his breath away. He had only seen her from the neck up in their vidphone conversations. She had been always wearing horn-rimmed glasses with her hair up in a bun that he thought was rather severe. But now long locks were flowing down her shoulders like a vision of a Botticelli fresco. As she came closer, he could see she had a long lean athletic figure and skin as smooth as porcelain. Without her glasses, her almond shaped green eyes were intoxicating to him. He could hardly contain his attraction to her, and this was something for which he had been not prepared. It put a new problematic dimension to their impending partnership.

"Welcome to Hawaii," he said, grabbing her bags.

"Thank you. It's so good to finally meet you in person."

"Same here," he replied noticing her entrancing smile.

"This weather is wonderful," said Sydney, with her arms stretched out in a gleeful embrace of the warm air. "What a change from the snow storm I left in Ann Arbor. I wasn't even sure I'd be able to get out today."

"Yes, I don't miss those Michigan winters either. You'll love it here," said Alex as he led her across the street to his car and began loading her bags in the trunk.

"How long have you been living here?"

"Almost ten years now, and I haven't regretted it for a minute, although you need to get off the island every once in a while to avoid island fever."

"Oh I don't know. I don't think I'd ever want to leave this place," said Sydney looking at the lush foliage and brightly colored flowers that grew everywhere.

"I'm so glad you were able to get here in time for my presentation."

"Me too. It was touch and go there with the snow. I had to leave a few days earlier than my Department Head wanted me to as well. How many physicists do you have coming?"

"As far as I know, around twenty-five have signed up. I consider this a major coup to have been able to get so many mainstream scientists to hear my so-called *radical theory*," said Alex making quote signs with his fingers and letting out a chortle.

"At least we have tonight to get acquainted and get you situated before the presentation begins tomorrow afternoon. Are you hungry? Would you like to get something to eat in town before we go to the hotel?"

18

"Sure, that sounds great. My flight from Detroit had was late and I didn't have a chance to eat anything during my layover in L.A."

"I know a nice place right on the water. Town is only a few minutes from here." Alex put the car in gear and smiled at the beautiful woman that was to be his new partner … perhaps in more ways than one.

Alex and Sydney were seated at a table for two that overlooked the harbor where the cruise ships came in. The sun was low and the sky was turning shades of plum, casting undulations of color on the gently lapping water. As they sat waiting to order, Sydney noticed how Alex's chestnut colored eyes twinkled in the waning sunlight. He was far more handsome than she had expected. Vidphone transmissions often don't do a person justice. She was surprised to find he was as fit as an athlete, with a tall, finely sculpted and wiry body … considering he was forty-six. His face was darkly tanned with high cheekbones and she wondered if his ethnicity might include some American Indian. He did not have short hair as she had thought, but rather it was long, jet-black, and pulled back in a ponytail. It gave him a Bohemian look that she hadn't noticed during their vidphone conversations.

She found herself strangely entranced and excited in his presence. This was a feeling she did not want to have in her life right now. Since her painful breakup with Mark over two years ago, she had put all thoughts of men aside. She had simply turned off. It was a skill she honed to protect herself from the pain, and it had served her well so far. Now, this feeling … this stirring, was unsettling. She tried to shift her focus. She was determined not to allow herself to feel something for a man ... not now and not anytime soon.

Still, Alex had a charisma about him. He had an engaging smile and intense eyes that when fixed on her made her feel like the only person on the planet. She shook her head and her long curls swept across her shoulders. It was all too dangerous personally, professionally and politically, so she redoubled her efforts to shut out the attraction.

Dinner out in a public restaurant was the first opportunity Alex had to talk with Sydney without fear of their conversation being monitored by the OEB police force. He was anxious to approach her on what was a forbidden subject under the tyrannical rule of the Office of Ethical Behavior. It was also an issue most scientists weren't willing to discuss publically. He needed to know how open Sydney would be to the true nature of his quest, and he had to be careful not to alienate her before she could come to these conclusions herself.

He looked into her intoxicating green eyes, trying to think of a way to broach the prohibited topic.

"It's great to have you on board. I had an extremely difficult time finding a mathematician with your background in physics willing to consider my theory. I can't tell you how many encounters I had with mainstream physicists that ended with them running out of the room screaming."

Sydney laughed. "Welcome to the wonderful world of scientific rivalry. I've been arguing with my colleagues for years about the way they've been dealing with infinities in mathematical equations, so I know what you mean."

"Tell me about it," said Alex rolling his eyes.

"Really, I don't understand how they can keep ignoring and renormalizing the infinities that are always showing up in the math."

"Renormalization, ha! That's what they tried to do to me in school!" Alex laughed and slapped his hand against his forehead. "Making arbitrary cut-offs to get rid of infinities in the math to make their equations work has kept mainstream science from understanding that infinities are fundamental to creation!"

"Your theory is quite a radical shift from the current theories. Everybody is doing particle physics, looking for the smallest 'God' particle. But your theory says matter can be divided infinitely, and that we need to look at the infinities and how the universe creates boundaries around the infinite space to make physical matter. How did you ever come to this?" asked Sydney.

Alex smiled sheepishly. *Perhaps this story would open the door to discuss the matter on his mind.*

"I've been pondering the concept of dimensions as far back as I can remember. In many ways, I've always felt that I've been interacting with other realities."

"Really, how so?" Sydney looked taken aback by his statement, and Alex wasn't sure how much he should reveal about his strange journey of discovery.

"Oh, you know, I was always day dreaming. I had been wondering what reality is, even when I was as young as eight or nine years old and everything they were teaching in school and church didn't seem to make much sense."

"I can relate to that," said Sydney, taking a bite of bread.

"There was one pivotal day when I had a profound experience after my first geometry lesson. I always had a lot of trouble in school because I wasn't interested in anything they were trying to teach me. I usually took a seat at the back of the class as close to the door as possible so I could make a quick escape," said Alex with an impish grin.

Sydney laughed. "You know Einstein didn't do well in school either when he was young." Alex smiled, flattered to be compared to the great icon and his personal hero. He cleared his throat and continued:

"One day the teacher announced that we were going to talk about dimensions and I got excited for the first time about something they were teaching at school. Finally, they were going to talk about a subject that was interesting to me. When the teacher got up to the black board, he drew a dot and said that this was zero dimension and it didn't exist and I got so ... so ... so ... disappointed!"

Sydney almost choked on her bread, she laughed so hard.

"I knew right then and there that I was going to flunk this class because I could see that dot on the board. So how could it not exist? Then the teacher said, if you take a bunch of these dots and string them together you have a line and that's dimension one ... and it too does not exist. If you take four of these non-existent lines and put them together you get a plane, and that's dimension two ... but that also does not exist.

Then the teacher said something incredible to me. If you take six of these non-existent two-dimensional planes and form a cube, now miraculously you have existence! All I could think was how can you get existence out of six non-existent planes? What we really have is non-existence to the fourth! I don't care if you take ten thousand non-existent dimensions, you can't get existence out of non-existence."

"I never thought of it that way. But doesn't a plane exist? Isn't there something that can be said to be two dimensional?"

"When you start talking about flat space, you have to ask: how flat? And you can't answer that question without adding volume."

"When you put it that way ..."

"This principle is at the heart of my theory, for it's a fundamental flaw in our thinking of mathematical constructs. Almost all of our science is conceived of in two-dimensional space and there's no such thing in reality. We think of a comic book as two-dimensional. Yet, even the ink on a comic book is three-dimensional if you examine it at the microscopic level. The ink has height, weight, and depth. But most of our mathematics and concepts in physics are conceived in two dimensions.

There's no such thing as flat space, and so we have to stop conceiving of physical reality as two-dimensional and creating mathematics that refers to things that way."

Sydney now moved forward in her seat, her chin propped up on her hands, elbows on the table, listening intently to him.

"Anyway, while taking the bus home from school that day … and it was a really long ride since I'd been thrown out of all the closer schools … which a friend of mine always says is how I *furthered* my education " Sydney and Alex laughed.

"Anyway, I had been sitting there trying to picture what dimensions really were. I knew at a gut level that what the teacher just said had been wrong. I started to imagine myself leaving my body and traveling into the sky above the bus until the bus appeared like a tiny dot below. I kept flying higher and higher until the entire continent had become a dot. Then the Earth itself receded in size as I soared farther out of the solar system. As I visualized myself nearing Pluto, the sun had become a tiny speck of light in the vast distance and the Earth had long since vanished from my view.

I pictured myself flying farther out in space until I could see the galaxy below me like a neon lit pinwheel. Then the galaxy began to shrink as I flew past it into the cosmos. Finally, it too had become a tiny dot of light. I continued in my mind's eye out into space and watched as even galactic clusters receded to tiny dots. Then I stopped. I started to imagine myself flying back into the galaxy, into the solar system, into the Earth's atmosphere, and into my body.

But my journey did not stop there. I decided to shrink in size until I was small enough to enter the pores of my skin. As I became smaller, what at first appeared as tiny dots grew and unfolded to reveal entire new worlds with billions of new tiny dots. First, I imagined traveling into a cell and saw a world of activity and billions of tiny dots that were atoms. Then I found myself diving into the atoms, which expanded into solar system-like configurations, as I shrank in size. As I became smaller, I realized that with each leap in scale another world – that first appeared as a tiny dot – expanded to reveal whole worlds within.

I understood at that moment that everything in existence was just different-sized dots that can be divided infinitely and that scale and density were important to reality. I knew from then on what I would do with my life. I needed to understand what matter was and how it came into existence."

"That's a pretty profound epiphany for a kid." Sydney's green eyes seemed enchanted as he continued telling his story.

"Anyway I remember getting home all excited to tell my mother about this revelation. She was thrilled that I was finally interested in school. But when I told her that the teacher had been wrong and I had figured out that everything was a dot and everything was infinite, she was so happy. She looked at me like only an Italian mother can and said, 'If you put that down on your test you're going to flunk that class, and you know I've been working for eight hours and I don't feel so infinite.' That's when I had another revelation because I realized she had a point. Why is it that if everything is infinite – things just don't collapse into each other? I didn't know it then, but I had been asking one of most debated questions in physics. How can infinities be compatible with finite structures?"

"Yes, exactly!" Sydney's face lit up. "That's the very question I've been struggling with for years! I keep seeing that infinities are always cropping up in the math. I mean take pi or the phi ratio for instance. These are fundamental constants that must be used to describe almost everything in the universe and they're infinite numbers!"

"Exactly. It took me many years to get a handle on this but I realized that the challenge was to find out how the universe creates boundaries around the infinities to create the material world, and if I understood that I would have the key to creation. Eventually I came to understand that the answer could be found in geometry and that this new way of looking at matter had profound spiritual implications."

This was the forbidden subject, and Alex leaned back in his seat watching for Sydney's reaction.

"Really?" Sydney looked perplexed. "You don't often hear physicists talking about spirituality."

Alex pursed his lips. He had to go slowly with Sydney and take care not to lose his credibility with her.

"If the universe uses geometry to create physical reality it would explain the concept of sacred geometry," said Alex hoping she could relate to his explanation.

"But isn't that just people putting a spiritual spin on what is, in actuality, a mechanical function of nature?" asked Sydney.

Alex could see that Sydney was not on a spiritual path and this disappointed him. He considered that scientists were almost as bad as religious fundamentalists in their outright rejection of anything not in line with their dogma when it came to spiritual concepts. But his theory brought science and spirituality together, and she would have to understand how he arrived at his conclusions to see the spiritual implications of his work.

"Think of it this way," said Alex. "If all matter can be divided to infinity, it means we are living in an infinite or open system, not a closed one."

Sydney took a sip of wine and Alex poured the red Merlot into his glass and took a sip as well. "In infinity, every point is the center. That means you center your own universe and I center my own universe."

Sydney nodded as if unconvinced. Clearly, Sydney did not comprehend the underlying meaning of his theory. It seemed to him that everyone who came through the formal education system had their brains stuck in a neat little box. It was too early to press the subject further, so he decided to shift the conversation to something more scientific.

"If all matter can be divided to infinity, it implies an infinitely dense energy field or a black hole at the center of every particle of matter in the universe. It would mean that there is an infinite field of energy underlying all of our physical reality. But first I needed to solve the incongruity of infinities and finite boundaries. I worked on it for years and finally realized that the geometry of the double-bounded tetrahedron was the key."

"You mean a six-pointed star?" asked Sydney, leaning back to let the waitress serve her grilled tuna.

"Yes, but the geometry that must drive the creation of

matter has to be able to grow in fractals and be in perfect equilibrium."

"How so?" asked Sydney, taking a bite of her dinner.

"Well if it weren't in perfect geometric equilibrium, cancelling each side out, we would be able to see it, and we can't."

"See what?" asked Sydney, now looking confused.

"The underlying energy field. While I know the geometry of the field has to be based on this tetrahedral geometry, it has to be able to expand and contract infinitely in stable geometric fractals. I still don't have the perfect shape of equilibrium. We have to find that perfect geometry before my theory can be complete," said Alex, waving the waiter over. "Are you ready for another glass of wine?"

"Absolutely," said Sydney. The waiter brought over another bottle, showed the label to Alex and pulled out the cork, pouring a small amount for Alex to taste.

"This is fine," he said to the waiter. Then he turned to Sydney. "I thought we'd do it up right on your first day in Kona. I think it's appropriate that we toast our new collaboration." He lifted his glass and smiled. They clicked their glasses and Alex looked deeply into Sydney's green eyes. *She is truly a rare beauty,* he thought. A surge went through him. It was a feeling he knew all too well. It was a sign that something profound, something of immense importance was about to take place. Then it hit him as if he were awakening from a deep sleep and remembering the wisps of a fading dream. He remembered their deep connection. He remembered their destiny.

By the time Alex dropped Sydney off at her hotel it was after 10:00 p.m. It had been a long day and she was now over-tired. She found herself tossing and turning, unable to sleep. She was excited about the prospect of working with Alex, and their conversation replayed in her mind. She had gotten a number of ideas from their discussion and wanted to get them into her computer before she forgot, but had been too tired and a little too drunk to do it. She would have to get some sleep first. One thing they talked about stood out and she couldn't wrap her mind around it. She never really thought of the infinities she had been finding in her math as having spiritual significance. Even if there is an infinite field of energy underlying physical reality, she didn't quite grasp how that had spiritual implications. She needed to think about it.

She put her computer on her nightstand and gazed around her room. It had only three walls with the outside being an open balcony, and a warm breeze wafted over her bed. They had told her at the desk that open-air rooms were common in Hawaii in areas that tended to get little rain. Her bed was made up with white linens and a fluffy white duvet cover. There was white mosquito netting pulled back around the tall iron bedposts. She felt as if she were enveloped in a cloud.

Sydney lay in her bed staring out at the brilliant conflagration of stars splashed across the black Hawaiian sky and marveled at the glory of the universe. There were so many galaxies, with so many suns and so many worlds in the vastness of space. Even our sun, a million times larger than the Earth, is but a grain of sand against the swath of glimmering lights that dot the heavens. It looked so peaceful and permanent, and yet she knew the cosmos is in constant and volatile motion.

In fact, it was more like a deadly pinball machine with galactic collisions and exploding stars. And the Earth is far from safe in this colossal game. She knew that humankind would have to learn how to leave the planet if humans are to survive for the long run. Planets are just too unstable, so a civilization needs to be able to travel to other worlds to endure. Earth has already experienced several extinction events and there will surely be another eventually. Just one deadly sun flare could suck up the atmosphere, not to mention the possibility of a hit by a comet or an asteroid! This scenario had always caused Sydney anxiety, and had been one of the main reasons she wanted to work with Alex so much. He claimed that his work would result in uncovering a new energy source and even anti-gravitational drive, which she believed was of utmost importance.

Sydney found it hard to still her mind. She felt as if she were drifting in and out of sleep as thoughts continued to swirl through her head. The night was quiet except for the sound of rustling fabric and chirping frogs. She found herself focusing on what looked like a star, but brighter than the rest. As she stared at it, she noticed that it appeared to be growing more luminous. *That's odd.* Then it seemed to burst, increasing at least a hundred times in size ... but just for a second. Her eyes grew wide in amazement. *What in the world could that be?* She continued staring at the light in the sky until her eyelids became heavy and she lost consciousness.

Her dreams were often colorful and intense but this time it was different ... almost real. She saw the outline of a tall Being, that seemed more shadow than substance, coming towards her. Sydney froze. Her first reaction was sheer fear that tore down her spine like a hot poker. It seemed to be at least seven feet tall and had a large round head. She couldn't really make out a face and she was petrified as it approached her. She knew she must be dreaming, but it felt real. She tried to calm herself. *It's just a dream ... just a dream. Wake up damn it, wake up!* But try as she might, she remained locked in position unable to move, unable to wake herself.

As the figure came closer, she could see that it looked humanoid but she could not determine its gender. Something about it seemed non-threatening, and Sydney calmed down. The Being's hand had only four fingers and was outstretched with an object in its palm. It was now just inches from her and Sydney could see that it was holding a sphere with a tetrahedral shape inside that looked like a three-dimensional six-pointed star. The Being let the object float in front of Sydney's eyes and smiled at her. Sydney could now see that the Being had large almond-shaped eyes and two slits for a nose.

"This is the key," Sydney heard it say, though its small mouth did not move at all. The sphere morphed into a many-sided tetrahedral structure that was square from her vantage point.

"There are clues in crop circles. I will make one tonight, and you will begin to understand" she heard it say. Then with a wave of its hand the Being showed Sydney a geometric design. It had multiple spheres, each containing an up and down tetrahedral design in smaller and smaller fractals of the same geometry.

Then the structure within the ball morphed into a much more complex geometric array, with many more tetrahedrons. It then started spinning, and turned into a shape that looked like two stacked doughnuts, a double torus, spinning with small beads spiraling back and forth between the two donut shapes. Sydney looked up at the Being, her brow furrowed, not understanding the significance of the object.

"Sixty-four," said the Being. "This number is the key." Then, the Being simply vanished into thin air.

When Sydney opened her eyes, she gasped. *What just happened? This had been no simple dream!* She was sure it had been a real experience, but she had to confirm it. She would do what the Being told her to do. She would look for the crop circle. If it was there, it would verify that this had been a visitation, not a dream. Sydney grabbed for her laptop and wrote down everything she could remember from her dream. Then she pulled a notebook out of her nightstand drawer and drew the crop circle.

She had never taken crop circles seriously and always dismissed the phenomenon as a hoax perpetrated by pranksters. She figured they were made by crazy artists stomping out their statements in the fields. That had been about as far as this kind of speculation had gone with Sydney until now. If she found this crop circle, it would prove she had had a visitation, not a crazy dream.

She started to go online, but then hesitated and closed her computer. Often people going to these kinds of websites were monitored and even arrested by the Brotherhood. The OEB believed that any interest in paranormal or UFO activity was demonic and crop circles would probably fit into that category. She decided to go into town and use a public access Internet connection that couldn't be traced back to her. This was tricky, but she knew how to do it. She would go into town during one of the breaks. For now, she had to keep this to herself.

CHAPTER 3

Two Steps Beach was one of Alex's favorite places on the Big Island of Hawaii. He put in long hours at his lab and kayaking was a refuge from his hectic days. He loved to paddle out to where the dolphins came to rest in the bay in the early morning, and he thought it would be a great place to take Sydney before the conference.

Alex was nervous about making his presentation to so many prominent physicists. He needed to gain their support, though he knew it would be difficult to bring them around to his radical view of reality. It meant that they would have to give up their ideas on mainstream quantum physics, and that had been a hard nut to crack. Still, he believed he was right and that his work, once accepted, would radically advance technology. In doing so it would completely transform human civilization because spiritual change that would also happen - though this could not be brought up with his audience, or even with Sydney. Not yet.

"It's so beautiful here," gasped Sydney as she looked out onto the placid bay. "Thanks for bringing me here. It's great to be able to experience the island before we go into the presentation." She helped Alex un-strap the kayak from the roof of his car.

"I thought it would be cruel and unusual punishment to not let you get a little sun and surf before we go into a darkened conference room for the afternoon," he said with a twinkle in his eye. "This will give us a few hours to enjoy the day before we have to get to work. If we're lucky, the dolphins will be out this morning. There's no better way to be initiated into Hawaiian life than a swim with our spinner dolphins. You can change over there in the tented area," said Alex pointing past the parking lot.

"That's okay; I put my bathing suit on under my clothes." Sydney pulled off her blouse and stepped out of her shorts, revealing her milky white skin and toned body.

"Whoa! You'd better put some sun screen on that skin!" Alex reached in his duffle bag and tossed her a tube of lotion. "It's only thirty-six SPF. With that white skin you might need fifty!"

"It's okay. I actually tan quickly and rarely burn," she replied squirting a dab of the cream onto her hand.

"Here, let me get your back." Alex gently applied the lotion and realized he had never touched such smooth, soft skin.

"Thanks," she said with her green eyes twinkling in the sunlight.

Alex lowered the kayak into the water off the rocky ledge and secured their gear to the boat. He got in first and steadied the kayak for Sydney as she climbed down off the ledge and took her seat behind him. As they paddled out through the coral reef, he spotted a dolphin about two hundred yards away doing its classic jump and spin as it frolicked in the water.

"They're here, look!" he said pointing toward the dolphin. "We can get a little closer to them, but so many people seek out dolphins that Hawaii has declared it illegal to approach them. It carries a $10,000 fine. So we have to stay at a good distance from them and wait to see if they come to us."

After a few minutes passed, he heard a loud splash as five dolphins rose in the air in perfect unison right in front of them. They made a high arc, dove into the water and went under the boat. Then they surfaced and started to swim in a circle around them, their dorsal fins skimming the gently rippling waves. Alex could see their intelligent eyes watching them as they passed by.

They dove under the surface. Again, the dolphins jumped in front of them and disappeared below the kayak. Alex tossed some snorkel gear over to Sydney.

"They're really being attentive today. Why don't you

jump in the water? I'll hold the kayak."

Sydney pulled on the fins, put on the mask, and slid her long legs over the side of the kayak while Alex put his weight on the other side for balance as she slipped overboard. Sydney swam with strong athletic arms away from the boat.

For a time, the dolphins seemed to have disappeared below the water. Then Alex saw two of them surface and swim straight for Sydney. They were on a direct collision course, then suddenly they parted, one going to her left and one to her right. Alex paddled a little closer to watch the elegant creatures jumping up in unison and swimming around her.

The watery dance seemed to go on for a long time. This was highly unusual. Alex had hoped that the dolphins would come to Sydney but he hadn't expected this much attention. This was a spiritual attunement, and when he looked at Sydney, he realized she was getting it. Her face had a look of pure ecstasy as the magnificent creatures moved around her in their ritual of initiation. Alex gazed knowingly at the spectacle. After an unusually long time, the dolphins swam away, and Sydney headed back to the kayak.

"That was the most amazing experience I've ever had," she said grabbing hold of the strap on the kayak and pulling herself onboard.

"Wow, you have really good upper body strength."

"Yes, that's from my climbing."

"You're a climber?"

"It's the one sport I truly love. Unfortunately, there aren't any mountains to climb in Michigan, so I only get a chance to do it when I travel. I keep in shape doing martial arts, so I have a lot of upper body strength."

"Excuse me, Miss Kung Fu mountain climber for underestimating you," said Alex laughing. "I'd better watch myself around you."

"Yes, you'd better," she replied with a wide grin.

"I've never seen the dolphins pay so much attention to someone," said Alex steadying the kayak.

"I feel high. It's like I've been put in a state of pure

love!" Sydney had a look of joy on her face.

"Welcome to Hawaii. You've just been dolphinized."

"Dolphinized? What's that?" she asked.

"It's what you just felt. They do something to you. Sort of makes you high. The police had to impose a fine on people chasing after the dolphins because people get addicted to the sensation and just crave more. If you're lucky, the dolphins approach you. That's why I love to come down here in the morning when I need to relax."

"I can see what you mean. But it's more than being high. It's love ... pure love."

Alex smiled at her. "Yes, I know."

Alex and Sydney headed back to the hotel where Sydney had been staying and where the conference was to be held later in the day. Alex's feeling that Sydney would be someone special in his life had been confirmed by her dolphin experience. He knew that dolphins were highly intuitive and did not behave this way around many people. He believed that everything had consciousness – even things not considered alive like rocks and minerals. So he was not surprised that beings like dolphins, that some believe have even higher consciousness than humans, would have such an effect on her.

Since Alex had been a young boy he lived in other dimensions, experiencing phenomena that most would call paranormal. He had a rational, scientific mind, but he could not deny his experiences. He was convinced there had to be more to reality than what people can detect with their five senses. His quest for answers had driven his physics research, where he had been searching for a scientific explanation for the phenomena he experienced in his life. Alex was on track to figuring out just that. But the knowledge did not come to him solely through study. It came to him from somewhere else, and he needed Sydney to be open to receiving such inspirations too. With her expertise, he believed he would find the answers to the most profound questions of existence: why life exists ... how consciousness arises ... and perhaps the very nature of creation.

Sydney looked over at Alex who seemed deep in thought as he drove up the winding road towards the hotel. She wasn't ready to tell him about her experience the night before. It could very well have been just a dream but she was curious to see if he saw any significance in her vision.

"Is there some importance to the number sixty-four in your theory?" asked Sydney.

Alex looked at her. "Sixty-four? Why do you want to know?"

"I don't know. I just have a feeling it might be significant to your work."

"Well, there are sixty-four codons on a DNA strand" he answered. "Sixty-four is the number of possible combinations in the I Ching grid of reality, and Hindus believe in Saraswarti, the Goddess of Sixty-four Arts."

"And there were sixty-four Runes in the Gaelic tradition," offered Sydney.

"Hey, I thought you were asking."

"I am," she said. "It's a brain teaser."

"Okay," said Alex. "Here's another one. It takes sixty-four cells before a living organism begins to differentiate itself."

"Do you think it has any significance for our work?"

asked Sydney.

"Well, it could. What are you thinking?"

"I'll tell you later after I've had time to do a little research. It's just a hunch." Sydney decided to change the subject. "I have to admit I'm surprised that you were able to get so many mainstream scientists to come to your event."

"I think the fact that it's in Hawaii helped my cause a great deal. There was a little method to my madness scheduling it in the middle of winter," said Alex, giving Sydney a wink. "I've been talking with most of them on a one-on-one basis for a long time, trying to gain their support for my theory. Most of those who are coming are also working on cutting-edge theories and are rebelling against the prevailing quantum theory. It had been a huge confirmation of my ideas when they were able to smash the Higgs Boson in two last years. That got me a lot of attention as I've been saying for years that they're never going to find a fundamental particle."

"The whole scientific community was upset when the Higgs didn't turn out to be the God particle they've been looking for," agreed Sydney.

"And the smallest particle will never be found, if I'm right. I believe you can keep dividing matter into smaller and smaller particles for eternity! Eventually, they will come to understand that matter can be divided infinitely! When they realize that there's a black hole at the center of all particles, perhaps then mainstream science will embrace my theory that black holes are the source of gravity, not the so called graviton particle."

"It's amazing," replied Sydney. "With all our scientific knowledge we still don't have an explanation for gravity, and the graviton particle has never been observed."

"Exactly. We have been inventing particles to make our math work for such a long time that everyone just accepts it. The scientific community ignores the infinities that keep occurring in the math and the three-dimensionality of reality… and this has kept us from a deeper understanding of creation. I believe there is so much more to reality than what we can observe with our limited senses. It's like we've been insects who skim the surface of the water unaware of the world below, unaware of a much deeper reality underlying everything," said Alex.

CHAPTER 4

The conference was being held at the Island Hotel, a lovely, but older complex right on the ocean. Like most hotels in Hawaii, it had an open-air pavilion with lush flowering plants everywhere. The entire lobby, restaurant and bar area were completely open to panoramic views of the water and volcanic shoreline.

Alex had dropped Sydney off at the hotel so that she could clean up, and he went back to his house to get dressed for the occasion. Sydney donned a conservative suit, pulled her hair up in a twist and put on her glasses. She thought it appropriate, given the astute colleagues she would be meeting, though totally inappropriate for the atmosphere of the Island. She checked her makeup in the bathroom mirror and pleased with the professional look she had conjured up, headed downstairs for the conference room.

Sydney walked by the formal restaurant with its white linen tablecloths and carved mahogany furniture, and went to check out the pool area and the bar that overlooked the rocky shore. She leaned over the wrought iron railing and could see six sea turtles basking in the late morning sun. Several people sat at the bar with colorful drinks topped with little umbrellas and cherry and pineapple garnish.

The large pool area was filled with white chaise lounges and blue market umbrellas that fluttered in the light breeze. There were several blue and white striped canvas tents around the pool. They offered welcome shelter from the bright sun beating down from the cloudless azure sky. Another bar, in the middle of the pool with a faux waterfall behind it, was offering drinks to swimmers, while three young native men with colorful shirts played soft Hawaiian music. Sydney noticed a large hot tub, and vowed she would find time to take advantage of it.

The vegetation everywhere on the spacious grounds was lush green with splashes of red, pink and lavender blossoms. Sydney, with her skirt blowing in the light breeze, was getting hot in the suit she was wearing. She started to resent the charade one had to put on at these scientific settings. She had fought all her professional life to be taken seriously by her peers. Being beautiful, people often tended to dismiss her intellect. Dressing this way was for her one of the necessary evils of the game.

A woman who looked to be in her late thirties, dressed in a colorful sarong, opened the large carved teak doors of the conference room and handed Sydney a folder filled with handouts for the presentation. There were about thirty men and women there, most of them middle aged or older. She recognized one of them. She had worked with him in the Physics Department at the University of Michigan.

"Brian Sheppard?" she said, tapping the distinguished looking Professor on the shoulder.

He turned around. "Dr. Stewart! Nice to see you. I didn't know you were coming to this."

"And I thought your field was particle physics, Dr. Sheppard. I'm surprised that you're here as well. Isn't this topic a huge departure for you?" asked Sydney teasingly.

"That's right. And that's why I'm here. Harmon's been telling me for years that I was never going to find the smallest fundamental particle and I didn't believe him. I had been sure it was the Higgs Boson. But as he predicted would happen, we were able to split the Higgs within a year. So I'm ready to listen now. Maybe he's right and we can throw all our super colliders away because matter can be divided to infinity. That's seven hundred billion dollars down the drain; enough money to stretch thousand dollar bills end to end around the Earth three times! And it could all be a total waste!"

"I didn't know that you knew Dr. Harmon," said Sydney.

"We know each other all right," said Brian raising his left eyebrow. "We've been friends for a long time. More like "frenemies" since he has always been such a naysayer about the mainstream quantum theory, and my work in particular. I gave him some space and access to my lab at U of M. several years before your time. Unfortunately, the authorities got wind of it and he had to leave. He came to Hawaii to continue his research. I had been intrigued with his theory, as it was the opposite of what I had been doing, and we were in a sort of race to prove each other wrong. After all these years I'm starting to think he may be the one who had it right after all; so here I am."

The woman in the sarong now stood at the podium. "I want to welcome you and ask that you take your seats. We're about to begin." The room quieted as everyone sat down.

"Thank you all so much for coming. I'm Dr. Susan Handy of the Institute of Alternative Physics, and we are honored to be hosting this important presentation on Dr. Harmon's theory."

Well maybe the dress code is different here on the Island after all, thought Sydney.

"I know it's a burden to leave the snow and come to Hawaii for a conference," said Dr. Handy sarcastically, and the crowd laughed. "As you are aware, Dr. Harmon has a theory that changes everything we understand about physics, our universe and our reality. This is a complete paradigm shift! We have observed for decades that the universe is expanding. However, it is doing so at such a rate that scientists have calculated that we must be missing ninety-six percent of the matter necessary to cause the galaxies to be moving apart at the speed we are observing. This means we do not know what makes up ninety-six percent of the universe! So our current physics theories are based on knowledge of only four percent of what we know must be out there. Let's face it, if we only know what four percent of the universe is, we haven't been working with a very good model." With this, a buzz went around the room.

"Isn't it the dark matter and dark energy that's driving that expansion?" asked Dr. Moody, a thin scientist in his mid-fifties

41

with a quiet demeanor and long graying hair that hung down to his shoulders.

"This is exactly the issue. Our current model assumes that there must be some particles or bits of matter called dark energy and dark matter causing the expansion of the universe. But these particles are completely theoretical. We've never seen one of these made up particles and we think that if we build bigger and bigger colliders, eventually we will find them. We don't know what dark matter and dark energy are ... but it must be dark because we can't see or measure it," she said sarcastically. The room broke out in laughter at this remark.

"Dr. Harmon has a completely different explanation. It's time for new thinking about the nature of reality, and how the universe creates physical matter. Dr. Harmon has done just that, and we are excited to put forth this information to you during our presentation. Many have been quick to criticize and discount his work. You are the brave souls on the leading edge, and we are deeply grateful for your willingness to consider this different concept of reality. So ladies and gentlemen, please welcome Dr. Alex Harmon."

As the room applauded, Alex walked up to the podium.

"Thank you so much for coming. During this presentation, I'm going to demonstrate that with some subtle shifts in the way we look at how the universe creates matter, we can open up a completely new level of understanding of creation and spur a giant leap in technology for mankind. If I'm right, and I believe that I am, the technology coming out of this new understanding will provide unlimited energy, unlimited natural resources, and anti-gravitational drive that will take us to the stars and much more!"

"Space travel? I thought we were talking about an energy source," said a thin, stern looking woman in the second row, with a disconcerted look on her face.

"My theory is based on the idea that black holes are intrinsic to the creation of matter, and when we are talking about black holes, we are talking about gravity. I believe a new understanding of black holes, or singularities, will lead to a breakthrough in controlling gravity. Conventional propulsion is too slow to be an effective means of reaching other solar systems. But with anti-gravitational drive we could open controlled black holes and fly through them allowing us to travel almost instantaneously throughout the galaxies," replied Alex. "I think you will start to see how this could be possible as you come to understand my theory."

"We keep thinking there is no way to travel efficiently to the stars, but we are thinking narrowly. Remember, as Dr. Handy mentioned, our current understanding of reality is based on only four percent of the total picture. In my research, I have uncovered some flaws in our basic understanding of reality that have been carried down through our educational system for literally thousands of years. These flaws have prevented us from discovering the other ninety-six percent of the universe in which we live.

"It begins with Euclid and our model of dimensions." Alex touched the virtual screen and an image appeared of the dot, the line and the cube.

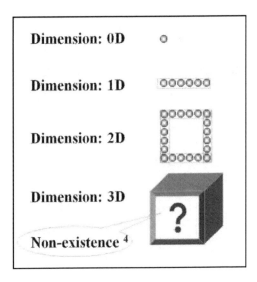

Alex explained the absurdity of the Euclidean concept of getting existence out of six non-existent planes.

"This concept is at the heart of my theory, for it's a fundamental flaw in our thinking of mathematical constructs. There's no such thing as one or two dimensions! There's no such thing as flat space and so we have to stop conceiving of physical reality as a two-dimensional flat plane and creating mathematics that refers to things that way. It logically follows ... if everything is three-dimensional, then everything in the physical world, all matter, can be divided ... divided to infinity. What that means is that every atom, every subatomic particle goes to infinite density, or an infinite amount of mass squeezed into an infinitesimally small dot; and that, my friends, is the definition of a black hole! In fact, we are living in a black hole, and everything in the physical universe is just a different-sized black hole ... including you!"

The room was dead silent. He had captured his audience's attention. He had also captured the attention of an Office of Ethical Behavior surveillance agent, Martin Scorely.

CHAPTER 5

John Croft, the Grand Master of the Office of Ethical Behavior, gazed out his office window that had a direct view of the Capitol building in had in Washington, D.C. From there, he could watch the mere puppets that scurried around the Hill, including the President he brought to power, who had no real effect that wasn't sanctioned by him. As the leader of the most powerful organization in America, Croft had been more effective than the Catholic Church in creating and enforcing religious law. And unlike the Vatican, Croft had at his disposal the firepower of the entire United Christian States of America's armed forces, not to mention his own OEB morality police: the Brotherhood.

Croft's rise to unrivaled power had been swift, and accomplished through a series of deftly crafted political maneuvers that had blindsided a naive and easily manipulated American public. First, the OEB had been able to engineer a complete collapse of the economic system under the reign of the previous administration. They had siphoned trillions of taxpayer dollars into the hands of private banking interests and other corporate entities aligned with them, and had created so much debt that they had all but obliterated the value of the dollar.

All entitlement programs such as Social Security and Medicare were discontinued, and the balance of wealth in America had all but wiped out the middle class and the ability of most citizens to stand up to the OEB. The devaluation of the dollar led to the creation of a monetary system that implanted cashless chips in everyone's arm. Croft's implants prevented anyone from buying anything that cost more than $200 without using the chip. If a citizen did not follow the OEB's dictates, the agency could simply turn off their chip, effectively thrusting the person into poverty. The economic hardships imposed on the non-believers served to silence and control them. Croft's ultra-extreme wing of the religious fundamentalist right had been able to capture the Presidency and a two-thirds majority in both the House and the Senate. They did this by preying on the fears of a gullible population who watched the body count rise day after day in an endless Muslim war that had already spanned an entire generation.

Croft had found his opportunity to grab power during the Iran incursions that ignited an all-out religious war that had been festering as the U.S. continued to exert its dominance in the Middle East. The OEB had been formed originally to consolidate the many agencies dealing with intelligence, and was first named the Office of Executive Bilateral-Intelligence. However, it had really been created to put the administration in control of all intelligence activities – especially the CIA.

Croft, appointed to head the new agency, had a specific agenda that was unknown to the public. His vision was to create a religious state, enforce the rule of "God" in America, and to keep a watchful eye on, and silence, anyone who did not accept his ideology.

America had succumbed to a minority that was highly organized, and controlled all of the nation's media outlets, allowing the OEB to push its agenda on a complacent American public. For Croft, it was the universe as it should be. It had been a twenty-year plan to reshape the American government into a religious state; one that could exert complete control over its people, and enforce "God's" law ... one nation, under God, as Croft believed it was meant to be.

Martin Scorely was short and slight with thinning hair, a prominent, pointy nose and skin that had not been out in the sun for a very long time. He wore a bow tie and looked the part of a scientist as he sat quietly in the audience taking copious notes. He had signed in as a physicist from Georgia Tech, but he had never even been to Georgia. At the break, he had gone outside to place a call, as he was to do throughout the conference.

Dr. Handy took the microphone. "I know it's killing you all to be in here while Hawaii is out there." The audience groaned. "So tomorrow we'll start at 2:00 p.m. so you can have a chance to take in the Island."

Great! thought Sydney. *This will give me some time to go into town in the morning and use a public Internet connection to check out the crop circle in my dream.*

Alex took the podium again.

"So if there's no smallest particle, and if all matter divides into infinity, it means that space or the vacuum is not empty at all, but filled with infinitely dense matter that is so dense that light cannot escape its gravitational pull, and so is a black hole. It means that there is a field we cannot measure attached to every particle of matter in the physical universe."

"Then how can we have physical things? Why doesn't everything just collapse into infinity?" asked Dr. Alfred Barlow, a man with thick curly black hair in his mid-forties.

"That's an excellent question, and one I asked myself early in my research," answered Alex. "I believe the answer is that the universe creates boundary conditions around the infinity of the vacuum, and that the boundary conditions are what we call physical reality."

"But aren't infinities and finite boundaries a contradiction in terms?" asked Dr. Barlow.

"I've found that finite boundaries and infinities are indeed compatible," replied Alex. "For instance, you can consider your body a boundary condition around infinity within you."

Dr. Barlow looked incredulous. "How is that possible?"

"I found the answer is geometry." Alex clicked on the next slide. "The universe makes spheres. It makes suns, planets, and such. However, a sphere isn't a stable geometry. I realized there had to be an underlying geometry that gives the sphere stability. I used an equilateral triangle, which is the most stable geometric shape, but as everything has a polarized pair - male and female, positive and negative charge, and so forth, I realized there had to be another opposing triangle. When I added that, I got one of the most ancient symbols in Western Civilization: the six-pointed star, the Star of David, or the Seal of Solomon.

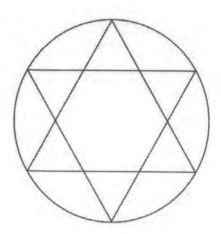

"In fact, this symbol is found in many cultures that even predate the Hebrews and the Star of David. Using this geometry, I can draw more spheres around each of the points, and continue to do that within each of the new six-pointed stars. If I could zoom in and create more circles around the new vectors, my computer could continue to do this to infinity for as long as it had power.

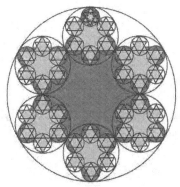

"This is how it is possible to have finite boundaries around infinities. Matter stays together because you can never, *ever*, exceed the original boundary that you set for yourself. Within the boundary condition, matter goes to infinity. However, the original boundary condition cannot be exceeded. In this way, you can start to see an entirely new way of thinking of dimensions as concentric geometric fractals. It's a much more elegant and simple explanation of the universe than the extremely complicated mathematics that goes into explaining quantum physics theories.

"When we thought the sun revolved around the Earth, we had to create a convoluted model with all sorts of loops and retrogrades to match the observations. However, when we realized it was the Earth that moved around the sun, the model became simple and elegant. The same thing has happened with my model – where everything, from the largest objects we can see to the smallest subatomic particles, operates on the same simple repeating fractal system."

Martin Scorely looked around the room. The audience seemed to be listening intently. But he was annoyed. *All the understanding we need of the universe is in the Bible. This is all blasphemy,* he thought.

Alex continued. "Infinity has been a concept we, as a scientific community, have been unwilling to embrace. We have renormalized it, or given it an arbitrary cut-off. This doesn't seem so unreasonable at the small end, where the numbers are so infinitesimally tiny, such as the Planck's length. It's much harder to ignore infinities at the high end. Perhaps that's why they call them the very scientific term: "*nasty*" infinities." Alex used his fingers to put quote signs around the word nasty." He shook his head at the sheer absurdity of the term, and the audience giggled.

"We all know infinities are everywhere in math. So what I'm proposing today is that we stop ignoring the infinities and embrace them as central to creation; and when we do this, we open up a whole new view of reality."

How could anything but God be central to creation? thought Martin writing down a note to himself with several exclamation points.

Alex continued: "Empty space or the vacuum isn't empty at all, but rather filled with an infinite amount of energy in a universe that has two sides. The expansive side is what we call reality and the hidden contracted side or black hole. This *other side* represents most of what is in the universe. In fact, the matter that we call reality is just a minuscule part of the whole. Think of it this way. Physical reality is made of atoms. But what is an atom really?"

"A proton, neutron and electron," shouted the corpulent Dr. Hanes, sitting in the front row and rolling his eyes behind his thick black-rimmed glasses. "If you don't know that, you need to go back to physics 101!"

The audience snickered.

"Not really," answered Alex, ignoring the rude remark. "An atom is 99.999999999 percent empty space! So if our reality is made mostly of space or vacuum, and matter is just the little fluctuation in the field, maybe we should stop looking at the matter and start looking at the space to understand our reality. Maybe the key to creation is how the space divides to create these tiny fluctuations ... not the matter!"

"Consider this: The relative distance between a neutron

and a proton in a single atom, taking into account its size, is about the same as our sun to the nearest star - 4.2 light years or almost twenty-five trillion miles! That means we're dealing with a lot of space or vacuum making up most of our physical world. If space isn't empty, but rather filled with energy as I believe it is, and we could harness just a tiny bit of that energy, we would have enough power to last an eternity!"

Martin Scorely left the room to make a phone call.

Alex clicked on the next slide.

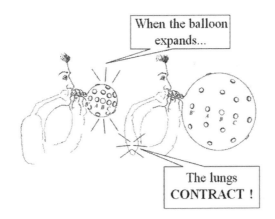

Illustration courtesy of "Gravitation" by Misner, Thorne, and Wheeler

"This is a page out of *Gravitation,* the bible of relativistic physics that illustrates our current model of the universe," said Alex clicking on his projector.

A picture appeared on the holographic imager of a man blowing up a balloon with pennies on it.

Dr. Henry Hanes, the large man from NYU who was sitting to Sydney's left, leaned over and said, "Boy, if he's got to go back to Physics 101, we've got a long, boring conference ahead." Sydney gave him a look of annoyance.

"This is our current model of the universe, Alex continued. "What I want to ask you astute scientists in this room today is: Where in all of your equations, in all of your calculations, has anyone explained who this guy is?" Alex pointed to the picture of the man blowing up a balloon.

Dr. Hanes choked on his coffee when he heard this. "Oh no, this isn't going to be some sort of lecture on the nature of God is it?" he said loud enough for the front of the room to hear him.

"Please!" said Sydney trying to quiet the irritating man, who was emitting a foul smell of dirty laundry.

"Seriously," said Alex, looking past Dr. Hanes. "Our current theory says the universe is expanding like a balloon, with pennies representing galaxies moving farther and farther apart. We know it's expanding at such a rate that we must be missing ninety-six percent of the matter and energy that would be necessary to drive this expansion. We've labeled that missing stuff "dark matter" and "dark energy" but no one has a clue as to what it is! No one can explain what is driving the expansion, or in other words, who this guy is," said Alex pointing again to the man in the picture.

"Well, let's explore this picture a bit further. If it really were a guy blowing up the universe, we would see that he would have to have lungs. What I'm saying is that for the universe to expand there has to be something that contracts, just as the lungs would be doing for the *guy* to force air into the balloon and cause its expansion."

Alex showed the picture with the rest of the man to include his lungs. "I mean, come on. What is the primary law of physics? For every action, there has to be an equal and opposite reaction. Thus, for the universe to be expanding something has to be contracting; and ladies and gentlemen ... I say there have to be two sides to the universe with one side contracting and the other expanding! I believe it's the dynamic of matter going to infinite density that causes the contractive force, and it is in a feedback-loop with the expansive side. It is this dynamic that is driving the expansion of our visible universe just like lungs contract as we blow up a balloon! What I'm saying is that there must be an interaction between the black hole side and the visible universe for us to be having this expansion effect. The two sides of the universe are communicating in a breath-like interaction with each other.

"Everything we know about physics is based on the expansive side of this equation. And since we already know that we are missing ninety-six percent of the matter and energy necessary to drive the expansion, our current model of physics is woefully inadequate, as it's based on just a fraction of what we know must be out there. And so is our technology, or for that matter our sociology, medicine and entire worldview!

"Currently, most of our technology depends on fire and explosion … the expanded side of the universe. If something does not expand energy, it does not exist in our world. That's why we think the entropy of the universe tends to increase because when things expand they get more and more disorderly. When you look at our universe, does it look disordered? Look at your own body. In order to work, our bodies are highly organized. They operate for the most part without our conscious participation. For our bodies to function, every atom needs to know what to do. This is a lot of organization! In fact, there's enough DNA in one body to stretch end to end around the Earth five million times! Maybe it's the energy in the contracted side of the universe that is taking care of all of these functions in the human body.

"When you ask the religious community how the world came into being, they say God did it. When you ask the scientific community, they say the Big Bang – which is the God of physics – did it. Both are equally unsatisfactory and vague answers. If the universe is expanding, then something had to contract to gain the energy to cause the expansion. For there to be a Big Bang, there had to be something there to bang, something compressed so tightly that it was infinitely small … like a black hole!

"This had been my first clue to the nature of the gravitational field and its relation to the visible universe or the electromagnetic field. If I'm correct, all our technology and understanding of energy is based on only what is out and not what is in. What will we find when we look into the contracted side of the universe? I say we will find an infinite energy field – one that we can tap, that will fuel our energy needs to infinity!

"If you take a ball on a stick and spin it, you will feel a centrifugal force. But if you look up centrifugal force, it will say it's an imaginary force. But that can't be right. Something has to be holding the ball to the center. The expansion side or the electromagnetic force can only exist with a force that holds it to the center. I'm saying that this force is the black hole dynamic at the center of all things. You can think of where the mouth meets the balloon as the event horizon or rim of the black hole, and the black hole as the lungs. Thus, in my model of the universe, there are two sides: a radiated and a contracted side; and there's a flow of energy between the two sides creating a feedback-loop of information."

Sydney's heart skipped a beat. *Doesn't an enormous energy field that feeds back onto itself imply consciousness?*

Alex continued. "So I'm saying that this feedback dynamic between the black hole side and the radiated side of the universe is what causes gravity. Current scientific theory has no explanation for gravity or even for why water curls when it goes down a drain. I believe that there are torque and coriolis forces in this black hole dynamic between the two sides, so that the field not only curves, but it curls and spins."

Dr. Reizen in the back row spoke up. "Einstein said gravity is caused by the exertion of the weight of an object on the fabric of space."

"Yes, and this is where I go further. The weight is caused by the gravitational dynamic of the black hole in the center of matter; and I say that it also curls. This, I believe is the source of the spin of all things."

"I thought it was the Big Bang that caused everything to spin!" Brian Sheppard sat forward in his chair as he offered his

54

objection.

"Think about it Brian. Things only spin if they're in a frictionless environment, and the universe is far from frictionless." Brian nodded in agreement. "It's like how you can spin a hardboiled egg easily, but not a raw egg. The viscosity plays a key role.

"It's counterintuitive to believe that everything's been spinning for fourteen billion years from the force of the Big Bang. If we don't consider the black hole dynamic in the center of galaxies, it's like trying to describe a car without accounting for the V8 engine! However, a black hole exerting a huge gravitational pull could do the trick!"

CHAPTER 6

The next morning Sydney got up early. She hailed a taxi and headed down the bumpy, winding road into Kona with its beautiful vistas and bohemian atmosphere. There weren't any high buildings, just a few blocks of art galleries and jewelry shops, some restaurants, cafés and a plethora of trinket shops mostly filled with T-shirts, clogs, sarongs and other typical fare of any tourist area. It was a refreshing change from the up-tight university environment she had lived in most her life. She could almost forget about the repressive government here, as she hadn't watched television or listened to the news. Only the occasional sighting of a Brotherhood agent in his red and gold uniform would bring back the reality of the current state of the government.

Everything was casual on the island. People wore shorts and tank tops and she only rarely spotted someone wearing a skirt or jacket. Many of the women looked like they weren't wearing bras, though this was not allowed in public. At the university, all women were required to wear skirts and nylons; bare legs were not allowed. But no one seemed to enforce that ridiculous law here on the island.

When Sydney arrived at the Internet café, she chose the computer that was the most isolated in the far corner of the room. She didn't want anyone looking over her shoulder. She typed in crop circles and found nothing. The OEB was probably censoring this kind of search. She would have to find the information in a more roundabout way. Everyone knew that you had to go through backdoors to get to sites considered heresy by the OEB. She typed in just the word circles. Over seventy thousand choices came up. Sites used a great many code words to avoid problems with the police, so she would have to spend quite a while sorting through the possibilities. Since her dream said to look for a crop circle made the night before, she narrowed her search by putting the parameters of the last twenty-four hours. That cut down her choices to less than 250. She scrolled through them looking for anything that looked like a code for crop circles. Then she saw the word, *grains*. She clicked on the site and there it was! A whole catalogue of crop circles popped on the screen. She downloaded the file onto a chip. She didn't want to spend any more time than necessary with this sort of thing on her screen in a public place. She slipped the chip in her wallet, bought a coffee, and left the café.

A few minutes later, a Brotherhood agent entered and told everyone to step away from their computers. Three other people were working at terminals, and a young man stood behind the counter. The three immediately pushed away from their holo-imagers and put their hands out where the officer could see them. This was standard protocol when being confronted by the OEB, and no one dared to bring attention to themselves by not following their orders.

The officer went to each computer and checked the sites they had accessed. When nothing of interest showed up he told them they could go about their business. Then he checked the two other terminals that weren't in use. When he found the site that Sydney had been using, he turned to the young man behind the counter.

"Who was using this machine?" he demanded.

"A woman, but she left about three minutes ago."

"How did she pay?"

"With cash," the young man answered shaking nervously from the interrogation.

"Figures!" The officer grunted and copied down the information on the site visited by Sydney. "Do you have surveillance cameras here?"

"No, sir," the waiter answered. "You can look around if

you want."

The officer scanned the premises, and when he didn't see any cameras he asked, "What did she look like?"

"Hey man, I wasn't paying that much attention. It's just a coffee shop. She was pretty, long curly blonde, thirty-five or so I don't know."

"Would you recognize her if you saw her again?"

The young man scowled and shook his head. "I don't know, maybe."

The officer handed him a card. "You call this number if you ever see her in here again. Is that understood?"

"Yes, sir." Everyone was sitting quietly at their machines watching the unfolding scene. No one dared to work until the officer left. When the door closed behind him, the four looked at each other and rolled their eyes as they let out a collective sigh of relief.

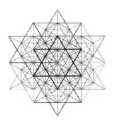

Sydney didn't have much time before the presentation started, as her taxi drove up to the hotel. She was anxious to look at her images. She pressed the elevator button impatiently, hoping she would have enough time to see what she had downloaded. She was staying on the fifteenth floor, and as she entered the elevator, a young oriental woman with three children followed her in. The little boys were giggling and bouncing around, and before Sydney could say anything one of them started pressing the buttons to every floor. She tried to compose herself while cursing her bad luck to have gotten in the same elevator with this child.

When Sydney finally reached her floor, she ran down the hall to her room. She popped her chip into her computer and waited impatiently for it to boot up. "Come on! Come on!" she said tapping nervously on the keyboard. When the images failed to appear, Sydney let out a shriek. "No, damn it, no! This better work!" Her heart was pounding, and she took a deep breath to calm herself while checking her settings. Before she had time to get more upset, the images appeared in three dimensions projected above the keyboard.

A whole slew of crop circles were on the disc and not in any particular order, as she had downloaded the entire site. Sydney had to go through them one by one, checking the dates and the locations. She was amazed by several of the intricate geometric designs, though some clearly seemed like they had been made by people stomping through the fields at night. Each circle had a commentary attached with analysis of the design and the molecular structure of the stalks. She read that, aside from a few people who confessed to making some of the crop circles, the vast majority – and there were tens of thousands found all around the world – remained unclaimed. Some had such intricate designs she didn't see how anyone could do that with some boards tied to their feet in just one night.

As Sydney read on, she learned that the molecular structure of the stalks had been altered in many of the circles. Some were done in such a way that they created a three-dimensional effect when viewed from the top. Clearly, this would be difficult, if not impossible for pranksters to accomplish in the space of a few night hours. When she read that there had been over fifteen million sightings of UFOs over the past ten years in the Western Hemisphere alone, she was taken aback. She had no idea that there had been that many. She had assumed there had only a few hundred of them at most.

Sydney continued to scroll through the crop circle images. Many seemed to be variations on the same theme of geometric fractal relationships. One had a sphere in the middle with six arms swirling out of it in a galactic formation made up of small circles, becoming larger in the middle and then smaller again toward the end of the arm. Off each circle in the arm, were three circles in decreasing size, attached to the top and the bottom of the larger circle in the arm. The design looked like a pinwheel of circles. Another seemed like a close up of just one of the arms, but was larger with more circles, laid out in similar fashion. Then she gasped in awe when the one she had seen in her dream appeared before her eyes. It was a double torus shape like two doughnuts with small spheres curling around both doughnuts and feeding into a vortex at the top and bottom.

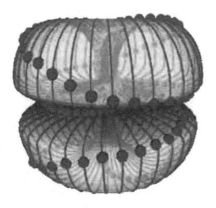

Now she knew her dream was not just a dream. It was something far more profound. Chills ran down her spine as she contemplated the implications of a dream that was not a dream at all!

CHAPTER 7

Sydney wanted to tell Alex about what she had found on the Internet, but there were several people standing around him and there was no time. Alex had spoken of the spiritual implications of his work, but this wasn't a spiritual experience; this seemed more like an extraterrestrial encounter!

As Alex adjusted the microphone, Sydney took her seat and tried to quiet her rapidly beating heart. All she could think about was the Being who had visited her, and what it all meant.

"If our reality is mostly this infinitely dense energy field, the next question is, how dense is it?" asked Alex as he resumed his presentation. "I found a way to calculate this, and discovered that the "vacuum" is filled with an infinite amount of matter. Even if we use the arbitrary cutoff point of the Planck's length as the accepted smallest measurement of a particle, which is billions of times smaller than an atom, we can calculate that the entire visible universe can be compacted down to fit into less than one cubic centimeter of this unseen energy in the vacuum."

Alex clicked on the next slide.

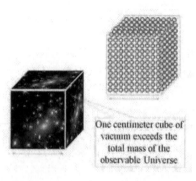

One centimeter cube of vacuum exceeds the total mass of the observable Universe

"That's 10 with 94 zeros after it, grams! That is a lot of matter! That is a lot of energy! Actually, if it weren't for renormalization or the arbitrary cutoff of infinite numbers, it's an endless amount of energy! And I'm not the first to say this.

"Let me read you a quote from the book *Gravitation*." He picked up the book feigning it to be heavy. "It's called *Gravitation* because the minute you pick it up you can feel the force of gravity," said Alex pretending to struggle with the four-inch thick book as if it weighed a hundred pounds. The room broke out in laughter.

"...Present-day quantum field theory gets rid by a renormalization process of an energy density in the vacuum that would formally be infinite if not removed by this renormalization."

"The Casimir experiments support this conclusion as well. This experiment shows that when you measure down to the subatomic level, you cannot press two plates totally together, indicating there's mass in the vacuum. Even Einstein thought this was the case with his Cosmological Constant. It's ironic that he thought this had been his biggest mistake. Now it's looking like he had been right after all. If Einstein was right, as many quantum physicists now believe, and this energy density in the vacuum does in fact exist, it means that we are living in a sea of energy, and all we need to do is to learn how to tap into it."

"If there's so much stuff in the vacuum, why can't we see

it?" asked Dr. Hanes, wearing a gray and peach Hawaiian shirt with armpits stained from perspiration. Sydney noticed it was the same shirt in the window of the hotel's gift shop.

"I'm glad you asked that because I've put a great deal of thought into that exact question. I found, after years of research that the answer is that the vacuum has to be in perfect geometric equilibrium, so that one side cancels out the other to appear empty. I believe this geometry is based on the tetrahedron and the six-pointed star, but I have not yet discovered the perfect geometry that can expand and contract in fractals to infinity.

"Buckminster Fuller had been studying this same question, and believed, as I do, that the universe has a mathematical geometric blueprint to it. He had been working with the shape of the vector equilibrium, as he called the cube octahedron, as one of the fundamental geometries, because all its vectors are in perfect equilibrium."

Alex pulled up a holographic image of the vector equilibrium. "Here you can see that all the vectors are the same length, making it the most stable geometry.

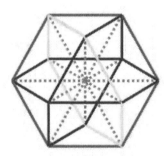

"Bucky had also been working with the isotropic vector matrix, which is a tetrahedron that has twenty other tetrahedrons within it. As you can see, it also contains a vector equilibrium or a cube octahedron. I believe the universe uses this geometry to take matter to infinity both large and small. But as I've said, this is not yet complete."

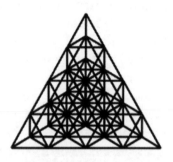

Martin Scorely had taken copious notes, and was secretly recording the sessions as well. It was his job to monitor the conference, and report to the OEB any breaches of party-line protocol or religious transgressions. This whole lecture seemed like one blasphemy after another to him, and he wondered if Croft would have his Brotherhood police raid the conference and arrest everyone there. At the break, he ducked around a corner and made his report of the morning's discussion.

John Croft hung up the phone after speaking with Martin Scorely. Perhaps this is what he had been waiting for so many years. It was too soon to know. Certainly, a new energy source had been something he was eager to control. However, there was something else that piqued his interest far more – something he believed would afford him power beyond his wildest dreams. Croft thought he had a destiny, one even larger than the grand scale of what he had accomplished so far. A psychic had predicted his fate many years before. Though under his regime he had outlawed such "witchcraft," he knew that some people had genuine psychic abilities. Croft had been told he could be the most powerful man on Earth if he controlled a technological device that used a geometric matrix. It would be invented within the next twenty years, and would bring him immense power. That is why he decided to go back to school to study physics.

The mystic also told him that a Class 19 psychic, one of the most skilled, would be instrumental in the creation of the device. Since then, Croft had put in motion a search to identify all Class 19 psychics, and had sent his minions to all university and public physics symposiums to look for the technology. Now Martin Scorely had just reported on a new technology based on the supposed geometry of the vacuum.

Croft controlled America, but it was not enough. He wanted an even greater destiny. He wanted to control the entire world. The President was a mere puppet under his influence. He chortled as he thought about how easy it had been to take over an American population more interested in their television shows and music than what was really happening in the world. It had been a simple matter of organizing a dedicated and politically active minority who showed up at primary elections, and gaining control of the media outlets.

Now, no one under twenty-five knew much about the America of old and the freedoms that were once enjoyed, as all mention of it had been purged from the educational system. Those who lived through the change didn't think it could happen in America. They trusted the government, and gave up their freedoms willingly, believing it was necessary in times of war. They never thought the government would use the power they abdicated in the name of national security against the American population. But Croft had consolidated power in such a way that no one really understood the full ramifications of these changes until it had been too late to oppose him.

The onslaught started somewhat benignly. Pervasive wire-tapping of Americans had been first tolerated, and then made legal. The right of Habeas Corpus, that prevented one from being arrested without being charged with a crime, had been abandoned – first for those suspected of being terrorists, and then for anyone the government arrested. Soon, the entire country lived in fear of being falsely accused.

The ambush on religious freedom had started rather innocuously as well. Legislation had been passed requiring all public school children to say morning prayers. Although there had been decades of protest from those who wanted clear separation of Church and State, the measure prevailed. The effort to remove the words "under God" from the Pledge of Allegiance had been not only defeated, but its inclusion had been mandated through an Amendment to the Constitution, as had been the illegality of gay, inter-religious, and inter-racial marriage. The majority of Americans were in agreement with these measures.

When the OEB declared that legal testimony by atheists could not be heard because their oath on the Bible would be invalid, the tide started to shift, as many felt the OEB had gone too far. By this time, there was no organized power base left to fight the righteous indignation of the OEB. Most Americans felt that the measures taken by the OEB did not impose restrictions on religions that believed in a deity – at least not in the beginning – so there had not been much opposition from people of faith.

No one really believed that Croft would take the movement to such an extreme position. It wasn't until the "examinations," that outlawed any religion other than the OEB's version of Christianity, that people had become incensed with the restrictions. By that time, it was too late. Croft had consolidated power to the point where nothing could be done within the framework of the prevailing system to stop him. Croft began reshaping the country into his vision of a society in which his rule of God and strict moral code infused all facets of daily life. It was his answer to crime and the wanton behavior that had been running rampant for so long in America. It was also the end of freedom.

The OEB with Croft as its sovereign leader had become the most powerful force in America. Croft accomplished this by rallying the largest and most highly organized, passionately committed group in the country – created on the shoulders of the powerful religious right wing of American politics. As he pondered Scorely's report, he could see his true destiny was soon to unfold. He picked up the phone and called Brandon Tarnoff.

"I want full surveillance of physicist Alex Harmon."

After a short break, Alex returned to the podium. "The next question I asked was if there's so much stuff … so much energy and matter in the vacuum, is it random or is it organized? To answer this question I developed a scaling law."

Alex pulled up another slide.

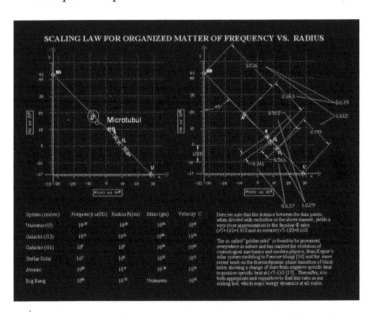

"I took the size or radius of various data points of matter, from the smallest measure of the Planck's length to the visible universe. In this example, I plotted galactic clusters, galaxies, solar systems, planets, down to cells, atoms, subatomic particles, and then down to the smallest measure, the Planck's length, and compared it with the energy level, or rate of oscillation of each of the data points. What I found was that they fell in a perfectly straight line indicating that the universe is highly organized and not random as is currently the view.

"Not only did they line up in perfect scalar relationships, but the distance between the data points - the sun compared to the solar system compared to the galaxy and so on - lined up in phi ratios! Now, this is a remarkable finding!"

Sydney looked at the graph in amazement. An organized universe had huge implications. She had been taught it was quite random, that there had been a huge explosion from the Big Bang, and everything is just swirling around making random collisions like a giant pinball machine. But if the universe has a highly organized structure as this graph indicated, it meant that the universe was created according to a very specific design. She knew Alex had been hinting that there were spiritual implications to his work, and she had not been willing to go down that road. But for the universe to be so organized, something had to be guiding that organization ... something intelligent. The thought sent a chill down her spine.

"What's that point in the middle?" asked Dr. Reizen, squinting to see the display.

"That's a microtubule."

"You mean the biological entity is right in the middle of the graph?" she asked, her eyes widening.

Sydney gasped. *My God, this implies that the biological cell has to be pretty important to the universe. Perhaps life is not rare at all But rather, central to creation. Maybe the universe makes biological life as ubiquitously as it makes stars!*

When the conference broke for an early dinner, Alex came

over to Sydney.

"How about another little tour instead of dinner? We can get a box meal from the concierge and have a picnic."

"That's perfect. I have something I need to talk with you about," said Sydney, thinking this would be a good time to tell him about the crop circles and the Being in her vision. "What do you have in mind?"

"It's the Place of Refuge, a preserved ancient Hawaiian village. It's thought to be a sacred place, and it would be a nice break."

Alex and Sydney drove to Pu'uhonua o Honaunau, a park that juts into the Pacific and lies in the black lava flats of the southern Kona Coast. Tall royal palms surround a temple complex that sits on a twenty-acre finger of lava, bordered by the sea on three sides. The ancient Place of Refuge lies firmly protected behind the mortar less masonry of the sixteenth-century Great Wall.

They walked down a path that wound through the village, passing the palace, with its fishpond and private canoe landing, and three heiaus: grass hut burial sites, guarded by large carved effigies of gods – reproductions, still in their original setting.

"This is a special site on the Island" said Alex. "It's considered sacred ground by the natives. In ancient times the only access to the Pu'uhonua, which means temple of refuge, had been by swimming across a bay known as the sharks' den. Those who broke ancient Hawaii's intricate system of kapu, which was often simply the offense of treading on the shadow of a Chief, or fishing in the wrong season, could expect summary execution unless they fled to the sanctuary of this place. The Kings lived on this land and transgressors had to swim through the shark-infested waters to get here. If they survived, they would be absolved of their crime."

Alex and Sydney continued on the path. "This is part of an ancient system of trails that encircled the island to serve as trade routes."

"It's really beautiful here," said Sydney. "Even the air feels different."

"There's intense energy in this place. It lies at exactly 19.6 degrees latitude on the planet; right on one of the vectors of the six-pointed star I believe constitutes the inner geometry of the planet ... *and* every particle of matter, actually. I believe energy is more intense on these points and that is why there's a volcano here."

"Yes, I can almost feel it," said Sydney taking in a deep breath of the ocean air.

Alex stopped and faced Sydney. "I'll move you up to the complex after the conference,"

"Aren't you concerned about the OEB having a problem with my living there?" asked Sydney. She was expecting her living quarters to be in Alex's house. She knew that the OEB policed relationships between men and women, and it was prohibited for couples to cohabitate if they weren't married.

"The staff quarters are separated from the main house. I've already registered you with the OEB as required by law. Anyway, they don't give us too much trouble here on the Island. Things are way more relaxed here than on the mainland."

Sydney couldn't help but feel a little nervous about this arrangement. She had a run-in with the OEB in Ann Arbor, when they started to scrutinize her relationship with Mark. It was the main reason they broke up, as the law would have forced them to marry if it could be proven their relationship had gone on longer than a year. The passion was just not there for her, and in the end, she had been unwilling to compromise to save the relationship. Leaving Mark had been one of the hardest things she ever had to do. But now, here in Hawaii with Alex, she was starting to see the unfolding of a larger picture.

Sydney stopped and turned toward Alex with a serious look on her face. "There's something I need to tell you. I had a strange dream." She looked down at her feet finding it hard to find the words to describe her bizarre experience.

"How so?"

"I had what I thought had been a dream, but now I'm sure I have proof ... it wasn't a dream; it was real."

Alex looked perplexed. "You had a lucid dream?"

"I had ... I don't know how to put this ... a visitation?"

"What kind of visitation?"

"I saw some sort of ... I don't know what. It was a Being. I couldn't tell if it was male or female and it was very large. It was almost like a shadow. At first, I was sure it had been a dream. But then I found what it showed me."

"Found what?"

"It showed me a crop circle."

"A crop circle? I didn't think you were interested in that sort of thing," said Alex warily.

"Well, I'm not ... I mean I wasn't. This Being told me this crop circle would appear that night, and this morning I went into town and used the Internet, and it was there! So it had to be real!"

"Then it probably was real," said Alex in a matter-of- fact tone.

"It didn't look like an angel. It looked more like an extra-terrestrial." Sydney scrutinized Alex's face for some sort of reaction. But there was none.

"Were you able to get copies of the crop circle?"

"Yes, I downloaded everything I could."

Sydney was surprised by his casual response. She realized Alex thought his work had spiritual implications, but ET's were a completely different story. She continued telling him about her experience but Alex didn't seem surprised at all. She couldn't help but wonder what this man was all about. Clearly, there was much more going on here than scientific research, and it was thrilling and frightening at the same time.

"So you've had an experience like this too?" she asked.

"Yes, I'm interested in crop circles. I've been so busy preparing for the presentation that I haven't had time to check out the latest formations. They are important communications."

"Communications for you?" she asked shocked.

Alex stopped to watch a turtle trying to climb out of the water onto a large flat rock. As Sydney watched Alex, he seemed shrouded in mystery. And for the briefest of moments, she wondered if he was human.

A young couple approached, and Alex waved at them.

"I'd like to get a picture of us together Sydney. What do you think?"

"I think that is a great idea," said Sydney smiling, flattered that he would want to do this.

"Excuse me," shouted Alex to the couple, continuing to wave them over. "Would you mind taking a photograph of us?"

"Sure, no problem," said the young man.

"Come on then." Alex pulled a small camera out of his rucksack and handed it to the tall young man.

"Come on Sydney. Let's get this beautiful scenery in the picture."

"Just stand a little over to the left," said the young man. "I don't want the glare of the sun in the picture. Yes, that's great; now stand a little closer."

Alex and Sydney stepped back onto the large, flat volcanic rocks that formed a ledge to the ocean. Alex put his arm around Sydney and smiled down at her. He saw a twinkle in her eye that suggested she was attracted to him. He smiled and his heart skipped a beat.

"That's perfect," said the man as he clicked the shutter. "Oh, wait a minute," he said as he checked the view screen. "There must have been something on the lens," the man said, noticing some round, bubble-like anomalies all over Alex and Sydney. "Let me take another one." He wiped the camera lens with his shirt to clear the lens and snapped another photo.

"Gosh, the smudges are still there." He handed the camera back to Alex. "Sorry, there must be some dust on the lens, but I couldn't get it off."

Alex looked at the two pictures. "Hmm," he said as he scrutinized the round, translucent globes on the image. He handed the camera back to Sydney without further comment, but he had seen these round images before and he knew they weren't smudges. They were something of great significance, something that couldn't be seen with the naked eye but showed up in the infrared spectrum of digital cameras. There were at least twenty of them in the photograph, and Alex knew that this meant something special. He had come in contact with orbs many times before. He had even communicated with some of them. Alex had learned that orbs were multi-dimensional Beings of many different species. When cameras using the infrared spectrum came into use, the orbs could be detected in the pictures. He found they often gathered at auspicious events, acting as harbingers of wondrous things to come.

CHAPTER 8

It was the last day of the conference and Alex paused and looked around the room with a serious expression, as he had a deep passion for what he was about to say.

"These are difficult times. We have exhausted most of the planet's fossil fuels, and we have not succeeded in creating sufficient alternative energy sources to meet the needs of even the immediate future. The Earth's population has exploded and people are dying of starvation and thirst. We need to do something radically different, and we need to do it now. I'm hoping that you astute scientists in this audience will help me to further this work because with an accurate understanding of the fundamental structure of the universe, we can create a whole new technology that will solve many of the world's problems.

"We need to tap only a tiny bit of the vacuum energy field to fuel our entire planet indefinitely. It's time for our civilization to get out of the age of fire and using brute force that we have been stuck in for thousands of years. Currently, our most sophisticated technology is a phallic symbol with a lot of explosives at the bottom; some ... *volunteers*," he said making quote signs with his fingers, "and a match to light the bottom, set off a huge explosion and hope the volunteers survive the experience!

"All of our technology is based on explosives, using fossil fuels that pollute the environment and use finite resources. The new technology I am presenting here would harness and work with the forces of creation, not against them, to create a completely sustainable way of life for all people on the Earth."

"But won't this take years?" asked Dr. Hanes, who had moved away from Sydney and was now sitting in the middle of the room.

"No, I believe I'm close to knowing how to do this."

"What exactly are you talking about in terms of technology?" asked a woman with white hair pulled back in a bun.

"I'm talking about harnessing the energy in the vacuum."

With this, the room broke out in a lot of talk. Many hands were waving in the air.

"How exactly do you plan to do that?" asked Dr. Hanes.

"By opening a controlled black hole," answered Alex. This statement created a lot of commotion in the room.

"Are you out of your mind!" shouted Dr. Hanes. "You'll blow up the Earth! You can't go messing around with something like that!"

Everyone started talking at once.

"Please, please hear me out," said Alex, trying to gain control of the room. "This is not as far-fetched as it may seem, and I think by the end of the presentation you'll agree with me."

"Well I've heard enough. This is just damned irresponsible!" Dr. Hanes shouted, his face now red with rage. "You better not mess around with black holes! You'll kill us all! I won't be party to this insanity!" The heavy man pulled himself out of his chair clumsily, knocking over his notebook, and stormed out of the room.

The room grew quiet as the door slammed behind him. Alex tried to regain his composure. This kind of reaction was not the first he had experienced in his many years of trying to put forth his ideas. He had hoped it wouldn't happen with these scientists, as they were all pushing the edges of scientific discovery and were mostly open to his theory.

"So I assume you have some idea how you would control this black hole?" asked Dr. Reizen. The room broke out in an uneasy laughter.

"Well, certainly that will be the challenge, and yes, I think it can be done," said Alex. I don't believe that black holes are the

78

monsters they are made out to be. In fact, I believe they are intrinsic to creation. I believe we live in a black hole, and that black holes are at the center of all matter."

The group adjourned to have dinner at a restaurant a few miles away. Sydney walked with Alex along the large, black volcanic rocks that rimmed the shore by the hotel to the parking lot. The ride took them past block after block of beachfront condominiums as they made their way to the dinner site. They turned into a long driveway lined with palm trees, and pulled up to a stately white house that had been converted into a restaurant. The air was filled with the scent of flowers, and Sydney stopped a moment to take a deep breath.

Alex led her through the estate, which had been built in the 1890's, and out the back to a beautiful patio in the midst of a garden filled with flowering trees. The patio was made of cobblestones, and surrounded by limestone walls covered with lush green vines. The restaurant had assembled several long tables covered with pink linen tablecloths for the group. Festive lanterns hung from the lattice above the patio, and the sound of soft island music filled the salty, humid air.

The water came up to the walled edge of the outdoor eating area and was lit from below, casting a blue-green hue on the waves as they lapped against the wall.

"Watch carefully," said Alex, leading Sydney to the wall and pointing to the water.

Sydney looked and didn't see anything unusual. Then she let out a gasp as a huge white-winged Manta Ray came to the surface and then did a graceful back flip under the water.

Its wingspan must have been at least fifteen feet. Then

she saw them. There were at least ten beautiful angelic creatures that seemed to be all mouth and wing. Her eyes lit up with delight. She had never seen anything like it before.

"They put the lights in the water there and drop in food to attract them. Aren't they incredible?"

Sydney nodded her head.

"Swimming with them is like being in another world," said Alex. "We'll have to do that sometime."

The waiter seated them at the table closest to the wall where they could continue to watch the creatures dance in the blue-green light and where several other conference attendees were already seated. The scientists exchanged introductions as more of the group filed in.

"Fascinating stuff," said Dr. Barlow from Duke University. "Let's assume you're right, Alex. If there's so much stuff in the vacuum, how come we've never detected it?"

"Well actually we have. It's what has been mistakenly labeled dark matter and dark energy. The reason we can't measure it is three-fold: Firstly, we are looking for particles instead of the gravitational dynamic of the space-time manifold. Secondly, it's in the contracted black hole and therefore the immeasurable side of the universe. Thirdly, as I said earlier, I believe the vacuum is in perfect geometric equilibrium and so appears to be empty. Figuring out this specific geometry is essential to building the technology that will access the vacuum energy."

Dr. Barlow's wife Beverly looked perplexed. "I'm sorry Alex, but what do you mean by space-time manifold?"

"Einstein believed there is a fabric of space. You can think of it like a trampoline. When a body of mass interacts with space, it's like a bowling ball on a trampoline and causes a curvature in space."

"Honey, I guess you'd need to be in the conference to understand all this terminology. She's astute scientifically, Alex, but this is all new territory," said Dr. Barlow.

"No problem." Alex smiled at her. "That's a good question. I'm happy to clarify it for you."

"So wouldn't your model have some ramifications on the way we conceive of dimensions?" interjected Dr. Barbara Edwards, a petite blonde woman.

"Yes, dimensions under this model are concentric, infinite and progress much like the slide I showed of the six-pointed star in the circle."

"Infinite? That blows the eleven dimensional string theory out of the water doesn't it?" laughed Bert Mar, a rather rotund and affable professor from Stanford. "You're going to put every mainstream quantum physicist out of business!"

"Well, Bert, we all know that model is full of holes or we wouldn't be here!" piped in Dr. Calvin Harris, a scientist who had worked on the super collider in space until he had become painfully aware that they were getting nowhere.

"Yeah! Black holes!" shouted Calvin with a chortle.

"Good one," laughed Bert.

"Really!" said Calvin. "There are so many patches upon patches to hold up string theory, I'm surprised we're still even talking about it. We may be talking Nobel prize here, Alex."

Alex grinned sheepishly. "Well, that's a bit premature, but thanks for the vote of confidence."

"I find this whole idea of a geometric matrix in the vacuum fascinating," said Bert, stuffing a piece of bread in his mouth. "What exactly do you mean by that?"

"I believe the universe uses geometry to spin matter into creation from the vacuum. You can think of the vacuum – remember that is not empty – but rather filled with an infinite density, like a vast lake. Matter is like a vortex in the water. It is a dynamic of the field - made of the same stuff and not separate from it. The universe uses a geometric matrix as the building blocks of matter."

"When it's not matter, what is it?" asked Katherine Wexel from the University of Liege, in Belgium.

"It's in pure potential. It's in the infinite vacuum state. When the vacuum comes into coherence, we call it matter," answered Alex.

Alex stood up and clanged his wine glass with a fork. "I

want to take this moment to thank you all for coming and to introduce my newest colleague. Sydney Stewart has just joined my team and will be helping me work out the math to prove my theory," said Alex, motioning to Sydney to stand up and be acknowledged by the group.

Sydney stood up and took a reluctant and shallow nod as the group applauded.

"That's some task you're taking on," said Bert, taking a big gulp of wine.

"I don't know how you convinced her to do this," said Brian Sheppard. "She was my brightest student ever and leagues above her colleagues in the math department at U. of M."

"Well Sydney, even if you find Alex's theory has some holes in it - like some big black holes - at least you'll get a damned good tan!" said Bert in his characteristic jovial manner

"I'll drink to that," said Sydney, laughing and tipping her glass to salute the group.

Martin Scorely wrote her name down in his notebook.

"So Alex," said Bert. "If I'm hearing you correctly, you're saying that this theory is going to mean an unlimited source of clean energy?"

"Certainly, that's one of the practical applications of my theory, but this is about energy and a lot more. In fact, it will revolutionize our civilization."

"Better be careful," said Sheppard with a serious look on his face. "I mean it. The OEB may not take kindly to any changes in the status quo. They've arrested several of our faculty in the last year alone!"

"That's why I'm holding this conference. We need to get these ideas out and in the hands of as many scientists as possible. We need to do this for the sake of all humanity. We are reaching a critical juncture where our civilization can no longer sustain the population using conventional forms of energy. We need a change and soon. I'm hoping you'll go back and share these ideas with your colleagues. It doesn't have to be me that brings this new technology to the world; it just has to be someone."

"Aren't you going to patent this?" asked Sheppard. "You

might be talking billions of dollars for a technology like this."

"Yes, but only to keep it out of the hands of those who would suppress the technology. This has to be given freely to mankind."

"What if this gets into the wrong hands? Wouldn't someone be able to weaponize this technology?" asked Dr. Barlow.

CHAPTER 9

Sydney stood at the hotel entrance with her bags as Alex drove up. He got out of the car, grabbed one of her suitcases, and opened the door for her.

"Chivalry is not dead," said Sydney flashing a broad smile at Alex.

"I am here to serve," he said with a slight bow.

Sydney climbed in the car and they headed for his complex.

"I'm glad the conference is over," Alex said with a sigh.

"I thought you did a great job," replied Sydney.

"Everyone seemed excited."

"Except Dr. Hanes," said Alex mischievously.

"There's one in every crowd, isn't there? I can't wait for you to take a look at these crop circles I downloaded, especially the one that was in my dream," said Sydney as Alex drove her up the mountain – over a thousand feet in elevation.

"Did you make sure the OEB couldn't trace the search back to you?"

"Yes. I'm certain of it," said Sydney. Alex gave her a skeptical look.

They turned off the main road onto his land and drove up a winding dirt path past some grazing cows and goats.

"This is something," said Sydney. "You have quite a nice spread here."

"Thank you. I have twelve acres of land and I've been working on it for over ten years. I hope to make it completely self-sustaining. Every plant and tree on the land is edible, and I have my own power and water supply."

They drove past several small dwellings and then past a large garage-like structure.

"That's the lab. I'll show it to you tomorrow," said Alex pointing off to the left.

"What's that?" asked Sydney, pointing to the spherical structure with intersecting triangular lattices to her right.

"That's our geodesic dome. We have group events in there. There's usually something going on with the staff every night. They have dances, meditations, and presentations. It's a great facility. My friend, Asha donated it to the project."

Alex turned into the long dirt road that led up to his house that was situated about two hundred feet up from the lab building. It was three stories with porches, or lanais as they're called in Hawaii, surrounding each level. It had been built with a light colored wood and was propped up on pylons.

"What's going on up there?" said Sydney, noticing flashing blue lights at the house.

"Damn, that looks like OEB." Alex and Sydney looked at each other with the anxiety that always accompanied any run in with the Brotherhood police. These encounters rarely went well.

"Stop the car for a minute," said Sydney. She got out of the car and placed her bag that contained her computer in the bushes.

"Good idea," said Alex. "Better safe than sorry."

Sydney got back in and they drove up to the house.

Alex got out of the car and smiled. "Hello officer. Can I help you?"

"Are you Alex Harmon?" asked the officer.

"Yes, I am."

The officer walked over to the car and looked in at Sydney.

"Are you Sydney Stewart?"

Sydney swallowed hard. She didn't want to look frightened, but she was.

"Yes, sir. Is there a problem?"

"This is the *employee* that you registered to stay here?" He now turned to Sydney.

"Yes, she is."

"I see," said the young man. "She is quite attractive," he said scrutinizing her with a pompous leer.

Sydney was taken aback by his good looks that belied his harsh demeanor, but she knew not to underestimate his authority. He was young, probably only twenty-five or so as was typical of many of the OEB police. It had been much easier to convert the young people than those who had experienced the religious freedom of the past.

Sydney smiled at him uneasily. She was trying to remain calm, and praying the officer wouldn't search the car.

"Where are her quarters and where are yours?" he asked.

"Follow me. I'll show you. Do you mind if I unload her bags? She's just moving in now and her bags are in the car."

The officer looked on suspiciously as Alex unloaded the trunk. Sydney got of the car and picked up a smaller case.

"So you're a colleague of Dr. Harmon?" the officer asked, looking Sydney up and down as if inspecting a dinner he was about to devour.

"Yes. We're both physicists." Sydney twisted her hair nervously, trying to avoid his gaze.

"Oh yes, I see," said the officer. He rubbed his neatly shaped mustache, shifting his eyes between Alex and Sydney. "Are you married, Miss?

"No, I'm not," she replied.

The officer squinted and tightened his lips. "So you're a virgin at your age?"

"No sir, but I have been celibate since the OEB ban on sex outside marriage," she lied.

"Uh huh." said the officer now biting his lip. "You're very attractive."

Sydney felt a pang of fear in her gut as she noticed a large bulge in his pants. "Sir, I don't think that comment is appropriate."

The officer saw what she was looking at and cleared his throat. It was not unheard of for OEB officers to rape unmarried women and then turn them in for illicit sexual activity. With Alex in the room, she was safe for now. The officer abruptly changed his line of inquiry. "Show me your credentials!"

"Certainly." Sydney pulled out her identification from her purse and handed the papers to the officer. He looked them over, seeming to read every word while Sydney and Alex stood nervously watching the officer inspect the documents.

"All right for now," said the officer looking them both over suspiciously. He handed the papers back to Sydney. "Let me see the living quarters."

Alex led Sydney and the officer to the small dwelling that stood next to the main house. "This is the guest quarters," said Alex. "I stay in the main house." Both dwellings were surrounded by vegetation blooming with fruit, nuts and coffee. There were floor to ceiling windows around the entire dwelling that unfastened to create an open-air pavilion made out of light-colored teak. A covered lanai stretched around the house, providing more living space. The living room was furnished with a large, dark brown wicker couch and several wicker chairs with red, green, and yellow floral pillows.

"Where will she sleep?" demanded the officer.

Alex led them up a stairway to the second floor that consisted of an enclosed room and an open-air lanai with a ceiling but no walls.

Alex showed the officer the white wrought iron bed that was on the lanai, and placed Sydney's bags next it. The bed had a fluffy white duvet, and was covered by white mosquito netting.

The officer inspected the bed. He pulled a device out of his pocket and waved it over the covers then pulled them back and wanded the sheets.

"What are you doing?" asked Sydney, clearly perplexed.

"DNA testing. It's a base test that will be kept on file."

"For what?"

The officer gave Sydney a cold stare, and it dawned on her that he was going to be monitoring to see if there would be any sexual activity in the future. She had heard of Brotherhood police doing this kind of invasive scrutiny, but this was the first time she had experienced it. It sent a shiver through her entire body.

"We'll be watching," he said, and abruptly turned and left.

Sydney collapsed into a chair when the door closed behind the officer, and Alex closed his eyes and shook his head.

"Whoa, that was not fun!" he said. "At least he was only doing the morality thing. I was worried he was for my work."

The experience had been draining, for there was much to fear if an OEB officer decided to turn you in. People often disappeared after having been arrested – never to be heard from again. Their families were told they were taken to secret prisons, but there were rumors that many were executed. The OEB wanted to cull any nonbelievers out of the population, and you had better give the appearance of cooperating if you wanted to be left alone.

"Thank God he didn't search the car," said Alex. He looked out over the lanai and saw the officer had driven off. "Let me get your bag and you can show me what you downloaded." Alex ran down the stairs to the path where they had hidden Sydney's computer.

When he returned, he handed Sydney her bag. She pulled out her computer, turned it on, and displayed the crop circle that she had been shown in her dream.

"Does this mean anything to you?" she asked.

Alex's eyes widened. Then he gasped. "My God, it's a double torus! I've been thinking about this shape, but I'm not quite sure what it means. I don't understand how we go from tetrahedrons to this shape. This is amazing!"

Sydney put up another crop circle on the holographic

projector. "What do you think of this one?"

"This is a cube octahedron," answered Alex. "These are all fractal depictions of tetrahedrons within spheres. Here, look what happens when I lay the geometry on top of it."

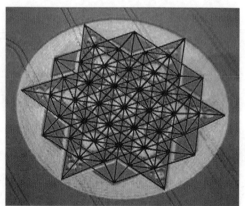

Photo courtesy of Steven Alexander

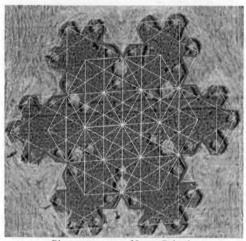

Photo courtesy of Lucy Pringle

"This is confirming of the direction I'm taking with my theory. These certainly are related to the geometry of the vacuum," said Alex, scrutinizing the shapes before him.

"Are you saying that these crop circles relate to *your* work?" Sydney was astounded at this notion.

Alex shrugged. "It sure seems that way."

"I downloaded a whole slew of these. Maybe you should take a look at all of them. I have to say I always thought crop circles were made by pranksters getting their kicks by making designs in the fields late at night. But if these designs are made by hoaxers, then they're guys who know a whole lot about your theory."

Alex grinned as he took the disc and slipped it into his computer. "I've known that crop circles have great significance for my work for some time now."

"Alex, what's the deal here?"

"Well, if it's a scientist working on the same theory that we are, he's got a strange publisher," said Alex laughing.

"Seriously," said Sydney. "These are uncanny. I mean I have a dream or a visitation, and I'm shown something that turns out to be real. I'm told these crop circles are important to your work. What do you think it was? Did I have an intuitive dream? The Being I saw sure didn't look like an angel. Do you think it was an encounter with an extra-terrestrial?"

Alex didn't respond. Instead, he scrutinized her face, tempted to tell her his secret; but it was too soon.

"What?" she said. "You're looking at me like I have two heads."

"It means we should investigate these shapes."

"Well, then you must have a theory about who or what is making these things," said Sydney, clearly unwilling to let the subject drop.

"The theory is that they're made by an advanced civilization that is trying to tell us something. It sure seems that way as I'm not aware of anyone else who is doing this kind of research," said Alex evasively. "All I know is there seems to be a code in some of these designs."

CHAPTER 10

"There she is – our guest of honor," said Alex dressed in an apron as he welcomed Sydney into the large circular eating area with its industrial style kitchen. Most of the staff was there for the evening meal. "This is Alicia, she's our main cook." Alicia, a slim girl of about twenty with short black hair and an Iowa farm girl face shook Sydney's hand.

"And this is Alan Highland a physicist from MIT who is working with me." Alan was a large man in his mid-fifties with a round friendly face. He was wearing a Hawaiian shirt and a straw hat, which he tipped in greeting to Sydney.

"This is Millie," said Alex pointing to the young girl with long brown hair. "She's our gardener and has planted everything in accordance with the geometry that is most conducive for optimizing crop growth." Alex introduced Sydney to the ten other staff of scientists and grounds keepers that had gathered for the evening meal. The camaraderie between them seemed genuine, and Sydney felt at home and welcomed into this obviously close-knit group.

"The meal is made entirely from food grown or raised on the land" said Alex. "I'm a stickler on not eating anything that is not organically grown. Most of the food supply on the Island has been tainted with genetically engineered crops that are causing all sorts of health problems in the population. This practice has gone unregulated for so long that cross-pollination is running rampant, overtaking most of the vegetation. The only way to ensure our food is untainted is to grow it ourselves."

"Kevin, say hello to Sydney," said Alex calling over to the

young man sitting on a couch reading a magazine. Kevin looked up rather sheepishly, and acknowledged Sydney.

"Kevin is our resident handyman. So if there's anything you need, Kevin is our 'go-to' man."

"That's good to know," said Sydney. She felt something odd about this quiet young man but shook it off. Kevin went back to reading his magazine and remained quiet throughout the evening meal.

"So how did the presentation go today?" asked Alan passing a large salad bowl to Sydney.

"We had quite a lively debate on some of the theories in quantum physics that my theory blows away," said Alex. Even though most of these guys are open minded, there's still so much resistance to letting go of some of these basic principles that are simply wrong from my point of view."

"What specifically did they have a problem with?" asked Alan.

"The problem with our current model is that they don't realize that everything is happening in a field – an infinitely dense field – not in empty space. It's hard for them to accept that all things are interrelated within the system, because it is all embedded in a larger system."

"Didn't you show them Dr. Moon's quote in *Gravitation*?" asked Alan.

"Yes, but they still needed a lot of convincing. A vacuum that is filled changes everything we understand about what's happening at the quantum level. For instance, take the Schrodinger's cat thought experiment where a cat is placed in a box. Inside the box, there is a poison pellet and a little hammer. A random function will either cause the hammer to release the poison pellet and kill the cat, or not. The current thinking in quantum theory is that until the observer sees whether the cat is alive or dead, it is in quantum limbo; neither alive nor dead."

"Yes, it takes an observer to witness the event before the event can be said to have happened. This is at the core of the uncertainty principle," said Sydney.

"Yes, and I think it is wrong," said Alex. The problem

with that concept is that they're assuming the cat is completely isolated from the observer because it is in a box. But according to my theory, everything is connected through the vacuum, so nothing exists separately from anything else."

"Einstein also had a problem with the uncertainty principle and famously declared that he didn't think *God played dice with the universe*," added Alan reaching for another helping of grilled mahi-mahi the staff caught that morning.

"Yes, and I certainly agree with him," said Alex. "If everything is connected through the vacuum, then the field knows what everything is doing at all times, and just because there's a box around the cat, it does not isolate the cat from the vacuum."

"What about the double slit experiment?" asked Sydney. "You know, the one where you take a board with two slits and beam light through slit A and it makes a pattern on the wall behind it. But when you open slit B, the pattern that slit A had made on the wall changes. It implies a communication between the two beams of light even though they're not interacting. They also found that the pattern changed anytime they added an observer, implying that you can't determine whether the light going through the slit is a wave or a particle until you add an observer."

Alex swallowed a bite of salad and wiped his mouth with his paper napkin. "Here again, our current model does not take into consideration that everything exists in a connected field. It's just like when you toss a pebble into a lake. It causes waves on the surface because it's interacting with the water, and it's creating a vortex as it falls through the water. So in a sense it is both. It is a particle but it also is creating a wave. The same is true when you add an observer, because the observer is creating a wave too."

"I see," said Sydney, her green eyes lighting up. "It makes perfect sense and explains why there's a communication between particles that aren't touching. That explains the seeming connectedness of particles at the quantum level!"

"And it also means that the universe knows what's going on everywhere at all times," said Alan.

Sydney hesitated for a moment. "Are you saying the universe is conscious? I thought that was what you were implying during your presentation," she said turning to Alex.

"In a sense," said Alex. "There's a feedback-loop of information between physical matter and the vacuum state. If you remember the picture of the balloon and the *guy* that I showed as the model of the universe, there's an exchange between the lung and the balloon for it to expand. If you apply that concept to my model, the lungs represent the contracted – or back hole side of the universe – and the balloon represents the radiated side and is what we call reality. There is an exchange of information or energy to cause the expansion of the universe. I believe this is the universe learning about itself. It gathers information and feeds it back onto itself."

"I thought that was what you were implying in your talk." Sydney took a bite of fish and chewed it slowly. Alex tried to gauge her reaction. He hoped she was starting to realize that his theory had profound spiritual implications, as he was going to need her help to research religious texts in his quest for perfect geometric equilibrium.

"Okay, you've been giving me a lot of things to think about, but a conscious universe? I'm finding it hard to take the leap from information flowing between the contracted and radiated sides of the universe to consciousness. I think you'd better stick to finding an energy source in the vacuum if you want the physics community to take you seriously," said Sydney with a look of skepticism.

Alex was disappointed with her statement, and Alan shot him a knowing look. They always hit the wall with scientists when it came to questions of creation. He had hoped that she was opening up to the spiritual implications of his work, especially with her recent experience with the visitation and the crop circles. Unfortunately, she still seemed to be stuck in the typical mindset of most scientists.

"I'm a scientist, Alex. In a true Newtonian sense, I believe the universe is an intricate machine and all its moves could be calculated with precision if we knew all the dynamics

96

involved in the system," said Sydney.

"Science and religion are seeking to answer the same questions," said Alex. They both seek to understand how the universe came into existence and how it operates. Religion will tell you God created the universe. Scientists will tell you the Big Bang did it. The scientific explanation is just as much a matter of faith as the religious one, as it fails to explain what caused the Big Bang. I believe both explanations are inadequate and that the black hole dynamic at the center of all particles is what is fundamental to creation and what caused the Big Bang. I don't know about you, but an infinite, conscious energy field underlying all of physical matter seems to have spiritual implications to me."

Sydney shrugged her shoulders. Alan started to talk, but Alex signaled for him to stop. He didn't want to push her too far with a debate over religious questions. It was one thing to talk about ETs and another to tread on someone's religious beliefs.

The blonde officer threw his brown leather bag that was strapped over his shoulder on his desk in the OEB office in downtown Kona. He pulled out his electronic notebook where he had written copious notes on the conversation he had with Alex Harmon. He dragged his chair forward, waved his hand to turn on his computer, and typed *Sydney Stewart* into the search engine. Within seconds, a complete dossier on Sydney appeared chronicling her career. But Patrick Deheney wasn't interested in her work. He wanted to know about her personal life so he did a more detailed search. There he found a complete chronology of her life since birth including a dossier on her parents and links to friends and other relatives. He also found what she studied in school, all her grades and legal activities such as applications for licenses and tax returns, and links to all Internet activity.

He wanted to know whom she had been involved with romantically in the last few years and was interested to find a link on her relationship with someone named Mark. Evidently, the OEB in Ann Arbor, Michigan had been spying on her for possible morality breaches but had never made any charges. *This was more than two years ago,* he thought stroking his mustache. *She's not been married, and she claims she's been celibate. I don't believe that for a second. A woman that attractive needs a man.*

He had seen her looking at his manhood, and knew she wanted him. He touched the screen, printed out a picture of her, and traced a finger over her breasts. Then he placed the picture in a folder.

CHAPTER 11

Sydney found Alex huddled over his laptop at the breakfast table, already working when she came into the kitchen of the main house.

"Good morning sleepyhead," said Alex looking up from his screen.

"Sleepyhead?" said Sydney somewhat surprised.

"It's eleven o'clock!" said Alex pointing to the clock on the wall.

"Oh my God! I had no idea. I never sleep this late," said Sydney embarrassed to have overslept on her first day on the job. "I'll have to get an alarm clock. I had no sense of the time at all, which is odd for me."

Sydney grabbed a mug and poured herself a cup of coffee. She joined Alex at the breakfast table on the lanai that overlooked the ocean in the distance. Below them, a lush paradise of vegetation stretched all the way down the mountainside to the beach. Sydney felt giddy enveloped in all this beauty. Her senses seemed elevated. The colors of the fronds were intensely green, and the sound of the birds resonated like a symphony. The light glistened on the ocean, and the turquoise and rose floral tablecloth flapped lazily in the light breeze. It was akin to sensory overload being in all this splendor after the unending gray skies of Michigan.

Alex had toasted some bagels and brewed a pot of the aromatic Kona coffee that grew on his property. Sydney hadn't had a man make breakfast for her since her relationship with Mark had ended. In fact, she hadn't even thought about being with another man until she met Alex. She couldn't deny her attraction to him. There was something about him, a kind of charisma, that was inescapable, and she found herself energized just being around him.

"This is so beautiful," said Sydney.

"I love being close to the Earth. Being in the midst of all this natural beauty has helped me to formulate my theory. Plus, I love just being able to throw on some shorts, sandals, and a cotton shirt," said Alex, tugging on his brightly colored Hawaiian top.

"I was surprised to see Brian Sheppard at your conference. I didn't know you knew each other," said Sydney taking a sip of coffee.

"I was at U of M before your time, that's for sure."

"It had been really traumatic for him when they split the Higgs Boson," said Sydney. "He had been certain he had found the smallest thing the universe makes."

"Oh yes, it was supposed to be the ultimate "God" particle!" Alex said with an air of irony. "I remember many late nights and many rounds of beer at O'Reilly's when I would tell him that was going to happen." Alex chuckled, thinking of his world renowned, completely inebriated colleague. "One night he got so mad at me he almost broke his leg going up two steps to his apartment."

"Did you know his wife died four years ago?" asked Sydney taking another sip of coffee.

"Yes, he had been terribly distraught for a long time. But he seems to be doing much better now," said Alex. The last I heard from him, he was dating Annie Haskell. Did you know her? She was that tall, slim beauty in the Psych Department."

"Oh yes, I know her. She's very nice and very nurturing too."

"I'm sure she is good for him and for Beth. Beth is such a sweet child," said Alex reaching for another bagel.

Sydney adjusted her blouse and let out a chortle. "Beth, oh my God; you must not have spoken to him lately."

"Well, it has been about two years, and he didn't say anything about her at the conference," said Alex. "What's going on with her?"

"Well, when she hit seventeen she turned into a wild child. She's been doing drugs, having sex, along with a host of STD's. Brian sent her to an American College in Switzerland but they've been threatening to kick her out."

"Oh that's too bad, said Alex concerned. "She was such a sweet little girl, and smart too."

"She's turned into a beauty too," said Sydney. "But that sweet little girl has morphed into a full blown rebellious teenager."

"Stories like this make me glad I never had kids," said Alex. "I don't know how Brian handles it."

"Didn't you ever want children?" asked Sydney turning to face him – surprised to hear such a statement coming from a man as compassionate as Alex.

"Well, when I was younger I always thought I'd have a family, but my wife had problems and couldn't get pregnant, so that was that," said Alex.

Sydney noticed a gloom descend upon Alex like a shroud. His face actually turned ashen.

"How long has it been since you divorced?"

"I'm not divorced. I'm a widower."

"Oh, I'm sorry," said Sydney embarrassed by her assumption.

"It's been eleven years. I can hardly believe so much time has gone by." Alex grimaced.

"What happened if you don't mind me asking?"

"Cancer. It was pancreatic cancer, and she didn't have any symptoms until it was too late." Alex looked off into the distance, and Sydney could see this was still an open wound in his heart.

"Have you had other relationships since then?"

"Oh, sure. But the time I spend on work is always an issue. It was an issue with my wife too." Alex shook his head as if trying to shake off his remorse. "What about you? Have you ever been married?"

"I was involved with someone for many years, but when

the OEB started cracking down on unmarried sexual activity we were forced to either marry or breakup ... so we ended up doing the latter." Sydney still found it painful to talk about Mark and decided to change the subject.

"So where do we start?" Sydney asked pouring another cup of coffee.

Alex seemed relieved to leave the personal subject as well. "I've been struggling for years trying to find the perfect geometric equilibrium of the vacuum. I need to find that specific geometry to complete my theory. It's the key to understanding how the universe creates boundary conditions around the infinite vacuum to create physical matter. If we can figure that out, we can figure out how to make these boundary conditions ourselves, and then we'll be able to create matter at will!"

"Create matter?" asked Sydney clearly shocked by this revelation.

"Yes, and we may actually be able to create physical matter directly out of the vacuum – something like the replicators on the old Star Trek programs.

"So you're saying space is the infinite field and the boundary conditions are the matter and follow a specific geometric pattern?" asked Sydney.

"Exactly," said Alex. "Space defines the matter, not the other way around!"

Sydney's face became bright with this new understanding. "Theoretically, we may be able to not only tap into an unlimited energy source, but also create anything in the natural world. In a sense we would be Gods."

Sydney sat at her desk in her living quarters working on her computer. She had been in Hawaii for a month. She and Alex worked so well together it was almost as if they were telepathically linked to one another. She finished an equation she had been struggling with for three weeks and was startled by the result. *Well, I'll be! He is right! The math is showing that gravity may well be coming from another dimension – or as Alex theorizes, the other side of the universe.*

Sydney and Alex had spent pretty much all their days and nights together since she arrived in Hawaii, and Sydney's feelings for him were growing with each passing day. He never ceased to amaze her with his quick mind and depth of knowledge. He could talk intelligently about such a wide range of topics, and she found every day to be a new learning experience.

Sydney was finding it more and more difficult to control her desire for him. She had to admit to herself that she was falling in love, but she knew that to act on her feelings would be too dangerous. Still, she wondered if Alex even returned her affections. She had been finding this hard to determine as he was a bit shy and rarely talked about his feelings or his personal life.

The sun was starting its descent into evening and Sydney decided to go over and join Alex in the main house to show him the results of her equations. Typically, the workday was over at 5:00 p.m. but she thought he would be as excited as she was to see the outcome of her work. She found him sitting on the lanai on a large white wicker couch. Below them the sun was glimmering in purple and red hues on the surface of the water.

"I have something I want you to see," said Sydney handing Alex her laptop. "The math is definitely corroborating your theory that gravity is coming from a hidden dimension. According to these calculations, that would make it the strongest force in the universe, not the weakest."

Alex looked over her calculations and grinned. "See," he said looking up at her. "I told you!" He took her hand. "Come sit here and enjoy the evening. This is great. You've done a fantastic job!"

Sydney sat down beside him gazing at the light show in

the sky. "It looks like something out of a Rousseau painting."

"Yes, it really is amazing. I come out here on the lanai often just to watch nature. The process of creation is all around us."

The two of them sat gazing out at the dance of nature as it unfolded before them. They spoke in whispers so as not to interfere with the sounds of the beauty around them. Alex put his hand gently on Sydney's knee in what seemed like the most natural of warm gestures, but it sent a fresh wave of desire through Sydney's body. They were close enough for her to feel the heat of his body. She moved to place her hand on top of his when he turned to her.

"I spoke to Brian Sheppard last night," said Alex. "He's been scrutinizing my papers and is finally seriously considering my theory. I'm amazed he showed up for my presentation. It was a big leap for him, but I'm glad he's not been spending any more time at the accelerator. With your math, we may now be able to convince him to co-author the paper. His name on the work would be a big bonus in getting some serious consideration by the mainstream physics community."

Sydney's pounding heart slowed down abruptly at this turn in the conversation. She had expected him to say something personal But once again, as so many times before, their talk was about work.

"That's fantastic," said Sydney trying to hide her disappointment.

Alex smiled at her and Sydney saw something in his eyes again – something leading her to believe there might be more than being mere colleagues in their future. He had gentleness about him mixed with the kind of raw masculinity that made her melt. She felt another wave of passion course through her body.

"Your expertise has been invaluable to the work. We've made a lot of progress since you got here," said Alex, the look in his eyes turning serious.

His words burst her bubble yet again. *My expertise? Maybe he's not interested in me after all,* she thought. *I better not get myself too excited about this guy. It has been a month and he's never approached me in that way. Maybe he's too paranoid about the OEB to cross that line.*

Sydney was concerned about the OEB too, but she doubted it would stop her from responding to Alex should he ever make a move. Alex patted her knee and pulled his hand back. He then stood up. "Stay here as long as you like. I've got to go down to the lab and check on the clean room. We're getting close to a vacuum state." He smiled at her as he closed the door behind him. Sydney let out a sigh. Her heart felt like it had a hole in it.

CHAPTER 12

Sydney woke up when the droning, didgeridoo-like sound in her head became so loud she could no longer ignore it. She really hadn't thought much of it before, but the sheer persistence, and the fact that the sound was getting more intense was starting to worry her. She decided she better go to the doctor and check it out.

She found Alex at the breakfast table reading the paper when she came into the house.

"Alex, I've got to go to the clinic this afternoon."

"Are you okay?" he asked with an air of concern.

"Oh I'm sure I'm fine, but I've been hearing a sort of ringing in my ears and I thought I'd better have someone check me out."

"How long has this been going on?" asked Alex.

"Actually, ever since I got to Hawaii."

"You mean for a month? Sydney you had better get yourself to the clinic! I can't believe you've put off something like that for so long!" The look on Alex's face was one of deep concern and incredulity.

"I know, I know," she said. "But I doubt it's anything serious."

"I'll come with you," said Alex as he got up and reached for his car keys.

"No, really! I'm fine. Please, you have a lot of work to do and there's no need for you to sit around the waiting room all day for me."

Alex sat back down and sighed. "Okay, but only if you're

sure you'll be okay." Sydney was touched and a bit surprised at Alex's concern.

"I'll be fine. I'll call you if I need anything," said Sydney.

Alex pulled the keys to the car off the wall hook and handed them to Sydney. She headed for the door.

"Well, you are beautiful on the outside," said Alex. "I'm sure they'll find you beautiful on the inside as well."

Sydney smiled at him and blushed. He had never said anything like that to her before. In fact, she didn't think he was even attracted to her. She was self-conscious about her height and flat chest and had always been surprised when a man found her attractive. She had been such a gangly kid and had been called *beanpole* in grade school. She had never been part of the clique of "cool" kids, and that early experience damaged her self-confidence to this day – even though almost anyone would surely call her a beauty.

Sydney had resigned herself to the fact that their relationship was professional, and that was probably a good thing – especially since she was living so close to him and the fact that he had never made any advances whatsoever. Nevertheless, she found herself falling in love with him, and it was getting to be painful holding her emotions in check all the time. Living with him here on this lush island was like paradise.

Sydney never thought she could feel so at home and comfortable with someone. She had lived on her own for so long that she was afraid she would never be able to tolerate someone else in her space. Of course, this was Alex's space, and she had her own quarters; but they spent so much time together that it really had been as if she was living with him.

She walked over to Alex and leaned down giving him a soft kiss on his cheek. Alex looked up at her somewhat surprised at her gesture. Their eyes met for a split second that seemed like an eternity. Sydney withdrew, feeling awkward. "I'll be back soon," she said, hesitating to look back at him before closing the door.

The clock read 7:00 p.m. when Sydney finally returned from the clinic. Alex was in the living room sitting on the couch and looked up when he saw her come in to drop the keys off.

"Is everything okay?" he asked softly. "You've been gone all day."

"I won't know for a while," she said coming over to him and sitting on the arm of the couch. "They did a lot of tests. They saw something unusual on the MRI, but felt it was too out of the ordinary and that something must be wrong with their equipment."

Alex's eyes showed concern. "Did they tell you what it was?"

"No, they were so convinced the results were due to an equipment failure that they want me to go to Hilo and get retested. They said it wasn't anything that would put me in danger like a tumor; just that it looked strange."

Sitting on the arm of the couch so close to him, she felt her passion shoot through her like a firestorm. She gazed at him with a desire that consumed every fiber of her body. She wanted to lean over and kiss him but she was afraid he wouldn't return her affection. Alex sat up and gently pulled her down to the couch. He looked in her eyes and stroked her face tenderly. Then he kissed her on the lips hard and long, and the passion in Sydney exploded! She returned his kiss with lustful abandon, and Alex took her in his arms and laid her down on the couch, unbuttoning her blouse and kissing her neck and breasts. He was so forceful Sydney felt swept away and totally out of control. The weight of his body on top of her made her hunger for his touch. He ran his hands down her body while his tongue caressed her nipple and he reached under her skirt.

Sydney was keenly aware this was a dangerous complication for their working relationship. But there was nothing she could do, or wanted to do, to stop him. She desired him with every ounce of her soul. He touched her like a man who knew how to please a woman, and she was swept away in a passion so intense she felt transported to a world where only the two of them existed. She couldn't remember a time when she felt so in sync, so perfect with someone. Their lovemaking lasted for hours, both of them finally indulging their unfulfilled desire until it exploded in passion. They laid wrapped in each other's arms silently as Alex stroked her forehead and smiled down on her.

"Oh Alex, we shouldn't have done this," she whispered.

"Are you kidding me, we should have done this ages ago. I don't think I could have gone another hour without having you. Don't think. Just be," he said. Then he whispered, "I love you" in Sydney's ear. Sydney smiled and closed her eyes.

"I love you too."

Dr. Harrison shook his head as he scanned the MRI.

"This is impossible! I simply can't accept what I'm seeing on this brain image. Mary, could you come in here please?" he said rolling his chair over to the doorway where he could see his lab assistant thumbing through some files. Mary looked up from her work and came into the lab. Where did these tests come from?" he asked looking at her above the rim of his tortoise shell glasses.

"They were sent over from Kona General," she replied.

"And this set was taken here?' he asked his brow narrowed in disbelief.

"Yes, Doctor."

"So let me get this straight. These films were taken on two different MRI's?"

"Yes, I know it's rather unbelievable," she said.

Dr. Harrison let out a snort. "Unbelievable just doesn't describe this. This woman's brain has thirty percent more area activated than a normal brain."

"I know," said Mary. "But haven't you ever wondered how the brain evolved to have more capacity than it uses in the first place? Doesn't that kind of fly in the face of evolutionary theory? I mean, nature adapts to give a creature a certain advantage, but does nature build in capacity that it isn't even using?"

"Well, this woman is certainly using her capacity! This is a medical miracle. Let's get her in here. We need to find out what she can do with all this extra brainpower. Let's keep this to ourselves for a while until we run some more tests. We have a once in a career opportunity with this." Doctor Harrison leaned back in his chair, his hands behind his head. "Yes indeed, what is this woman capable of doing?"

Sydney and Alex walked up and down the narrow aisles of the library looking for the ancient civilization area. Hardly anyone ever used a library anymore with so much available on the Internet. However, a library allowed you to research subjects without leaving a trail – as long as you didn't check anything out of the library. Alex didn't really know what he was looking for but trusted he would know it when he saw it.

The library in Kona was small and the resources sparse, but they found two shelves of books they thought might be important for their work. Almost by instinct, Alex pulled out a thick, heavy book filled with color photographs called "The Secrets of The Mexican Pyramids" by Peter Tompkins.

"Let's take this one over to the desk," he said to Sydney.

The only other person there was an old man sitting at one of the seven tables, that sat six each, in the small reading room. The room was stark with white walls and orange plastic folding tables and chairs. The only sound was the squeaking coming from the old man shifting about in the uncomfortable plastic seat and the buzzing of the overhead neon lights. They walked over to a small table at the far end of the room. Alex sat down beside Sydney so that they could study the book together. He opened the book at random to a diagram of a geometric structure within a sphere and let out a gasp!

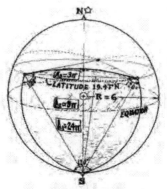

Illustration courtesy of *The Secrets of The Mexican Pyramids"* by Peter Tompkins

"Do you believe this?" he said, his jaw hanging open. "This is an isotropic vector matrix in a sphere! I can't believe this is on the first page I opened!"

Sydney gazed at the diagram, her face filled with astonishment. "What is this doing in a book about Pyramids?" Alex pulled his reading glasses out of his pocket and positioned them on his face as he read on. "This is amazing."

"Who drew this?" asked Sydney.

"It says here that the diagram was made by Hugh

Harleston Jr. who had been commissioned by the Smithsonian to do a major study of the ancient ruins of Teotihuacan, north of Mexico."

As they leafed through the book, a diagram of the layout of the city caught Sydney's eye. She started reading.

"Evidently, Harleston Jr. spent over twenty years working out the mathematical relationship of the buildings and discovered the city was an accurate representation of our solar system, including Pluto!" Alex looked over at Sydney and watched her eyes dart back and forth.

"How could this be? Pluto hadn't even been discovered until the 1930's, and this city had been built two thousand years ago. How could they have known this at a time when civilization didn't even know the Earth revolved around the sun?"

"It also says here that the builders had to have knowledge of spherical trigonometry to construct this city," said Sydney clearly flabbergasted.

Of course, Alex already knew where the knowledge had to come from.

Sydney leaned back in her chair and looked at the ceiling. "Well it certainly raises some questions," she acknowledged.

"It says here that they had to carry these blocks – some of them weighing over seventy tons, that's 140,000-pounds each – over a hundred miles through the jungle to build these structures," said Sydney looking over at Alex. "How could they do that, and why would they cut such large blocks to work with?"

"Maybe they had some sort of technology," said Alex. "Why would you work with blocks so large as to make the task virtually impossible? Why not cut them into five hundred-pound blocks or even one thousand-pound blocks, not 140,000 pound blocks, for God's sake! It just doesn't make sense to me unless they had some sort of technology making it much easier to handle," said Alex.

Sydney shook her head and flipped through a few more pages.

"Here it says the pyramid at Chichen Itza is aligned so perfectly with the solstice that the sun casts a shadow that appears like a serpent descending the stairs. Such a precise alignment would be pretty hard to do thousands of years ago. It's not like they could say, Hey Joe, move that seventy-ton block a little to the right!" Alex chortled at his own attempt at humor.

Alex found the section on the Egyptian pyramids at Giza. "It says here that the Great Pyramid at Giza is thirteen acres at its base and only a quarter inch off center at its apex at four hundred and eighty one feet, and is built with two million three hundred thousand blocks. The space between each block is so perfectly cut and aligned that you can't even put a credit card between the cracks!"

"Let me look at that," said Sydney leaning into Alex to read the passage. "My God, it says here the King's chamber is built with two hundred ton blocks! That's four hundred thousand pounds each! I don't believe we can move anything that large even today."

"Yes, and they supposedly hauled those puppies and then *stacked* them!" Alex said rolling his eyes. "And did you know that they never have found a body in the Giza pyramids?"

"Well, that's probably because of grave robbers," countered Sydney.

"Grave robbers? Right!" said Alex sarcastically. "So you really think grave robbers dynamited into the pyramid long before dynamite had been invented and found a way to cut the top off of the sarcophagus which weighed over two tons. Then they took the crumbly, icky mummy out, for God knows what purpose, and put the lid back on and resealed it? After that, they supposedly *rebuilt* the entrance so it fit exactly with the other blocks. I don't think so! There's also another problem. If you do the math, these workers had to quarry, transport, and put into place two blocks every nine seconds to have built the Great Pyramid in the twenty-year period that archeologists say the construction took place."

Sydney shrugged her shoulders with reluctant acknowledgement that something was wrong with this story. "Well, when you put it that way, it really doesn't add up, does it? So where did the mummy go?" asked Sydney.

"Well that's the point, Sydney. There's only one mummy,

that of Queen Shesheshet, that has ever been found in a pyramid. That's a common mistake. Maybe the pyramids were built for another purpose entirely." Alex read to her: "The sarcophagus is made in such a way that it could have been a conductor of a high energy source."

"It was?" said Sydney. "Let me see that." Alex pushed the book over toward Sydney.

"Well, I'll be! So it is!"

"Maybe it wasn't a tomb at all. Maybe it housed an energy source," said Alex watching for Sydney's reaction. "It could have been the energy source that I'm seeking to build – one that used the knowledge of the geometry of space-time. I mean, think of it. The ancients went to incredible trouble to build giant tetrahedrons! Hollister's diagram is significant, Sydney. He's drawing an isotropic vector matrix in a boundary as a representation of the layout of the pyramidal structures found at Teotihuacan."

"What! Let me see that." Sydney pulled the book in front of her.

"It also says here that the only reason history believes the Pyramids were built by the Pharaoh Khufu is because of an account by Herodotus written thousands of years after they were supposedly constructed, as he lived between 484 and 425 B.C. Actually, there is no ancient Egyptian record claiming they were the builders even though the Egyptians documented just about every aspect of their lives. Maybe we need to explore why so many ancient civilizations were building pyramids. Maybe the builders were trying to tell us something important and wanted to preserve the knowledge for thousands of years," said Alex.

Sydney sat up straight in her chair. It was as if she had a sudden epiphany. "These people must have had the ability to control the vacuum. Infinite density causes the gravitational pull of the black hole. Harnessing this force would produce anti-gravity capability! That could be it! They levitated these blocks! That's the only thing that makes any sense. Why else would someone build with such unmanageably sized stones unless they weren't troublesome to move at all! If they had anti-gravity technology, they would have had no problem bringing these stones here and stacking them like this," said Sydney, her tone getting into the higher pitch she used when she was excited.

"Alex, you know you may be right! There's a lot more here than meets the eye."

"They weren't the only civilization to go to such trouble to build pyramids. In fact, there are pyramids, not only in Egypt and Mexico, but all over the world." Alex continued studying the book while Sydney leaned back in her chair, deep in thought.

"So if the ancients were able to levitate these enormous blocks they had to understand the force of gravity, and somehow it's mixed up with the tetrahedral shape ... whoa!" gasped Alex."

"What?" Sydney looked over at him startled by his outburst.

"Look at this!" Alex pointed to a diagram of the layout of the pyramids in Giza, the pyramids in Teotihuacan, and the pyramids in China. They were laid out exactly the same way, with the three pyramids aligned exactly as the tree stars of Orion's Belt.

"I knew of the theory that the pyramids at Giza were laid out supposedly to correspond with the stars in Orion's Belt. But I never knew that this had been done in two other places on opposite sides of the Earth!"

"That's amazing!" said Sydney turning the page. Then she stopped, dumbstruck at what she saw. Alex looked at her, shocked at her expression. "What is it?" Alex asked looking over.

"This is a picture of the so-called face on Mars, but notice what's next to it a little off to the left! This is a satellite photo taken by NASA of three pyramids on the surface of Mars near the face, laid out in the same configuration as Orion's Belt!"

CHAPTER 13

John Croft leaned his corpulent body back on his leather chair with gold leaf crosses inlaid into the dark wood strips that ran down the sides of the thick armrests. His office was paneled with mahogany, and the hunter green velvet drapes were mostly closed, shrouding the room in partial darkness. The only illumination came from the low desk lights with their dark green shades. Croft didn't like the light.

He reached over to his large black onyx and pearl humidor with his stubby fingers and pulled out a large Cuban cigar. He savored the smell for a few minutes before sticking it in his mouth and lighting up.

"Sir?" bellowed the voice of his assistant Gertrude over the COM system. "The Surgeon General is on line one."

Croft clicked his vidphone on. "Dr. Remick, what can I do for you today?"

"As per your directive, I'm passing on information received today on a Class 19 event." The doctor cleared his throat and Croft could hear the nervousness in his voice.

"Class 19?" he asked raising an eyebrow.

"Yes, sir. It came to me from Hilo General Hospital in Hawaii. A patient named Sydney Stewart has presented with a brain scan indicating the mutation for a Class 19 psychic."

"Do you have the report and the scans?" asked Croft.

"Yes, sir. I've already sent them to you."

"Good. I want to put surveillance on her."

"Sir, we already have surveillance on her. She's been working with Alex Harmon."

At this, Croft's cigar almost fell out of his mouth. *This is it. These must be the scientists who will bring my technology to fruition!*

"Good work. I will remember your loyalty."

Croft hung up the phone. Only six other Class 19 cases had been discovered, and none of them had been working on anything close to a technological device. Alex Harmon and Sydney Stewart had to be the ones the seer had predicted, and he needed to watch their every move. His future and the future of the world depended on it.

Class 19's were psychics on steroids. Their potential was like nothing he had ever seen before. They were possibly the most highly evolved humans on the planet. The seer who told him of his destiny had warned that someone with enhanced brain activity would be involved in the creation of the technology that he sought to control. That technology would either lead the world to a true understanding of creation that would destroy his extreme fundamentalist translation of Christianity, or it would place power in his hands alone ... power that would enable him to rule the entire Earth.

Now, after years of searching he had found a Class 19 working with Alex Harmon on some sort of technology. This was it! For now, Croft needed to watch, not destroy them. He had to let them build the device and then take it from them. *Sydney Stewart, Kona, Hawaii*, Croft wrote on his desk pad. *Who are you and what can you do?* Croft pushed a few keypads on his computer and up came a complete dossier on Sydney.

Alex heard a heavy knocking at the front door. He peered out the window and saw the flashing blue light on the motorcycle.

"Yes, is there something wrong?" asked Alex opening the door to the police officer who was wearing the red and gold uniform with the matching helmet of the OEB Brotherhood police. He had on dark sunglasses and his mouth was partially covered by the helmet strap so that Alex could hardly see his face ... and that made him look menacing, as it had been intended to do. When Alex opened the door, he could see it was the same blonde officer that had come by the day Sydney moved into the complex.

"Yes. What can I do for you, officer?"

"This is an inspection. Where is Miss Stewart?"

"She's not here right now. I think she went to the beach."

"Which beach?"

Alex was taken aback by his question. Why did he need to know her exact location? It was disconcerting to him.

"She usually goes to Two Steps Beach."

"The officer pushed past Alex letting himself into the house.

"The bedrooms sir!"

"Yes, yes, come this way," said Alex as he led the officer up the stairs. Alex hated the Brotherhood for their tyrannical invasion of personal liberty. They had the right to enter anyone's house at anytime, without warning, to enforce the strict laws against sexual relations outside of marriage. Alex showed the officer his bedroom. The officer sniffed around his room for the scent of a woman's perfume. He then took a device from his pouch and began scanning over the bed.

We'll know if she has been in your bed or you in hers."

Alex was furious. '*How dare they!*' Yet he dared not anger the officer. He had the power to arrest him and send him to God knows where, without any specific charges. He could rot there for years without the right to an attorney and nobody would even know his whereabouts. One messed with the OEB police only at one's own peril, so Alex kept a quiet and respectful tone to his voice. Alex led the officer to the guesthouse and showed him Sydney's living quarters, where again the officer scanned her bed with the device.

"She's very beautiful. Are you not attracted to her?"

"We have a professional relationship," answered Alex his blood starting to boil with anger.

"Are you gay?" asked the officer with a surly tone.

What a catch twenty-two. If I'm attracted to a woman, they'll accuse me of having sex with her, which is illegal. If I'm not having sex with her, I'm gay, which is also illegal! Alex didn't even answer this inquiry. He gave the officer a steely glare.

"You say you work together? Can you prove that?" asked the officer.

"Yes, certainly." Alex could now feel a drop of sweat trickle down from his forehead. "You'll have to come with me to my lab. It's across the garden in a separate building."

Sydney pulled herself onto the rocks at the small, secluded beach down the road from Two Steps and threw her mask and flippers onto the ledge. She grabbed the towel she had left and made her way over to her favorite spot that was across from where most people sunned. It was a small landing hidden behind some rocks and gave her enough privacy to be able to undo her bikini top and work on her tan. She pulled out her book and lay down on her stomach to bask in the sun. It was a hot day and it felt wonderful just to be able to relax and cool off in the ocean and then bake in the sun.

"You!" came a deep voice that startled Sydney. She grabbed for her bikini top and held it to her chest as she looked up. To her horror, she saw the blonde OEB officer who had interrogated her at the house.

"It's illegal to be nude in public," he said with a menacing tone. He seemed to be aroused as he was wearing swim shorts and she could see that bulge in his pants. Sydney's heart began to beat rapidly. They were alone. He must have seen her and followed her. No one could see them in this small cove.

The OEB operated with impunity. With all their rhetoric of morals, they were known to be the worst offenders, and often harassed women and even raped them. Every nerve in her body told her she had to get away. She grabbed her towel and started to run, but the young, strong officer grabbed her, put his hand over her mouth, and pushed her to the ground. She knew that if she fought him, he would come after her later and arrest her.

"Touch it!" he shouted as he pulled his manhood out of his pants. Sydney tried to scream. If there were witnesses she would be okay. But he was too big and too strong, and she could not pry his hand off her mouth.

"If you scream, you'll be sorry; so shut up and enjoy it. You know you want it," he snarled.

Sydney could not fight him. Just as she resigned herself to the rape, she heard something in her mind. *You need to transform him! This is a man who had been hurt deeply by a woman and has turned this hurt to hate and anger. Send him love and compassion.* Sydney closed her eyes and with all her might and being tried to envision him surrounded by golden light. As she did this, she felt his grasp loosen from her arm. He had stopped, still holding her under the weight of his body. She opened her eyes to find him looking at her with a most disoriented expression.

She continued to concentrate on thoughts of love, compassion, and appreciation. She tried to understand what damage done to this young man would drive his violence, and continued to send him compassion. She visualized holding him in her arms and comforting him like a mother. As she did this, she could feel a pressure building in the center of her forehead. Suddenly she could see in her mind's eye, rays of light reaching from her temple to his, filling him with the radiant, golden light of love.

Without a word, he loosened his grasp and stood up. He

continued to look at her as if he was stunned and confused. His eyes lowered as if he was in the presence of divinity itself. Tears were streaming down his face as he turned and walked away.

Sydney gathered up her things and returned home. She went into the bathroom and looked at herself in the mirror for a long time. Something profound had just happened to her. She didn't even know where the idea came from to send him love. But it worked! It was powerful. A sense of complete freedom overtook her. All her fears melted away. It was as if she had been reborn.

After reading about Hugh Harleston Jr.'s study of Teotihuacan, Alex realized the isotropic vector matrix was somehow fundamental to the geometry of the vacuum. He had been spending countless hours trying different permutations of the shape attempting to solve the puzzle.

The geometry would need perfect equilibrium, so he reasoned that the tetrahedron was the stable geometry that must form the basis of any such shape. He already knew that a double tetrahedron, or Star of David within a sphere, was the geometry the universe uses to go to infinity. He was fairly certain that the cube octahedron that Buckminster Fuller called the vector equilibrium was involved as well, but he couldn't put it all together.

He noticed that the isotropic vector matrix, with its twenty tetrahedrons, had some negative spaces that he could not explain and this nagged at him. He tried putting two together end to end, but when he drew a boundary around it, he got an egg shape, not the expected sphere. He knew this could not be right.

"What are you working on?" asked Sydney as she entered

the lab eating an apple.

"I'm still looking for perfect equilibrium. I can't figure out what these negative spaces are or how the universe would use this shape alone. It has got to have its polarized pair."

Sydney stood behind Alex studying the shapes on the holo-imager. "What would happen if you take the two isotropic vector matrix shapes and push them together?"

"How so?" Alex stood up and offered Sydney his chair at the keyboard. She sat down and started to move the design around, merging the two tetrahedral shapes together until it formed a star shape.

"Oh my God!" said Alex, flabbergasted as the negative spaces interlocked perfectly when the two shapes merged.

"Look, Alex; it forms a cube octahedron at the center! That figures – as the cube octahedron is the only geometry in which every vector is the same length."

"This is amazing! But it still can't be the shape of perfect equilibrium. There are all these points that are exposed. This shape can't grow in fractals," said Alex scrutinizing the geometry.

Sydney started to play with the shape adding additional tetrahedrons to the exposed edges. When she finished, she had added three tetrahedrons to each of the eight edges.

"That's it!" exclaimed Alex.

"We have twenty tetrahedrons in each of the isotropic vector matrix shapes and twenty-four that we've just added," said Sydney, the significance of the number just starting to dawn on her. She looked at Alex in awe and amazement ... sixty-four! The sixty-four tetrahedral grid is the shape of perfect equilibrium! The universe uses the star tetrahedron to grow outward to infinity and the cube octahedron to contract inward to infinity!"

Sydney lay in her bed watching the stars for a long time. Her eyes were growing heavy and she found herself drifting off to sleep. The Being appeared before her once again. Sydney sat up in her bed and pinched her arm but felt nothing. "Is this a dream?" she asked. Sydney looked around trying to ascertain if she was sleeping or awake when the Being answered her thought.

"There are no dreams; there is only travel into the vacuum."

"What do you mean?"

"During the sleep state, your consciousness is able to travel in hyperspace, where we can communicate with each other. I will help you remember what has transpired after you awaken. I have come with some important information. You are close, but there's another vital piece to unlocking the physics of creation. You have not addressed this issue and it must be added into your equations." A holographic image of another crop circle appeared above the Being's hand. This one was different from the one it had shown Sydney before. It had multiple swirling spheres laid out in a fractal procession.

"Spin is everything," the Being said. "It's at the foundation of why everything works the way it does. Why do planets spin? Why do galaxies and electrons spin? There's a fundamental force causing the spin."

A new image appeared above the Being's hand. Sydney didn't recognize it at first, but then she realized it was the solar system when she saw the blue planet of Earth and the ringed Saturn. She noticed the solar system was doing something she rarely thought about ... it was moving forward as it spun around the sun becoming a vortex.

"Of course! The solar system isn't static and two-dimensional. It's traveling around the Galactic arm, which is moving around the Galaxy. It has angular momentum! Everything has momentum and spin!" Sydney gasped as she realized that this important element had been left out of their equations.

"Why does water curl as it goes down the drain?" asked the Being.

"Even Newton couldn't figure out why that happens." Sydney furrowed her brow. "I don't understand why you are so cryptic. Why don't you just tell me the answer?"

"I'm not allowed. I can point you in the right direction. That is all. There are strict rules governing contact. I am sorry. Take a close look at how Einstein's theory was solved for spin. There are two major omissions. Solve these and you will have the answer you seek."

"But what do? ..." The Being turned to vapor before Sydney could finish her question.

Sydney opened her eyes as she awakened from a particularly deep sleep. The memory of her dream started to flood her consciousness. The Being was not only appearing physically, it was able to communicate with her in her sleep. She looked at the clock. It was 4:00 a.m., but she couldn't wait to tell Alex. She threw on a robe and ran barefoot across the path to the main house.

"Alex?" she whispered peering into his bedroom. He didn't answer. She walked over and touched him gently on his shoulder.

"What? What's wrong?" asked Alex startled.

"I'm sorry to wake you like this but I have to tell you now, before I forget."

"Forget what?"

"I had another encounter with the Being."

Alex sat up in the bed. "Okay, I can see this is going to be a long conversation. We had better do this in the living room. We can't have your DNA in this room." Sydney nodded in agreement. Alex grabbed his robe that was draped over the chair beside his bed and they went downstairs.

"Alex, this time it was specific. The Being told me to investigate spin! It said there were errors in how Einstein's equation for spin had been solved."

Alex hesitated before answering her. It was something he had only shared with a few of the most trusted people in his life, as it was something that could seriously damage his credibility as a scientist. Now he had to decide whether he could trust Sydney enough to include her in that privileged group. She just had her second direct experience. It was clear to him they wanted her to know. Hopefully, she was ready. He let out a long breath before speaking.

"You've worked with me for over a month now. You know I'm a rational person, a competent physicist."

"Not just competent, brilliant!" she countered.

Alex smiled at the complement. "Well, there's something you need to know about me." Alex folded his arms across his chest, looking at her somewhat defensively.

"I uh, I know some things, not just because I have studied them, but because I have been getting help."

"Help from whom?"

"Other-worldly Beings."

"You mean you've been visited by these Beings too?"

"Yes, quite often as a matter of fact." Alex hoped she could handle what he was about to tell her.

"Is this Being an angel?" she asked. "It seemed God-like."

"Actually they're from the Galactic Federation."

"The what?" Sydney's eyes widened in disbelief.

126

Alex hesitated again but decided this was the time for disclosure.

"I've had contact with Beings from other worlds for a long time. In fact, since I was a young boy." There it was. He hoped she wouldn't run away screaming like some other women in his past had done.

"ET's? You're talking about people from other planets?" Sydney had a look of incredulity on her face. "I was sure the Being was an angel."

"Actually, angels, multidimensional beings, extra-terrestrials, and the Galactic Federation are all one and the same. They can come from other planets and other dimensions," said Alex.

"You mean angels are from other dimensions and extraterrestrials are from other planets?" asked Sydney furrowing her brow, struggling to comprehend this radical shift from all she had been taught.

"Well, here's the big news Sydney. There's no difference."

"No difference?"

"Actually this is one of the greatest misunderstandings. Beings humans have called angels through the millennia are really space faring races capable of transcending dimensions – many of whom live for tens of thousands of years. In fact, you can't really talk about religion without talking about the Galactic Federation. If you start to look at Biblical stories in the context of extraterrestrial Beings, like the story of Ezekiel, who "ascended" on something that sounds much like how an ancient might describe a spaceship, or Moses who comes down from Mount Sinai with radiation burns, they don't seem so mystical anymore."

Sydney looked at him unable to speak. Her whole worldview was unraveling before her eyes. She had been prepared to accept an angel or some spiritual being, but she was not at all prepared for ET contact.

"Once the Galactic Federation has made contact, like they did with you last night and during the conference, you will never be the same."

Sydney looked panicked at this revelation.

"You don't have to be afraid. This is something quite wonderful, and you will find yourself opening to a whole new level of awareness and a whole new realm of information."

Sydney paused for a moment. "But what does that do to the whole concept of God? Are you saying that throughout history we have been worshipping ETs?"

"Certainly that has happened. However, you have to remember that some of these Beings are thousands if not millions of years ahead of human development. They understand the universe and creation and the oneness of everything – and like you and me – are part of it. No species, in fact nothing can be, or is, separate from the conscious Source that connects all things. So this does not negate the concept of a higher power And in fact, validates it. Is it so hard to think that the Beings that we might call angels could be from highly advanced civilizations that have a complete understanding of the mechanics of the universe and can interact with it and engineer it?"

"What do you mean engineer it?"

"I believe the universe operates within a specific system. Don't get me wrong, this does not minimize the consciousness of the vacuum. After all, you are conscious and yet your body operates under specific parameters. It's just like when we learned how the heart worked; we could create a mechanical heart. In the same way, when a species understands how the universe works, they can create, or shall I say manifest, things at will. I call it *engineering the vacuum*."

Sydney was astonished by Alex's revelation.

Alex's face took on a serious expression. "From your description, it sounds like you met a Being from the Galactic Federation. They had told me that they would be contacting you directly as it's important for you to understand the true ramifications of my work. I'm not just trying to create technology. I'm trying to create something much more profound."

Sydney leaned back into the floral cushions of the couch, and Alex turned to face her directly.

128

"I'm looking for the fundamental principles of creation. I'm looking for the scientific equation for creation."

"Alex, you better be careful. If the OEB learns of this, they'll kill you. They're not going to allow anyone to mess with their dogma," said Sydney, clearly worried for Alex's safety.

"The OEB is an abomination!" This was a sore subject for Alex. "The beauty of the holy teachings has been so distorted over the millennia by men who are seeking money and power over the people. So much violence has been committed in the name of religion throughout history. Now that America has become a religious government, it's happened again.

"One word gives them the moral imperative to do so much harm. Did Jesus say *I am THE* way, or I am *A* way? This simple change would have made such a difference in how those of other faiths have been treated down through the ages. This one word gives them the moral superiority to dismiss the validity of other faiths and to persecute those who did not follow their way. Certainly, it's possible that this one word could have been altered through the thousands of years and by the many corrupt Popes who controlled the Church."

"But there are a whole lot of people who are buying into this," said Sydney.

"My work will show once and for all that there are many ways to God. We can reach God through our own vessel. We don't need a priest or a Pope to find God. Our bodies are boundary conditions around the vacuum that is essentially God. We need only look within to access the conscious infinite field. The sooner people realize this, the oppressive control religious institutions have wielded will be lifted."

If they don't kill you first!" said Sydney shaking her head as if to say, *you had better not go there*.

"It doesn't matter what happens to me. What matters is that an accurate understanding of creation gets out to the people."

"So our work is not simply about creating a new technology?" said Sydney sardonically.

"The technology goes hand in hand with the understanding of creation. I believe this was the true message of the masters that had walked the Earth throughout the ages - and is the birthright of all men and women. It is a birthright that's been stolen from us, depriving us of our intrinsic and amazing power to interact with the Universe."

"I was brought up Catholic but have trouble accepting so much of what the Church, and for that matter, all organized religions have to offer," said Sydney. "But I still believe in God and Jesus."

"I'm not saying that Jesus wasn't highly plugged in," said Alex. "For all intents and purposes, He is divine. But so are you and so am I. If you listen to what Jesus said, and throw out what has been said about him, a very different picture of Him comes forth. Remember that many gospels were omitted from the doctrine of the Church by Pope Constantine in the Third Century. If you read the Gospels of Thomas and Mary Magdalene, you get a very different picture of what Jesus actually taught."

Sydney nodded in reluctant agreement.

"So much of the story around the birth and death of Jesus is mere myth as far as I'm concerned," said Alex. "The validity in Christianity is in the actual teachings of Jesus, who talked of the importance of love, forgiveness, and the meek inheriting the Earth. Most of what was said after His death is where I part company with traditional beliefs.

"In fact, my understanding from a movie called *Zeitgeist* by Peter Joseph, is that the whole nativity story had been really based on celestial movements, and the story reaches far back into antiquity thousands of years before the time of Jesus. If you look at mythology around the world, you'll find that in ancient times many cultures worshipped the sun. The stars also were also seen as deities and were catalogued into the Zodiac. The sun with its life saving properties had often been referred to as the God Son and a savior, for it brought light and life to the world.

"In Egyptian mythology, Horus, son of Osiris, was the Sun God around 3000 B.C. and was thought of as a Solar Messiah. He had an enemy called Set who represented darkness as every evening Set would battle Horus, and every morning Horus, the Sun God, would be reborn victorious. Horus was also baptized, like Jesus, at thirty years of age by Anup.

"The birth stories of Osiris and Jesus are also almost identical. Just like Jesus, Osiris was born around the winter solstice. The similarities of the myth do not stop here. Osiris was a teacher, healed the sick and walked on water. And he too had been murdered, and then resurrected by Isis and became the Lord of the Realms of the Dead."

"Really? I had no idea," said Sydney, clearly astonished by the parallels in the two stories. "That can't be an accident."

"It's quite uncanny! I realized that this story had to be a celestial allegory referring to the movement of the stars, and is why so many myths around the world are so similar to the Christian birth story."

"You mean there are others?" asked Sydney, now clearly intrigued.

"Oh yes. Scores of them. It's because the story really relates to the movements of the night sky. Sirius is the star in the East and is the brightest star in the night sky. On Dec. twenty-fourth Sirius aligns with the three stars in Orion's Belt which, in antiquity and today, are referred to as the *Three Kings.*"

"Oh my God!" exclaimed Sydney. "I had no idea!"

"It gets better. They all point to the place of the sunrise on December 25th. This is why the three kings are said to follow the Star in the East in order to locate the sunrise or the birth of the sun/son. The Constellation Virgo or the "virgin" was known as the house of Bread whose translation is Bethlehem; not a place on Earth, but a place in the sky. By December 22nd the sun reaches its lowest point in the sky and appears to stop moving South for three days. To the ancients, the sun seeming to stop its movement across the sky symbolized death. During the three-day pause, it resides in the Southern Cross or Crux Constellation. Then on December 25th it appears to move north or rise again.

"So it is said that the sun/son died on the cross, lay dead for three days, and then rose again; which is the origin of the birth myth. This is why so many ancient myths share the virgin birth, death on the cross, three days dead and resurrection story. The resurrection, however, had not been celebrated until the spring, as it's in the spring equinox when the light overcomes the darkness, and the days become longer than the nights."

"What other cultures have this myth?" asked Sydney, still unwilling to accept what Alex was saying.

"Many ancient myths are exactly the same as the Jesus story including Krishna who had also been born of a virgin with a star in the east and had been resurrected after death. Dionysus also had been born of a virgin on December 25th as was Mithra of Persia who was also said to have had twelve disciples, performed miracles, died, and been resurrected. There are many other God Beings who share a similar story such as Indra of Tibet, Bali of Afghanistan, Jao of Nepal, Sakia of India, Osiris, and Horus of Egypt, Odin of the Norse, and a host of others."

"I still believe the basic teachings of most religions are true…that there's a God, that what we do and say matters, and that we are immortal infinite beings," protested Sydney.

"I don't disagree. And removing the dogma doesn't change that, but it changes things politically!" exclaimed Alex.

CHAPTER 14

Under the glaring light of the large office filled with computer screens and monitoring devices, Elton Newhardt sat eyes half-glazed with boredom. His screen lit up with different colored lights indicating threatening words that filtered through the billions of fiber optic communications on the island. He pointed to the green light and the conversation filled his headphones. "Kill the President" were the words the system picked up.

"This man is so out of control," said the female voice. "America is gone. There's no freedom anymore. We might as well be living in the Soviet Union in the 1960's."

"Ain't that the truth," said the coarse male voice with a southern lilt. "Someone should just shoot the President and his crony Croft!"

"Yeah, if wishes could come true."

Elton, realizing this conversation was not a real threat to the President marked it D code for *dissenter,* which would put both parties on a list of people to be stripped of their financial privileges.

Another light flashed on the grid. This was from the phone of Sydney Stewart. He was assigned to monitor her phone communications and those of Alex Harmon. So far, he couldn't figure out what the big deal was with these two. But all of a sudden, his board lit up with red lights – indicating target words were being used – words like *Galactic Federation* and *telepathy.*

"I received a download from the Galactic Federation last night," said Alex. "It is important to our work."

"Did you have a visitation?" replied Sydney's voice.

"No, it was a telepathic transmission .... "

"Holy Jesus!" Elton cried. "I got me a hot one!"

He immediately routed the conversation through to headquarters.

"Brandon Tarnoff, is he in?"

"Sir, do you realize what time it is in Washington?" came the voice of the White House operator.

"Yes I do, "said Elton. This is a code RA1 for Brandon Tarnoff. Did you hear me? Code RA1!" he shouted.

The operator knew the rules on code RA1 and immediately connected him through to Tarnoff's home.

"This better be good," said the gruff voice of Tarnoff with the annoyance of someone who was roused from sleep.

"Yes sir. I picked up an RA1 at the Harmon house. They were talking about being contacted by an ET."

"Anything more?"

Elton played back the entire conversation.

"I want a man on their conversations continuously, not just when there are trigger words. Do you understand?" ordered Tarnoff. "And record everything!"

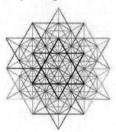

"Alex, did you know that the Kerr Newman Solution that solved for spin in Einstein's Field Equations uses a fixed frame of reference to account for rotation?" asked Sydney looking up from her computer at Alex who was huddled over his desk.

"No, that can't be. Let me see that." Sydney put the equation up on the holo-imager.

Alex studied the equations in silence for some time and then rolled his chair away from his desk. "Well I'll be! Those little sneaks! How did they get away with that for all this time? They eliminated all the shearing, torque, and coriolis forces to solve Einstein's Field Equation for spin."

"Exactly!" exclaimed Sydney. "By using a fixed frame of reference, which doesn't exist in nature, they have distorted the way nature actually works. They can count the rotations, but they've discounted all the forces that come into play in the real world."

"This is a truly outrageous omission," said Alex. "Just think what would happen if you were stupid enough to grab onto a piston spinning at five thousand rpm."

Sydney gave him a look of incredulity. "There would be a lot of shearing effects, that's for sure!" said Sydney laughing. "You'd catch on fire and your skin would start flying off. There would be a lot of force!"

"Exactly," said Alex. "But by fixing the frame of reference, it's moving at exactly the same rate as the rotating vector: like a rod bolted onto the spinning piston, it would eliminate all the torque and coriolis forces. I can't believe they did this." Alex leaned back in his chair and let out an exasperated sigh. "I can't believe the scientific community hasn't noticed the flaws in this solution for spin in Einstein's equations for so long!"

"I have to admit, I didn't know about it. We were given the equation in school and no one questioned it. Frankly Alex, we've seen this repeatedly. The scientific community keeps coming up with ludicrous solutions just to make their math work. Just think how using arbitrary cutoffs like the Planck's length, instead of accepting the infinite nature of matter, has screwed up our understanding of reality. The Plank's length is the arbitrary measurement for the smallest piece of matter, so the omission seems infinitesimal. But think of how skewed the results get when they use this renormalization at the large end."

"Sydney, do you think you can add torque and coriolis forces back into Einstein's Field Equations?" asked Alex.

"I think I can – and once we've done it, I think we might get our unified field theory!"

Sydney had been putting in long hours every day, working well into the night for months trying to write torque and coriolis forces into Einstein's Field Equations. *No wonder Kerr and Newman left these out. This is damned complicated,* sighed Sydney as she sat staring at the mathematical equations trying to persevere despite the extreme complexity of the task at hand. She was certain getting the correct equation would be vital to understanding the way matter comes into being.

She and Alex had come to believe that the structure of the vacuum was the sixty-four tetrahedral grid. *But how does the universe use this structure to create matter? Everything spins, from galaxies to particles. Matter is in constant motion ... angular momentum, really. Everything is spinning and moving at the same time. The solar system isn't a fixed two-dimensional rotation that is usually pictured. The planets are circling the sun while the sun is circling the galactic arm and the galactic arm is circling the galactic center while moving around the galaxy, and the galaxy itself is moving. It must look more like a vortex than concentric circles.*

Sydney continued to develop her mathematical construct. Alex wanted to know what shape the sixty-four tetrahedral grid would form when they spun it. He kept saying that would be the shape the universe uses to spin matter into existence. It was Sydney's goal to find this shape. She ran calculation after calculation in an effort to account for all the forces that would play on a moving body of matter. It was no easy task.

She tried to imagine what the form would look like. It was with this thought that she remembered the shape that the Being had shown her. It was a double torus; two donuts stacked on top of each other. The diagram showing some sort of energy progression between the double torus appeared in her mind's eye. *Could that be it? A double torus with the black hole in the middle of the two donut shapes with energy radiating around it like an infinity sign?* She could see it so clearly now. It made perfect sense.

If the visible universe is the expanding balloon, and the vacuum is the "guy's" lungs contracting, the interaction back and forth suggests a feedback-loop, and that would mean matter is constantly being informed by Source where all information and all time exists all at once. Thus the feedback-loop of energy, which is information, must be flowing between the radiated side and the contracted side of the black hole. The shape could definitely be a double torus, the topological model for consciousness! Information that feeds back on itself is the definition of consciousness.

She ran the calculations and it worked. The sixty-four tetrahedral grid formed a double torus when it spun. An enormous chill went down her spine, and Sydney took in a deep breath. This was a huge breakthrough. She realized in that moment that she just discovered the scientific proof that the universe is conscious. She let out a squeal of delight, grabbed her computer and ran over to the house to find Alex.

"What?" he asked looking up from his book as Sydney burst into the living room.

"Look at this." She placed her computer on the coffee table in front of him, put up the holographic depiction of the sixty-four tetrahedral grid and began to spin it. As Alex watched, he could hardly believe his eyes as the tetrahedral structure took on the shape of a double torus.

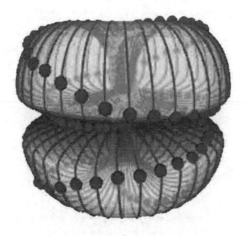

"And look at this," said Sydney as she rotated the torus to show the top view. Alex's eyes lit up with delight as he watched the yin and yang sign form.

"Remember when I said I didn't think it was a coincidence that a religious symbol, the six-pointed star, is the model the universe uses to go to infinity?"

"Yes. This is getting eerie," said Sydney. "A Yin and Yang sign and the Star of David are fundamental to the geometry of space-time!"

"Quite frankly, I'm not surprised. Delighted, but not surprised. I have been looking at symbols from a variety of religions. I was playing with the Kabalistic Tree of Life. Look what happens when I take eight of them and merge them together."

Alex leaned over and picked up his computer that was lying on the floor next to the couch. He pulled up a file that showed the geometry of eight Trees of Life. As the trees came together, Sydney gasped. "Look at that! It forms a sixty-four tetrahedral grid! It's been there all along, hidden in plain sight in many of the world's religious symbols."

"You see, Sydney … I've been trying to tell you! This is far more than just accessing a field of energy. The ancients used this geometry when referring to God!"

Alex watched the way Sydney's lips moved when she spoke and how her long golden hair cascaded over her shoulder. *She was so beautiful.* He got up and stood behind her chair, leaned over and began kissing her neck.

"You're a genius," he whispered in her ear.

Sydney dropped the pen out of her hand and leaned back to receive his caress. She let out a shudder of desire and turned around grabbing his neck and kissing him hard on the lips.

Alex began unfastening her blue cotton shirt, running his hand over her chest and feeling her nipples harden. He pulled her up off her chair and lifted her small frame over to the table that was strewn with diagrams of geometric structures. With one hand he pushed the papers onto the floor and laid Sydney down, her blouse now open, exposing her creamy skin. He kissed her deeply and felt the wetness between her legs as he lifted her white skirt out of the way. Sydney wrapped her legs around him and took him in with a gasp.

CHAPTER 15

Alex and Sydney took the last turn up the 4,200-meter high summit of Mauna Kea when the white Keck Observatories became visible on the horizon. The temperature had dropped dramatically on the mountain and frost had formed on the windshield of their car. From this height, they could see wispy clouds passing by below them.

"I told you that you would be glad you dressed warmly," said Alex as he pulled into the parking lot in the shadow of the cylindrical structures. "Most people don't realize that this is the largest mountain on the planet. It's even higher than Mount Everest if you count the part of the mountain that's below water."

Sydney zipped up her ski jacket and stepped into the ankle high snow. It was surreal to have been swimming in warm water and sunbathing in the morning, and then walking in snow in the afternoon.

"The Keck Observatories are not in high demand anymore since they built the Sagan telescope in Tibet, so we can have access to one of the best facilities on the planet to view the universe. Albert said he could fit us in right away today. I'm hoping that we will be able to see the geometric structures in the Super Nova they saw this week," said Alex looking over at Sydney as they walked up to the large round building.

Inside, Alex signed in and they were ushered to the waiting room for their time slot to use the telescope. The "Dog" super nova had just been reported in the Milky Way, and they were privileged to get telescope time to view such a rare event that happened only once or twice every hundred years in the Milky Way Galaxy. It was paying off that Alex had befriended many people at the Keck who help him get access to the telescope rooms.

"Actually, there's a super nova somewhere in the universe almost every minute," said Alex. "But getting to see one this close is a treat!"

"Once a minute? Really?"

"Yes, it gives you a feeling for how vast the universe is."

Sydney nodded in agreement, taking a seat in the waiting area outside the observation room.

After almost an hour, Alex looked up at the clock. "We've been waiting an awfully long time!" exclaimed Alex in an irritated tone.

Sydney looked at her watch. "Does it always take so long?"

"No. This is unbelievable. Albert told me I would be first in line if I showed up before 1:00 p.m." Just as Alex started to fume some more, a thin, mild mannered clerk with a receding hairline poked his head through the door and told them they could go into the telescope room. As Sydney and Alex approached the viewer, the clerk went back to his office, turned on a surveillance camera and began monitoring them.

"Do you see anything?" asked Sydney as Alex gazed through the lens quietly for some time.

"It's absolutely amazing. Here, I'm sorry, take a look," said Alex as he moved over and let Sydney get into the viewing seat.

"Oh my God, it's more amazing than I ever imagined. You were absolutely right. You can see the double torus dynamic happening in the super nova. Look, you can see the two donuts and the singularity point in the middle!"

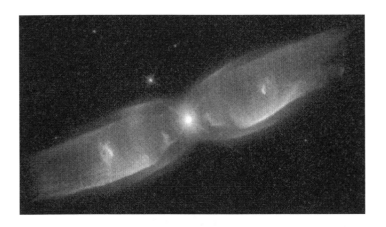

"I told you," said Alex beaming. "If the universe does the same thing at all scales, this is exactly what I expected we'd see – and there it is! You can see the point of singularity between the two toruses. And you can see in the red rings the torus or donut shape that it would form."

"This is very confirming, Alex," said Sydney with a triumphant nod.

They watched the super nova for some time, and then Alex switched the view to Saturn. He had read that Saturn's North Pole had a hexagonal structure, but he had never seen it for himself.

"Look, Sydney! There it is!" Sydney took over peering into the huge telescope.

"Oh my God! It's still there!" exclaimed Sydney.

"Scientist first saw this during the Cassini space probe fly-by decades ago," said Alex. This is remarkable evidence that there's a sixty-four tetrahedral structure supporting the spherical shape of the planet. Look at the South Pole. You can see the vortex. That also supports my theory. These formations cannot be flukes and still be there after all these years! It's also predictable that the ring would form around the equator where matter and energy are expelled and re-circulated around the black hole at the center of the double torus."

Sydney continued to stare at the blaze of stars that lit up the night sky.

"There are so many stars up there it's hard to fathom."

"Actually, there are so many stars up there, the sky should be white, not black," said Alex.

"What?" said Sydney looking over at him with a surprised expression.

"Think about it. With all that light being generated by all those billions of galaxies why isn't the sky white?"

"I've never thought about that," replied Sydney.

"Our universe behaves like a black hole. Light bends around the mass and can't escape it," said Alex.

"You mean you think we are living in a black hole?" asked Sydney pulling away from the telescope to look at Alex.

"Exactly. In fact, I think everything, all material reality, is a different sized black hole."

"You have said that before."

"Well, I've been thinking about it for a long time. Perhaps everything we are seeing in the universe is just the electromagnetic or radiating side of a black hole. Think about it, Sydney. The very definition of a black hole is an infinite density. Infinite! And what is infinity? Infinity is everything all in one – the whole – not the hole or emptiness. So everything we see in the universe, or more likely the infinite multi-verse, is just a black hole or 'whole' inside a larger black hole/whole and so on to infinity. The Super Nova dynamic certainly demonstrates the characteristics of a black hole dynamic. We've seen the same dynamic happening at many different scales. Now we've just seen it at one of the largest scales."

"It certainly supports your theory that the universe is fractal in nature," agreed Sydney.

"I've believed for a long time that black holes are intrinsic to the nature of the universe – that they are the source of creation, not the result of it. We've known for quite a while that there are super massive black holes centering every galaxy. By looking back billions of years into the early formation of the universe, we've been able to detect that black holes were there first, before matter started to form."

Sydney thought for a few minutes. "You know, the way

light bends, the universe does kind of behave like a black hole," she replied.

Alex nodded in agreement. "The super massive black hole at the center of galaxies produces smaller black holes we call stars, which produce smaller black holes, or planets, and then atoms and so on."

"But if we're living in a black hole, wouldn't we be spagettified?" she asked referring to the theory that all matter gets elongated as it gets sucked into a black hole."

"No, I don't agree with that theory," said Alex. "I believe that's just a factor of perspective when one is outside of a black hole watching matter go into it. I think if we were somehow to ride the matter into the black hole, much like Einstein envisioned riding on a streak of light, the view would be quite different. In fact, we've seen that stars are being produced very close to the event horizon of black holes, which goes against the current model that they would be ripped apart by the tidal gravitational forces.

"What do you think of running the math assuming there's a black hole in the center of an atom? Let's see if it's enough force to hold the atom together."

"Alex, everyone knows it's the *strong force* that holds the atom together."

This statement pressed one of Alex's buttons. "The *strong force* is just another theoretical cop out!" he fumed. They just calculated how much force would be necessary to hold the atom together and called it the *strong force*. But no one knows what is causing this so-called *strong* force. I bet you'll find that a black hole in the center of an atom accounts for the force."

"Gee, Alex. I can't believe this gets you so angry." Sydney positioned herself behind him and rubbed his shoulders in an effort to calm him down.

"I'm sorry, honey. I'm just sick and tired of the ridiculous made-up particles and forces mainstream physics uses to make their math work. They give me so much flack for my theory when they commit the most outrageous transgressions!"

"Well, if we could get the math to work, it would provide

some real proof that black holes are a fundamental component of matter," said Sydney. "Let's do it!"

As Sydney and Alex left the Keck, the clerk monitoring them saved the surveillance chip and sent it off to the OEB.

"Mr. Croft?" came the voice of Gertrude Aarhus as she knocked lightly on the door. Croft reached over for a fat cigar with his stubby fingers, browned with age spots. The knock at the door stopped him from lighting up. "Yes?"

"Sir, excuse me." She poked her head in his door. "Mr. Tarnoff is here to see you."

"Good, send him in." Gertrude showed Tarnoff into the cavernous mahogany paneled office, and he stood before the large carved desk, his hands clasped in front of him, waiting quietly for Croft to look up from his paperwork.

Brandon Tarnoff was one of Croft's top aids, but still was treated with the formality that Croft had demanded from everyone. Brandon headed the Domestic Surveillance Agency, the feared "DSA," and answered directly to Grand Master Croft, an honor few others enjoyed.

Brandon was a slight, boyish-looking man in his mid-forties. He had a grayish pallor, probably from the eighteen-hour days he spent indoors pouring over surveillance reports. He had reached his position because of his dogged commitment to Croft and the OEB. Many had lost their jobs, their families, and some had lost their lives trying to stand in Tarnoff's way. He was paranoid and perceived his colleagues and targets alike as possible enemies.

Tarnoff looked somewhat green and his hands were quivering as he waited for Croft to acknowledge him.

Croft had little patience for meekness. "Well?" Croft demanded.

"We had an operative over at the Harmon lab yesterday. He had a good look around. He placed the surveillance equipment per your request sir."

"Good," said Croft, lightening up a bit. "Very good. Now we'll be able to find out what he's up to."

"The operative slipped bugs onto their computers, so we should be able to monitor everything they do," said Tarnoff clearing his throat. "They were overheard talking about an extraterrestrial and a diagram. We found pictures of crop circles in Stewart's computer."

Tarnoff handed Croft a stack of pictures that he had taken from Sydney's computer.

"Crop circles? What do you make of these, Tarnoff?" asked Croft, pulling another large cigar out of the humidor on his ornate desk. He offered one to Tarnoff.

"No thank you sir."

What a little weenie, thought Croft.

"I don't know sir. They're just made by some crazies that like to stomp around in fields at night."

"I don't think so" said Croft. These have some specific geometric shapes. They may mean something."

"They're just designs," replied Tarnoff.

Croft knew they were more than that, but he didn't want to tell Tarnoff. He wouldn't understand anyway.

"It looks like they're working on some sort of energy source sir."

"Yes, yes. I've known about Harmon for years. But this Sydney Stewart. She's a Class 19 psychic and she's talking about ET contact? This is more than an energy source." Croft's tone was incredulous.

"I don't know sir. Maybe they're a bit crazy. I mean talking about ETs and all."

Croft looked up at Tarnoff, but said nothing. *Need to know*, he thought. He didn't need to tell Tarnoff about the extraterrestrials.

Croft scowled, his eyes shifting back and forth as he tried to get a handle on the significance of Harmon and Stewart having contact with an ET. *Which species was it?* he wondered.

"Keep watching them and let me know everything."

Croft had known about the ETs for years. He had much to fear from them for the Galactic Federation was not actively working to bring about a change on Earth. It was a change that would benefit mankind but dissolve the power of men like Croft who needed to keep the people ignorant of their true power in order to keep their own.

Croft was a divinity student before he went back to school to study physics. In his examination of ancient scripture, he started to believe that what had been contained in the Ark of the Covenant was a device that accessed the power of God, but a device just the same. Those who had the device had great power. It had been the power of the Pharaohs of Egypt. As he learned more, he found that Alexander the Great, Napoleon, Hitler, and many other men of history sought the device believing it would give them ultimate power.

As a divinity student, Croft had studied the prophesies, not only in Christian texts, but those of the Mayans, American Indians, Chinese, and other ancient civilizations. He came to believe that once mankind reached a certain level of scientific understanding there would be profound changes in human civilization. He also believed that this time was at hand and that the change would be brought about through a technological device such as the one housed in the Ark of Covenant.

He needed to control the device and keep it from the masses, for the knowledge that came from understanding the technology would bring down the status quo and his hard built empire with it. Now, he suspected Alex Harmon and Sydney Stewart might be working on creating such an ark device.

It was months later when Sydney ran excitedly into the lab. "Alex! Darling!" she squealed.

Alex looked up from his computer amused by her giddy animation. "What is it?" he asked raising an eyebrow and giving her an impish grin.

"The math, it works," she gushed.

"What math?"

"I think I've come up with the mathematical proof that a black hole in the center of the atom is the source of the force that holds the proton and the neutron together, not the theoretical *strong force.*"

At this, Alex pushed back his chair and swung around.

"Really? Let me see."

Sydney handed him the computer card and he slid it into his laptop.

"You were right. We can do away with the strong and weak forces. There are only two forces in the universe: gravity and electromagnetism – not four. Take a look at this, Alex. If you assume there's a black hole at the center of all protons, the force it would exert exactly equals the theorized *strong force.*"

"And the *strong force* is just a hypothetical construct in the first place," added Alex.

"Exactly. They came up with it backwards: simply calculating the force that would be necessary to hold the atom together, not knowing where the force was actually coming from," said Sydney shaking her head at the absurdity. "The so called "strong" force is an explanation of nothing. Our black hole theory describes the actual force.

"Here's what I did." Sydney cursored to the first page,

and the diagrams and equations appeared in the projection. "I decided to call our black hole proton the Schwarzschild proton, since Schwarzschild was the scientist fighting on the Russian front in World War I who solved Einstein's equations for a black hole, calculating how much mass is necessary in a certain radius glossary to cause it to collapse into a singularity."

"I think that would be a proper tribute to him," agreed Alex.

"It's just pure luck that he had been able to send his calculations off to Einstein before he died shortly afterwards from illness.

"Alex, look at what else I discovered," said Sydney as she cursored down to another equation. "If you compare the Schwarzschild, or black hole proton, with the current standard model you can see that the black hole theory is far more credible. Look how it lines up with the other data points on the scaling law while the standard model is way out in left field! It resolves the unification problem – that Einstein's Field Equations and Quantum Physics don't seem to operate by the same laws of physics – by eliminating the need for the *strong force*."

"Yes," agreed Alex. "The current model created the problem in the first place!"

"It also eliminates the missing mass problem that we call dark energy and dark matter as it explains that the black hole dynamic is causing the expansion of the universe, not these theoretical particles," continued Sydney excitedly. "It explains why the force is nearly infinite at the quark level close to the singularity and does away with the need for a so-called *color force*. And it starts to explain the communication between atoms at the quantum level that seemingly have no physical connection, whereas the current model has no explanation for this." Sydney had a look of triumph on her face.

Alex leaned back on his chair and threw his arms in the air laughing with satisfaction. "I've been blessed to have found you!"

Sydney grinned. "You're the one who's always saying there are no accidents in the universe!" Sydney cleared her throat trying to regain her train of thought. She had worked hard and wanted to fully share her results with Alex.

"I found something else that is truly remarkable. When I calculated the velocity of two black hole protons orbiting each other with their centers separated by a proton diameter, and if I utilize the gravitational force to calculate the associated acceleration, I get that they are orbiting each other at the speed of light at the event horizon! So in a very real way we are made of light!"

Alex watched Sydney as she went through her calculation, grinning from ear to ear.

"This is it! We have the mathematical proof that a black hole proton exactly equals the theoretical *strong force*. This is going to turn the scientific community on its head!"

Alex jumped up, threw his arms around Sydney and kissed her deeply. "God, I wish it was the old days and we could publish this! This is an incredible confirmation. You're a genius baby!"

Sydney blushed and her heart was racing once again. She knew that this indeed was it. They were on the threshold of a whole new understanding of creation. Everything would be different.

CHAPTER 16

Sydney lay in the wide hammock on the lanai next to Alex gazing out on the horizon in awe of the scene before her. The sky looked as if it was painted with fluffy ribbons of deep melon and dark pink.

"Look Alex," she said nudging him.

"Wow, this is a particularly colorful sunset," he said looking up from his book to take in the evening's show.

As they watched, the pastel hue of the clouds blinked out one by one leaving them a gray-blue as the sun disappeared into the ocean. It was all so magnificent and so brief.

The sky became dark. Sydney and Alex put their books down and lay silently in the hammock in each other's arms. In silent reverie they fell into a deep sleep. As they slept, a white beam of light descended to the lanai. Its brilliance hit Sydney's eyelids waking her. Sydney looked at Alex, trying to get up, but she was paralyzed. The light began to spin and the form of her previous visitor stepped out of the light. She stared at the white wispy swirls as they dissipated behind the Being. Though its form was scary, she had come to realize it was not to be feared. She tried to catch Alex's eye, but realized he was in a deep trance.

The Being stood beside her and began to speak. Sydney could hear its words in her mind even though the sound of her heart pounding in her chest dominated her consciousness.

"Am I dreaming or are you real?" She wanted to nudge Alex to awaken him but she couldn't move. Now the features of the Being came into clearer focus and it appeared to be male.

"My name is Leytar. Was the crop circle there as I told

you it would be?" he asked.

"Yes, it was," Sydney replied without speaking.

"Then you know that I'm as real as you."

"Yes, Alex has told me you're from the Galactic Federation," answered Sydney realizing she only had to think her conversation.

"Yes, I'm from the Galactic Federation. We are a conglomerate of sentient space-faring races from across the galaxy. We are here to help you. This is a pivotal time for your species, and what you are working on is the vital link."

"What do you mean?" asked Sydney.

"Alex's work will change the future for mankind. In fact, it is we who have sent you many of your inspirations that have led to your calculations."

"What do you mean? No one has helped me."

"We whisper in your ear and come to you in your dreams. We have done this for millennia. We helped Isaac Newton, Albert Einstein, the founding fathers of America, and many other great thinkers in your history. Now we are here to help you. I'm coming to you with a dire warning. You are not ready, Sydney. You will not be able to survive exposure to the field."

Sydney felt a deep pang in her stomach. "I won't survive?"

"You are not resonating as high as Alex. You must be trained before you go any further with your work. You are getting close. Soon you will understand enough to be able to build a resonance chamber that will access the Divine energy field. But it is deadly to those who have not reached a certain level of resonance."

"What do we have to do?"

"You must journey to Tibet and complete your initiation. There's a man you must find. His name is Gieshe-le Tanzen Darghe. He will train you both."

"You mean stop our work ... just drop everything and go?" asked Sydney.

"Yes, you cannot accomplish your work without first being fully initiated. We will help you as much as we can, but

154

some of the work you must do yourself."

"How will we find him?" asked Sydney.

"Begin your journey towards Tibet and he will find you." With this, Leytar receded, its form dissolving into mist as if its molecules were spreading out, until it vanished completely.

Sydney lay there silently for sometime afterward looking over at Alex who still seemed to be fast asleep. *Initiation was a strange word, she thought. Initiation into what? Initiation is something you need to do to be included in some sort of group. But what kind of group? If she needed to be initiated, why didn't Leytar take her off to its planet to do this initiating? What did she have to learn from a Buddhist monk?*

It suddenly dawned on her that this must be a dream. She pinched herself and it hurt, so that meant she was indeed awake. She looked over at Alex again and wanted to wake him to verify the experience, but then realized he could be part of her dream too. She needed to verify that this was not a dream because when she went back to sleep she would never be able to be sure – especially since Alex appeared to be in a trance or a deep sleep throughout the whole event. Sydney decided to write herself a note. She reached over for a pen and paper on the table next to the hammock. "You need to be initiated by Geshe-le Tanzen in Tibet," it read. *Unless I'm writing in my sleep, this will be my physical proof.*

Before long, her eyes closed and she drifted off. In the darkness, a light beamed through the overhanging ceiling of the lanai into the crown of her head and began to download information, equations, graphs, and maps into the sleeping mathematician.

Sydney's eyes popped open as she awakened. She shook Alex who was still asleep beside her.

"Alex, wake up!" she said excitedly. "Wake up!"

Alex sat up startled by her abrupt disruption of his sleep. The hammock almost tipped them both over the edge as Sydney tried to sit up.

"What is it? Are you all right?"

"Did you see Leytar? Was it a dream?"

"See who?"

"The Being. He was here last night. Didn't you see him?"

"No, I'm sorry I didn't."

Alex looked around perplexed. "Did we fall asleep in the hammock last night? I don't remember anything."

"Damn. Maybe I was just dreaming. No, wait a minute. I wrote myself a note." Sydney ran her hand over the table next to the hammock searching for the piece of paper, but it was not there.

"It was so real! It couldn't have been a dream. Is this how the Galactic Federation behaves?"

"Galactic Federation?"

"Yes, he specifically said he was from the Galactic Federation."

"Really?"

"Alex! You've been telling me there's a Galactic Federation and now you're looking at me like I'm crazy. What gives? And where is that note? I know I wrote a note!" Sydney looked down at the floor searching for the paper.

"It doesn't matter necessarily if you can't find the note. They often come in the dream state. It doesn't make it less real."

"But Alex, it's really important that we know if this was real because he said we had to go to Tibet right away! He said if I didn't get initiated I would be killed if I'm exposed to the field."

"What else did he say?"

Sydney filled Alex in on the entire conversation. She remembered it vividly and in detail. Alex pulled himself off the hammock. "Honey, I've got to take a shower and think about this

156

for a few minutes."

Sydney lay back in the hammock looking at the sky and trying to make sense of the night's events. She could hear the shower and realized she was sticky from sleeping in night air without netting. She pulled her legs over the hammock and rocked herself to a standing position. Her barrette that had been hanging loosely on a few strands of hair fell to the floor. She stooped down to pick it up and stopped. Her mouth dropped open in awe. There it was ... the note was there!

CHAPTER 17

The armed Chinese guard at the border of the Tibetan checkpoint gave Alex a suspicious stare.

"What is your business here?" he asked looking over Alex and Sydney's passports.

"We're visiting – on vacation really," answered Alex, trying to hide his nervousness. He knew getting into Tibet would be tricky and up to the whim of the border guard. Sydney smiled at the guard from the passenger seat of the rented Mercedes.

"Where will you be staying?"

"At the Len Dau Monastery."

"Oh, so you are here on a religious quest?"

Alex almost forgot that anything having to do with religion was a criminal offense in China, and practitioners were hunted down, often jailed, and worse. He shouldn't have revealed he was going to a monastery.

"No, no. We merely have an acquaintance there who has kindly offered to let us stay for a while. We're hoping to do some climbing mostly."

"Open your trunk, sir," ordered the guard.

Alex pushed the button on the dashboard that opened the trunk, and the guard moved toward the back of the car. Alex leaned over to Sydney and gave her a reassuring smile, trying not to show his apprehension.

The guard leaned against the Mercedes and then poked his head into the car. Alex could smell the vodka and cigarettes on his breath.

"I don't see any climbing gear, sir," said the guard as he

surveyed the contents of the car.

"Oh, it's been shipped ahead, you're right; we don't have it with us."

"Who are you visiting at the monastery?"

"Gieshe Le Tanzen Darghe," replied Alex. "I met him in the States several years ago."

The guard's demeanor changed radically, becoming stiff and gruff.

"Sir, Madam, please step out of your car."

Alex was nervous now and felt sweat begin to form on his brow. Sydney was visibly shaken as they both exited the car. Alex didn't know why naming Gieshe Le Tanzen would make the guard suspicious of them. Whatever the reason, if they weren't allowed into the country they wouldn't be able to fulfill Leytar's instructions and Alex's life's work and the future of mankind possibly hung in the balance.

"Come with me," said the guard as he maneuvered Alex and Sydney into a windowless, sickly green colored room with just a small wooden table, one folding chair behind it and two chairs in front of it. Another guard, shorter and stockier, followed them in and closed the door behind them. Alex glanced nervously from one to the other and then to Sydney. He could hear his heart pounding, and sweat forming on his lip.

"Sit down here," said the guard pointing to the two wooden chairs. The guard motioned to his comrade. "Tung, get everything out of the car and bring it here." Clearly, the taller guard was the one with more authority.

"We must check through your things," said the guard with a slight English accent.

Alex's eyes shifted downward and he felt his stomach tighten, but he kept a polite smile as he tried to maintain a calm demeanor. After all, they didn't do anything wrong; they weren't carrying contraband. The worst that should happen is that they would be denied entry into Tibet.

"Have you ever been to Tibet before?"

'No, this is the first time." Alex noticed a long scar on the guards left cheek, obviously from a knife wound.

160

"Yes, the first time," chimed in Sydney with a nervously high voice.

"Where were you born?"

"Geneva, Switzerland" Alex replied. But I became a U.S. citizen thirty years ago. You'll see in my papers. I have a U.S. passport."

"I'm American," said Sydney.

Tung re-entered the room with their three cases, which he placed on the floor along with Alex's large, brown leather, accordion briefcase. He then handed the briefcase to his superior. The guard opened the briefcase and started looking through it.

"What is it you are looking for?" asked Alex.

"You will speak only when I ask you a question," snapped the guard with a terse snarl.

Alex leaned back in the chair compliantly and remained silent as the guard continued to rifle through everything in his case. Sydney rolled her eyes upward and let out a long anxious breath through her nostrils. It seemed that the guard was looking for something specific. He kept pulling out binders and flipping through each page, tossing them carelessly on the floor after he finished each one.

"What is this?" The guard held up a binder filled with Alex's geometric drawings of the crystal container, mathematical equations, and had a diagram of the sixty-four tetrahedral structure on the cover.

"It's our work. We are scientists. It's just something we were going to work on while we are here."

The guard gave Alex a long, cold stare as if he was trying to read his reaction. Then he started speaking with Tung rather heatedly. He picked up a phone and called what appeared to be a superior, judging by his tone and demeanor. Alex wished he could understand what they were saying to each other. He didn't know why the diagrams would be of any concern to this Chinese military man, but something about them seemed to set off an alarm.

"Alex, what is going on?" whispered Sydney, her voice now clearly trembling.

Alex merely shook his head, "shhh." He didn't want to do anything to cause the guards to lash out at them. He thought the less they said the better. He was horribly worried about Sydney. He didn't care what they did to him, but he couldn't bear the thought of Sydney being subjected to harsh treatment or worse.

At the end of the call, the guard turned to Alex and grabbed him roughly under his arm.

"Get up!"

"What's wrong? What did I do?" stammered Alex.

With this, the guard punched him in the face.

"I told you not to speak!"

"Don't hurt him, don't hurt him!" yelled Sydney as they dragged him out the door.

Alex's jaw ached with pain, and blood was spurting from his lower lip. The guards threw him into the back of an old van and drove him to a larger building not far from the border checkpoint. As they ushered him through the steel door, he saw that it was a jail and his heart sank as they threw him into a tiny, filthy dark cell.

Alex sat in the corner on the cold cement floor, as there was nothing in the cell. He had no idea why they had detained him. *Maybe Gieshe Le Tanzen was a criminal. But why would the Galactic Federation have us seek him out if it meant trouble?* He started to wonder if this Being that had been contacting Sydney was really a positive entity. After all, it hadn't shown itself to him even when he had been sleeping next to her. He squeezed his eyes closed and wiped the blood off his mouth with his shirtsleeve. *How could they know of my work? And even if they did, why would they be interested in it?* Alex just couldn't fathom what the problem was.

Alex woke up hungry and thirsty with his jaw still throbbing with pain. He looked at his watch and saw that it was 6:00 a.m. He had been in this cell for almost eighteen hours. He was filled with anguish at the thought of what had happened to Sydney and by the hopelessness of their situation. They had no way of contacting this Tanzen. The Being said Tanzen would find them. But how would he know to look for them here? How would he know they were in trouble? Alex looked up with trepidation when a large man in uniform, his weaponry making a loud clanging sound as it accompanied each step, stopped in front of his cell.

"Alex Harmon?"

"Yes?" replied Alex grabbing a bar to help him to his feet.

"Where is this monastery that is hiding Tanzen?" demanded the guard.

"I don't know," said Alex. "Someone is supposed to contact us at our hotel in Lhasa and take us to him," Alex lied.

"What hotel?" The officer glared at Alex.

Alex could not betray his contact, and he didn't know hotels in Lhasa at all.

"The Hilton downtown," offered Alex. He was hoping that there would be one in Lhasa.

The officer seemed somewhat pacified. "When?" he shouted.

"Sometime between this Thursday and Friday," lied Alex.

"You say you are not here to aid the religious rebels. So what are you doing with this?" shouted the man holding up Alex's notebook.

"It's my work. I'm a scientist; a physicist."

"This symbol," said Alex's interrogator pointing to the sixty-four tetrahedral structure, "is on the ball under the lion's foot that guards the Forbidden City. The rebels think it has power and that it's the entry key to the land of their *so called* Gods!"

Alex's eyes grew wide. "What do you mean? I don't know what you are talking about."

"This kind of religion is strictly forbidden in China."

Alex was not sure what to divulge to the man. It seemed that any answer was going to dig him deeper into trouble.

"It's not about religion. It's about science. It has to do with geometric fractals." Alex doubted that this man would have any idea what he was talking about, especially with the language barrier. "Science, not religion," repeated Alex.

"Don't think you can lie to me," shouted the man. "You Westerners think you can come here and spread religion now that our people are finally liberated from the yoke of false beliefs!"

"Honestly, sir. Really, this isn't about religion at all. I would be happy to show you, or someone who can understand it, that this is science. I don't know anything about any gateway to the Gods. I'm a scientist. I work in Hawaii. You can check. I'm well known in the States as a physicist. You have made a mistake. In fact, I would be most interested to hear about your lion and the Forbidden City. I know nothing of it."

"Look at this!" said the guard pulling a paper out of his pocket and shoving it in Alex's face.

"What does this design have to do with your so-called work?" asked the officer, his tone softening somewhat.

"Energy. I'm developing an energy source."

The officer stared at Alex for a few minutes and then he turned abruptly and left.

"Please, sir. Call the American Embassy. They will clear this up," Alex shouted after him, but the officer did not reply.

Alex sat back down on the cold cement floor and put his head in his hands. He had no idea what he had gotten into. His jaw was still pounding and he was hungry. He thought they might have trouble getting into Tibet, but he never anticipated this kind of treatment. He wondered if the OEB was somehow wound up in this situation. *But this was China. Surely Croft's grip did not extend this far. That religious fanatic would have no common ground with atheist Communists in China.* Then he looked up as he heard the clanging of the officer's footsteps returning to his cell. He had a statue in his hand of a lion with a ball under its paw.

"Here," he said as he opened the cell door and handed the object to Alex. Alex looked at the ball and saw that it had the same sixty-four tetrahedral structure carved on it.

"Well, Sir, I, uh, it's the same design, but this is hardly reason to detain me. It's a common geometrical shape. I'm sure this was just decorative. Why is this such a big thing?" Alex tried to keep his voice calm, but in fact, he was amazed to see this rendering – the one he had come to understand to be the pattern that organizes all of nature and the universe was there under the foot of yet another religious symbol!

"No, this is no simple trinket," said the officer. This is a Buddhist religious symbol. The sphere under the Foo dog's foot that carries your drawing represents all knowledge; and the Foo Dog, which is a representation of the Buddha, guards it. Before the Cultural Revolution, many considered this structure to be sacred object. Of course, the People's Republic has outlawed this idiocy. We do not tolerate this kind of treachery to the State."

"I think we've had a simple misunderstanding. I'm interested in this geometry from a purely scientific point of view."

"Science? You're seeking an energy source from a symbol of knowledge? Perhaps you are a sorcerer, not a scientist!" said the officer, giving Alex a cold glare.

"Well, if you believe in sorcery, perhaps you are not such an atheist yourself. Perhaps the line between science, magic and religion isn't so clear," said Alex looking at the floor, hoping his statement would not enrage his captor. With this, the officer's eyes squinted in contemplation. He looked at Alex for what seemed like a long time and then he turned to leave the cell.

"Can you tell me where my companion is? Is she all right?"

The officer stopped and turned, but he did not answer Alex. Then he turned and walked away. As the clanging of the officer receded, Alex was filled with foreboding. *What have they done to Sydney? Why isn't this Being, Leytar, who got us into this mess, protecting her?* He feared the worst and was utterly powerless to do anything. He lay plotting an escape – trying to figure out how he would overcome the guard the next time there was an opportunity, until exhaustion put him into a deep sleep.

Alex counted the scratches he had made on his cell wall. There were six of them. He made one for each time he slept, figuring it was the end of the day. There were no windows, so he couldn't tell whether it was day or night. Only the guard who delivered his daily meal of contaminated rice and a glass of water that had given him Buddha's revenge interrupted the monotony of his days.

He hadn't seen another soul in the jail except for the guard. There had been no one to talk to, and the guard would not speak to him. He didn't know what kind of system of justice they had, or, if they had one at all. For all he knew, they would be detaining him for months, even years. He had to get out and he had to rescue Sydney. To do that, he needed to plan to escape from his jail cell. He decided he would try to overcome the guard when he brought his next meal, though he had little strength after days of near starvation.

Alex could hear light footsteps down the hall, not the usual clanging of the enormous key chain carried by the guards. He tried to poke his head out through the bars to see who it was but could not see anything. As the footsteps grew closer, he braced himself for his escape.

A slight young man appeared and held his finger up to his lips indicating that Alex should be quiet. He slipped a key into the cell door and opened it. Alex grabbed him by the neck and threw him to the floor.

"Please stop, I'm here to help you!" pleaded the man. Alex could see from the look on his face that the man was sincere and loosened his grip. He helped the slight man to his feet.

"Come with me," he whispered.

"Who are you?" asked Alex.

"It is better that you do not know my name, but I am here to help you." He signaled not to speak again, and guided Alex through a door that led to a dark, narrow passage. There were chains on the walls indicating this was probably where they tortured prisoners. The walls were made of thick stone through which no sound could penetrate. Alex imagined the futile screams of the unlucky souls who had been there. For now, it was silent. He could hear only the squeals of what seemed like a herd of rats as he and the stranger made their way through the damp passageway.

The young man carried a small flashlight that lit their way. At the end of the long corridor they hit a dead end, and the man showed Alex a metal ladder on the wall and started to climb it. He motioned for Alex to follow. They scaled the thirty-foot wall and Alex's companion lifted a manhole in the ceiling. As Alex peeked his head over the rim, he could see it was nighttime. The moon cast a low light on the tree-lined landscape. Alex strained to pull his body up with his weakened arms onto the terrain. The man motioned for Alex to stay low as they moved quickly into the trees. Alex looked back to see that they had emerged from a tunnel outside the high brick walls crowned with barbed wire that encircled the prison.

"Where is Sydney?" asked Alex in a whisper. The man looked back at him, his finger on his lips and motioned for Alex to follow him. They made their way through the thick, jungle-like growth. In the distance, they could hear a siren and the sound of barking dogs. They were being pursued. Alex ran after his rescuer as fast as he could, trying not to stumble on the thick growth on the ground. The sound of the dogs grew louder and Alex felt his heart would burst out of his chest. He didn't know how much further he could go. He was exhausted. He had hardly eaten while he was imprisoned and his body felt weak. His muscles ached in places he didn't even know he had muscles. He was panting heavily, and signaled to the man that he needed to stop for a minute to catch his breath. He leaned on a large tree and buckled over in pain.

The man pulled a small leaf out of his pouch and handed it to Alex, motioning to put it in his mouth. Alex chewed the bitter leaf reluctantly, and within minutes he could feel his strength returning and the pain subsiding. He wanted to ask the man what this miracle plant was, but before he could utter the words, the man hushed him yet again.

His rescuer took some powder-like substance from a pouch and sprinkled it all around where they had stopped, then motioned for Alex to follow him. The two men continued on when suddenly the barking stopped and the dogs began to squeal and howl in pain. The man looked back at Alex and winked at him.

Alex and his rescuer emerged from the thick growth into a clearing where they could see smoke rising from a small dwelling in the distance. The man patted Alex's back and smiled, pointing at the wooden shelter. As they drew nearer, the smell of saffron filled the air. Alex hadn't realized how famished he was until the aroma filled his nostrils. The last one hundred yards to the shack seemed to take an eternity. His companion reached the house first and flung the door open, revealing the figure of a woman dressed in blue Mao garb running towards him. His first reaction was to run the other way. But then his eyes focused and he realized it was Sydney. He ran to meet her and collapsed in her arms, tears of joy streaming down his dirt-caked face.

"Sydney, Sydney! Are you all right? What did they do to you? I imagined the worst."

Sydney smiled at Alex and held his bruised face in her hands.

"No, darling, I'm fine. I have been so worried about you. They were taking me somewhere in a truck and all of a sudden I just wasn't there anymore. I found myself here, in this house, sitting on a couch instead of the bench in the truck. I've been here ever since waiting for you. They couldn't transport you in the same way because the walls of the building you were being held in are lined with lead. Kala has been trying to get you out for days," said Sydney bowing slightly to Alex's rescuer.

Kala bowed slightly to Alex.

"Thank you so much, and I'm sorry for grabbing you in the cell," said Alex returning his bow. "I thought you didn't want me to know your name."

"Kala is not my real name," he replied bowing once again.

"Well, Kala, it's good to have any name to go with your face, and I am in your debt."

Sydney took Alex's hand and led him into the small but clean and brightly decorated house. There were prayer flags hanging from the ceiling and incense burning in a large statue of the Buddha. Oversized pillows and brightly colored throw rugs covered the floor. A rather plump, older woman tended a pot of something cooking on the stove that smelled delicious.

She didn't speak English but smiled welcomingly. She led Alex to a room with a large tub of steaming water and handed him a towel and a bar of soap. There didn't seem to be any running water and Alex realized this must have taken a great deal of hard work to prepare for him. He bowed to her in gratitude. The woman motioned to him to clean up and then indicated they would eat afterwards. Sydney came in behind the woman.

"Darling. Let me help you. I'll give you a bath."
Alex smiled and pulled off his clothes and stepped into the soothing water. It felt like heaven after the captivity he had endured for the past several days. He was relieved beyond measure that Sydney had somehow escaped unhurt from the situation.

Teshe was a stocky young man of about thirty-five with a friendly face. He bowed as he greeted Sydney and Alex. "Gieshe le Tanzen has sent me to guide you to the monastery."

"They took our papers. How are we going to get into

Tibet?" asked Sydney.

"We cannot go the way of the roads," he said. "We must travel through the mountains." He looked down at Sydney's high-heeled shoes and then reached into his bag and pulled out a pair of women's hiking boots. "These are a gift from Tanzen." He said you would probably not realize how we are going to get into Tibet."

"Ah ... what do you mean?" she asked taking the boots and noting that they were indeed her size.

"We will be hiking."

"All the way?"

"I'm afraid so. And it's a hard trip. It will take us at least a week."

"A week!" Sydney rolled her eyes at Alex. "How are we going to make a week's trek on foot?" Sydney was visibly panicked at the news. She was in good shape, but she was not prepared for a weeklong journey by foot.

"Do not worry Miss Sydney. We will have several Brothers to assist us. If you get tired, we will have a yak for you to ride."

"A yak! Oh brother, Alex! This isn't going to work." Sydney's face flushed bright red, aghast at the thought of such a difficult journey.

"Surely there must be an easier way," said Alex.

"Please have faith my friends. We will have much help, and you will be all right," said Teshe with a look of serene confidence that seemed to quell Alex and Sydney's trepidation.

"Come on Sydney. For God's sake! You've been on climbing trips before. You can do this; you're in great shape!" said Alex surprised at Sydney's resistance. Usually she was pretty much up for any kind of adventure, be it rafting in class five rapids, or taking a safari in Africa. Her martial arts skills were not too shabby either.

"I know Alex, it's just that after all we've been through I just need to collapse in a hot tub in a five star hotel, as opposed to going on a week long trek through the Himalayas! My nerves are frazzled! I know this isn't like me, but surely you must be feeling the same way."

Alex nodded with understanding, but he was anxious to get to their destination – And whatever obstacles had to be overcome ... well, he would just deal with them.

Teshe put his hand on Sydney's shoulder. "I will help both of you to prepare. We will not leave until morning and I can help you to fortify your strength."

Sydney gave Alex a quizzical look, which he returned with a shrug as if to indicate that he didn't know what Teshe had in mind. Teshe led them back into the house. Please join us for our evening meal and then we will begin.

Teshe led Alex and Sydney into a small sanctuary across the yard from the main house. It was simple, with a wooden floor covered with several brightly colored mats. There seemed to be hundreds of candles burning in the room, and the musty smell of incense filled their nostrils. Alex could feel a difference in the atmosphere. It seemed to have an immediate calming effect on him. This was a feeling he often had when he entered a dwelling where people habitually meditated. The vibration of the space seemed somehow altered.

A large white translucent bowl sat in the middle of the room. Teshe motioned to Alex and Sydney to sit down as he kneeled at a simple altar of candles and a small Buddha figurine. He took a drumstick and rolled it along the edge of the bowl. As he continued, the sound grew from a slight murmur to a loud eerie deep drone that resonated for several minutes after he had stopped stroking it. Alex fell into a trance-like state. Sydney too was relaxing into the serenity of the room.

Alex closed his eyes and listened to Teshe's soft chanting.

When he opened them, he let out a gasp. Teshe was levitating five inches above the floor with his legs crossed underneath him. Alex had heard tales of monks levitating, but had never witnessed it. The actual sight was beyond belief, though it fit with his understanding of the effects of gravity when interacting with the vacuum. He nudged Sydney who had her eyes closed. When she opened them, her jaw dropped and her eyes bugged out. She almost fell backward as if in the presence of some sort of evil apparition.

Alex grabbed her hand and mouthed the words, "I've been trying to tell you ...."

The sound of Teshe's chanting now took on an otherworldly quality. The low-pitched tone did not sound like something that could come out of a human being, and the candle flames began to flicker simultaneously. Moonlight poured in through the window illuminating Teshe's body. Then Alex saw what looked like a large orb, appear around Teshe's head. It made him look like he had a halo.

Suddenly, the room was filled with what seemed like hundreds of orbs of every size from the tiniest points of light to at least five feet in diameter. They were translucent with a variety of different textures and hues. They appeared to be non-corporeal, more like vapor, moving through the objects in the room.

Sydney didn't seem to notice them. She was still transfixed on Teshe's hovering form. But now she had a look of serenity on her face as if she had surrendered to the moment.

Later, Alex and Sydney retired to their small room.

"My head seems to be reverberating with the sound Teshe made," said Sydney as she pulled back the covers.

"Yes, me too," said Alex climbing into bed.

"I feel like my brain is being reprogrammed."

"It sounds like a didgeridoo reverberating between my temples," agreed Alex.

As they drifted off to sleep, the sound continued and so did the programming.

A loud commotion woke Alex and Sydney. Several monks in saffron and red robes had arrived and were loading luggage and supplies into a cart. Quite a caravan began to form as more men and animals lined up in front of the small house.

Sydney looked over at Alex. "I feel amazing. I'm filled with energy."

Alex looked into Sydney's face. "You look younger."

"You too," she said tilting her head to the left as she perused his face. Most of his bruises had disappeared.

"I feel engulfed in a sensation of deep joy," she said as she looked out the window at the mountainous and thickly forested scenery surrounding them. "Everything seems filled with wonder."

"Yes, I feel it too," said Alex taking in a deep breath of the clear mountain air.

"Whatever Teshe did last night, it completely rid me of any fatigue and seemed to purge my nervous system of all the trauma of the past several days," said Alex.

Sydney could see the serenity on his face and could feel her own sense of calm emanating from the depth of her being. Then she noticed a glow radiating around Alex's head.

The group had been hiking for three days. The monks chanted continuously as they trekked through the rugged landscape. Sydney was holding up well. She seemed to have limitless energy, and the beauty of the mountains kept her transfixed in awe and immersed in a state of reverence. The mountains seemed to breathe and the trees seemed to bow as they passed by. Everything appeared to be alive, even the ground beneath their feet. Sydney marveled at the beauty of the snow-capped mountains towering like cathedrals into the blue sky. She felt a deep sense of respect for the living, conscious Earth.

"This seems like a good place to stop for the night," said Teshe pointing to a small clearing sheltered by a rocky cliff. The group dropped their packs and began setting up camp. The monks quickly built a fire and began preparing the evening meal of rice and vegetables. The smell of curry filled the air and Sydney realized she was hungry.

The meal was simple but tasty, and the monks seemed in good humor as they spoke and laughed among themselves. Sydney noticed Alex starring at her. "What?" she asked. "Is something wrong?"

"There's something on your head.

"What do you mean there's something on my head?" Sydney brushed off her hair as if trying to swat a fly.

"No, not a bug ... an orb." said Alex.

"I guess that's what I have seeing around your head. You know what this is?" she asked in an almost angry tone.

"Yes, I have seen them many times."

"Them? What do you mean? Why didn't you say anything?" demanded Sydney, now growing somewhat aggravated with him.

"Well, you know how you are about these things. I just didn't have the energy for another one of our little debates."

"What are they?" she asked.

"Not it, them. I think they're Beings," said Alex hesitantly. "I had heard about them several years ago at a presentation in Trout Lake, Washington." He watched Sydney's face for signs of skepticism, but her face remained expressionless.

"It was a presentation on enlightened contact with extra-terrestrials."

"You've convinced me that there are extra-terrestrials," said Sydney. "But now you're saying there are little round translucent things flying around that are also conscious?"

"Yes. I didn't want to get into this with you, but in light of all that has happened it's time you broaden your awareness to include these Beings."

Sydney shrugged and bowed her head, her long blonde hair tumbling over her face, surrendering to yet another blow to her concept of reality.

"At Trout Lake we picked up thousands of them on our digital cameras. I couldn't see them with my naked eye, but they show up all over our pictures."

"Why do you think they're Beings?" asked Sydney.

"Well, the speakers at the presentation claimed to be familiar with them and claimed they had telepathic contact with some of them. One speaker had a slide show and pointed out which ones were from other planets, which were Earth spirits, and even some that were viewing machines from other planets. Since then, I've picked them up on film on numerous occasions. The first time I ever saw them with my naked eye had been when Teshe levitated. I didn't say anything before, Sydney, because in the not so distant past this kind of conversation would have sent you storming from the room."

"I can't deny the experiences of the past few weeks with Leytar and then with Teshe levitating. I guess I have no choice but to open myself to the possibility that reality extends beyond what I used to think it did."

"What's so amazing is that they're multi-dimensional Beings and so are wound up with our concept of angelic Beings and other spiritual entities," said Alex.

Sydney stopped and thought for a moment. "Multi-dimensional Beings? Leytar mentioned this."

"Yes, they're resonating at a higher frequency and are less dense than us. That's why most people can't see them. Our frequencies must be higher now since we are seeing them with

176

our naked eyes."

"Leytar told me that ETs and angels are one and the same. I guess it does make sense that if there are Beings who have evolved and advanced their technology to the point that they're able to interact with the underlying energy field in a highly proficient way, they would be God-like themselves."

"Beings that have learned how to engineer the vacuum," said Alex raising his eyebrows as he did whenever he attempted to drive home one of the points of his theory.

"I must admit, they do look an awful lot like halos depicted in religious art," said Sydney. "How can you be sure they're good and not some sort of evil entities?"

"Well, all I can say is from my own experience," said Alex. "When I'm aware of their presence I feel a sense of well-being and love. So I doubt they're bad."

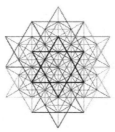

The activity in the camp woke Alex. "Come on sleepy head," said Alex as he gently shook Sydney's shoulder. Sydney opened her eyes and stretched languidly. The smell of coffee filled the air.

"Coffee? Who's got coffee?" she asked. They had nothing but tea during the journey and Sydney had been dying for a latte.

"Well, it's not a latte," said Alex, "but one of the monks gave me a can of French mocha mix, and I thought it would make a good surprise for you."

"You're an angel darling. Let me throw some pants on and I'll be right there."

There was no milk for the coffee, but it tasted good just the same. Sydney savored it as she warmed herself with the coffee mug. After a small morning meal, the group packed up and began another day's trek.

"Today we will have many difficult obstacles to overcome," said Teshe. "We will have to do some climbing with ropes."

Sydney looked over at Alex and took a deep breath. She felt fit and energetic and had experience with rope climbing. She felt like she could do it without a problem. But as the day progressed the climbs became steeper and steeper with snow and ice on them, and she felt a sense of trepidation. Her fingers started to tingle with pain from the cold, and her nose seemed frozen solid. Teshe handed Sydney a woolen scarf, and she wrapped it around her face, and bowed her head slightly in gratitude. The monks were chanting as usual as Alex and Sydney pushed on in silence.

Soon they approached a high cliff with what looked like a forty-foot overhang. This would require some difficult moves to maneuver under it. Teshe went first. He scurried up the sheer rock face quickly with his lean body moving like a spider monkey. He stopped and pounded in the pitons and threaded the rope through them as he ascended the mountainside. The overhang took him a particularly long time, but he prevailed. As he stood at the summit, he gestured for the others to follow him.

The monks hauled up as much of the gear as they could on their backs as they scaled the cliff. Teshe motioned for Alex and Sydney to start the climb. Sydney looked up at the challenge with a determined grimace. She grabbed hold of the rope and began pulling herself up. It took a lot of upper body strength, and she hadn't been working out for some time.

Her arms ached as she continued to pull her body weight. Slowly she inched up to the overhang. This was the hard part. She would have to suspend herself from the ropes and shimmy the forty feet hanging upside down. Teshe called down to her. "How are you doing?"

"I'm okay, so far," gasped Sydney trying to get enough breath to speak.

Alex had started his assent behind her. "You can do it

Sydney; just take your time."

Sydney started into the overhang. She fastened the ropes to her harness and grasped the rope above her that Teshe had laid out. She began to shimmy with her arms and legs wrapped around the rope, pulling herself a few inches at a time. Her arms were now strained to the limit of her endurance. She wanted desperately to rest them to get a respite from the piercing pain, but it was impossible in this position. She had to keep on going – there would be no turning back now.

She pulled on with all her might, but her muscles gave way and she lost her grip. In terror, she began to free-fall and then felt sharp pain in her sides as her harness stopped her fall. She dangled helplessly, too far from the rock face to grab onto it.

"Sydney! Are you okay?' shouted Alex from below.

"What do I do now?" She looked at the thousand-foot crevice below and terror overwhelmed her.

"Stay calm. Collect yourself and then you'll have to start rocking as if you're on a swing, until you can grab the rope again," shouted Alex.

Sydney closed her eyes and tried to calm herself. "*Dear God help me*," she whispered over and over again.

"I'm coming. I'm right behind you. We'll get you. Just stay calm," shouted Alex as he sped up his climb. "Start to swing. Just a little at a time. You will build up momentum. Pretend you are a kid on a rope over a beautiful pond."

Sydney complied, doing her best to block out the danger from her mind. She swung her legs back and forth and started to build up some speed. In her heart, she didn't think she had the strength to get as much height as she would need to get to safety. Then suddenly her swings seemed to have a power outside of herself, and she moved easily higher and higher almost without effort. She felt hands on her back pushing her, though she knew that couldn't be possible. Alex watched in awe as she flipped her body upwards, grasped the rope and pulled her legs around the line like an acrobat.

Teshe had climbed down to help her up the rest of the way to the top, finally pulling her over the edge. She lay sprawled out on her back looking at the clear sky, saying, "Thank you, thank you," repeatedly.

"It's okay," he said. "You did well."

"But that's just it," she said looking up at him. "It wasn't me."

CHAPTER 18

Gieshe Le Tanzen was a young-looking thirty-eight year old Tibetan man of short stature with a cheery round face. He opened the large carved wooden doors of the monastery and welcomed Alex and Sydney in with a bow. They both returned the gesture.

"I'm so pleased to see you master Alex and Miss Sydney. I have heard much about you and your work, and we are all excited about it."

"Really? I'm flattered."

"Yes, His Holiness himself is most interested in your theory," said Tanzen. "I have heard that the Dalai Lama has been following your work with great enthusiasm for some time. Science and religion are really seeking the same answers, only with different vehicles of inquiry. Both science and religion seek to understand the nature of reality, and in the end they are one and the same. Those who seek a religious path choose to use the method of accessing knowledge through inner contemplation. This is actually a more accurate method of inquiry than the Western double blind test, as so much of reality cannot be measured or observed with our limited senses and instruments. However, most Western scientists would never accept this."

Sydney thought that she too had been one of those Western scientists who didn't quite buy the inner-inquiry method, but Alex nodded with an acknowledging expression.

"Yes, and that is why you're here," said Tanzen looking at Sydney, and then throwing a quick wink at Alex.

"Did you just read my thoughts?" asked Sydney,

somewhat shocked by his statement.

Tanzen smiled and turned walking towards a tall armoire in the back of the dimly lit room. "Have a seat." said Tanzen as he waved Alex and Sydney to the large red pillows on the floor. There were no chairs in the small room, only an array of red and yellow pillows. Two low lying tables, the armoire, a great many candles, and a bed that looked more like a mat in the corner of the room, was the extent of the furnishings. There was one large window with wooden shutters and brass trim. It looked out to the snow-capped Himalayan peaks and the sun flooded the room with bright light through its warped pane glass. Tanzen reached into the armoire made of darkened bamboo and pulled out a large papyrus scroll. He unraveled it on the table in front of Alex and Sydney.

"You Sydney must be initiated to be able to withstand the force of the Source energy. Your time here will entail a series of trials and you will need to trust me ... completely trust me. Alex already is vibrating at sufficient frequency." Sydney shrugged in resignation.

"So that's why they call you my better half," she said smiling at Alex. Sydney felt a bit chagrined at being one upped in the higher consciousness game, but she could hardly argue with the fact that Alex had long been on a spiritual quest and had meditated for years.

"We will begin your first trial tomorrow morning Miss Sydney."

"Will it hurt?" asked Sydney with a laugh.

"It might, but that will be up to you."

This was not the response Sydney expected.

"What kind of tests are we talking about?" asked Sydney, starting to wonder if coming here had been such a great idea.

"There are two sides to all things and in the Source there's both good and evil. You must learn to distinguish between the two and to be strong enough to ward off the evil if you are to survive the encounter with the Source. Alex, you must learn the knowledge contained in these scrolls while Sydney undergoes her initiation training. This is an English translation and is the only

182

such one in existence. For now, you should rest. I understand you have had quite an arduous journey."

Tanzen handed the scroll to Alex and led them to another small room down the hall. It too was sparse, with only a few pillows, a mat-like bed, a small table, a chest of drawers, and many candles. As far as Alex could see, there was no electricity, no outlets, no phones, no lamps or computers. This was true isolation from the outside world.

"I'm very tired Sydney, but I really want to start reading the scrolls. He opened one and began to read. Sydney was curious too, but she could not bring herself to study just now, and curled up on the mat and quickly fell asleep.

"He what?" Croft screamed angrily into the receiver.

"He escaped sir," stammered the voice on the line.

"How on Earth does someone escape the Chinese police?"

"I don't know sir. No one seems to know how it could have happened."

"Well those guys are more incompetent than I thought ... so much for the feared Chinese. If they can't even hold a Professor for a few nights they're not much of a threat are they?"

"No, sir. I guess not."

"You're damn straight! Shit! Where is Harmon now?"

"We've lost him sir."

"How could you lose him? We can see a dime on the moon!"

"We lost all transmission of him the night he escaped. It just blipped off the holo-imager."

"Blipped off the holo-imager! Where's Tarnoff?"

"He's not here right now."

"Well, you have him call me; and I mean ASAP!

The bright white light of the rising sun streamed through the small window and woke Sydney. She felt the space next to her and found Alex was already gone. She bathed herself with the water and soap left in a large basin by her bed, and put on the red and saffron robe that Tanzen had laid out for her the night before. There was no mirror in the room, but she imagined that she looked quite out of character in this traditional Tibetan monk's garb. She hoped Tanzen would not ask her to shave her head like the female monks she had seen. That is where she would have to draw the line!

A light knock on the door indicated it was time to go to the great hall for the morning meal. Sydney put a few things in a carry bag and fell in line with the many monks as they made their way to breakfast.

Tanzen was waiting for Sydney at the entrance to the hall.

"Miss Sydney, good morning," he said with a slight bow. Sydney returned the bow clasping her hands together to form the prayer position.

"After your meal, meet me in the garden by the great tree." Sydney nodded and entered the dining hall.

The meal consisted of green tea, bread, and an oatmeal-like substance, though it tasted like nothing she had ever eaten before. She tried to get down a few swallows of the odd tasting mash, but found it difficult. The monks all ate in silence, their eyes down, as Sydney scanned the large room. The air felt different in the monastery. There was a sense of great peace and tranquility. Sydney finished her food and headed out into the courtyard. She found Tanzen standing by the tree motioning her to sit down.

"I want you to sit here and look at the tree until you really see it," said Tanzen.

Sydney looked at him as if he was kidding, but Tanzen's demeanor indicated was serious.

"How will I know when I have really seen it?" she asked.

"You will know," replied Tanzen. With that, Tanzen left Sydney alone in the courtyard to stare at the large Banyan tree with its winding, lumbering limbs.

It's a tree. Just a tree. What am I supposed to see? But despite the seemingly futile task set upon her, Sydney relented and began to stare at the tree. As time went on, she felt the sun get hotter. Hours passed and she began to get hungry and thirsty, but Tanzen did not come to offer her anything. She continued to stare at the tree until it started to blur. At one point, it seemed to divide into two trees and then into three and four and back to one.

The sun started to fade and Sydney was very hungry and thirsty, but still Tanzen did not come out to see her. The moon rose in the sky and a canopy of stars filled the night as Sydney continued to stare at the tree. Several times she felt like falling asleep and tried to steady herself and continue her task. She stared and stared at the tree until finally she did not see it at all. She started to see it as a composite of an infinite number of component parts. Each nook and cranny of the bark seemed to come alive, moving with incredible energy, and breaking down into smaller and smaller parts. As she penetrated the essence of the tree, she saw the entire courtyard and everything in it, including herself, merging into one great swirling organism. There was no difference between herself, the bark and the branches, the sky, or the ground on which she sat. She now knew she had finally seen the tree.

At that moment, Tanzen appeared with a tray of hot food and a pitcher of water. He silently set it in front of Sydney, smiled and slightly bowed his head.

The next morning Sydney felt somehow reborn with a new understanding of herself and the world around her. It all looked different. The green of the leaves were more vivid, the pattern in the pillows seemed to jump off the fabric. Everything was moving, undulating, and alive. It was as if she could see the component energy in all things ... animate and inanimate.

A light knock on her door let her know it was time to get up. Once again, Alex was already gone. She poured some water from the large pitcher on the table and drank it in almost one gulp. She still felt dehydrated. Sydney dressed quickly and headed down to the dining hall. Tanzen was waiting for her by the entrance.

"Good morning to you Miss Sydney."

Sydney bowed and smiled at him. "What do you have planned for me today?" Sydney asked with some hesitation in her voice.

Tanzen gave her a crooked smile. "It was bad for you yesterday?"

"It was both wonderful and horrible."

"Ah yes. Then you had a good day! Let us eat first and then I will tell you."

They entered the great hall, filled with the smell of curry, and steam coming from the huge pots of tea. Sydney had not really gotten to know any of the monks there, but they always acknowledged her and smiled when she came to sit at the table.

She now understood what Alex meant when he said the air in the monastery was different. It had a texture that permeated the atmosphere and gave her a sense of well-being and serenity. She felt as though there was a pressure in the middle part of her forehead – as if her so-called third eye was bursting through her skin.

The meal was simple but at least it wasn't the tasteless mash that she didn't like. There was brown rice and vegetables, some fish, and a few sauces. She ate greedily in case Tanzen decided to starve her again today. She drank more than she would have for the same reason. Tanzen glanced over at her with a look that told her he knew what she had been doing. He even started to giggle.

"How do you do that?" asked Sydney.

"Do what?" replied Tanzen not even trying to hide his mischievous intent.

"You know, you seem to read my thoughts."

"They're not difficult to read," replied Tanzen. "Your thoughts are written all over your face."

Sydney gave him a resigned smirk. She knew Tanzen would never admit to any special abilities, but she was sure he had many. In fact, she wouldn't have been surprised if Tanzen leapt up and flew away.

Tanzen pushed his plate to the center of the table and wiped his mouth with the starched white linen napkin. "Are you ready to begin?" he asked.

Sydney got up and they went out into the extensive gardens. They walked for about ten minutes until they came to a small pagoda by a stream.

"This is so peaceful," remarked Sydney.

"Yes, it's one of my favorite spots. I have spent much time here," said Tanzen. "Your task today is to sit here and ask yourself 'who am I?' until you know the answer."

With that, Tanzen bowed and turned, leaving Sydney sitting on the stone bench in the middle of the small pavilion. She could hear the gentle babbling of the stream and feel the warm air on her skin.

Who am I? That's an odd question and it shouldn't take all day to figure that out. Who am I? Well I'm Dr. Sydney Stewart. I'm thirty-seven years old. I have blond hair and green eyes. I'm 5'5". I was born in Detroit, Michigan. My father was a dentist and my mother was a teacher. I'm a sister and a daughter. I'm a mathematician and a professor. I love Alex. I'm kind and good-hearted. I'm a positive person and good at what I do. Okay, some of the bad things ... I have a quick temper that I have trouble controlling. I'm impatient with people. I'm a workaholic ....

Sydney continued to think of all the things she believed she was - all the things that defined her life. But with each of these answers, she realized that she was really none of these things. She would still be herself if she wasn't a sister or a mathematician or if her hair were red or she were 5'8." This continued for some time. Each time she finished an answer she'd repeat the question: *Who am I?*

Who am I? Who am I? The hours passed as she repeated the question and kept coming up with answers – and just as quickly rejected them. As the day wore on, she felt hunger creep upon her and she started to ask, *Am I the person asking the question, or am I the person hearing the question asked?* She listened to herself ask the question repeatedly.

I'm neither the voice asking the question nor the person hearing it. I'm not even the person having thoughts because my thoughts change with differing circumstances. Is the true me my feelings? I feel calm now, but my feelings change with each passing moment. I cannot be my feelings. Who am I if I take away my thoughts and my feelings? Am I my experiences? If I am the sum of my experiences, then I change every moment as well. Am I my physical body? If I lost my arms and legs, I would still be me. Am I my head? Am I my brain? If someone cut my brain open would they find me? I don't really know that I have a body. For all I know, I could be dreaming this life. Is there anything that is the core me? Who am I? Who am I? Am I the dream?

Sydney kept asking the question, peeling away the layers of her mask of identity, trying to understand what truly defined her. Nothing – not her thoughts, experiences, loves, hates, quirks, physical being – none of those were truly her. The day wore on and the daylight started to dim and the setting sun could be seen over the hills beyond the gardens. The sky filled with pink and bright red swirls as the sun hung low over the horizon. She gazed directly at this yellow ball that gave life to all things on the Earth. For a moment, she had no thoughts as she stared at the sun. Then it came to her. She is simply awareness – a non-thinking, non-judgmental awareness. *I am consciousness. That is all!*

After a hot breakfast of rice mash, Tanzen took Sydney out to the courtyard once again. Sydney gave Tanzen a wary look.

"Oh, I see. You think I'm going to torture you today."

Sydney laughed. "Well, actually, yes."

"I think you'll find today's exercise difficult, but comfortable."

Sydney relaxed a bit. She was finding the training fascinating, but grueling, to say the least.

"Today, I want you to practice controlling your thoughts," said Tanzen sitting down in front of Sydney.

"Okay." Sydney didn't think that would be difficult.

Tanzen handed her a notebook and a pen. "I want you to meditate now. As you well know, you'll have thoughts. But the task today is to be aware of your negative thoughts. When you become conscious of a negative thought, make a note and jot down the amount of time that you indulged in that negative thought before you became mindful of it."

Sydney raised her eyebrows and sighed in compliance.

"I will check on you in three hours at lunch time," said Tanzen as he rose to leave Sydney under the tree.

Sydney closed her eyes and began to focus on her breath as she had been taught to do. She felt her heart rate slow and her breath become shallow as she reached a meditative state.

Sydney knew that in normal meditation it was natural to have thoughts. She would simply and gently shift back to concentrating on her breath as soon as she became aware she was having thoughts. Sydney had done this many times, and so the exercise seemed to be a bit too easy for her. She tried to focus on the space between her nostrils and upper lip as she gently exhaled her breath.

She was anxious to get back to Hawaii, and to get back to the lab. She wanted to finish the work on the resonance chamber, but she knew these exercises were necessary for her to withstand the field that would emanate from the device. *It has been so incredible working with Alex, and our personal relationship has been all I could hope for. I can hardly believe that I'm able to have such a beautiful relationship with a man, especially since my relationship with Dad had been so difficult. He had been so cold to mother; absent for me most of the time. It still feels like an open wound and has always permeated my relationships with men over the years. I've always been afraid to love. It was the reason things didn't work with Mark, and I pray it doesn't ruin my relationship with Alex. I resent Dad for this. It seems that I've suffered so much over the years because of Mom and Dad's bad relationship. Shit, what am I thinking?*

Sydney noted in the book, "neg. thought – five min." By the time Tanzen came to get her for lunch, her notebook was replete with notations. She had a total of ninety minutes of thoughts that had gone negative in three hours of meditation.

"So how did you do?" asked Tanzen?

Sydney looked up shaking her head. "Not well, I'm afraid," she said handing her notebook to Tanzen.

He looked at her notes. "This is normal for a first time." Tanzen extended his hand to help Sydney to her feet. "The untrained are unaware of how may negative thoughts cross their mind each day. If you weren't meditating, the number could be multiplied significantly counting worries, fears, speculations, and such."

"Yes, in fact it seemed that most of my thoughts

190

degenerated into some sort of negativity. I had no idea."

"Now that you see how often you indulge in negative thoughts, you must practice to the point that you can become aware before the thought has had a chance to fully form. This is crucial so that you can be exposed to the feedback-loop of the Source energy field."

CHAPTER 19

Alex sat on a large red pillow studying the scrolls laid out before him on a low table. It was so much to take in. There were sacred writings from ancient civilizations that claimed to be as much as twenty-five thousand years old – cultures he had thought were only myths. They were the ancient civilizations of Atlantis, Lemuria, Mu, and many more. They had all written of the sacred geometry and the oneness of Source, and it was all starting to come together for him.

There were tales of an extra-terrestrial scientist who had travelled to Earth 250,000 years ago and conducted genetic experiments mixing her DNA with that of early bipedal animals on Earth. It had been from these experiments that humans evolved, and why there was a so-called "*missing link*" in our evolutionary development.

The texts spoke of the Seal of Solomon, the Black Sun, and the Stone of Mu – all referring to an object that brought the power and word of God to Earth. Alex realized that this must have been a contained black hole, which he was sure was the technology he was working on. It was a portal to the infinity through which the power of the Source energy could be manifested on Earth. It was technological … it was a device!

The Seal of Solomon was a Star of David – an exact representation of Alex's model for infinity – with a six-pointed star within a circle, thought to be a gift from God that conferred great power to King Solomon. *Certainly, anyone who had the ability to access and engineer the vacuum would indeed have such power*, thought Alex.

Thoth, the author of the Hermetic Tradition, spoke of building the Sphinx as a marker where he buried his spaceship thousands of years prior to the time current science claims it had been built. He also indicated that the Great Pyramid of Giza had been constructed above an entrance to an inner Earth civilization, and was in essence a resonance chamber.

As Alex read on, he learned about the Emerald Tablets that are thought to have been written by Thoth. Thoth was the first Hermes (there were three), and was the Egyptian God of learning and hidden knowledge. The Emerald Tablets are the basis of the Hermetic tradition fundamental to Alchemy. It has long been thought to be the code for transforming reality. The main message of the Emerald Tablets is that there is an archetypal consciousness that creates all physical reality-one that can be accessed through knowledge of the workings of the universe.

Alex realized this directly corresponded with the theory of an underlying infinite energy density that is in a conscious feedback-loop with all physical reality. The Emerald Tablets read:

1. True, without error, certain and most true.
2. That which is below is as that which is above, and that which is above is as that which is below, to perform the miracles of the one thing.
3. And as all things were from [the] one, by [means of] the meditation of [the] one, thus all things of the daughter from [the] one, by means of] adaptation.
4. Its father is the sun, its mother [,] the moon, the wind carried it in its belly, its nurse is the Earth.
5. The father of all the initiates of the whole world is there.
6. Its power is integrating if it be turned into Earth.
7. Separate the Earth from the fire, the fine from the dense, delicately, by [means of/to] the great [together] with capacity.
8. It ascends by [means of] Earth into heaven and again it descends into the Earth, and retakes the power of

the superior[s] and of the inferior[s].
9. Thus[,] you have the glory of the whole world.
10. Therefore [,] may it drive-out by [means of] you of all the obscurity.
11. This is the whole of the strength of the strong force, because it overcomes all fine things, and penetrates all the complete.
12. Thus [,] the world has been created.
13. Hence they were wonderful adaptations, of which this is the manner.
14. Therefore [,] I'm Hermes the Thrice Great, the three parts of the philosophy of the whole world.
15. What I have said concerning the operation of the Sun has been completed.

Alex paused to take all of this in. It was clearly a code and the Emerald Tablet was supposed to contain a formula for accessing the Source of Creation. Perhaps if he could decipher it, he would be able to open a portal.

"That which is above is as that which is below" is certainly a reference to the fractal nature of the universe. "All things were from the one" referred to the infinite energy field that connects and creates all matter. The reference to the sun was important because if all matter goes to infinity, the sun is the largest mass in the solar system by far, and so would have the largest black hole ... the largest entrance to the infinity.

Alex could see great parallels between his unified field theory and these words. It was becoming clear to him that the knowledge he had reconstructed had been here on Earth many thousands of years ago. As he read on, he learned how this ancient knowledge had been given to the Sumerians by the Sun Gods – who were known to be Beings from another world. After all, with gravitational drive they would travel through singularities, and the largest singularity in any star system is the sun. They literally must have come out of the sun!

Evidently, this knowledge passed into the Egyptian civilization and had become the foundation of the mystery schools. It went into the Hebrew tradition next, and Alex wondered if Moses took it with him when he left Egypt in the Exodus. Moses was the adopted son of the Pharaoh and would have had free access to the pyramid. *Perhaps that's why Pharaoh changed his mind and went after the Hebrews. Perhaps that's how Moses had been able to split the Red Sea, which certainly qualified as an antigravity event.*

The Hebrews encoded the knowledge into the Kabala. The code may have been re-discovered by the Templers during the Crusades to the Holy Land. When the Templers were under attack by King Phillip of France, they formed another covert organization, and named it the Free Masons. The reconstituted Free Masons embedded the knowledge and codes of the Templers into the decorations and architecture of the churches of Europe. The knowledge was passed into the American tradition by the Founding Fathers, the majority of whom were Free Masons.

As Alex read on, he realized this secret knowledge that had been passed down through the ages was a code for how the universe works, and the method for creating a portal to the infinity … the Source … the vacuum, both spiritually and technologically. The knowledge, though known to be sacred, was not fully understood, though it had been embedded in plain sight in the world's religions. This is because it was coded and undecipherable until civilization reached a level of understanding of physics that included relativity and quantum mechanics, and most importantly, the physics of black holes. Alex realized *that* time is now. This is the moment that we finally have enough knowledge of physics and the cosmos to develop the technology that will allow humanity to interact with the Source to create our own reality, travel the stars, and manifest whatever we need in our physical world. With this technology, civilization will completely transform. It will bring an end to want, to toil, to hunger and strife, and the reason for most wars, which is most often born out of limited resources and the desire to obtain as much as possible.

Tears rolled down Alex's face as he realized the full implication of what lay ahead. He now knew that his theory was the key, and that he and Sydney were clearly the ones who would bring about this new age. At that thought, he felt as if the crown of his head had opened and energy was pouring down his spine like a great shiver. He sat frozen, in a trance, as equations and diagrams flashed in his mind's eye.

Tanzen bowed to Sydney. "You have completed your initiation. Now you and Alex must return home to complete your work. The future depends on you. Alex received a great gift last night."

Alex looked surprised. "Yes. Something special happened last night. I don't know what it was, but my mind is so clear. I can see what I have to do."

"You received the final download from the Galactic Federation."

Sydney looked at Alex in awe. "Oh? What is a download?"

"Alex has received them many times before," said Tanzen.

"You have?" Sydney looked confused as her world was rocked once again by Tanzen's words. Alex shot her an impish grin.

"A download comes from the Galactic Federation. It's how they send information."

"But who exactly are the Galactic Federation and what exactly are they up to?" asked Sydney wanting to get another opinion on this ET organization.

"You must realize by now that there are thousands of intelligent civilizations in our galaxy alone," replied Tanzen. "Many of them have advanced to the point that they are star faring races. The Galactic Federation is an organization regulating the conduct of these races and their exploration of less advanced planets, like the Earth."

"How advanced are they?" asked Sydney.

"Some are millions of years advanced beyond Earth. The Federation has civilizations that traverse the galaxies in planet sized ships of light."

"With ships as big as planets? How is that possible?" asked Sydney.

"That's right, with anti-gravity technology weight would be no obstacle to space travel," interjected Alex.

Tanzen continued. "They have determined that you are ready and worthy, and have given Alex the information he needs to complete the technology. Alex has been on this mission his entire life."

Sydney looked at Alex pryingly. "How long have you known about this?"

"For a long time," he said shoving his hands in his pockets looking a bit uncomfortable. Sydney shot him a look of irritation.

Tanzen continued. "What you're soon to realize for mankind has been promised for thousands of years. It's your destiny too Sydney, and always has been."

"I didn't know anything about ETs until I started working for Alex." Sydney protested.

"But you were driven to understand the infinities in the math. Isn't that true?" asked Tanzen, his eyes penetrating her soul.

"I guess."

"Why do you think that was?"

"I don't know. Numbers have always fascinated me. They seem to hold the secrets of the universe," she shrugged.

"Yes," said Tanzen.

Sydney's eyes widened as she began to understand yet another level of her constantly expanding reality.

"The knowledge and technology you and Alex are seeking is the beginning of a whole new age of technology and spiritual understanding for humanity. It will change human civilization more profoundly than any other discovery that has come before."

"How do you, a Buddhist monk, know so much about the Galactic Federation?"

"We know many things." Tanzen gave Sydney that enigmatic smile that usually meant he had volunteered as much information as he was going to at the time.

"But Buddhism isn't about technology. It's about spirituality," she protested trying to get a little more information out of him.

"Don't you see yet that it's all one and the same? And that much of our understanding of life and spirit has come from these other Beings?"

Tanzen bowed to Sydney and Alex. "I must take my leave now. I will see you at the afternoon meal."

Sydney and Alex returned his bow and walked into the garden to the small wooden bridge that lay over a narrow stream. Alex broke a prolonged silence.

"I see it all now." His gaze was fixed on the wispy clouds that hovered above in the bright blue sky. "I can see the ships. I remember traveling the cosmos in an instant. This is our birthright, and it's been hidden for so long that human-kind has forgotten the promise!"

"Do you really think we should build it?" asked Sydney.

Alex looked at her, shocked by this statement.

"Alex, after all we've been through at the monastery, can't you see that this energy field is as close as you get to the definition of God?"

"Yes and no. It's a force ... a force that can be harnessed and engineered to create material reality. This is the technology of God."

"I don't think we should tamper with this." Sydney shook her head ... her face contorted with apprehension.

"But why do you think the Galactic Federation contacted us? Why do you think we were sent to Tibet to go through initiation? It's all been so that we can complete the work. We need to build the technology. It's the key to the future of humanity! You heard Tanzen!"

Alex could hardly believe Sydney's reluctance. "We have to. Think about it, Sydney. The technology means unlimited energy and anti-gravity technology. The device will give civilization the power to manifest material reality. After all we've been through there must be a purpose. I believe we were meant to complete this mission."

"It just seems like we're tampering with something that's sacred, Alex."

"Yes, we are and it's our birthright! We are 99.999% God! The vacuum permeates your atoms and cells. There's no separation."

"I understand that, but it still seems dangerous. How are we going to build the device anyway? Do you really know how to do it yet?" asked Sydney.

"We have to open a mini black hole. We have to spin plasma in a perfectly cut crystal at just the right resonance frequency and create the right amount of torque to get the vacuum to form the dynamic. I know how to do it. I don't know how I know, but I can see it in my mind."

"Is this because of the download?"

"This morning I woke up and I could see it all. I could see diagrams and schematics as if I was looking at a book.

"Building something like that will cost a fortune, Alex. Where are we going to get the money? It's not like we can apply for a grant to build this kind of technology. We'd have the OEB all over us."

"I've never told you this, but my father was an investment banker. He left me a lot of money."

"A lot of money? How much are we talking about?"

Alex laughed. "Enough to build the device and more."

"Alex, you're rich?"

"Well, yes, I guess you could say that," he laughed and gave Sydney a wink.

"Honey, you just got a lot more handsome!" giggled Sydney.

"I'm not in the habit of bragging about how much money I have. Anyway, I wanted to make sure you loved me for me and not my money."

Sydney frowned affectionately.

"And I wanted to keep it from the OEB. When they took over I put it all in a bank account in the Cayman Islands. I'm really glad I did, given how they've been trumping up charges, imprisoning people, and taking their assets."

Sydney leaned over and gave Alex a long, deep kiss. "You're amazing!"

CHAPTER 20

Boxes and workers started arriving at the lab on a daily basis with equipment from all over the world. Alex and Sydney were riding on pure adrenalin for months on end, working day and night to put the machinery together.

Alex could see all the schematics in his head to create a device that would have the capacity to generate a vacuum energy field that could be induced into crystals of specific molecular alignments generating a charged field.

Sydney had flown to the Czech Republic several times to meet with the finest crystal manufacturers to have them made to their specifications. The crystals are the most important component necessary to the resonance chamber, and had taken months to create with just the right geometry. It had to be perfectly spherical and cut in a precise relationship to its molecular alignment.

Alex was working with his digital tooling machine to input the three-dimensional computer drawings from which he would be able to manufacture the many other components needed right in his lab. He was also busy with his team creating a "clean room" with zero contamination, as well as a gold-lined room to contain the energy field the chamber would produce. He needed a clean room in order to create an environment for placing the ionized gas into the spherical crystal. He would have to open the crystal, put the gas in, and then seal it back together. The ions would have to follow the magnetic field as he pulsed the wire coils around the machine. Absolute zero contamination was essential, as a single speck of dust could crack the crystal while it is spinning.

The geometry of the coils was another important component. He would have to construct them in a double torus configuration. The relationship of the ribs of the device was also crucial in creating the proper geometry within which to spin the plasma.

As Alex worked diligently on the equations and measurements, he realized he was writing the math for the magic of the universe. Kevin stood behind him looking over his shoulder and mentally taking notes.

Sydney and Alex walked along the City of Refuge. It was where they went to speak freely without fear of being overheard by OEB snoops.

"I'm surprised the OEB hasn't been around more," she said glancing at Alex with a worried frown.

"My guess is that they're watching us," said Alex

"Don't you think this is rather dangerous? We're causing a lot of questions to be asked, with all the people and equipment coming and going so often."

"If they wanted to interfere, they would have done so already. I think they're waiting until we have something operational, and then they'll try to seize it. I'm going to keep the staff working on some superfluous projects while I'm running the frequencies. Hopefully, that will throw off anyone who is watching and will make them think we're still in a building stage."

Alex's words did not ease Sydney's concerns. She didn't like the idea of being watched, as she knew all too well the kind of tactics the OEB was capable of using against them.

"I wonder if they've bought our cover story that we're building a replicating machine?"

Alex laughed. "I don't see why not. Quite frankly, I don't think they could begin to conceive of what we're really up to. It's so far from their sense of reality."

"I hope you're right, Alex. I just can't help feeling uneasy."

"If all goes well, we'll be ready to start running frequencies next week," said Alex. "We'll beat them at their own game."

"Do you have anything new for me?" asked Brandon Tarnoff, as he looked over the surveillance reports on his cluttered desk.

"It seems Miss Stewart has been making several trips to a crystal manufacturer in the Czech Republic," said the voice on the other end of the line.

"Have you been able to get anything out of any of the workers there as to what they're up to?"

"Not really. It seems they been told the patent for the work hasn't been finalized and so no one has been given full information about what it is that they're building. Some of them think it might be some sort of replicator like in the old Star Trek series. It looks like they're keeping the staff pretty segmented, so no one knows the whole picture. Do you want me to send some men up there to grab their equipment sir?"

"No, not yet," answered Tarnoff, biting a hangnail on his thumb. Croft wants them to continue. I need to know when they finish building whatever it is."

"Yes, sir. We're keeping a close eye on them, and I'll let

you know as soon as we see anything starting to happen."

CHAPTER 21
PRESENT TIME

Sydney awoke, startled from a deep sleep in her hotel room in Honolulu where she was attending a conference. She was soaked in sweat and her heart was racing. *It was a dream ... no, a nightmare!* She was in the middle of a room engulfed in flames and felt she was about to die. It seemed so real she needed to get up for a glass of water to shake the feeling, when the phone started ringing!

As Alex's bloodied and ashen face appeared on the holo-imager, she realized it was not a dream at all. She had been there with him, witnessing the explosion in the lab. *I must have acquired some degree of telepathy in Tibet,* she thought.

"My God Alex. Are you all right? Where are you?"

"I'm in an ambulance. One of the medics loaned me his phone. Mine was lost in the blast," he said looking at his cut palm. "I've got a lot of cuts and bruises, but I think I'm okay. That doesn't matter. Something incredible happened in the lab."

Alex told her what had transpired, and that it seemed they finally had some semblance of tangible proof of Alex's theory.

"I think I transcended a dimensional boundary! I told you this would happen. If we're messing with the gravitational field, we're messing with the God Source energy field. I honestly didn't think it was possible to pierce a boundary condition. But it seems that is what happened. Sydney, the back-ups in the floor safe may be all we have left from this particular sequence. An ambulance came to get me and there must be fire trucks and OEB police all over the place."

"I'm sure they've used this opportunity to ransack the place," said Sydney, her voice filled with distress.

"It's even worse than that," said Alex. "I heard the men in the ambulance saying that two men disappeared after entering the lab. They must have been transported to the same place that I went, but I don't think they came back, from what the medics were saying. The OEB will be asking a lot of questions."

"Those poor men!" said Sydney, horrified that she was now party to unintentional deaths.

"They may not be here, but I'm sure they're somewhere, and fine. If I came back, there must be a way to bring them back."

"My God Alex, we've done it! The world will have to listen."

"We don't have anything unless we can get the backups and find out what frequency I had been running at the time. Nothing counts until we can reproduce the effect. Right now, we have an explosion, two missing men, and a swarm of OEB creeps at the lab. Our equipment has been destroyed and we have to reconstruct out work," muttered Alex more to himself than to Sydney.

"What about Brian Sheppard? He has a lab. We could go there, back to Ann Arbor," said Sydney.

"Yes, that might work," Alex said, perking up with this bit of hope. "You need to get back to the house as soon as possible and get the backups and the other crystal spheres. You also need to call Brian Sheppard on a secure line, and by that I mean a line that cannot be traced back to either of us, and see if he will let us use his lab. He has a clean room and a digital tooling machine. I know what we need. It will be much faster and much less costly the second time around."

"Brian will be flabbergasted by what has happened tonight," said Sydney.

"How fast do you think you can get back to the house?"

"I'll leave as soon as I can pack my bags. I can be there within the hour using the air car."

"See if you can salvage any equipment from the lab, though I doubt there's much left. We've got to think about the dangers involved in moving this to another venue." Alex glanced at the two medics who were sitting in front of the thick glass that separated him from the driver's area. He spoke in a whisper so as not to be heard. "Don't come to the hospital until you've secured the work. Remember to do it the way we planned."

" All right, honey. Which hospital are they taking you to?"

"The one off of Queen Kaahumanu Road."

"Okay. I'll be there soon. I'll call Brian and arrange everything. As soon as you're released we can meet him in Ann Arbor."

"We better not talk on the phone anymore," said Alex. "For all we know, the OEB may be monitoring even this conversation, though I'm not using my own phone," he said, trying to see if the men upfront were paying any attention to him. They weren't.

"Yes, we can't be too careful. Take care Alex, I'll be there as soon as I can." Sydney clicked off the phone, and fell back onto her bed. There were so many questions running through her head that she was immobilized. *Where did he go? Was it another dimension? Was it Heaven? And where were the two HazMat men? Were they still alive?* Excitement began to well up within her. They now had something concrete, and soon the world would have to accept the possibility of a reality far more profound than anything mankind has dared to imagine.

The double doors by Alex's feet flung open, and two men jumped in and began un-strapping the gurney.

"On my mark, mark," said one of the men, and Alex was jolted around as they hoisted the gurney out of the vehicle.

Alex was blinded by the bright neon light as they pulled into the hospital emergency entrance bay. The medics wheeled him past the waiting lounge, and into the receiving area.

"Alex Harmon," said the medic as he handed some paperwork to the attendant behind the plate glass window.

"Oh yes," she said peering up at him above her eyeglass

rim. "We've been expecting Mr. Harmon."

The attendant lowered her voice to barely a whisper, and Alex could not hear what they were discussing. "Take him to A22," she said in a louder voice.

The gurney wheeled through the white corridors. There was not much activity in the hallway, just two men dressed in black suits and dark sunglasses who watched as Alex rolled by.

The medic maneuvered his gurney into a small, isolated room.

"Why aren't I in the ER?" he asked.

"Hey man, looks like you're special," said the young medic.

Alex didn't like the sound of that, but before he could ask another question, a doctor came in the room with a hypodermic needle.

"What's that for?" Alex asked. The doctor didn't answer and shot the contents of the needle into Alex's IV drip. Within seconds, Alex's world went black.

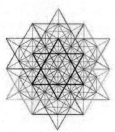

"Just sit down Tarnoff; I'll be with you in a few minutes." Tarnoff took a seat in the large leather chair in front of Croft's desk, tapping his fingers nervously on the chair arm as he waited for Croft to finish his conversation with the President.

"Well, I'm just not going to do it and that's that. I told you how this is going to be handled, and that's my final word. Well sir, your apology is accepted. You have a nice day now." Croft hung up the phone and turned his attention to Tarnoff, who then briefed him on the information he had received on the lab incident, and his take on the implications.

"How do you want me to handle this, sir?" asked Tarnoff.

"You say two HazMat men just disappeared into thin air?"

"Yes, sir. All I know is that they were seen going into the lab, and when the other men looked in to check on them, all they saw was a vortex in the middle of the room. Then the vortex closed, and the men weren't in the room. There were no other exits. Whatever they're working on in there must have vaporized those men."

"This doesn't look like replicator technology to me," said Croft sucking on a fat cigar.

"No, sir, it doesn't, unless it replicates people into thin air! We've detained everyone there and have been interrogating them. Sydney Stewart was not home, and it seems like Harmon has been keeping everything so fragmented that no one has the whole picture of what is really going on over there. We searched the house, copied their hard drives, and confiscated anything that seemed relevant. I have men going through their data now. It seems they were working on something called resonance energy, but my men haven't been able to figure out what they're doing yet. It seems like their main information isn't on the computers. They must be hiding the data somewhere else."

"Well, find it. I want to know what they're up to. Let me know when you have something."

"I knew you would want that, so I already dispatched an agent to take position watching the house and lab. We're keeping an eye on Harmon and Stewart day and night. I can take them out whenever you give the word."

"No, not yet. I want to know what they have first. This may be a new technology that we can use. I want to know what happened to those men," said Croft, as he led Tarnoff to the door.

Croft closed the door behind him and returned to his large mahogany desk. Then he reached for the day's list of enemies. At the top he wrote in the name Alex Harmon, and began circling it over and over as his curiosity intensified.

Croft didn't want to say anything to Tarnoff, but he believed that the two men who went missing into a vortex weren't vaporized at all, and the fact that they had disappeared into a vortex had enormous implications. He had read of this same phenomenon happening in an ancient alchemical text, and he was becoming more certain that Harmon and his Class 19 associate were creating the technology that was his destiny to control.

As a young man, Croft had studied ancient religions and had become interested in the Hermetic mystery schools, as well as texts on the Alchemists. He read that the power of transmutation and transportation was a power that could be accessed, not only by the mind of highly initiated masters, but also through a technology.

Croft believed such a device had been brought to Earth by the Sun Gods, common to so many of the world's ancient religious traditions. This device remained in the hands of some of the early Egyptian Pharaohs, and conferred to them their vast power. He suspected this was the alien technology that had been used to build the pyramids. He also suspected it was what Moses used to get water out of rock and part the Red Sea.

If Harmon had created an effect that caused the two HazMat men to disappear into a vortex, he might have created a similar technology. His heart began to pound as he realized that the technology he had been seeking for so long might be within his grasp. If it was what he suspected, it would not only be a transportation machine, but it would give its possessor power beyond imagination. For, such a device would have the capability to lift the veil between the material world and the spiritual domain.

It suited his purposes to keep his people in the dark for now. This was something he could not allow to become public. If people understood the truth, it would bring down his empire that was based on a religious certainty he knew to be false.

CHAPTER 22

Sydney drove up to the house to find it deserted. She had expected OEB agents to be swarming around the property. But it was quiet. There were no staff members around either. This stuck her as odd. She tried to call Alan but got his answering machine. She started going down the list of employees, calling to find out what was going on, but couldn't reach anyone. This was not a good sign, but it was the middle of the night. She figured they probably turned off their phones.

She couldn't stop thinking about what had happened to Alex at the lab. However, she had to get to the task-at-hand and she would have to figure things out later. She was filled with both excitement and trepidation. They may have just opened a portal, but she also knew they had just brought themselves into the direct spotlight of the OEB, and it would be difficult to avoid their scrutiny from now on.

Sydney needed to call Brian and arrange to use his lab. His cooperation would be essential to completing their work. Hopefully, with Brian's help, and his access to university equipment, Alex would be able to build another chamber and reconstruct what had taken place in the experiment. *The geometry in the chamber must have been off for it to have exploded. Or, it could have been that the size of the chamber not large enough to handle the energy field. Nevertheless, they had achieved an amazing result, even though the effect lasted only few seconds.* With a few alterations, she knew they would be able to stabilize the chamber.

Brian's lab had most of the equipment they would need,

so she didn't think it would take too long to get things up and running again. There was so much to do, and she had to pack up as much equipment and data as possible. She figured the police had searched the lab, but she hoped they hadn't found their secret hiding places in the house. If anyone had been monitoring their call, they might be there soon. So she had to be careful to leave no important data there.

She tried to put the night's events into focus. *If Alex's theory was right, and he had just witnessed proof, this would have enormous impact on not only the world's religions, but on humanity's concept of reality. The OEB would never tolerate this. If they found out what the two of them were working on, their lives would be in extreme danger. Even Alex didn't yet know exactly what he saw and what it meant! They'd have to do further testing before they could answer so many questions.*

When Sydney opened the door to the house, her heart sank. The house had been ransacked! Drawers were hanging open and their contents strewn across the floor. Rugs were pulled aside, and books had been thrown off the shelves. The office was in shambles, and the computer had certainly been compromised by the thugs who raided the house. Alex and Sydney knew there was a possibility of an OEB raid, and so never left sensitive information on their computers. They used backups that were hidden, along with the crystals, in a safe under a tile in the kitchen floor.

As Alex instructed, she went to the safe to retrieve the backup chip and made two copies. She then put the original back in the safe, and placed one in a small airtight locket which she strung around her neck. She placed the third in a small plastic casing, keyed in the address of the only other person she trusted, and slipped it into the mail tube. She took the two crystals and placed them in thick velvet bags, put them in a shoebox, and placed it among the boxes strewn about her closet floor. Then she set the lock on the safe.

The sun was just starting to rise over the ocean far below the hillside house. Sydney was tired, but she didn't have time to sleep, and needed a shower to wake up. She wanted to get over to the hospital as soon as possible. She turned on the faucets, placing her hand inside, feeling the temperature of the water when she thought she heard a bang. She listened closer and heard another bang. With this, she turned off the water, pulled on her robe, and walked quietly out to the hallway. She stopped and listened again for any sound, peering carefully around the corner. She didn't hear anything.

"Hello?" she shouted, thinking it might be one of the staff. Sydney started down the stairs to the second level where the office was located. "Hello? Who's there?" She peered into the office and stopped. Her heart started to beat faster. Someone had been at the desk. The papers that she had just straightened up were askew. She backed away slowly, and started moving towards the security alarm on the wall.

As Sydney backed into the hallway, and peered around the corner, an arm grabbed her by the neck from behind, and pulled off her chain with the back-up chip. She bent backwards into his grasp, and did a back flip over his shoulders, turned and kicked him in his kidney with all her might. The gun and the chain flew out of his hands, and slid across the wood flooring of the landing as he stumbled forward. The chain dropped over the edge of the landing, and fell to the foyer below. The man turned and lunged at her, grasping her shin, and pulling her to the floor. She scissored her legs around his neck, and swung him away from her. He tumbled backwards against the stair rail. Now she could see that it was a young man in his mid-twenties.

Sydney saw the gun just out of reach. She went for it. She could see the look of terror on the intruder's face. He slid halfway down the stairway banister, and then leapt the rest of the way to the floor below. He bolted for the door as Sydney fired two shots into the air just to show him she was serious.

Who is this guy? Is this just a robbery or has the OEB come for me?

Sydney ran down the stairs – gun in hand. She saw him bolt around the house to the left. She pursued him around the bushes to the back of the house, but her bare feet slowed her down as she stumbled over twigs and debris. She lost sight of him, then turned on her heels, as the roar of a motorcycle engine firing up pierced the air. The intruder appeared from behind a thicket of trees. Her eyes followed him speed down the dirt road with a hail of dust kicked up by the back wheel of the skidding bike.

Sydney bent over and clutched her knees as she struggled to get back her breath. As she calmed down, she became aware of the pounding pain in her neck and shoulders. She looked down at her hand and realized her palm was split open and her vidphone receptor was gone. She used the bottom of her tank top to stop the bleeding, and stumbled back to the house and into the kitchen for some water. As she entered, she noticed the floor tile where the safe had been pulled up. She found her chain lying on the floor and stooped down to pick it up. She opened the locket to find the chip in shards.

"That bastard must have been watching me all night!" she said under her breath. She rushed to the closet to see if he had found the crystals. They were still there. She let out a sigh of relief. *Damn, all the backups are gone. I'll have to go to New York to get the one I sent to Louis. It's our only backup now.*

She needed to let Alex know what had happened, but she couldn't call. He wouldn't be allowed to use a phone in the ER anyway. She also couldn't leave a note saying where she was going now that she realized the OEB was after their work. She needed to tell Alex what was going on in person.

CHAPTER 23

Sydney walked through the emergency area doors and approached the reception desk. There was no nurse there, and Sydney scanned the hall to see if she could find anyone. The hospital seemed to be deserted, and so quiet she could hear the buzz of the neon lights. It was a small facility that probably didn't see much action, especially at seven o'clock in the morning. She walked down the white corridor and entered a round area with a nurse station in the middle, and curtained patient areas circling the room. There was no one at this desk either. All the curtains were drawn, so Sydney started to peek behind each one to see if she could find Alex.

"What do you think you are doing?" The booming voice of a corpulent Hawaiian woman in a nurse's uniform startled Sydney. The nurse's stomach was so large her breasts appeared to be lying on a shelf. Sydney jumped backwards, and let out a yelp.

"I'm sorry. I couldn't find anyone, and I'm looking for Alex Harmon. He was brought here several hours ago."

"No one is allowed in this area without first signing in and getting a badge!" scolded the nurse. "You'll have to go to the front desk and sign in."

"But there's no one there," objected Sydney.

The nurse gave Sydney a grimace, and peered down the hall at the empty reception desk.

"Lord, has Carol gone to the powder room again? I swear that girl leaves her post every other minute! Come over here and I'll get it for you."

She led Sydney to the round nurses area and sat down in front of the computer.

"Harmon, you say? How do you spell that?"

Jesus, how many emergencies did they get here overnight anyway? By the looks of it – just Alex. You'd think she'd know where he is! "H..a..r..m..o..n." Sydney spelled out Alex's name, pausing between each letter.

The nurse searched the computer and then stopped abruptly. Sydney could swear the look on her face was fear, but it quickly turned to a supercilious smile. She looked up at Sydney and stuttered, "Oh yes, here it is! He was taken up to X-ray. He has … ah … a few broken ribs and they're checking for internal bleeding. They'll have him back in a few minutes. Just wait over there," she said sternly, her eyes darting back and forth as she pointed to a row of leather seats. Sydney nodded and took a seat. She tapped her fingers on the steel frame of the chair, and gazed at the clock as she anxiously waited for Alex to be brought back to the ER.

An orderly entered the station carrying a small urn. "These are Mr. Arlo Flynn's ashes. His wife is supposed to pick them up here."

"What are they doing here? Shouldn't these be at the funeral parlor?" asked the nurse.

"He was an enemy of the state, I think," answered the orderly. The family does not have the privilege of a funeral. They're lucky they're getting the ashes," snorted the man.

" All right then. Let me have it." The nurse put the urn on the corner of her desk between her lunch bag and a stack of papers.

Sydney looked up at the large wall clock as it rang out nine bells. She had been waiting for over two hours. While she sat there, she started to do something she had never done before. She fixed a vision of Alex's essence in her mind's eye and began to wrap him in a vortex of the brightest white light she could imagine. Somehow, on a gut level, she knew her visualization had power. She heard the monks in Tibet talking about how the mind has tremendous healing power. They believed all people

218

possessed this ability, and that anyone who had been trained correctly could do the same. However, under the rule of the OEB Fundamentalists, anyone who spoke of psychic healing would be labeled demonic.

As the hour grew later, Sydney heard that the OEB were detaining Alex, and that flicker of alarm she detected on the nurses face came back into focus. There were many horror stories of procedures being performed in hospitals on people without their knowledge. One had to keep constant vigil over loved ones, especially if they were being anaesthetized for surgery. Her mind went wild imagining all the things they could do to Alex. She couldn't sit still any longer and got up to approach the nurse's desk. She noticed the tag on her uniform with her name, Dorothy Kelly.

"Miss Kelly, do you have any idea when Mr. Harmon will be brought back to the ER?" asked Sydney in the calmest voice she could muster.

The nurse, who was eating a large meat sandwich, looked up at Sydney with an irritated expression. She clearly didn't want to put the sandwich down, and held it in her hand a few inches from her face as she answered Sydney. "I'll have to call to see what's happening, Mrs. Harmon."

"Oh, I'm not Mrs. Harmon. I'm his colleague, Sydney Stewart."

"Well, why didn't you say that before?" blurted the woman, crumbs falling out of her mouth. "You can't even be in the ER if you're not related to the patient."

"What? I've been waiting here for hours, you could have told me that ...."

"I'm sorry Miss," said the nurse cutting her off before she could finish her sentence. "The rules are the rules. I'm not even allowed to give you any information on the patient. I've already done more than I'm supposed to." The woman waved Sydney away and went back to eating her sandwich. Sydney stood in front of the nurse, staring at her, dumbfounded by this turn of events. The nurse ignored her, refusing to look up, and Sydney finally walked away.

Sydney was furious, but she knew she would get nowhere with this woman. She thought about trying to find a Supervisor, but then decided it was better not to draw attention to herself. She scribbled a note and approached the nurse again.

"Would it be at least possible to get this to him?"

The nurse reached for the paper, knocking over the urn on her desk. "Damn it!" she grunted, bending down and using Sydney's note to clean the ashes off the floor, and then throwing them back in the urn. Sydney watched in silent horror at this act of desecration as the nurse put the note on her desk without looking up at her.

The note said Sydney would meet Alex at B's. She hoped he would just go on to Ann Arbor when he got out of the hospital. Right now, she had to get some rest though her heart had was racing so hard she didn't know if she would be able to lay still. After she got a few hours' sleep she would have to get the backups or all their work would be lost.

With the OEB obviously watching, communicating with Alex and Brian would be difficult for her. She couldn't call Brian from any of her phones. The OEB was certainly monitoring them. She would have to go to her friend Nalassa's to use her phone. *Hopefully no one monitored the call Alex made to me from the ambulance, and no one knows of our plans to go to Ann Arbor. Hopefully ...*

It was two o'clock in the afternoon, when Sydney finally was able to pull herself out of bed. She had tossed and turned for hours before finally dozing off and got only a few hours of sleep. She checked the phone. There were no messages. Alex hadn't called, and that worried her. She threw on some blue jean shorts and a pink camisole, gave her hair a quick brush through, grabbed her purse, and headed out to go to Nalassa's house. She'd just have to drop by unannounced.

Nalassa was an artist and worked in a studio adjacent to her home, so there was a good chance she would be there in the afternoon. Sydney saw Nalassa's car as she drove up the rocky dirt road and breathed a sigh of relief. As she approached the house, Nalassa came out looking like a welcoming angel. She was thirty-five, short with a round fresh face. Her straight light brown hair was closely cropped to her face. She was wearing shorts and a tee shirt covered by an apron stained with paint. She smiled broadly, as Sydney approached her.

"What a pleasant surprise! I saw your car drive up from the studio window." Nalassa gave Sydney a big hug. "What's been going on with you? I haven't heard from you in such a long time, and there's so much buzz on the island about what you and Alex are up to over there."

"Well, that's a long story." Sydney felt her body relax for the first time since she received the call from Alex. It was a relief to be in the presence of a good friend.

"What's the matter, Sydney? You don't look good."

"There's been an accident at the lab and Alex is in the hospital. The OEB has ransacked the house and the lab. I just need to use your phone to make a call as mine is surely being tapped."

"Oh my God. Is Alex all right?"

"I think so. He sounded okay when he called, but they wouldn't let me see him at the hospital and wouldn't give me any information either."

"Geez. Come on in. Let me get you some tea; and of course you're welcome to use the phone."

The two walked into the small home that was filled with Nalassa's colorful paintings of island scenes. The furniture was white wood with canary yellow cushions. Nalassa handed Sydney the phone and went into the kitchen to make some tea.

"Pick up, pick up," mumbled Sydney to herself as the phone connected to Brian's office.

"Brian Sheppard's office," answered a voice at the other end.

"Is he there please? This is Sydney Stewart."

"Just one moment, Miss." Sydney tapped the phone nervously as she waited for Brian to pick up.

"Sydney Stewart! Are you still out in Hawaii with that dog Alex?"

"Brian. Thank God you're there."

"Is everything all right?" asked Brian, his voice filled with concern.

"There's been an explosion at the lab. Brian, we're on the threshold of something astounding and we need your help."

"What's happened?"

"I'm not sure. It seems like Alex opened a portal. But the resonance chamber blew up. We must have had the geometry off somewhat or it may have been too small for the frequencies we were running. Anyway, we need your help and your lab to reconstruct the experiment."

"Whoa. Slow down," said Brian. "Alex opened a portal! What do you mean?"

"He called me from the ambulance and told me that he had been sucked into a vortex, that everything changed, and that he was not in his lab anymore. He went somewhere else. Two HazMat men went into the room afterward and disappeared, and as far as I know have not reappeared!"

"Are you serious? I thought this device he's been working on was an energy source."

"It's an energy source all right, but it's much more. We've been on an amazing journey, Brian. I have a great deal to tell you when I get there. But right now we're being watched by the OEB. We need to get out of here. I've got duplicate crystals and I'm going tonight to get the back-ups."

"You're going where?"

"Listen Brian, it's all complicated and I don't want to stay on the phone too long. Can we come there?"

"Absolutely. I've been studying his equations since the presentation and I have quite a surprise for Alex. I was going to

222

call him and invite him out here, but it looks like you beat me to the punch."

"Really? What is it?"

"You'll see when you get here, but you're going to be really happy when you see it. When do you think you will get here?"

"Tomorrow ... probably in the early evening. I'll go straight to your office. Brian, don't tell anyone that we're coming. I mean no one!"

Sydney threw her suitcase into the back of the air car, locked, and set the alarm. The silver vehicle lifted up vertically into the air. When she reached ten thousand feet, she put it into horizontal mode and veered off over the deep blue Hawaiian waters. It would take about four hours to get to New York. As soon as she kicked into forward drive, the ocean below became a blur and the automatic pilot took over.

If the OEB was interested in following her, they could easily track her flight by satellite so she disabled the auto flight system and started to enter a flight plan by hand. This would disconnect her from the GPS tracking system and keep the OEB off her trail. She couldn't let the last copy of the data slip away. It would take them years, not weeks, to recreate the experiments without the backups that contained all the specifications on how to build the resonator.

The air car, she couldn't see anything from the windows ... just a blur of blue and green streaks. Her head was still pounding but she knew she had to get to New York and retrieve the only remaining data chip. She hoped they wouldn't think to trace the mail tube routing.

Sydney knew the young man who attacked her had to be an OEB operative. It couldn't have been a simple robbery. He didn't try to pry the money chip out of her arm as most robbers do. He had been messing with her computer, and he took the safe in the floor. He must have been watching her to know where it was. *He'll get a surprise when he tries to open that,* she chuckled to herself.

Her glee at this thought was short-lived. She now had was a fugitive and had to take every precaution to elude capture. She dreaded what would happen to Alex. After all, he was at their mercy in the hospital. Surely, the OEB will detain him and even kill him. The thought that she might never see him again filled her with dread. She might even have to complete the work without Alex. It is too important for all of humanity, to not finish what they had started together.

She wanted desperately to call Alex to see if he was all right, and to let him know where she was. But she couldn't call him without giving up her position. Her phone was broken anyway. She wondered how long the OEB had been watching them, and how much they knew about what she and Alex were really doing in the lab. They had taken great care to keep everyone on the staff in the dark about the true purpose of the technology. So even if they were interrogated, and she was sure they would be, she doubted the OEB would learn anything of value.

Still, she worried for the employees' safety and especially for Alex. Fear started to grip her. But she had to remain calm now. She needed to think about what had happened in the lab. *Alex opened up a portal. But a portal to where? Was it another dimension? Was it heaven? Was it a wormhole to another world? Tanzen had talked about how the Galactic Federation and what we call angels are one and the same. What did that really mean and what did that mean about the nature of heaven, life after death, and spirituality? Alex believes that there are an infinite number of concentric dimensions, and that we are confined by our original boundary ... our visible universe. Did he find a way to transcend that boundary condition?*

Sydney's experience in Tibet and all this time with Alex had opened her to a whole new understanding of spirituality. She had never followed any particular organized religion, especially not the brand the OEB had been selling in America. She had pretty much rejected her Catholic upbringing and had become an atheist. She did not believe in a personal God or life after death.

Her favorite line had been one written by John Fowles in his treatise, "The Aristos": *"If God created all this just to teach us a lesson in theology, he was greatly lacking in both humor and imagination."* But Sydney had taken a 180-degree turn since her journey to Tibet. Clearly, there was so much more going on in the nature of reality than she had ever considered before her trip. Her understanding of how consciousness impacts our lives had now expanded to include multi-dimensional orb beings, extra-terrestrial life forms, the Galactic Federation, Earth spirits, and so much more. It truly boggled her mind. This knowledge was so far beyond current scientific understanding that she knew she would have to be careful about what she said to Brian.

Alex had completely transformed her world-view. *We are living in an open, infinite system, where all matter, including every human being, goes to infinity. But what and where or perhaps even when Alex had accessed, is still a mystery.*

It was 7:00 p.m. when Sydney arrived in Manhattan and landed at the rooftop port of Bishop Tower Hotel located in SoHo. She was greeted by a porter, who grabbed her bags and led her to the reception desk, where she registered under the name of Ellen Ballard, greeted her. As they passed down the hallway, she excused herself telling the porter she would meet him at the front desk. She ducked into the ladies room, reversed her coat so that the brown side, not the gold side showed, then she took off her brown tam, and put it in her pocket, letting her hair tumble to her shoulders.

Sydney paid the desk in cash, and followed the porter to a large room on the thirty-first floor. The room had a floor to ceiling window that looked out over the city. She pulled the drapes all the way open to reveal the city lights starting to glisten against the darkening sky. Tired and drained, she kicked off her heels and lay down on the king sized bed. Her head still hurt, but she felt safe for the first time all day.

Hardly anyone even knew she had a brother … not even Alex. Louis was really a half-brother and much older, as he was her father's son from a relationship before marrying her mother. Sydney didn't even know of Louis until he showed up at her father's funeral ten years ago. She had been shocked that her father had kept his existence a secret. Evidently, Louis' mother had never told Sydney's father she had his child, and had been too proud to ask for any help from him.

When Louis turned sixteen, he began to look for his father, and found him living in Ann Arbor with Sydney's mother. Her father embraced Louis as a son after learning about him, and kept in close contact, helping with his college tuition, and talking with him often. However, he kept this a secret from his wife and family. It was inconsistent with his kind and open nature. Sydney assumed he had been afraid of devastating her mother who wouldn't have been able to handle it well. Her mother passed away a year before her father, and never knew about Louis. Sydney couldn't fathom how her mother would have reacted had she lived to meet Louis at the funeral.

For Sydney, finding she had a brother turned out to be wonderful. Louis was a successful doctor, funny, and smart, and they connected right away. Louis reminded Sydney of her father, and being with him was like having a bit of her father back.

Sydney had sent the data chip addressed to Louis' nine-year-old daughter. She breathed a sigh, thanking the universe that she didn't call first to let him know. The OEB was certainly listening in on her conversations. She would have to be extremely careful not to put Louis and his family in any danger. She had to think this through ... how she would contact him ... how she would retrieve the data chip, and how she would get it to Alex without alerting the OEB. She was confident the OEB would not link her to Louis, as there was no public record of their relationship to each other. Yet, the OEB's reach was so pervasive that it was always risky business trying to do something without their knowledge.

Sydney's wakeup call came at 8:00 a.m. on the dot. She opened the curtains to let in the sunlight, but found little in this city shrouded in shadows cast by the cloud-high monoliths of steel and glass. From her window on the thirty-first floor, she could see piles of dirty snow lining the cold drab streets. "This certainly isn't Hawaii," she said under her breath.

She put on her coat and took the elevator down to the lobby. A doorman tipped his hat and opened the door for her, and she walked out into the gray slush of the morning. The city was noisy and the streets were crowded with people. Sirens wailed from all directions and angry drivers blared their horns. Piles of garbage bags lined the streets in yet another strike, and the air had the scent of rotting vegetables.

As she turned the corner, Sydney smelled a stench so vile she had to pull her scarf over her mouth to keep from gagging. She looked around to locate its source but didn't see anything. As she continued down the street, the grotesque stench intensified with each step. Then she stumbled and looked down at what had tripped her. Her eyes bulged in horror as she gazed upon the wrinkled arm jetting out from below a pile of garbage. Then she saw the eye sockets that had been picked clean by the local rodents, and the face that looked several days decomposed … about the time it had been since the garbage trucks last picked up. Sydney gagged as she backed away in horror; and started running down the block. She finally stopped by a fruit stand, her chest, and waited for her heart to stop racing.

An old man dressed in rags and only old socks that were soaking wet held his hat out to her. She reached into her purse, and gave him some money. He bowed his head to her, his watery eyes filled with gratitude. Sydney had given him enough to stay at a shelter and eat for the day. Two elderly women having seen his success came running up to Sydney, begging her for some money too.

Sydney gave them the rest of her small bills. It was horrible that elderly people were forced to live on the streets as beggars. There were tens of thousands of them in New York alone. So many of these people had no children, no savings, and no safety net. Most had worked their entire lives, paying into the now defunct Social Security system after the government had bankrupted it on purpose. This thought always made her blood boil. The thugs who ran the OEB enriched their friends and the large financial institutions, spent the country into the dirt with their Muslim wars, and then bankrupted all the entitlement programs.

It was what they had wanted all along. They hated entitlements. "No handouts!" they chanted at their rallies. The people – now relegated to the streets – had paid into this system for most of their lives. Now when their investment should be paying dividends, there was nothing for them to live on. It was not a handout; it was their money; and the government had stolen it from them. Sydney shook her head in disgust at the horrific outcome.

One of the many OEB doctrines was that "one's fate was sealed by God." If you found yourself on the streets, it was where God had placed you for committing some sin. Good people had good fortune, according to the OEB. So it was not unusual to see elderly people lying dead in the streets in a city like New York. It was all part of the urban landscape of the new order.

Sydney hailed a cab and asked the driver to take her to the Plaza Hotel. She caught his dark eyes in the rear view mirror as he nodded and put the car into gear. The streets of New York were jammed with cars and irate drivers. The sidewalks were a teaming swarm of humanity. Nearly twenty million people now called this small island home. Sydney hated it. It made her feel trapped.

The filth of the city permeated her skin and clogged her nostrils. The drive from SoHo to the Plaza Hotel seemed to take forever as the taxi tried to weave through the tangle of traffic. Finally, they pulled up to the historic hotel. A doorman opened the cab door, and helped Sydney out.

Inside she scanned the large foyer for the sole payphone, a true remnant of the past as most people had vidphones these days. She had to call Louis, and this was the only way to do it without being tracked by anyone who might be attempting to locate her. Yes, they would know it was from the Plaza Hotel, but she wouldn't be there long enough for anyone to notice her. They would probably be able to identify her from the hotel security cameras, but that would take some time. She tried to stop this negative train of thought. She realized she was being overly paranoid, as there was no way for the OEB to know she was going to visit Louis.

"Hello?" Sydney recognized the warm, friendly voice of her brother.

"Hi Louis, it's Sydney. How are you?"

"Great," he replied cheerfully. "I haven't heard from you in a long while. I'm surprised you lifted your nose up from your lab experiments long enough to call your brother." He laughed.

"Actually Lou, I'm here in New York right now and would love to see you. How's your schedule?"

"Wow, you're here? This is a surprise. Why didn't you give me some notice?"

"It's a long story and that's why I have to see you."

"You're in luck little sis. I just finished my rounds and I was going to the health club to work out. But for you I'll sacrifice a little sweat. Where are you staying?"

"I'm at the Plaza, but why don't you meet me at that cute little café we went to last time I was in town. You know the one by your office."

"Oh yeah. Sure, what time?"

Sydney sighed in relief that he didn't say the name of the café on the phone.

"Well it shouldn't take me more than twenty minutes to get there. Oh and Lou, I sent a little gift to Sandra, but I want your opinion on it. I sent it by tube to your office. Would you mind bringing it?"

"Why didn't you bring it in person?"

"Well I really hadn't planned to be here today and only found out I would be coming late last night."

"Ohhhhkay, I'll see you there in twenty minutes," said Lou as he shook his head. "I shouldn't be surprised at yet another example of your impetuous lifestyle!"

Sydney stepped out the front door of the Plaza And as expected, there was a line of taxis waiting. One moved out from farther back in the line, and the doorman poked his head in the window, said a few words to the driver, and then opened the rear passenger door for her. Sydney saw the doorman put some money into his vest pocket, and thought it was odd that the taxi driver had paid him. *Well maybe that's the way you get to go to the front of the line*, she thought.

"Seventy-second and Broadway," she said to the driver.

230

The streets were a tangled mess of honking traffic as the taxi slowly weaved its way up Broadway.

It takes twenty minutes to go a few blocks and only a few hours to go six thousand miles. The irony made her laugh aloud. She could see the driver's dark brown eyes look at her through the rear view mirror. She turned her eyes away while he continued to look at her through the mirror. It always made her uncomfortable when men stared at her. But there was something about the way he looked at her that made her stomach swell with anxiety. *It's only another Middle-Eastern man ogling you,* she thought to reassure herself. Then he took an abrupt turn towards Riverside, sending her sliding to the other side of the cab.

"I think you're going the wrong way," she said with a trace of apprehension.

The driver did not respond, and so she said it again – this time slower, thinking that perhaps he did not understand her.

"Short cut," he said with a thick accent that sounded German, not Middle Eastern. Sydney froze as she realized she had seen those eyes before. This same driver took her from her hotel to the Plaza. Then she saw something metallic catch the sun reflecting off the chrome on the dashboard. It was a gun, and he had his hand on it.

Her heart was pounding with fear. She hadn't given the driver the name of the restaurant … just the cross streets. Hopefully, Louis would be safe. When the taxi stopped for a light she opened the door and bolted from the cab into the street. A cacophony of horns began to blow, as the angry New York drivers shouted for her to get out of the way. Her driver leaped out of the taxi and ran after her, leaving his car in the middle of the street.

The horns and shouts increased to a roar as more irate drivers became stuck behind the abandoned car. Sydney ran through the hoard of Christmas shoppers that packed the sidewalks, elbowing people out of her way. She gasped for breath as she looked over her shoulder to see if her pursuer was still in sight. She could see him pushing people over as he followed her about a third of the way down the block. She ducked into a women's shop – grabbed a blouse off the hanger – and asked for the fitting rooms.

The young sales girl dressed in black leather and sporting bright orange hair, pointed toward the back of the store. Sydney scurried in and pulled the curtain shut. She stood with her back against the mirror and gasped for air. Her heart was pounding furiously. She waited a few minutes and then peered out from behind the curtain. The sales girl looked at her with concern.

"Are you okay?" she asked.

Just as Sydney was about to answer, her pursuer appeared in the window. The sales girl caught her look of horror as Sydney pulled back the curtain and stood on the seat inside.

"Have you seen a woman ... uh ... my girlfriend?" he asked scanning the store. "She has long wavy blonde hair."

"No sir," the girl answered with a calm voice. There's been no one in here for the last half hour."

"He grunted and pushed open the door, and then disappeared into the crowded street.
Sydney peered out again, and the sales girl motioned that he was gone.

"Was that man harassing you?" she asked Sydney looking concerned.

"Yes, and thank you so much for what you did for me.

"Men!" said the young girl as she rolled her eyes and cracked her gum.

"Is there a back way out of here?" asked Sydney.

The girl led her out through the stock room. The double steel doors led to an alley behind the store.

God, I hope I lost him. Sydney took off her coat and reversed it, changing it from the brown side back to the gold. She pulled a long black scarf out of her purse, wrapped it around her head, and put on her oversized sunglasses. She thanked the sales girl again and walked out into the alley and then into the sea of people, feeling safely concealed in their midst.

Sydney was sure he was the same driver that took her to the Plaza. That meant he knew where she was staying and he would be watching for her. Sydney hoped he didn't know what

232

room she was in, and hotel security wouldn't give it out. Still, it was now too dangerous to stay there. She would have to figure a way to get out of there without anyone seeing her. *This guy obviously has a lot of resources to have known my travel route from Hawaii,* she thought.

"What's that for?" asked Alex eyeing the large needle the doctor was preparing.

"Just, er, um, a little something to help you relax," the doctor answered, his voice cracking as he swabbed Alex's arm.

"Wait a minute, I don't want .... "

The doctor injected the needle into his arm before he could finish his sentence.

Alex's eyes fluttered and rolled back into his head as he passed out.

"Is he ready?" asked the man entering from behind the curtain.

"Yes, sir." The physician lowered his head and left Alex alone in the room with the OEB agent.

Tarnoff slapped Alex's face a few time to bring him back to consciousness.

"Alex Harmon. Wake up!" Alex's head rolled side to side

as the room started to come back into focus.

"Is your name Alex Harmon?"

"Yes," he heard himself answer involuntarily.

"Do you live at 123 Plantation Road?"

"Yes."

"What kind of experiment were you running when there was an explosion at your lab?"

Alex realized he was being interrogated, and he didn't want to say anything. But he couldn't keep himself from answering.

"Uh, I'm looking for energy in the vacuum," he heard himself answer.

"What do you mean energy in the vacuum? The vacuum is empty."

"No, it's not. There's energy … infinite energy." Alex started to nod off and the man slapped him again.

"What did you do with the two HazMat men?"

"I didn't do anything. I saw them go into the lab when I was in the hall."

"They're missing; gone. What happened to them?"

"They went into the vortex."

"The vortex? What kind of vortex?"

"The chamber creates a field with a vortex."

"Where does the vortex go?"

"I don't know."

"Did you go somewhere?"

"Yes."

"Where did you go?"

"Another place, another time, another dimension, heaven … I'm not sure."

"He's delirious," said Tarnoff clearly impatient to get more valuable information. He called the doctor back into the room. "Put him under and complete the procedure. Call me when it's done."

Dr. Jergensen made a small incision under the hairline of Alex's left temple. Blood trickled down his comatose face. The nurse handed the doctor a tiny nanobot clasped at the end of a long silver prong. The doctor carefully took hold of the probe and inserted it into the incision. He then inserted a tiny chip.

"This has got to be lodged precisely behind the optic nerve. There, got it."

The nurse handed the doctor a second nanobot and chip, and he inserted them deep into Alex's ear canal. "Easy does it," he said and then smiled, satisfied with his skill. The doctor walked over to a device on the other side of Alex's bed, turned on the holo-imager, typed in a command and the tiny robot began to perform its intricate task of connecting the chip to Alex's optic nerve.

He then directed the second nanobot to a precise location in Alex's ear canal. When he was done, he opened the door and nodded at the two men who stood guard outside the small hospital room.

"Is it working?" asked the man wearing sunglasses in the middle of the night.

"It seems fine. But we need to wait until he awakens to be sure."

The man in black got out his phone and placed a call to Brandon Tarnoff

Alex woke up with a hellacious headache. The neon lights above his bed hurt his eyes, and he struggled to sit up.

"Whoa honey." The older, heavyset Hawaiian nurse came over, and helped him up to a sitting position. "You've been sleeping a good long time."

"What happened? Was there someone here asking me questions or have been I dreaming?"

The nurse turned her back to him and arranged some tools on the tray against the curtain. "Now you must have been dreaming honey. There hasn't been anyone here to visit you."

"Where's Sydney? Did she come?"

"Oh, now yes, actually there was a young lady last night or rather really early this morning. She wasn't allowed into the ER as she was not kin. You know the rules; only kin get into the ER. I believe she left you a note. I'll go get it for you. First, you need some liquids. Here drink this." She handed him a glass of juice.

Alex hesitated. "Now honey its just juice. Go on and drink it all up."

Alex's mouth was extremely dry, and although he was wary, he took in the welcome liquid.

Alex wanted to fly out to meet Sydney as soon as he was released from the hospital, but he couldn't muster the strength. He felt exhausted and his body simply lost all of its energy a few minutes after he got home. His arms suddenly felt so heavy he could barely lift them. He stumbled over to the sofa and lay down. *Just for a few moments,* he told himself as he tried to collect his thoughts, but he slipped into a deep sleep almost immediately.

When he awoke it was after 7:00 p.m. He'd been sleeping all day.

"Damn!" he exclaimed when he saw the clock. He reached for the phone to call Sydney, but then realized she'd have it turned off, not wanting to be tracked by the OEB.

CHAPTER 24

Alex's cab pulled up to the University of Michigan campus. He paid the driver and made his way into the Physics building. There were the usual guards at the entrance to check his bags for security. He opened his brief case to let the guard look through it. Alex hated the invasiveness of this process. The guard then waved him into the building.

Alex took the lift to the seventh floor and knocked on Brian's office door. There was no answer. His next knock pushed the door open. "Brian, are you here? It's Alex." There was no reply.

Brian's office consisted of a small reception area and a large office just beyond. He noticed some papers scattered on the floor, and caught the faint odor of a noxious chemical, but he couldn't place it.

The office was empty but the lights were on, as was Brian's desk computer. Alex thought it was odd that the file cabinets were open. Upon closer inspection, he suspected that someone had rummaged through Brian's things. However, Brian was not the most organized person, and often had piles of paper scattered around the office. *It isn't like Brian to be late for an appointment. Maybe he's already out with Sydney, but they would have at least left a note or called me.*

He heard a rustling sound at the door and turned around in alarm. He relaxed when he realized it was Sue, Brian's research assistant, carrying a load of books in one hand and a cup of coffee in the other.

"Hello? Can I help you?" she asked, appearing somewhat

put off that Alex had let himself into the office. She plopped the books down on her desk and pulled her purse off her shoulder.

"I'm sorry, the door was ajar and Brian was expecting me. Do you know where he is?" asked Alex.

"Oh, you must be Alex Harmon! Brian told me you would be coming by. He had an emergency with his daughter this morning. He told me to tell you he would call you as soon as he could get free."

"Beth? I hope she is all right," said Alex with concern. Brian's daughter was a pretty eighteen-year-old girl. Alex had been witness to many of her milestones growing up. He considered Brian and his wife Katherine two of his closest friends. When Katherine died, he knew it would be hard on Beth. Brian couldn't care for her himself, so she was sent to a boarding school, and then to the American College in Leysin, Switzerland. All his friends agreed this would be the best thing for her.

Brian had told Alex about how the town was four thousand feet in the Vaud Alps, literally built on the side of a mountain. Hiking, climbing, and skiing were everyday activities. He started to worry that there had been an accident. Brian talked about how one slip on a narrow mountain path in some places could send you tumbling thousands of feet to the valley below.

"Do you know if Sydney Stewart has arrived yet? We agreed to meet here."

"No, I'm sorry, I haven't heard from her. Do you know how she was coming in? I could check the flight schedules for you." Sue sat down behind her desk and waved her hand in front of the virtual holo-imager to turn it on.

"No, she took the air car, and quite frankly we made only vague plans to meet here, and I haven't been able to get in touch with her all day. She doesn't even know where I've booked our room," said Alex, realizing all he had was the scribbled note saying to meet her at B's.

"You're welcome to make yourself at home until Brian gets back," said Sue.

Alex looked at his watch. It was almost 4:00 p.m. "No, that's all right. I'll get a beer at O'Reilly's. But please leave a note on the door for Sydney when you go. She may not get here for a while, and she'll be expecting Brian and me to be here. Tell her that I'll be at the Marriott." Alex was nervous letting Sue know about Sydney and his whereabouts, but coordination without using vidphones or any other electronic communication was going to be extremely difficult. It was a necessary evil.

"Sure, I'd be happy to do that."

Alex walked out into the frigid December air. The campus was lit up with white Christmas lights and looked like a fairyland with a glaze of glimmering ice outlining the branches of the trees. He looked enviously at the young students as they rushed by all bundled up. *Ahhh, to be that young again and so unaware of the realities of life.* His heart was heavy with the many disappointments life had thrown in his path over the years.

He thought of his wife and how her death left a hole in his heart. They had met and fallen in love during college on this campus. Being here brought back many bittersweet memories. He felt some remorse that he had not had children with Karen. *Sydney is still young enough,* he thought. *Maybe there's still a chance for a family yet.*

He had spent so many years, working day and night on his theory that there had been room for little else. Karen had suffered for his dedication to his work. *Once I bring the technology to fruition there might be time for family.* His success depended on Brian right now.

He wondered how his discovery would affect all the young people that scurried around him. He winced remembering the enormity of why he was there. His steamy breath against the cold air made him wish he had a cigarette, though he had given them up years ago. He needed something to calm his nerves. The thought that there was trouble with Beth gave him a sharp pang of anxiety. *I guess I'll just have to wait until Brian or Sydney call me,* he thought as he shrugged his shoulders and pulled his collar up over his freezing ears. He forced himself to shift his thoughts.

Alex headed over to his favorite pub on State Street. He hoped it still had that great cider ale. That would hit the spot right about now, and he could go for some of their grilled sweet sausage too. He hailed a cab and climbed into its welcome warmth.

The taxi pulled up in front of the Tudor style building with bottle glass windows etched with snow, and steamy from the heat inside. Alex leaned over to pay the driver, then slipped on his warm gloves and headed into the pub. It was the place of choice for the scientific crowd in Ann Arbor – with a collection of students, professors, and scholarly types debating topics that the average person would need a library of reference books to decipher. That's what he loved about this place. He could think of nowhere else where there was scintillating debate going on just about twenty-four-seven. He loved the energy, and it lightened his mood.

He took a seat at a small rough-hewn table against the mahogany wall by the fireplace. Alex could finally feel his body relaxing. The server came by with a large stein of cider ale, and Alex drank the whole thing in almost one gulp. *Why isn't Sydney here already? She had a two-day head start on me. Perhaps she's dodging the OEB.* Both Sydney and Alex had honed their telepathic skills in Tibet, and he started to concentrate on sending her a thought message to let him know where she was. Hopefully, he would pick something up from her. But as he sat there he felt nothing.

He was aware that he had many so-called paranormal abilities since he had been a small child. He could even feel the presence of spirits of people who had passed away. This convinced him that consciousness continues after death, and that a person's infinity remains when their boundary condition – or body is lost. It is much like a super nova that reveals a black hole after the explosion, but at a different scale and density.

Scientists often say that when a star goes super nova it creates a black hole. However, Alex had come to understand that the black hole was always there, and when the star sheds its boundary condition, the black hole becomes visible. He believed that humans have to be truly endless beings if all matter goes to infinity.

He had been struggling since the explosion to make sense

of what had happened within the context of his theory. He had been in another place. A place with people and buildings. Was it occupying the same space as his lab? Somehow, he had managed to access another level of existence, and there seemed to be another reality there. But had he actually been teleported somewhere else? Had he been in another dimension? Had he been in another time? Did he experience heaven? He needed to know.

He wondered if the HazMat men were still in that place, or trapped in some netherworld, or worse, dead. Would they ever return on their own? Maybe it was Heaven. Were the people he saw deceased souls? Clearly, he had found something much more profound than an energy source. There were so many unanswered questions. The light streaming out of everything in that place reminded him of something. He felt like he'd seen it before. He squeezed his eyes shut trying to remember.

CHAPTER 25

It was a Sunday morning after an abundant snowfall and Beth decided to go skiing. She loved to ski by herself when she was stoned. There was at least six inches of fresh snow the night before, and the trails would be beautiful. She went into her closet, took a shoebox down from the shelf, got out a pair of shoes, screwed the heel off the left shoe, and pulled out her bag of marijuana. She poured a thimble full into a small pipe, placed it in a sealable baggy, and stuffed it in a pocket of her yellow and white ski suit. She lifted her skis out of her locker and headed out the front doors of the school, waving innocently at Mr. Pagan, the math teacher.

Beth had become an excellent skier after three years living in the Swiss Alps. Leysin wasn't the greatest ski area, but she was just a few hours drive from some of the world-class ski resorts like Davos, Chamonix, Gestade, and Verbier. She would often go for weekends with her friends, sampling the best of Swiss, French, and Italian ski resorts on a student's budget. She didn't mind flopping on the floor of some friend's place, but often could take over someone's parents' posh chalet. At eighteen, she was adventurous, carefree, and prone to act impulsively if it sounded like fun. She was just starting to become aware of her allure to boys. She was pretty with long dark hair, turquoise eyes, and a long, sleek athletic figure.

Beth headed up the mountain to the gondola that goes up to the ski area with her skis on her shoulder. This was the lousy part, the uphill walk carrying skis! She had to walk about a quarter of a mile uphill to the gondola station. When she reached the ticket booth, hardly any skiers were there and she boarded the lift alone.

Once at the top, she snapped her boots into the ski bindings and eyed her target area where she could light up without anyone seeing her. Beth leaned forward and took off gracefully down the mountain. She stopped by a thicket of trees and sidestepped up to a small ledge that was out of sight. Beth pulled her pipe and baggy out of her pocket, lit it up and inhaled deeply. *This is heaven,* she thought, with a smug grin – knowing she was being bad and getting away with it.

"Hey, you over there!" shouted a man's voice. Beth's heart leaped into her throat as she turned around, holding the pipe behind her back.

"Are you all right?" The slender figure of a young man appeared just above her.

Whoa, he's cute, she thought as she brushed the hair out of her face trying to look sophisticated and mag.

"Wait a minute. I smell something," he said with a sly grin. "Do you share?"

Beth heaved a sigh of relief. "Sure, thank God you're not a narc!"

She handed the pipe to him as he slid down to be adjacent to her.

"My name is Seth. Are you skiing alone?"

"Well, I was," she said looking at him coyly, noticing his deep blue eyes and strong jaw. She could tell he was older and that was exciting to her. She tried to act older herself, hoping he would think she was at least twenty.

"Are you a tourist?" he asked her.

"Pa..lease, no one is a tourist in Leysin. How utterly boring. No, I'm a teacher's aide at the American High School," she lied. "And you?" she asked, now taking notice of his wide shoulders, slim hips, and long wavy hair.

"I'm here on business, and I don't know anyone at all. To tell you the truth, I don't much like skiing alone. It's always so much nicer to share," he said glancing at the pipe as he handed it back to her. "Would it be all right if I tagged along with you?"

"Sure," said Beth, elated at the suggestion of male attention.

"It's probably not a bad idea to have a buddy anyway when you're skiing stoned," he said. "This mountain looks a bit treacherous."

"Well I hope you can handle it," she said teasingly, and then they pushed off and headed straight down the steep slope laughing with her marijuana buzz intensifying her senses.

Seth was a good skier, much better than Beth, but she was determined to keep up with him. She thought she would throw him off a bit by taking a narrow back trail. She slid by him and yelled for him to follow her.

"I'm going to take you somewhere mag. Watch out for the bare patches; this isn't groomed." she shouted over her shoulder, her long hair now blowing wildly as she increased speed.

They weaved in and out of the trees through a narrow, steep pass, and then through an open slope and around a bend. They could now see the old chalet down below with smoke streaming out of the chimneystack.

"There's Le Fendent! Beth pointed at the chalet. Seth swung to a stop beside Beth.

"What's there?" He planted his poles and blew into his gloves to warm his hands.

"It's an old chalet. I think it dates back to the 1700's. They serve the best Fondue in Switzerland and I'm hungry!" she shouted, already heading down the slope toward the rustic building.

They stacked their skis against the wall, brushed off the snow, and entered the welcome warmth of the quaint old chalet. Beth asked for the table in the back, by the window, adorned with a frilly red-checkered curtain. They ordered cheese fondue and a bottle of white wine. The waitress quickly brought a stand with a lit sterno and a large basket of cubed crusty bread to the table. She then brought a ceramic pot with the hot, liquid cheese soup.

"Bon appetite, Monsieur, Mademoiselle," she said as she turned and left them.

"Do you know the secret to making fondue?" Beth speared a piece of the thick Swiss bread with the long fork. "You have to heat the wine first, not to the point of boiling, but just to the point when you see small bubbles forming. You have to grate the cheese and mix in a small bit of cornstarch. Then you add it to the wine slowly. That keeps it smooth and allows the cheese to dissolve evenly. And you must use Gruyere cheese and a Fendent wine. I learned that from Paulo at L'Horizon Tavern. I worked there last summer because I had to stay in Switzerland. My dad was real busy with some experiment. He's always busy with some experiment!"

Gawd, I'm babbling, she thought as she rolled her bread around in the cheese and raised the fork to her mouth with her pinky in the air. "Ow!" she moved her hand to her mouth. "That's hot!" She was trying to act sophisticated and older, but she had a nasty feeling she wasn't pulling it off. But she noticed happily that Seth still seemed interested.

Seth touched her hand gently and smiled at her. "You're pretty…did you know that?"

Seth had a slight accent that made him seem exotic. She gazed back into his eyes and smiled, her heart pounding with excitement.

"So what does this mean dad of yours do?"

"He's a professor at the University of Michigan. He's a physicist, and he's always working on something more important than me."

"How could he not treasure such a beautiful gem as you?" asked Seth as he filled Beth's glass up with more wine.

"Oh, I'm sure he loves me. It's just that it doesn't do me any good. Ever since my mom died, it's like he can't deal with me."

"I'm so sorry to hear that you have lost your mother."

"Yea, that was a big bummer. And that's why I'm here. My dad sent me to the American High School and then the College here." Beth realized she was about to contradict her story of working here, not being a student. "Anyway, when I graduated I started working here," she lied again.

"What is your last name?" Seth put his hand on hers and drew it to his chest.

"Sheppard, why?"

"Just curious," he said with a smile.

"And what's your last name?" she asked

Seth dropped her hand and cleared his throat. My name is Seth Benet and I'm very happy to make your acquaintance."

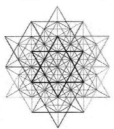

Brian Sheppard, his black winter trench coat dripping with melting snow, found his way through the crowded restaurant to Alex's table.

"Alex, I'm so sorry I wasn't at the office to meet you when you arrived."

"Sue told me that you had an emergency with Beth. Is she all right?" Alex noticed a worried look on Brian's face.

"She's okay for now. You know she's eighteen going on thirty. She was caught with drugs and the school was threatening to expel her. I've been on the phone all day begging them to keep her in school!" Brian's eyes darted back and forth as he explained his delay. Then he shrugged and shook his head. "What am I going to do?"

Alex detected something else in his manner. Something beyond worry about his eighteen year-olds' drug incident.

"Did you hear from Sydney yet?" asked Alex.

"No, I stopped by the office and saw your note, but nothing from Sydney. Where is she?"

"I don't know. Did she tell you about the explosion at the lab?"

"Just briefly. She said she had to go somewhere to get the back-up chip."

Alex remembered the broken floor safe, and realized she must have sent off one of the chips to a safe location.

"The OEB is watching Sydney and me. We have had to go to some extremes to cover our tracks. They ransacked the lab and the house. They even found our floor safe where we had hidden back-ups. I hope to God Sydney saved another copy or everything will be lost."

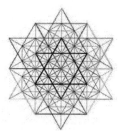

Seth could see the clouds below him hanging over the valley and could hear the clanging of the cowbells. Beth lay sleeping in his bed at the Hotel Leysin. He sat in a large pine chair on the veranda and lit up a Galois. If he was going to die from lung cancer, he was going to do it smoking a good cigarette.

He looked over at Beth's innocent face as she slept. She had full pink lips that curled upward at the sides in the most provocative way. She was lovely. He knew he had to keep her with him. He was hoping she would come with him willingly. If not ... well he had ways.

Beth squinted as she opened her eyes to the bright sunlight. She gave a smile to Seth and crawled out of bed.

"I hope you don't mind," she said as she threw on his shirt that lay crumpled over the chair.

Seth looked up from his smoke. "Will they miss you at school?" he asked.

"Its Saturday. No one will notice until class on Monday morning."

"Well that's good," he said. "Why don't you drop by your place and pack a few things and I'll take you to Zermatt for the night. I have some business there tomorrow afternoon, and I would really like your company."

"Completely mag!" she squealed. "What is it that you do?" she asked stretching her arms out in a long languid arc as she walked out to the veranda to join him.

"It's top secret," he said putting his finger up to his mouth as if to say, "shhhhh." He rolled his eyes and leaned over and grabbed her onto his lap, kissed her deeply and then lifted her up and carried her over to the bed.

"Can you handle me again?" he said in a sly, seductive manner as he slowly unbuttoned the shirt that was the only barrier between his skin and hers. Beth threw her arms above her head in a submissive gesture, inviting his caresses. As he kissed her slowly, unfastening each button, he felt himself get hard with excitement.

This is one damn pleasant assignment,' he thought as he ran his hand over her supple young breasts. *'If I wasn't on assignment they'd have me arrested for this.* Then he thrust himself into her. They moved together as she moaned with each plunge, penetrating ever deeper.

"Hello?" Brian Sheppard turned on his vidphone to see Sydney's face.

"Sydney, thank God," he said. "Alex has been trying to reach you."

"Yes, do you know where he is?"

"He's here with me." Brian handed the phone to Alex.

"Sydney, where are you? What is happening? I've been trying to reach you all day. The house was a wreck when I got back from the hospital. Are you all right?"

"I'm fine, but I was attacked. All the backups were destroyed except for the one I put in the tube. I had to go to New

York to retrieve it. I've been followed here and my vidphone is broken. I'm on a pay phone. The OEB is after me Alex, and you can't be safe either. Do you think the OEB knows where you are?"

"I don't think so. I haven't seen any signs of them so far," said Alex.

"You need to be extremely careful," said Sydney. "They're definitely following me and seem to want to get their hands on our work. I guarantee they're looking for you too."

"Well there's nothing here for them to see at the moment. Brian and I need to retool the resonance chamber and that's going to take some time. As far as I can tell, no one knows I'm here. I didn't tell anyone where I was going. I rented an air car, but didn't file a flight report."

"It's not safe Alex; please be careful. I have to go now. I'm sure they're trying to track me. I'll have to reach you through Brian. I can't take the chance of calling your phone. It will lead them directly to you. It would be best if you throw your phone away. They can track it even if it's shut off."

"Don't worry, I don't have one with me anymore. The one in my palm was destroyed in the blast.

Sydney saw a Brotherhood agent entering the hotel. She hung up the phone without saying goodbye and hurried out to the safety of the crowded street.

CHAPTER 26

When President Frederick invaded Syria and Iran simultaneously, the rest of the Muslim world united to fight off the U.S. The battle quickly degenerated into a religious war, with the Christian European nations allied with the U.S. against the Muslim world's one billion faithful. Previous allies such as Saudi Arabia abandoned their relations with the West to join the greatest confrontation of Christians and Muslims since the Crusades.

With America in an all-out war, Frederick declared Marshall Law and the Congress and Senate voted to postpone elections indefinitely. With the war in its seventeenth year of bloody conflict and elections eliminated for the foreseeable future, Croft saw his moment of historic opportunity to recreate America as a fundamentalist Christian nation.

"The forces of good and evil are in a life and death struggle!" John Croft pounded his fist on the podium as he addressed Congress. "No longer can we allow the Godless of America to pull us down into degradation and divert our God-given mission. We stand at a crossroad. All of the signs are upon us. We must be unwavering in our fight. The God of our enemies is clearly the devil and his followers are the devil's minions. Either we submit to the forces of evil or we fight for God's kingdom on Earth!

"America can no longer equivocate. You are either with God or in league with the Devil. We will not have a vote today. For the fate of God's kingdom isn't subject to debate. Today, America is united under God not in words, but in law! This is our new Pledge of Allegiance, not to the state, but to God. And those who will not take the pledge will be exposed as nonbelievers and will be brought to justice!"

There was robust applause from many in the Chamber as Croft raised his arms in supplication. Those in agreement sprung to their feet. Those who disagreed began an outraged uproar of protest. Croft was prepared for this response. The doors of the Congress sprung open, and armed guards rushed in arresting all who protested. America was officially renamed The United Christian States of America – the UCSA – that day.

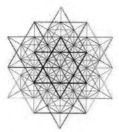

Alex and Brian decided to stay at O'Reilly's for dinner. They ordered two steaks with fries and another round of beers. The call from Sydney worried him. He was deeply concerned for her safety. He wouldn't be able to relax until she arrived in Ann Arbor, and hoped they would be safe there. He cringed and his stomach tightened as he contemplated the OEB's fascist conduct.

"You know Brian, we have lost everything Americans held dear in our zeal to protect ourselves against terrorism ... the conveniently never ending threat," he said with a look of profound sadness.

Brian looked around the restaurant uneasily. "We better not talk about this in public. You never know who is listening."

Alex bit his lip as he thought of how much things had changed since the Brotherhood came to power. He was amazed at how little time it took to disassemble democracy. He had seen it coming, but it seemed everyone else had been asleep. Croft and his OEB were brilliant at manipulating public opinion and obfuscating the truth, turning even words like *social justice* and *equality* into negatives. They poured trillions of dollars into propping up the financial market with the goal of thrusting the middle class into poverty – robbing the people of their tax dollars, savings, and homes.

They dismantled every social aid program, and put so many people into poverty that no one had the will or the means to protest against the OEB. By the time Croft made his move on Congress, it was too late. After twenty years in office without an election, President Frederick, Croft's puppet, had been able to replace all the remaining moderate judges on the Supreme Court with his cronies. He replaced Justice Murray when she resigned, too ill from cancer to hold out any longer. A year later, Justice Deeds died and just four months after that the two remaining moderate justices were assassinated on the steps of the Supreme Court. It did not surprise Alex when there had been absolutely no investigation into the murders. Frederick, and by proxy Croft, had virtually no opposition, and now the OEB was an unstoppable force.

"They were watching us! They God Damn even knew where our floor safe was! That son of a bitch and his religious thugs have been monitoring our every move! Can you believe it?" he asked Brian, trying to contain his anger. "I hope to God Sydney is okay."

"She's probably okay Alex, and will get in touch with you when it's safe."

"Yeah. That's probably it. That Bastard Croft thinks he can do any damn thing he wants with impunity, and you know what? He can!" Alex fumed. "We might as well be living under Stalin! Big Brother is here and his name is Croft! Shit, they're so damn cocky; they named their organization the Office of Ethical Behavior! Doesn't anybody notice the irony?"

Brian leaned across the table. "Shhh. Hey man, you've got to keep it down."

Alex's face had turned red with anger. It outraged him that Croft had been able to wean freedom away from an unsuspecting public who trusted that those to whom they gave extreme power would not abuse it.

"They don't get it. People will always abuse power if

they can! What is it that they say? Absolute power corrupts absolutely! Those Bible thumping hypocrites have justified their rape of America in the name of God. If they knew what I know now about the true nature of the force underlying creation … that we are all part of one great consciousness – that we are not separate – their dogma would crumble, and all this nonsense would end."

"That's why they're after you and Sydney," said Brian nodding his head in agreement.

Brian led Alex into the basement of the Physics Building. It was a cavernous expanse of corridors laid out in a maze-like configuration. They passed rows of doors – probably to storage closets given how close they were to each other.

"I think you'll be surprised by what I have to show you," said Brian scanning his card to open door 504B.

Alex followed him into the darkened room. Brian fumbled for the light switch. When the light came on, Alex gasped at what he saw in the center of the room.

"What in the world!" he blurted. He walked around the large device, noticing a mess of equipment strewn around the room. This was no closet. This room was at least fifty square feet. "What is this place?"

"It's my secret lab," replied Brian with a sly grin. I've been buying up consecutive storage closets for years and taking out the walls to have a place to work in private."

"And nobody knows about this?"

"Not really. No one ever comes down here. It's just a storage facility for old files, books, and equipment. I haven't run into a soul down here in years."

"This looks like my prototype, but what have you done to it?"

"I've been busy since I came back from your conference in Kona. I remembered you had left a prototype in my storage unit, and I got an idea about how to improve on it. I've been tinkering with it for quite a while. I wasn't going to say anything to you unless I was able to get it to work. But then you called ... and well, here it is!" Brian gave Alex the look of a proud parent presenting his newborn offspring.

Alex walked around the device inspecting Brian's modifications.

"Well my friend, you're a hell of a lot smarter than I've ever given you credit for."

Brian scowled.

"That didn't come out right," said Alex somewhat embarrassed at his clumsy statement. "I mean this is close to our final design. It's taken me years to come up with some of these modifications, and this is quite good."

Brian grinned. "You shouldn't have underestimated your old friend."

"The geometry of the coils is off however, and you don't have a crystal!"

"I haven't gotten that far."

"That's not a problem. We have a crystal. Brian, this is amazing! I had been thinking it was going to take months to rebuild the device, but with this, I think we're only talking weeks. I'm impressed you were able to do this," said Alex crouching down to get a better look at the copper wiring that circled the device.

"I remembered you saying at the conference that Walter Russell had been working on a similar concept in the 1920's. So I read up on him and started to think I could make some modifications to your prototype that might work.

"Look at this," said Brian wheeling a dishwasher sized device out of a closet.

"What do you have there?"

"The answer to your prayers," said Brian giving Alex a

wink. "This is a Faber. It can manufacture just about anything, using claytronics to create a form of programmable matter. It uses tiny catoms that are submillimeter computers that make up the basic units of claymatics. The tiny ball-like units can assemble themselves into anything you want. You can even program the color!"

Alex's eyes widened. "Where did you get that? I thought those things were only prototypes."

"Yes, they are; and I just "borrowed" this from the Department. If we have it back in a few days, no one will be the wiser. With this machine, we will be able to manufacture all the parts we need to complete the resonance chamber right here!"

"Let me take a closer look at the geometry you used," said Alex stooping down to examine the chamber.

I used the tetrahedral structure you spoke of at the conference."

"This is close, but it's not right. Sydney and I were able to work out the complete geometry of the vacuum since you came to the conference. What I had before was incomplete. You don't have enough tetrahedrons. We need a sixty-four tetrahedral array to have complete geometric equilibrium. We're going to have to modify that in the structure. I also found that it should follow a double torus configuration. It will take some work, but it's a start. When were you planning on telling me about this?"

Brian cleared his throat and Alex noticed his eyes shift.

"Oh, I've just been tinkering. I was only half convinced of your matter going to infinity theory. Like I said, I wasn't going to bother you unless I got it to work."

Alex's eye's narrowed. "You weren't trying to steal my idea now were you?" Alex felt a twinge of anxiety in his gut, which was never a good sign. He had known Brian for years and he had always been a good friend. He was sure Brian could be trusted and yet something didn't feel right. He decided to shrug it off. There really wasn't much choice at this point. He had to trust him.

"Hey buddy, if I got anything I would have given you full credit," said Brian punching Alex's shoulder playfully.

258

"You might be interested to know that Sydney and I have come up with the math that proves the black hole dynamic is causing the gravitational pull, holding atoms together. I've named it the Schwarzschild proton. The math shows that when you calculate the force a tiny black hole at the center of a proton would exert, it exactly equals the so-called '*strong force.*' Therefore, we don't need a theorized strong or weak force. There are only two forces in nature, gravity and electromagnetism."

"Alex, that's a major discovery. Have you published?"

"Not yet. I want to wait until I have the device up and running. That will be the real proof."

Sydney could see Louis through the frosty window of the café. He smiled and waved as he caught sight of her.

"What's with the incognito look? Are you playing spy today?" he asked as he gave her a hug.

Sydney didn't want to worry him, and she didn't want to tell him too much. The less he knew, the safer he'd be, so she laughed off his comment.

"Oh, I'm just frazzled. Trying to get through the Christmas crowd on the streets is an incredible ordeal! There's hardly room to breathe."

"Where are you staying and how long are you in town? You know you're welcome to stay with me."

"I'm at the Plaza," she lied. "And I'm only here for tonight. I'd love to stay with you, but I have to be back in Hawaii tomorrow." She lied again, hating to do so but it was for his protection.

"I brought the envelope you sent. What kind of gift is a data chip?"

Sydney moved her body across the table and whispered to Louis. "It's something I need for work. I'm sorry for the little lie, but we're concerned that the OEB doesn't like our research, so I have to be careful what I say on the phone."

"Why did you send it here?" he asked with a look of incredulity.

"It's a long story, Lou. It's better that you don't know too much."

He looked at her saying nothing for a few moments. He didn't have to, his eyes showed his worry and concern for her.

"Has this Alex gotten you involved in something dangerous? This guy is really pushing the envelope. Maybe you two shouldn't be working on research that is controversial in these times. You know how ruthless the OEB can be. Did I tell you how my friend Marc Getter was arrested because of some atheistic passage in his latest book? They won't even let him speak to his lawyer! We are living in dangerous times. This might as well be the Inquisition. People just disappear and you never hear about them again. They erase all traces of their lives."

"If we allow ourselves to crumble, they win," said Sydney with her characteristic look of defiance. "Our work may be what is needed to bring them down."

Now Louis' look of concern turned to a look of sheer fear.

"Sydney, you must be careful. Don't say anything to anyone."

"I know," she said. "Let's make this our special meeting place, and don't mention the name of the restaurant or my name the next time I call. That's why I wasn't specific when I called you. It's amazing how fast they can track you down."

Sydney leaned in towards Louis and took a deep breath. "I need to ask you for something and it might be dangerous for you."

Louis looked down and his body tensed. "What?"

"The truth is the OEB are all over me. I was attacked in Alex's house in Hawaii, and I was followed here."

Louis started looking around, his face filled with panic.

"No, don't worry, I lost them."

Louis clenched his jaw and lowered his face into his hands. "You need a new identity implant, don't you?"

Sydney whispered, "Yes."

Louis shook his head. "Sydney, you know I love you, but you're asking me to do something that could cost me my career … could cost me my family. If it were just me at risk, I would do it. But this may well affect my family. I can't do that to them."

For the first time since she left Hawaii, Sydney felt utterly hopeless.

"Lou, you're afraid of them, I'm afraid of them, we're all afraid of them. But what Alex and I are doing could change the world! This is bigger than you or me." She looked down at her lap, wishing she could just dissolve away the feeling of anxiety that rippled through her body.

Louis pulled out a piece of paper and pen from his jacket pocket.

"I know a guy. He was fired. He's not a bad guy. In fact, he was a good doctor. There were rumors that he had been performing abortions, but it was never proven. He lost his job anyway. I heard he was selling identities. I'm not sure if it's true. Anyway, here's his address and phone number. Don't call him. Just go there. Tell him the Knife sent you."

"The Knife?" Sydney asked with a look of disparagement.

"It's an old surgeon's joke. He'll know it's me."

Louis passed the paper across the table and folded it into Sydney's hand. He kept his hands on top of hers for several moments and gazed into her eyes as if he wanted to protect her.

Sydney looked at the address on the paper. It was all the way down on the Lower East Side. "Let me leave first," she said. "Don't leave for at least five minutes after me. If there's anyone watching for me, I don't want them to see you with me. They know I'm somewhere in the area and they have satellite surveillance that is incredible."

Sydney kissed Louis goodbye, gave him a hug, and headed back out onto the crowded street. Seventy Second Street was lined with shops and restaurants, and one caught her eye on the other side of the street. It was a wig shop. *That might be a good idea,'* she thought, *'especially if they're watching the hotel.*

The bell on the door rang as she entered the shop. Sydney greeted the chubby man behind the counter. He wore a big Jewish star, a yarmulke, and spoke in a thick Yiddish accent.

"May I help you Miss? You have such pretty hair. Why do you want a wig?"

"It's for a party," she said. "I need a short, dark-haired wig. Do you have anything like that?"

He pulled out five wigs from a case behind him. "This one has real human hair. It's the finest quality for eight hundred dollars."

Sydney's eyes rolled when she heard the price. She wanted to be able to use cash. "How much are the synthetic ones? It's just for a party, and it doesn't have to be that good."

"Here, try this one," he said holding out a jet-black wig in the style of a short bob. Sydney stuffed her long hair into the wig and looked at herself in the mirror. She didn't look good as a brunette but she did look quite different, and that was the idea. It cost $165.00.

"I'll take this one," she said as she handed it to the man. He wrapped it in tissue and placed it in a colorful bag. She paid him with cash, and he looked at it as if it was something foreign.

"You don't see cash much anymore," he said. His thick grey eyebrows rose as he put it in a drawer.

"If anyone inquires, would you tell them that I bought a red wig?" she asked him with an expression that showed her distress.

"Don't worry Miss, I won't help those people," he said with a look of contempt that needed no further explanation.

"Merry Christmas," he said as he handed the bag to her.

"And Happy Hanukkah to you."

"It's not so good to celebrate Hanukkah these days." he sighed again and shook his head. My poor brother was arrested for nothing. Well, we don't know why. He's never been charged, and they won't let us speak to him. I think it may be because of a letter he wrote to the editor of the *Times.* I warned him not to do that, but he wouldn't listen to me."

Sydney gave him a sympathetic smile as she left the shop. She needed a contraband money chip and ID code. Without them, she would never be able to stay more than a step ahead of the OEB. She took the subway back to the hotel. The crowds would offer more safety after her experience with the taxi. She looked different in her wig and sunglasses, and hoped she would be able to slip in the back door of the hotel unnoticed.

When she got to her room, Sydney took the tiny data chip out of her purse. She needed to put it someplace where no one would be able to take it from her. She looked through her suitcase for her travel sewing kit and pulled out the scissors, a needle, and thread. She took her coat and began cutting a small slit in the hem, inserted the data chip, and then stitched up the slit.

Sydney hurriedly packed up her belongings, then looked around the room to make sure she left nothing behind. She put on her wig and her sunglasses and left the room. She just needed to make it to the carport without anyone noticing her.

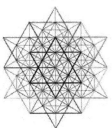

"I've lost her sir," the man spoke into his vidphone. The angry face of Brandon Tarnoff barked back, "You had her in your taxi; how could you lose her?"

"She must have gotten suspicious. She jumped out of the taxi and ran off! I tried to follow her, but there were too many people on the street. She could have gone anywhere."

"Well you better find her!" Tarnoff growled. "We don't tolerate failure here. Can you get a fix on her vidphone?" he asked

"I think she must have disabled it because I'm not getting a signal," said the man.

Tarnoff's face was tense and strained. Croft made it clear

263

to him that he wanted the data and he wanted Sydney Stewart.

CHAPTER 27

Beth waited for Seth in a small rustic tavern. She could see the Matterhorn with its famous jagged peak through the old warped window glass. This was so exciting for her. In fact, it was the realization of all her girlhood dreams. She was with a handsome man, not a boy, obviously with ample means, and infatuated with her. The thought of him made her ache to be in his arms again. She loved his blue eyes and the way he looked at her. How lucky could she be?

She wondered if anyone had missed her yet and decided to call her friend Giselle and let her know where she was.

She pulled out her vidphone and made the call.

"Hi Gizzy, it's me."

"Beth, where are you? Mrs. Bremmer was looking for you this morning. She's fuming mad and said she was going to call your dad. You're going to get thrown out of school."

"You won't believe where I am," Beth swooned into the phone. "I've met this fabulous guy. He's just mag! We're in Zermatt. He has business here and we've had this whirlwind romance. He seems to really like me, and Gawd I'm just crazy about him. I don't know if I'm coming back."

"Your dad will be furious," Gizzie fumed into the phone.

"I don't care. My dad can just kiss my you know what. He just dumps me here because I'm in the way. He doesn't care. He just wants me anywhere but with him. So really, I'm doing *him* a favor." Beth felt a tinge of deep sadness that came from the depth of her soul. She had felt abandoned by her mother when she died. She knew it wasn't rational, but that's how it felt to her.

And when her dad shipped her off, first to the American High School and now the College in Leysin, she felt rejected by him as well … and all alone in the world. She wanted to be loved, and Seth was giving her what she had craved her whole life.

"I hope you know what you're doing," said Gizzie. "Do you even know anything about this guy? Is he safe?"

"Oh Gizzie, he's wonderful … he's perfect, and I'm perfect now."

"Well, call me, please at least once a day, just to let me know that you're okay. And let me know where you are. It can't hurt, just in case."

"Oh, Giz, you're just a mother hen, but thanks. I know you have my best interests at heart."

Beth ordered her third glass of wine, and went back to reading her electronic magazine. Three-dimensional holograms emerged from the page as tall slim models walked down a runway displaying the new fashions for the upcoming season.

She was a bit high from the wine and feeling sexual. She put her hands between her thighs as if to quiet the passion that was welling up within her. Seth walked in with a broad smile on his face as he slid into the booth next to her.

"Hey gorgeous!" He leaned over, kissed her tenderly, and ran his hand over her thigh, which made her gasp. Beth felt herself go limp with excitement at his touch.

"Where would you like to go for dinner?" he asked looking deeply into her eyes.

"How about our room?" she asked giving him a hard stare of desire. Seth grinned back at her, whisked her out into the snowy, festive street, and back to their chalet.

It was snowing hard and Beth could hardly walk on the slippery street. She hung onto Seth as he pretty much carried her with his arm under hers, anchoring her shoulder. They shook off the snow, and entered the main hall of the old chalet with its large fireplace blazing and crackling logs piled four feet high.

The concierge behind the desk pulled out their key and handed it to Seth. "Monsieur, Mademoiselle." He looked at Beth with a lecherous leer, and Seth put his arm around her protectively as he led her to the room.

They entered the cozy room a four-poster bed and Seth locked the door behind them. He took her coat, threw it over the chair, and threw his on the floor. He lifted her up and threw her on the bed. He stood over her with a look of a wolf that had cornered its prey.

Beth looked up at him, her desire, turning to fear for just a moment. He ripped her blouse open and lifted her skirt while pinning her arms to the bed. "You're hurting me," Beth squealed from beneath his weight. Seth did not answer but began to kiss her tenderly as he made love to her.

"Where is she?" Brian demanded trying to hold back his anger and fear.

"We have her, and you'll get her back when you've delivered the device," came back the menacingly calm, raspy voice on the other end. There were never any holograms with these calls.

"I swear I'll kill you if you hurt her." Brian clenched his fist as if he could somehow pound the voice into submission.

"We will see who'll kill whom." the raspy voiced man replied coldly. "Believe me when I say that she will be tortured for a long time before she is killed if you try to cross us. Do you understand?"

Before Brian could answer, the caller hung up.

He lowered his head down to the table and put his hands over his eyes. He stifled a sob, then looked up to the waiter and ordered another drink. His stomach filled with acid as he wrestled with his conscience. *'Betray a friend? Betray this crucial work? It's for Beth.'* There was nothing he could do. He looked up, startled, as Alex approached his table.

"Are you okay, Brian?"

"Yes, yes, I'm just tired."

"Well you better wake up! I need you to make some modifications to the equipment. Come on."

Alex noticed the empty liquor glass on the table. "Drinking so early?"

Brian gave him a sheepish grin. "It's just one of those mornings."

"Tomorrow, I need to be in Dubai and I want you to come with me," Seth said to Beth as they lay together in the morning sun.

"But tomorrow is Monday and I really need to get back to school or they'll fire me, and my dad will kill me! When will you be back?"

"Well that's just it. I don't know. It could be months."

"Months?" Beth shuddered at the thought of not seeing him again for such a long time. And yet, she felt she had to get back to school for class the next day.

"I want you to come with me. You don't ever have to go back to school. I want us to be together." Seth held Beth's face in his hands and looked into her eyes. "I love you."

"I love you too, but I don't know ...."

"Would you rather be a teacher's aide than for us to be together?" he asked.

"No, um, okay, I guess." Beth had a strange feeling of trepidation rising within her. She was scared to go so far away from anything familiar. She wasn't even sure her vidphone would work in that location if there was a family emergency. Her

268

stomach hurt and she really didn't want to think about it. She just wanted to be with Seth. This was the man of her dreams. She couldn't be a winey baby or she would lose him.

Brandon Tarnoff had the look of someone who didn't have any good news.

"So" said Croft, his eyes so intense, they seemed to be shooting bullets at Tarnoff from across his desk.

"We've analyzed the information on Harmon's computer but we didn't find anything useful. We also found a floor safe where they had hidden a data chip but it self-destructed when we tried to unlock it. Krishkow was hurt by the blast. We believe Sydney Stewart has another data chip, but we've lost her for now."

"You've lost her?" Croft looked as if he could hardly contain his fury, but before he had a chance to chastise him, Tarnoff interjected: "We really don't need the chip. What we need to do is to monitor the experiments. We've got a surveillance device implanted in Harmon's eye and we know that he's at the University of Michigan. He's contacted Brian Sheppard and they're working to rebuild whatever it was that exploded in his lab. At this point, it is more prudent to watch them, as they obviously don't have the device fully functioning. We have Sheppard in our pocket. Our agent has his daughter, and he'll turn over any results to get her back. We will succeed sir."

Croft settled back in the overstuffed leather chair, his look of anger morphing into a steely glower.

"You'd better and soon."

"Yes, I won't let you down sir."

Croft looked at him with a glare that implied all too

clearly what Tarnoff's fate would be if he did not succeed with the mission.

"There's no room for failure here, Tarnoff. Failure means you have let the devil divert you; that you are weak and not worthy. We are doing God's work and so we must succeed."

"Yes, I ... I know," stuttered Tarnoff as he backed away toward the door. Croft swiveled his chair around turning his back to Tarnoff, dismissing him.

Outside Croft's office, Tarnoff made a hurried call.

"I want twenty more agents on Sydney Stewart and Alex Harmon, and now!" He didn't wait for a reply.

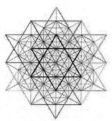

Sydney knocked on the door of the apartment on the Lower East Side of Manhattan.

"Who's there?" asked a male voice from behind the closed door.

"The knife sent me," answered Sydney.

"The knife you say?"

Sydney heard the clanging of several locks being unbolted. The door opened a crack, and a short thin man with a scraggly beard peered through.

"So you know Lou?"

"He's my brother, and he said you could help me."

The man opened the door fully and looked around warily. "You're in trouble?"

"I need a false identity chip. I need to evade the OEB for a while."

"Come in," he said grabbing her arm and pulling her into the apartment.

CHAPTER 28

Sydney's air car came to a soft landing on the roof of University of Michigan's carport. She hoped no one had followed her, but surveillance was so ubiquitous she couldn't be sure. She looked around nervously, half expecting men in swat uniforms to descend upon her. Luckily, the carport was quiet on this Monday morning.

Still afraid to give up her position by using a phone, Sydney decided to go directly to Brian's office, where she would be able to connect with Alex. She had the frequencies and schematics of the device. The tiny chip sewn into her coat was possibly the most precious cargo on Earth.

The air was cold and crisp on this Michigan morning and Sydney felt safe as she walked through the familiar campus to the East Physics Building. The students chatting happily seemingly without a care in the world made her forget the Brotherhood, and the fact that she was now a hunted fugitive ... at least for the moment.

She kept her face down and the hood of her microfiber coat low on her forehead, so as not to trip any face recognition cameras that now provided surveillance of just about every square foot of space in America. Sydney was anxious to find Alex. She wanted to collapse into his arms and simply relieve the fear of the harrowing past two days. Then a horrible thought came to her. *What if they've found Alex. What if he's not here and he's been taken?'* She hadn't been able to talk with him for over two days. *Anything could have happened in that time.* A wave of apprehension coursed through her body as she took the elevator to

Brian's office. The door was open. Sue looked up from her desk and smiled as Sydney entered the office.

"Hi. Can I help you?"

"Is Brian in?"

"I'm sorry. He's in class right now."

"Do you know if Alex Harmon has been here?"

"Oh my, yes. He's been occupying most of Brian's time since he arrived."

Sydney let out an audible sigh of relief and Sue gave her a startled look.

"Oh, I'm sorry. I've just been worried about him. He just was in an accident at his lab. Do you know where I can find him?"

Sue's expression turned serious and her body stiffened. "I'm sorry, who are you?"

"Oh, I'm Sydney Stewart, his partner."

"You wouldn't mind showing me some identification, would you? Can't be too careful these days," said Sue apprehensively.

"Sure, I understand" said Sydney fumbling through her purse for her ID.

Sue took a look at the holographic picture and a look at Sydney.

Sue's demeanor lightened up. "Just one minute, Ms. Stewart." She opened her desk drawer and pulled out a piece of paper and wrote down an address and phone number. "Brian's being awfully secretive about Alex. He told me not to enter any information about him into the computer. Normally I have to document everyone who comes here."

A shot of adrenalin surged through Sydney. "That applies to me too. If I were an operative, you just gave me all the information I would need to find him. You need to be more careful. You shouldn't let anyone know Alex and I are here."

Sue looked defensive. "I asked for your ID. I'm sorry. I'll be more careful. He's staying at Brian's. He should be there now."

Sydney sighed with relief. *He's okay – he's safe.* She put

the paper in her purse and went outside to hail a taxi.

As Sydney approached Brian's Cape Cod style house with its white siding and black shutters, she could make out the figure of a man standing on the porch as if waiting for her. Suddenly her blood went cold. *Could they have traced me here too?* She had taken so many precautions – gotten the new implant – not made any calls. How could they have found her? She thought about telling the taxi driver to turn around and then she saw something familiar: the scarf she had given Alex. It was Alex! She flung open the taxi door and rushed to embrace him.

She jumped into his arms and as she did he swirled her around, kissing her deeply and passionately. Sydney's body went limp with relief to finally be with him – in his strong arms – in his protection.

"Sue called and said you would be coming."

"Alex, I didn't think I'd ever see you again." A tear rolled down her cheek as he held her face in his hands.

"You don't know how much I love you. I can't even think of my life without you in it," he said gently kissing her tears. "It's going to be all right now." Alex put his arm around her shoulders and led her into his bedroom.

"Where's Brian?" she asked.

"He's still at the lab. Don't worry, we're alone." He closed the door behind them and leaned Sydney against the wall holding her arms above her head and kissed her with such passion, she could feel the heat from his body through her clothes.

He slipped her jacket off her shoulders and unsnapped her blouse, putting his warm hands on her breasts and kneeling down to put them in his mouth. Sydney gasped with desire. She could not think of anything but this moment, as if she was frozen in time in a universe that consisted only of the two of them. Sydney opened his shirt and ran her hands over his smooth chest as he lifted her and carried her to the bed.

His lips brushed over hers, while his fingers probed her supple body as he laid his hard muscular body down on her. He stretched her arms out in a wide arc and sat up looking down at her sumptuous body. He began to run his tongue ever so softly from her neck to her heat. Sydney gasped and heaved with his every touch sending her into higher states of ecstasy. Finally, they lay spent in each other's arms.

"Just like old times," said Alex, as he gently moved her hair off her face.

"I can never have enough of you," she sighed as she sweetly stroked his face.

"Tell me where you've been and what has happened, Sydney."

Sydney finally felt released from the tension and fear that had gripped her for the past two days. Her eyes filled with tears as she told Alex of her ordeal in New York.

In a dark room in Washington, D.C. the operative watching reached down and touched himself.

That evening Alex met Brian in the lab. Most people went home by 6:00 p.m. and the physics building was quiet. They felt there would be fewer eyes on them working at night. But this was wishful thinking. There were eyes on them that they would never have suspected. Vincent Shelby was watching as he had done earlier that day as Alex and Sydney made love. Vincent was a fifty-five year-old career bureaucrat with thinning hair, thick glasses and a stomach that looked like he was carrying a bowling ball under his shirt. He loved his work. It was the perfect job to satisfy his voyeuristic fetish. He was finding this assignment particularly stimulating.

The holographic image appeared as large as life in front of him. Brian Sheppard was kneeling beside the round device that stood about five feet high and four feet wide.

"Add another layer of wire," came the voice behind the eyes that were projecting the image onto Vincent's holo-imager.

"I don't know Alex, I think that might be too much."

"Brian, come on. I know what I'm doing. How's the clean room coming?"

"We're getting there. I'd say another day or two and we'll be at zero contamination."

Brian walked over and inspected the device. "How long until we can run the frequencies?" he asked.

"We're getting there," said the voice behind the eyes. "A few more days ... maybe a week."

Vincent took the viewing device off his head and called Brandon Tarnoff.

"A few more days sir."

CHAPTER 29

Sydney peered out of the bedroom window of Brian's house at the apple blossom tree that was bursting with new life. They were always the first to bloom and harkened the end of the grueling Michigan winter. Buds were forming on the other trees, creating a light green haze. The air felt still cool, and the sky was a bright blue. It was a welcome change from the all-pervading grayness of the past few weeks.

"We're almost ready to go," said Alex yawning and pulling himself out from under the thick duvet that covered their bed.

"Really? So soon?"

"Soon?" said Alex sarcastically. "It's been several months."

"I know. I've been so busy working on the theoretical papers, I've lost track of the time," said Sydney. You've made good progress. I thought it would take much longer to reconfigure the resonator."

"Brian did a lot of work on his own before I even got here, so we had a big head start. He also has a Faber machine, so we've been able to manufacture everything we need right in the lab. Anyway, from my point of view it seems like we've been working for years! I'm ready to take this baby out for a spin."

Sydney laughed. "Boys and their toys!"

"Yeah ... some toy!" said Alex sardonically.

Sydney threw on her robe and went to the kitchen to make some coffee.

"Alex, do we really know that being in the presence of

this field we are creating is good for living organisms?" asked Sydney as she poured some water into the coffee maker. The late March wind outside rattled the kitchen window and sent a stream of cool air through the small crack. Alex tried to force the window fully shut without success.

Brian's kitchen was sleek and modern with black granite counters and black lacquered cabinets sporting pewter knobs. Alex and Sydney took their coffee over to the square glass kitchen table with its stylish black leather chairs.

"We're spending a lot of time around this device. We need to know whether it's harmful or not," said Sydney taking a sip of her coffee.

"We can test it," he said settling back into his chair.

"How?"

"Let's put organic material, say a cut flower, in water that's been exposed to the field, some regular tap water, and some distilled water – and see what happens."

"Yes, that would be a good test. All we need are three Petri dishes and a fresh flower."

"I'll do a test as soon as we have the device running."

They dressed quickly and grabbed another cup of coffee before heading over to Brian's secret lab in the basement of the physics building.

In Vincent Shelby's thirty years of service, he had never seen anything like this before. What was happening in this lab was nothing like the scientists he had watched in the past. The others used terminology he could understand and were mostly working on alternative energy sources. But the guy he was watching was talking about things he thought were in the realm of science fiction. He could hardly believe what he was hearing. He took another bite out of his pepperoni pizza and then placed a call to Brandon Tarnoff.

"Sir, I've picked up something strange. I don't understand what they mean, but I think this is something you should see for yourself."

"What do you mean you don't understand?" growled an impatient Tarnoff.

"It's just I can't believe what they're saying could possibly be real!" They sound like mystics or maybe wackos ... not like scientists!"

Tarnoff stiffened. "Show me," he said sitting forward in his chair.

Vincent played back the holographic recording of the scene he had just been watching:

"Alex have you told Brian he can't be in the room when we turn on the machine?"

"No, not yet. That's going to open up a whole can of worms. We'd have to tell him about Leytar, the Galactic Federation, the initiation in Tibet and all of that."

"Exactly my thoughts. I don't think he needs to know about that right now. I'm glad you haven't said anything."

"He's been acting a little strange. Have you noticed that?"

"He seems a bit distant, now that you mention it," said Sydney.

"I'm concerned. I think the less he knows the better for now," said Alex

"Not to mention that whoever controls this device holds the key to ultimate power," said Sydney, a worried expression now overtaking her demeanor. "I just dread to think what would happen if this device fell into the hands of the Brotherhood. It could be used for so much evil."

"I don't think we have to worry about the Brotherhood using the device."

"Of course they would be able to," said Sydney looking surprised at Alex's remark.

"Remember there's the feedback-loop!" said Alex.

Sydney raised her eyebrows knowingly. "Yes, the feedback-loop."

Vincent turned off the hologram. "That's it sir. They changed the subject after that. Are these guys crazy talking about a Galactic Federation?"

"It's probably code for some sort of underground group that is working against the Brotherhood," replied Tarnoff. "Keep watching and let me know if they talk about this feedback-loop again."

"Feedback-loop? Sir?"

"Yes. I want to know what they mean by that," said Tarnoff turning off the connection.

"Galactic Federation, anti-gravity, ultimate power? This just got a lot more interesting," said Tarnoff under his breath. Now he knew why Croft had put so much of his personal attention on these scientists. *This isn't just another free energy source that Croft wants to suppress. No, this is something far more important!*

Tarnoff saw his destiny unfold before him. It was the opportunity of a lifetime. Perhaps he, not Croft, could rule the UCSA and its territories that now controlled half of the Earth's population. He could be King, not the subservient number two. *Whoever controls this device holds the key to ultimate power.* The words reverberated in his head. These words were his ticket to greatness. He could beat Croft at his own game.

Brian Sheppard sat in the neon glow of the laboratory lights. His gut was twisted with conflict and remorse. Beth was all he had left in the world since his wife died, and now he faced a terrible decision. Betray his friend and deny the world the most important discovery in history, or lose the one person in the world he loved.

His relationship with Beth had been strained ever since her mother died. She was a rebellious and angry young lady. They hadn't had a warm conversation since she hit her fifteenth birthday. But she was his flesh and blood; and in the end, the bonds of blood trump everything else. He could not imagine life without her ... although he couldn't imagine life without Katherine either. Yet, here he was, living and breathing while she lay cold in her grave. Katherine had been his whole life. He had depended on her heavily. They had met during their freshman year at U. of M., and he could count on his hands the days they were apart after that.

Katherine had a difficult time getting pregnant, and they were in their late thirties before conceiving Beth – and that had been after many disappointing rounds of in-vitro fertilization. Beth made them a family at last, and was the most precious blessing in their lives. Brian had been a man who finally had it all: a beautiful wife, a daughter, and a prestigious position in the physics department of U. of M.. He led the research team that found the coveted Higgs Boson, and was respected as one of the foremost physicists in America.

Then his world came crashing down. Katherine got sick, and though she fought valiantly against the lymphoma that consumed her bit by bit, she finally succumbed on a hot August morning. His parents were gone and he was an only child himself. Now, Beth was his only family.

Then, just a year after his team found the Higgs Boson, another team in Switzerland had been able to split his coveted particle, robbing him of his lofty status and proving the Higgs was not the ultimate building block of matter. His life's work had gone up in smoke, *and* his wife had died. So the world be damned! There was no world for him without Beth in it.

As Sydney and Alex entered the lab, Brian was turning up the frequency of the spin. In the center of the lab was a large containment area made of titanium and gold that surrounded the device. Brian sat behind a barrier made of thick cement working at the control panel.

Brian smiled broadly when Alex and Sydney entered.

"Hey guys, I'm ready to go. Get behind the barrier."

"Weren't you going to wait for me?" asked Alex grabbing Sydney's hand and hurrying behind the barrier they had constructed to shield them should there be a blast.

"I've been working since three in the morning on some calculations. I think this is the frequency you used to create the effect in your lab," said Brian.

"Yeah, but that blew to Kingdom Come," shouted Alex. "We're not ready for this."

"Trust me," said Brian. "I've run the calculations, and the new chamber is large enough to handle the frequency."

"Brian, turn this thing off now! You should have waited for me! What the hell do you think you're doing?" Alex lunged for the control panel, but Brian blocked his path.

"It's going to be okay. Trust me!"

"No Brian! Not yet. Shut it down! We're not even sure what this will do to human tissue yet."

Brian ignored him and the chamber started to shake violently, making a high-pitched hissing sound. Alex shoved Brian out of the way trying to reach the control panel to shut off the machine.

Then he stopped as something quite unexpected began to transpire. A three-dimensional image appeared in front of him allowing him to see the resonance chamber in the protective containment compartment. As the plasma in the crystal spun at a higher and higher frequency, a geometric shape began to form in the crystal. A schematic depiction of the sequence appeared in intricate symbols and numbers.

"Sydney, come look at this." Alex pointed at a formula running in the right upper corner of the image. "What do you make of this?" Brian stood behind her, looking on.

Sydney squinted to see the image as she pulled her reading glasses off her head and placed them on her face to look at the numbers flashing in front of her.

"This is wrong! This can't be right, can it? These readings are off the scale! The time ratios are all askew. It's certainly not working within normal parameters."

"It will be fine," said Brian fuming.

Suddenly, the loud hissing noise turned into a thunderous roar. Streams of light began to emanate wildly in every direction from the core. The white light shooting from the device started to become uniform, coalescing back into tetrahedral patterns. Soon the geometric figure began to stabilize into a sixty-four tetrahedral shape.

Alex entered in the last sequence that he had run before the lab accident, and the geometric array began to divide into smaller and smaller fractals until they appeared like tiny dots. The crackling sound increased and bolts of white light were now ripping through the display. Then the tiny dots started coalescing into one point like a whirlpool of water going down a drain. When the last of the shapes slid down the virtual drain, a circle of light began to grow outward from the middle. The room was now undulating as if the structure of the matter was altered.

"That's it. We've got to shut it down now," yelled Alex.

"I'm trying to! It's not working!" shouted back Sydney, furiously manipulating the control panel.

"What do you mean it's not working?"

"Look, I'm hitting the cancel, but it's still spinning."

The noise in the room became deafening, and Alex was shouting. "We need to go into the room and shut it down manually."

"That could be suicide," shouted Brian. "You don't know what will happen!"

"Brian, you stay here!" shouted Alex. "Stay out of the containment area!"

Alex ran out from behind the barrier wall and pulled on the latch that sealed the door of the containment room.

"Alex, you're crazy! Get back here! You're going to kill us all!" shouted Brian.

As the door flung open, beams of light shot out and everything in the room began to levitate. Alex was flying through the air trying to reach the resonator to shut it down. He could see a vortex forming above the spinning crystal, and waveforms shooting out from the device distorting the walls and floor. He tried with all his might to reach the chamber, but the force of the machine kept pushing him away. The walls were now buckling heavily as though they were made of rubber. He looked in amazement at his arm that also losing cohesion. His was racing, and his breathing became labored. The sound was sending a piercing pain through his eardrums. His foot hit the sidewall and he used it to kick off, propelling him towards the chamber. Then he hit the floor with a thud.

"Got it," yelled Sydney. "The device is off."

Alex came out of the containment room and brushed himself off. "Brian, promise me you won't run this again without me."

CHAPTER 30

It was day fourteen and the flowers Alex had placed in the tap water and the distilled water were brown and decayed. The one that was in water exposed to the resonance field still looked as fresh as the day it was cut.

"What is he looking at?" asked Vincent Shelby, looking over the shoulder of Wendy Simon, the junior surveillance officer assigned to monitor Alex Harmon that day. Wendy took off her electric blue-framed glasses and looked up at Vincent.

"They're running an experiment to test how organic matter fares that has been exposed to the field their device emits."

"Field?" Vincent looked perplexed. "What do you mean?" "Well sir, it seems the chamber emits a field unlike anything previously known to science. They keep talking about a vacuum energy. Quite frankly, I think they're trying to open a black hole."

"What the hell?" Vincent looked clearly alarmed. "A black hole? Isn't that incredibly dangerous?"

Wendy looked blankly at her boss. "I don't know sir."

Vincent picked up the phone and called John Croft.

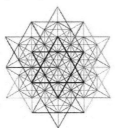

Do you think they've gotten any tangible results?" asked Croft as he exhaled a cloud of cigar smoke that curled around the phone.

"I'm not sure what to make of this. I've never seen anything like it before," said Vincent as he gazed at the tetrahedral shapes that floated in front of him in the holographic image. When Croft saw the image, his heart started to pound. He had seen this shape before. He knew it had tremendous significance.

"Let me see that," Croft said pulling the image closer to him.

"What the hell are they doing sir?

"I believe they're trying to create a singularity."

"Won't this cause some kind of rift in the space-time continuum, sir? I think we should go in and stop this."

"Not yet," said Croft. I don't think that will happen. "Have you seen how they are doing this?"

"From what we can tell they're spinning plasma in a crystal at a million rpm. They mentioned that the crystal has a pocket of pure vacuum within it."

"They're causing some sort of anti-gravity effect!"

"Yes, sir. It certainly appears that way. Something went wrong and they shut it down."

"Is everything okay in there?" asked Croft.

"Yes, sir … at least for now. But this looks dangerous."

"Well, it's their risk, not ours. Let them go. I want to see what this thing does when they stabilize it."

"Yes, sir. I'll keep you informed."

"Yes, yes," said Croft.

He hung up the phone and reached across his desk for a large gold paperweight. Croft screwed open the bottom. Inside was a small compartment that held a key. Croft took the key out and examined it thoughtfully. He put it in his pocket and headed out of his office.

"I'll be back in an hour," he said to Ms. Aarhus, poking his head back through the door as he left. Croft took the hallway elevator to the basement twenty floors below. The elevator door opened with a ping and he exited, hurriedly walking down a long corridor to another elevator. This one required a fingerprint scan to activate it. When the wide cargo doors opened he said, "Sub-Basement twenty-six." The elevator descended another twenty-six floors. He exited to a dimly lit corridor that felt damp and smelled of mold. He walked down the long corridor for what seemed to be about a quarter of a mile to a large door marked "TOP SECRET CLEARANCE REQUIRED."

There was an iris scan at the side of the door, and Croft bent down to place his chin on the plate below the scanner. The sound of heavy bolts unlocking echoed through the silence of the basement. "Entry granted," came the computerized voice. The doors parted revealing a small foyer with another set of doors and a scanning pad. Croft placed his hand on the scanner and the electronic voice said, "Welcome Grand Master Croft." The next set of heavy steel doors opened allowing him access to the top-secret warehouse.

The room was the size of an airplane hanger, with row upon row of boxes stacked in shelves that went from the floor to the thirty-five foot high ceiling. Croft passed shelves labeled numerically until he found Row sixty-four. Halfway down the aisle, he slid one of the ladders over to Stack 21 and climbed up until he was at eye level with a metal box. He reached in his pocket for the key and inserted it into the latch that sealed the box.

There was a slight burst of musty mist as he opened the airtight seal and pulled out the ancient text. Its pages were yellow and brittle, and the sheepskin cover was inscribed with the Hebrew word for "code". He opened the book to find page after page of mathematical equations that heretofore had no meaning for him. But now, he thought he knew the significance and his pulse sped up with the thought of it.

CHAPTER 31

"What's the frequency of the spin?" asked Alex

"600,000 rpm," said Brian.

"And the viscosity of the plasma?"

"Optimal," replied Brian looking up above his horn-rimmed glasses.

"Let's try to get the frequency up to 700,000 rpm!" shouted Alex as he moved out of the containment room and behind the retaining wall.

"Why not go all the way to one million?" asked Brian.

"Not tonight," said Alex as he plugged the frequency into the control panel. "Ok, here we go!" Alex turned on the device and they could see the plasma start to spin on the monitor. The structure lifted and hung in the air between the magnetic poles spinning faster and faster.

"Look at her go!" shouted Alex, placing his earphones on to protect against the high-pitched squeal that emanated from the device.

Brian shot him back a thumbs-up.

"I think we can go faster," said Brian.

"I think we can. But let's not get impatient," said Alex, the shaking of the room making him uneasy.

"No look, it's starting to create an event horizon," shouted Brian. "Look, the plasma is being pulled into the vortex."

"Increase the speed to 750,000 rpm and hold it there," said Alex.

Brian complied. The chamber began to glow brighter and brighter, like a miniature sun. Both men gazed at it, mouths agape and eyes wide, as the plasma formed a double torus shape. A bright white light emitted from the point where the two toruses met in the middle. The effect appeared to form a rip in the fabric of the space around it. But as soon as they saw geometry form, it collapsed.

"It's working Alex! It probably won't collapse if we get the spin to the full one million rpm! Let's let her rip!" shouted Brian above the sound of the technology.

"No, I don't think the geometry is quite right. We might shatter the crystal. There shouldn't be so much turbulence in the room. We have to wait," said Alex.

"I think it's working fine just as it is." Brian protested.

"I don't want to take the risk," replied Alex. "If the lab blows we'll be back to square one and our secret lab will be exposed." Alex ran over to the control panel and shut down the device as Brian looked on with teeth clenched and eyes shifting.

Brian's vidphone rang and when he saw who was calling, he left the lab to take the call in the hallway.

"Dr. Sheppard?" asked the voice on the phone.

"Yes. What do you want?"

"Why did you shut it down?"

"Alex thinks the frequency is still off. But we are close."

"May I remind you that time is running out on your daughter's life."

"It will take as long as it takes," protested Brian.

"It better be soon for your good and hers. We know you have the ability to open the rift now. So do it. Good night Dr. Sheppard."

"But …" Brian heard the click as the caller disconnected. He shut his eyes and sighed. His stomach was contorted and his hands were shaking as he opened the door to the lab.

"Come on Brian. That's enough for tonight. Let's go get some sleep and we'll go over the simulations again tomorrow," said Alex grabbing his coat and heading to the door.

Brian walked with Alex back to the house, but he did not go to his room

Brian flicked on the lights of the lab. It was late and he was sure no one else was in the building. It was cold – they turned the heat in the building off after 9:00 p.m. – so he kept his coat on. The crystal was locked in the wall safe. Brian scanned his eye on the lock and opened the container. He carefully lifted out the crystal and placed it into the chamber.

Brian realized that Alex didn't think the frequency was exactly right, but he had to take the chance. Beth's life hung in the balance. He put on his protective glasses, went to the control panel, and set the device to run at the last frequency. The plasma began to spin creating an otherworldly whirring sound whose pitch grew increasingly higher as the plasma formed a double torus shape inside the spherical boundary.

Here goes nothing, he thought as he moved the controls to a higher frequency. He knew the magic number was a million rpm. The room began to shake as a small black disc formed in the middle of the double torus. Then a bright white sheet of light shot out of the disc, flooding the room and causing Brian to leap away from the viewing window.

A flare sprung out of the center like an arm reaching out from the depths of hell, penetrated the containment room and then the thick retaining wall, striking Brian in the chest. He let out a scream and fell to the floor.

Sydney's eyes opened as she woke from a troubled sleep. She looked at the clock on the bed stand. It was 5:23 a.m.

"Alex, wake up," she said as she gently nudged his shoulder.

"Uh, what's wrong," he said wiping the sleep from his eyes.

"Something's wrong. I feel it. We need to get to the lab."

"The OEB?" he asked in alarm.

"No, something else. Brian's in trouble."

"Brian? He's home. We came home together."

"I don't think so" said Sydney. She pulled on her robe and walked down the hall to Brian's room.

"Brian, are you in there?" she asked, lightly knocking on the door. There was no response. "Brian, are you awake?" There was still no answer, so Sydney slowly opened the door and peered in the room. It was just as she feared. His bed was empty.

"Throw on your jeans. We need to go now!" she yelled to Alex.

They dressed hurriedly and went out into the dark morning.

As their car approached the lab, they could hear a high-pitched sound, and the ground was shaking under their feet. Sydney, filled with foreboding, hurried down the stairwell and opened the heavy doors to the lab.

"Oh my God, what has Brian done!" shouted Alex. He lunged for the controls and turned off the machine. Then he rushed to Brian's body that lay crumpled on the floor and listened for his breath. There was none. He listened for a heartbeat. There was none. He started to pound desperately on Brian's chest, giving him CPR trying to revive him. Brian did not respond. Brian was dead.

As Alex and Sydney knelt by Brian's side, Sydney started to sob.

"Why did he do this without us?" asked Alex. "I don't understand it. He must have doubled back here after he walked home with me. He did look agitated when I told him to shut it down. I told him I didn't think it was ready to go to full speed!"

"We should have told him that this would be dangerous for him," cried Sydney.

"I wasn't going to let him be in the lab when I ran it at full frequency. I never thought he would do something like this! He had been bugging me to go full out and I told him no."

"So it's ready?" asked Sydney.

"Yes. It's ready. The field must have been too much for him. He must have had a heart attack."

"What are we going to do? We can't call an ambulance and have anyone see the lab," said Sydney, tears still streaming down her face.

"We'll have to take him to the hospital ourselves. I don't want anyone checking out the lab. We'll say it happened in the car as we were driving to the hospital," said Alex. He pulled Brian's body onto his shoulders and carried him out to the car. Sydney and Alex didn't speak during the few minute drive to the hospital.

They drove up to the emergency entrance and watched in silence as Brian's body was zipped into a black body bag and hoisted onto a gurney. They both were in shock. Alex pulled Sydney gently into his arms and hugged her for a long time.

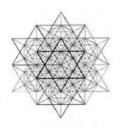

"He's what?" demanded Brandon Tarnoff.

"Dead, sir," said Vincent Shelby. "Brian Sheppard has been killed in an accident in his lab. Evidently, he was alone. Harmon and Stewart weren't there."

"Was the device destroyed?"

"No sir, everything is intact from what I can see. You wouldn't know anything happened in there except that Sheppard was DOA at the hospital."

"Did you see what happened?"

"No. All we have is from when Harmon and Sydney Stewart find his body in the lab. Our operative had contacted Sheppard yesterday and had put pressure on him to deliver results. From our feed it looks like Harmon wouldn't let him run the final frequency, and he must have gone back to do it on his own."

"What is the medical report?"

"They say his heart stopped. It could have been a natural heart attack, but we have feed of Harmon and Stewart talking about how he wouldn't have been able to withstand the field … whatever that means."

Vincent finished his report and Tarnoff turned off the phone. This put a big kink in his plans. He had been blackmailing Sheppard to ensure he handed over the device when it became operational. He had Beth in Seth's custody. Now she is a liability with no purpose, and he has lost his plant.

CHAPTER 32

The bright light from above woke Alex from a deep sleep, and blinded him as he opened his eyes. He shielded his face with his arm and sat up. When his eyes adjusted to the light, he saw Leytar's image hovering above him. Sydney too sat up in the bed covering her eyes.

"I'm sorry to intrude like this," said Leytar, his form moving like smoke.

"Your device is almost ready but you need another component."

"Oh God, I hope we don't have to go on another trek," gasped Alex, his eyes rolling back in his head. Alex laughed, but the look on Leytar's face told him that perhaps he was indeed in for just such an ordeal. "We haven't heard from you for a long time."

"No, but I have been watching."

"Oh really?" asked Alex, anger welling up within him. "What about Brian? Why did you let Brian die if you're watching?"

"There was a reason I sent you and Sydney to Tibet to go through an initiation. Sydney needed to raise her consciousness, raise her frequency, and learn to control her thoughts before she exposed herself to the vacuum energy. Brian had been compromised and he had fear in his heart and thoughts. The feedback-loop is immediate when exposed directly to the field, and so his own thoughts created the effect that killed him. I'm sorry. I know he was your friend, and I know you warned him not to be in direct contact with the field."

"What do you mean he had been compromised?"

"The Brotherhood took his daughter Beth and forced him to spy on you."

Alex stared at Leytar with a look of disbelief.

"He was in fear, and his fear was fed back to him by the vacuum," said Leytar, his large eyes reflecting deep sympathy.

Alex hung his head and sighed, trying to reconcile his feelings of betrayal and sorrow.

A holographic image appeared over the bed.

"What's this?" asked Alex, trying to regain his composure.

"It's the location of a Galactic Federation ship." As Leytar touched the image, the point zoomed into focus. "Stellar travel with gravitational drive requires that one journeys though the largest black holes to reach a given destination. To travel to or from the Earth, you must first go through the black hole at the center of the planet. The best way to do that is to travel through an inactive volcano."

"So that's why there have always been so many UFO sightings near volcanoes!"

"Exactly," replied Leytar now tapping on the sun. "Then you must travel through the largest black hole in the center of your solar system."

"You mean we have to go through the sun?"

"Yes, all interstellar travelers must travel through their system's star."

"So any visitors from other worlds would come out of the sun?" asked Alex. "Exactly. Here are the coordinates. You must move the singularity at the center of the double torus you create 3.654 degrees to the northern torus, 1.618 here, and 4.781 here."

Alex grabbed the notebook on the nightstand and began copying down the image and coordinates. "Yes, yes, I see. We're navigating through specific scalar systems in the space-time fabric."

"Correct," said Leytar. "The ship is close, being on the same arm of the galactic wheel as your sun. If you were to travel to another galaxy, you would have to travel through the galactic sun."

"You mean the black hole at the center of the Milky Way?" asked Alex. Leytar nodded.

"But won't I have to build some sort of spaceship that can withstand the heat? It's one thing to build the technology to open a portal to the vacuum, and another to actually travel through space."

"These are the specifications for a shell that will protect you." Another holographic image appeared. "You can create it with your fabricator. Place the resonance chamber in the center. The journey will be in the blink of an eye. You don't need oxygen or food. Everything you need will be awaiting you at your destination."

Leytar smiled as his image and the diagram faded away. Alex and Sydney looked at each other with amazement.

"We're going to travel through a volcano and then through the sun?" asked Sydney, her startled look now morphing into a wry grin.

"Seems that way," said Alex.

"With no oxygen, and no food or water?" asked Sydney.

"Looks that way," said Alex.

"Are you sure you trust these Beings?" asked Sydney now looking rather uneasy.

Alex took her hand and kissed her. "I do."

Alex was startled awake by the buzzing of the alarm clock. He rolled over and nudged Sydney who had wrapped the pillow around her face defying his attempts to wake her.

"Can you believe we finally got another visit from

Leytar?"

"What are you talking about?" Sydney wiped the sleep from her eyes and yawned lazily.

"You didn't see Leytar?"

"No, honey. You must have been dreaming."

"I wasnt dreaming! Leytar was here just a minute ago," said Alex angrily. He reached for his notebook. "Here, I wrote it down." He flipped furiously through the pages looking for the diagram he had made but couldn't find it. He went through the notebook page by page but the diagram was not there.

"Never mind," he said pulling the covers aside and grabbing the pen on the nightstand. I remember it as if it were seared into my brain." He began copying down the image that was as clear as a photograph. "I have to build a shell for the containment room."

"Yes?" Croft cleared his throat as he took the call.

"Sir, Brian Sheppard is dead," said Tarnoff.

"Dead? What happened?" Croft stood up from his large desk and started to pace.

"An accident in their lab at University of Michigan," replied Tarnoff.

"You mean those jokers blew up the equipment again?"

"No, sir; that is what is so odd. The lab is intact. You wouldn't think anything at all had happened there. But Sheppard is dead from a massive heart attack."

"It was the hand of God, Tarnoff." Croft knew this was possible. It was what happened when the Israelites were traveling through the desert with the Ark of the Covenant. Anyone who came into contact with it, except for the high priests, had been killed instantly.

"What shall we do about his daughter now?" asked Tarnoff.

"We can't have any loose ends. You know the protocol," said Croft as he sat back into his large leather chair.

"Sir, do you think that is necessary?" protested Tarnoff. "She's just an innocent young girl."

Croft took a large cigar out of the humidor on his desk and ran it under his bulbous nose. "It's an unfortunate necessity."

"But sir ..."

"Are you questioning my judgment, Tarnoff?"

"No, sir. I just think there must be another way."

"It's either the ... and he is traceable right back to this office. Quite frankly, Seth is a highly trained operative and we can't afford to lose him. The girl is of no value now that her father is dead."

"Yes, sir; I understand sir," said Tarnoff tersely. Tarnoff ended the call. He didn't like Croft's order one bit. He had been willing to go a long way for the OEB. He had always believed they were on the side of God and righteousness. But murdering an innocent girl was certainly not Godly. Suddenly he was filled with doubt about everything he believed in. He had revered Croft as a great leader, but he was having doubts for months. He had worked faithfully for years for a world that would bring Christ's justice to Earth. Had power corrupted Croft? This order to kill Beth was heinous, and went against every fiber of his being. He didn't think he could do it. Though, if he didn't, he knew there would be consequences – not just for him, but also for his family. All that he had worked for would be lost.

Tarnoff started to chew furiously on his pen as he struggled with what to do next. He looked at his reflection in the mirror of his private bathroom in the OEB building on Pennsylvania Avenue. His narrow, lackluster eyes stared back at him out of his pockmarked face. *So this is the face of a cold-blooded murderer; a murderer of the young and innocent.*

He had ordered the elimination of countless heretics and enemies of the Brotherhood. But Brian Sheppard's daughter was not one of these criminals. She was an innocent pawn. Tarnoff felt a pain in his gut as he thought about Stephie. She would have been about Beth's age, had she lived … had he not looked away for that fateful minute fifteen years ago. One lousy minute had been the difference between a little girl growing up and going off to college, and dying a horrible death. If only his phone hadn't rung … if only he hadn't dropped her hand to answer. Now he was being asked to snuff out the life of another young girl.

"Alex, come over and take a look at this," said Sydney pointing to the Petri dish experiment. Alex pushed away from his desk and walked over to the counter where they had laid out the three Petri dishes with the cut flowers.

"It's been four weeks and the flower in the water exposed to the Field is still alive. It looks as fresh as the day it was cut!" exclaimed Sydney.

"This is remarkable. I wonder how long it will stay this way," said Alex.

"This means that the Field is definitely beneficial to living things," said Sydney.

"It looks that way doesn't it? "It's not just beneficial, the field seems to be extending and enhancing life! Is the video still tracking the progress and marking the days?" he asked.

"Yes, the camera's in place. We'll have good documentation. When we're done we can send the water to a lab for a formal analysis," said Sydney.

CHAPTER 33

Seth was laying out his shirts on the bed, folding them neatly into his suitcase. Beth peered out from behind the bathroom door and watched him.

"Hurry up Beth, we need to get to the airport and you haven't even gotten dressed."

"I really need to stop by the dorm and get some clothes and things," she said, her voice a bit shaky. She was having great misgivings about going away with this man she hardly knew. "What about my passport? I don't have it with me."

"Not to worry, I pulled some strings this morning and got you one."

"So fast? Wow, you must really be important."

Seth gave her a quick smile and continued his packing. Beth thought about this for a moment. *How could he get a passport for me without any identification? It just doesn't add up.*

"I'm going to call my dad and at least let him know I'm leaving school. He's a pain, but I don't want him to worry about me."

"I don't think that's a good idea," said Seth. "He might call the authorities and stop you, and then we won't be able to be together. You want us to be together. Don't you, Love? You can call him when we get to Dubai."

Beth picked her purse up from the chair by the bed and started fishing around for her vidphone.

"What are you doing?" asked Seth.

"I'm calling my friend Gizzy to let her know where I'm

going. She won't tell anyone."

Seth grabbed the phone out of her hands and smashed it against the wall.

"I said no!" he said with an angry snarl. Beth recoiled, shocked by his sudden turn in behavior. Her eyes grew wide with fear. She wanted to run to the bathroom and lock herself in, but there was no way she could get past Seth.

"I don't want to go!" she screamed. Seth grabbed her arm and twisted it forcing her onto the bed. He reached behind him, pulled a revolver out from the back of his pants, and pointed it to her head.

"You're coming with me!"

"Why are you doing this Seth?" cried Beth.

"It's my job. Nothing personal."

"Your job? What are you talking about?" she shrieked. "I love you. How could you do this to me?"

"I'm OEB and it's something about your father. I really don't know anything more, Love. It's a need to know kind of thing," said Seth, feigning a sweet tone of voice.

"You're OEB! What? What would the OEB want with my father? He's just a professor at U of M!"

"As I said, I don't know the details. We need to hold you for a bit. Why don't you just settle down?" Seth threw Beth's tee shirt at her. "Here get dressed. We're going."

"For a bit? What does that mean?" asked Beth.

Seth, standing by the door, looked over at her but didn't answer. "Let's go." He held her arm tightly as they made their way down the stairway and out to his car. "Be quiet," he said, his gun still pointed at her. He forced her into the car and drove it to the front door of the hotel, rolled down the window, and waved over the bellman. "Here man," he said handing him a tip. Those are our bags there. Would you mind popping them in the trunk?"

The trunk door banged down and they pulled out of the Hotel parking lot and merged into the heavy traffic.

"You're a monster!" said Beth as she folded her arms in front of her and stared out the side window, tears now rolling down her cheeks. "You'll never get me by airport security. I'll

302

scream for help."

"That's okay," said Seth with a smirk. "We're not going to the airport. I have private transportation."

"You still have to clear your papers with the authorities before they let you cross over the border."

"I am the authorities," said Seth.

"The OEB doesn't have jurisdiction in Europe!"

"I hate to break this to you, Love, but we do!"

Beth looked at him with amazement. "What the heck is going on? Jeeezus!" she said under her breath.

Seth leaned over. "One more thing," he said.

"What the hell?" screamed Beth as Seth put a cloth over her mouth and her world went black.

John Croft reached over to the large vidphone on his desk and answered the call. Brandon Tarnoff's image appeared as a hologram.

"Your report?" said Croft pulling his cigar out of his mouth to speak and blowing out a plume of smoke that filtered into the holographic image.

"Sir, we now know that they're trying to open some sort of portal," said Tarnoff, nervously clicking his pen.

"A portal you say? A portal to where?" asked Croft, feigning ignorance.

"They keep talking about the vacuum. From what I understand sir, they think there's an energy field in the vacuum and it's a place – somewhere you can travel through. We've also seen things levitating when they run the device."

Croft sat back in his chair silently for a few minutes. This meant something specific to him, something he had read about in the texts from the warehouse. Now he was certain he knew what Alex was trying to create, and he needed to possess it. "Anything else?" he asked.

"They're trying to find the proper spin rate for the plasma. They have been running the device for short periods of time. They keep saying that they don't dare do a full run until they can get up to a million rpm. They're not there yet, but they're getting close."

"Good. Let me know. It's important that you have your men ready to grab the device just before they go for their full run. We need to have the exact sequence and frequency. But we can't let them run it."

"Sir?" said Tarnoff looking perplexed at this specific request.

"Need to know, Tarnoff," said Croft and clicked off the connection.

Need to know? What the hell does he mean, need to know? If I don't have a need to know, who the hell does? Tarnoff was furious. He was second in command of the most powerful force on Earth and yet Croft was telling him he didn't have a need to know. He still was being treated like a bootlicking lackey, and that's exactly what he was in the grand scheme of things. *I kiss the ass of John Croft day and night and still I don't have a need to know. Croft thinks he knows something I don't. But I've been monitoring everything Harmon is seeing and saying!*

He knew why this was so important to Croft but he couldn't let on. He wasn't sure how traveling through space was going to give anyone a political advantage here on Earth, but he was sure the device had some amazing power. He had to find out what it could do.

CHAPTER 34

Beth, still blindfolded, was pulled out of the car. Seth had a tight grasp on her arm and jerked her back as she struggled to free herself. She felt pavement beneath her feet and could hear the roar of engines as he led her forward.

"Where are you taking me?" she pleaded. Seth did not answer. She heard the voice of another man as he approached.

"Is this the package?" asked the man?

"Yes," answered Seth, and pushed Beth forward toward him.

Beth could feel another hand larger and more forceful, on her arm.

"Seth, what's happening? Please!"

"You're going on a little trip," said the man who was now holding her close to his body. She could smell cigarette smoke on his breath and clothes. His jacket felt like rough canvas, possibly military attire. The man led her to a narrow metal stairway and now was pushing her upward into what she believed was an aircraft.

She turned back towards Seth's voice.

"Seth, don't you care about me at all?" she pleaded as she heard him walking away.

"Please, sir. What have I done? Why am I a prisoner? Who are you?" she cried in anguish. Her heart pounded wildly as she heard Seth's car drive away.

"Things will go better for you if you remain quiet and don't resist," came the hoarse voice of a heavy smoker.

"But I'm just a kid. What could anyone possibly want

with me?"

"I'm just following orders, Miss."

Beth was piled into a narrow seat. The vehicle seemed small, like a fighter jet. The man buckled her seat belt and handed her a paper bag.

"Here, you might need this," he said.

"What for?"

"When you throw up."

"Throw up?" Beth heard the engines start up and within seconds they were airborne. It felt like they were taking off in a vertical ascent. Her stomach began to churn and soon she realized why he had handed her the bag.

"Can't you at least take this blindfold off me?" pleaded Beth.

"I've been told to keep it on. It's probably for your own protection," said her captor. She detected a slight tone of sympathy in his hoarse voice.

"If you know too much, then they'll have to kill you."

"Kill me!" Beth felt a wave of pure terror shoot through her body. *Why would anyone want to kill or kidnap me? It can't be for ransom. Dad doesn't have much money. He's just a Professor!* Nothing made sense and she started to sob uncontrollably.

John Darp could clearly see the Washington Monument and the Capitol Building from the rooftop-landing pad of the government building. Several armed guards approached the vehicle and opened Beth's door. As Beth stepped out, Darp pushed her against the side of the craft, pulled her hands behind her back, and cuffed them.

"Ow, that hurts! I haven't done anything. Why are you treating me like a criminal? I've been kidnapped!" she screamed. Darp made the cuffs even tighter and then led her to an elevator. Beth and her captor descended for eighteen floors. The elevator door opened to what seemed to be a large vacant area as the sound was reverberating off the walls in an echo. The floor beneath her feet felt like concrete and she could smell something acrid in the air. She heard a door open and they entered a carpeted room.

"Sit down," said Darp, pulling a flimsy chair up to her. He sat her down in the chair hands still cuffed behind her back, and left her alone in the room. She sat there for what seemed like an hour before she heard the door open again.

Eric looked around in stunned silence, his eyes darting back and forth between Josh and the scene in front of them.

"What the hell! Where are we?" he asked, filled with sheer wonder as he looked around.

"I think we're dead," said Josh, his voice deadpan with resignation to the fate that had befallen them after entering the smoldering lab with the strange vortex in the center of the room.

"We're sure not in Kansas anymore," said Eric looking down at the vegetation around them that seemed to glow and respond to them as they walked by.

"What the heck is that?" asked Josh, pointing to the bright glow in the distance.

"It looks like giant crystals," said Eric squinting to get his eyes focused. "It looks like skyscrapers made out of crystals! Is anyone else here?" He made a 360 degree turn surveying the landscape around them. He didn't see anyone.

"Do you think this is heaven?" asked Josh sheepishly. He looked at his hands and pinched himself. "Ow! I can feel myself. I still have a body or at least I think I do."

Eric pinched himself and winced with the pain. "I feel real. Hell I don't know. Let's head toward the crystals." When he said this, all of the vegetation seemed to lean in the direction of the crystal city. "Whoa! Did you see that?"

Josh nodded as if in a trance, and they started walking down the dirt path that led through a field of turquoise grass. They walked towards the crystal city for what seemed like hours. There was no sign of people and for that matter no animals, birds, or even insects. As they neared the structures, the dirt path changed into a road made of smooth stone that looked like marble.

"Look man," shouted Eric pointing to figures that seemed to be approaching from the distance. They had a glow around them, so it was difficult to make them out.

"Finally people. Maybe we can get some answers now," said Josh. They started to run towards the figures but instead found themselves transported instantaneously to them.

"Hello?" said Josh to the beautiful young man that stood before him, emitting a golden glow. "Where are we?"

"You have been brought here by accident. You must go back."

"But where are we? What is this place? Who are you?"

The young man did not answer and raised a staff that he was carrying in his left hand. Eric felt like he was caught up in a tornado. Everything around him began spinning at an incredible speed and he was enveloped in a funnel of light as bright as the sun. Within seconds, the whirlwind stopped and Josh found himself in the dark. As his eyes adjusted, he saw a red glow. It said *EXIT*. He realized he was been back in the lab.

"Josh, are you here" There were no windows in the lab and it was pitch black except for the red exit sign that gave off only a faint light.

"Yeah, I'm here. Are we back in the lab?"

"I think so" said Eric. It was so dark in this windowless room, he didn't know if it was day or night. He glanced at the glowing face of his watch and saw that it had stopped. The building was silent. No one seemed to be there.

"Follow my voice," said Josh as he made his way to the door that he remembered entering to put out a chemical fire. He had no conception of how much time had passed since then. It seemed like a lifetime. He felt changed.

Tarnoff's heart raced as the images clouded his mind. These were the images he had tried to forget for fifteen years. The more he fought to chase them from his consciousness, the more vivid they became, like a horror film playing inside his head.

First, he caught a glimpse of the balloon Stephie had been holding floating skyward. Then he heard the giggle as he caught sight of her teetering on the edge of the narrow railing. The stranger running towards her, hands thrust forward, eyes wild with terror. Then the scream as she fell to the pit below, and the sound he would never be able to erase from his memory of the growling, and her last shriek as the beast tore her to shreds before his eyes.

The scene played out repeatedly, and so did his regrets. If only he had not taken the business call. If only he had been paying more attention. It was his fault she was dead. There was no doubt in his mind. That was the day his life ceased to have any real meaning. It was the day his wife of twelve years left him, screaming "murderer" as she slammed the door.

Tarnoff turned over in his bed for the forty-third time that night. He thought if he counted the times he shifted, he would finally fall asleep. It wasn't working. He was feeling something he had not experienced for a long time. It was doubt. His stomach was in a knot. Sweat was pouring from his forehead and soaking his pillow. For the first time, he had reservations about the Brotherhood. It seemed he was always being asked to do something out of line with Christian principles to accomplish a higher goal: a time when righteousness and the rule of God would prevail on Earth. He was fighting against the Devil and sinners. It used to make sense. Not anymore. Tonight his world was in disarray.

He reached over and turned on the light, then sat up in his bed using his pajama sleeve to wipe his face. He let out a sigh, and reached for the Bible that was always positioned within easy reach on his glass top nightstand. He had placed tabs on the many passages he liked to reread - the passages that seemed to justify his mission. Tonight, he hoped that these passages would comfort him and let him sleep. He was looking for strength - something to help him do what had to be done.

What did Jesus say himself, and what had been said by others? He suddenly had a burning desire to make this distinction. It was starting to dawn on him that there had been so much done in the name of Christ that just didn't fit with the idea of a loving, compassionate Savior. So many lives were ruined, and so many killed since the Brotherhood came to power. Were they really doing God's work? Was John Croft the pious and righteous man he had believed was bringing God's law to America? He had doubts ... terrible doubts. Doubts, that if known, would ruin him, and even worse, cost him his life. He went through each and every tab looking for something that could help him make up his mind. When he closed the book, it was 6:25 a.m. and he knew what he had to do.

CHAPTER 35

"Who's there? What do you want from me?" screamed Beth, struggling against the ropes that tied her to the chair, and trying to look under her blindfold. "I want to call my father!"

"Your father is dead and they want you dead too," came the voice.

"He's dead?" cried Beth, not even registering the threat to her own life. "What do you mean he's dead? What's going on? What happened? My dad is just a Professor. We're not important. Why are you doing all of this?"

Unfortunately your father was involved with something very important and that made you important too."

"What? You're going to kill me? Help, help!" she started to scream at the top of her lungs, squirming and fighting to free herself. A suffocating feeling of sheer terror welled up inside her as she heard her captor come closer. "Let me go. I don't know anything, you bastard!"

She felt the clammy hand of her captor on her neck, felt the prick of a needle, and gasped for air as she lost consciousness.

Brandon Tarnoff needed to know more about what Alex Harmon's work was about and how it translated into political power. He needed to know what the device would do. It seemed that Croft had much more information on how it could be used, than he was letting on. Tarnoff started to search the Internet for anything he could find about Alex Harmon's theory. He clicked on The Harmon/Stewart Solution.

THE HARMON/STEWART SOLUTION
A UNIFIED FIELD THEORY
Overview

"According to the Harmon/Stewart Solution – a Unified Field Theory, all matter is three-dimensional. Concepts of one and two dimensionality are manmade and an error in Euclidean geometry that this theory corrects. Because all matter is three-dimensional, it can be divided to infinity, and the state of infinite density or a black hole, must exist at the center of all particles of matter at all scales. It is this black hole dynamic in the fabric of space-time that is the cause of gravity, not a theoretical particle called a graviton; that has never been observed ..."

"... You will find in our paper that if you assume a black hole centers a proton, it exactly equals the theorized "strong force" and eliminates the need for the weak force. Thus, there are really only two forces in nature: electromagnetism and gravity ..."

"... The two forces represent two sides of the universe that have a feedback-loop between them causing the expansion that we can clearly observe. The standard model depicts our universe as a balloon being blown up, with pennies glued to the surface. As the balloon or universe expands,

the pennies, which represent galaxies, move
farther away from each other ..."

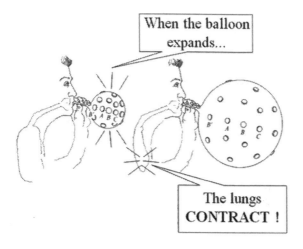

Illustration courtesy of "Gravitation" by Misner, Thorne, and Wheeler

"... For the expansion to occur there must be a
contracting force. Using the example of a man
blowing up a balloon, it is the lungs that are
contracting. The balloon represents our
expanding universe and the lungs represent the
contracting force, or the black hole side of the
universe. Therefore, gravity is the force of the
contracted side of the universe and
electromagnetism is the force generated by the
expanded side – or what we call physical
reality..."

"... The standard model does not explain the
contracted side of this dynamic. That is why it
looks as if we are missing ninety-six percent of the
mass necessary to cause the rate of expansion of
the universe, we can observe. Our theory does
away with the theorized dark matter and dark

energy. What we are observing is the force of gravity exerted by the feedback-loop from the contracted side of the universe to the expanded side of the universe. The contact point between the two sides (or where the lips contact the balloon) represents the event horizon of the black hole. Therefore, black holes are not the galaxy eating monsters that most people envision, but rather are fundamental to creation. In fact, everything in the physical universe is a different sized black hole, including our own bodies ... "

"... In infinity, all time, space and information exists at once, and much like a hologram or a strand of DNA, every point contains all information. Physical matter spins into existence creating embedded boundary conditions using the specific geometry of the sixty-four tetrahedral grid. This geometry can expand or contract in fractals to infinity ... "

Tarnoff cursored down.

"...We have found an error in the way Kerr and Newman solved Einstein's field equations for spin, in that they left out torque and coriolis effects. We have added these forces back into our equations to arrive at a unified field theory that does not require any theorized particles, but is complete using the geometry of the sixty-four tetrahedral grid. When we corrected for an accurate depiction of spin, we found the topology resembles a double torus – two stacked donuts with a singularity in the middle. The energetic feedback-loop follows this geometry at every scale from the subatomic to the universal."

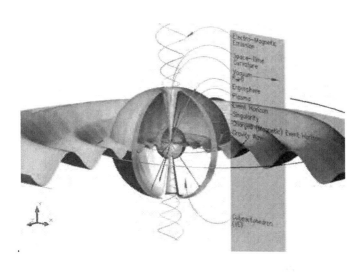

Beth opened her eyes to find herself buckled into an air car. She was no longer handcuffed and there was no blindfold covering her eyes.

"Are you all right?" asked the man piloting the craft?

Beth was dazed. Her last memory was that she was about to die.

"I'm alive, so I guess I'm fine." Then the fear returned. Her ordeal was not over. They hadn't killed her ... yet. She wasn't bound, but there wasn't exactly any means of escape. Maybe he was going to push her out of the air car.

"Let me go, let me out of here," she cried.

"Relax. I'm here to help you." The man of about 28 years with soft blue eyes smiled over at her. I'm taking you to Oregon."

She ignored his smile, certain it was a ploy. "Who are you and what happened to my father?"

"It's best that you don't know who I am. Your father was killed in a laboratory accident. That's all I know. You've been given a new name, and I have papers and a sizeable amount of money for you. If you want to live, you're going to have to start a new life as Sarah Miles. Beth Sheppard died in a car crash in Washington, D.C.

"But why Oregon? What am I going to do there?"

"You've been enrolled in Oregon State. Your tuition has been paid through graduation. You'll meet new friends. You'll be okay. But you must never let anyone know that Beth Sheppard is still alive."

Beth looked over at him speechless as tears rolled down her cheeks. She had never felt so alone. Now she wished they had killed her.

CHAPTER 36

Brandon Tarnoff lay in bed, computer on his lap, searching the Internet for more information on Harmon's theory, when he came across an obscure article written for a New Age magazine. Such publications had been banned for years, but as a high-ranking official, he had access to all information that had been pulled off the Internet. It was entitled *"The Scientific Explanation of the Spiritual, An Analysis Of The Unified Field Theory of Alex Harmon, Ph.D. and Sydney Stewart, Ph.D."* and was written by Donna Feeley, a New Age spiritual leader who was jailed when the OEB cracked down on such subversives.

Tarnoff needed to know more about why Harmon's work was of such interest to Croft. The information in the article startled him. It contained ideas he had never considered before. He started to realize that "The Harmon/Stewart Solution" might just be the scientific proof of the spiritual realm. More than that, they might be developing a technology to access it.

The Scientific Explanation of the Spiritual, An Analysis Of The Unified Field Theory of Alex Harmon, Ph.D. and Sydney Stewart, Ph.D.
by
Donna Feeley, Ph.D.

"Physicist Alex Harmon may have solved the greatest mystery of the universe. His unified field theory solves the unification between Einstein's Field Equations and Quantum Physics –

the Holy Grail of physics. In doing so he has discovered an infinitely dense energy field in the vacuum, producing a feedback-loop of information transfer (self awareness or consciousness) underlying all of physical reality. In other words, his theory is the scientific explanation of the spiritual realm, although he contends it's all one system and cannot be separated from the physics of the physical reality. Like vortices in a lake, he believes matter is a dynamic of this energy density, not something apart from it ...."

"... We are all intrigued that the observations at the quantum level seem to substantiate many New Age spiritual beliefs. Harmon's theory goes beyond quantum physics, creating a model far more logical and observable in nature. It is not reliant on theorized particles and complicated equations. According to my extensive research of ancient texts, this understanding of the universe appears to be encoded in the world's religions as the explanation of creation, or more accurately, the scientific proof of God ...."

Tarnoff skimmed the pages. He was looking for something specific.

"... Thus, what the theory implies is a conscious and infinite energy field underlying all of physical creation, attached through the black hole at the center of all particles, and in a constant feedback-loop with the physical world. Have you ever wondered how God could be omniscient and omnipotent? This field, whether you call it the vacuum, the universe, or God, is the fabric of creation ...."

Tarnoff continued to scan through the pages.

"... Harmon's 'Scaling Law' shows that the biological entity lies at the center of creation. Could it be that all biological entities exist to be probes for the Universe to learn about itself? Could biological entities be the event horizons for the universe? Could it be that life is not some fluke limited to planet Earth, but ubiquitous throughout the universe – as fundamental to creation as stars and galaxies? ...."

"... This knowledge of the physics of the universe or the geometry of space-time seems to be imbedded in the world's religions as the nature of God. The universe uses the geometry of the six-pointed star, or Star of David, within a sphere to go to infinity ...."

"... The Kabalistic Trees of Life come together perfectly to create a sixty-four tetrahedral grid. The seventy-two faces of God referred to in the Hebrew tradition, when doubled (as all particles have a polarized pair) add up to one hundred and forty-four, and equal the number of faces on a three-dimensional sixty-four tetrahedral grid ...."

"... The word for God in the Hebrew tradition is Yahweh. Yahweh in its Greek form means tetragrammaton – with tetra representing the four sides of a tetrahedron, and grammaton referring to gravity or grammar, which in Hebrew has numerical equivalents ...."

"... When the sixty-four tetrahedral grid is

spinning, it forms a double torus creating a Yin and Yang sign at the top …."

"… The Flower of Life is a sixty-four tetrahedral grid with waveforms or "petals" on its vectors …."

"... The I Ching uses a sixty-four grid of reality, and its short and long sticks used to guide the faithful form a star tetrahedron ...."

"... The ancient Egyptian Eye has a mathematical formula in its parts that are represented in fractals and add up to 1/64 ...."

The Sacred Egyptian Eye

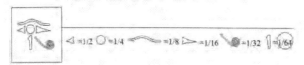

"... Harmon's theory implies that knowing how the universe creates boundary conditions to create physical matter will allow a civilization to create a technology to manifest anything. Is this how Moses manifested water out of rock? Is this how Jesus multiplied loaves and turned water into wine? Harmon believes that he can build a technology that can do this ...."

"... Here, we have an ancient Sumerian Relief depicting their Sun God, who gave them civilization. Clearly, the God is a giant compared to the supplicants. Before him is something referred to as a black sun – an appropriate name for a controlled black hole, which would have given this 'God' the power to manifest anything ...."

Then Tarnoff found what he was looking for. He read on:

"… Harmon's theory brings science and spirituality together to lift civilization to a whole new age, for they are fundamentally intertwined …."

"… This knowledge could usher in a leap in civilization more profound than when we discovered fire or the wheel. Possibilities include an anti-gravitational drive technology that would allow mankind to travel the stars through hyperspace. With this model of the universe, mankind will have access to unlimited resources, and most importantly, humankind will finally have a fundamental understanding of the nature of creation and how we as individuals interact with the infinite feedback of the vacuum structure to define our level of consciousness and co-create our reality with the universe …."

"… So what does this mean for you and your daily life? If all matter is infinite, it means you are infinite because you are made of matter. In fact, all matter, according to this theory, is just different sized black/white 'wholes' including stars, planets, and the atoms of which you are made. Just as with a super nova: when a star explodes, it is said to have turned into a black hole. Harmon says no, the black hole was always there, and when a star sheds its boundary condition, you can see the black hole that was always at the center. This means that within your boundary condition, or your body, is access to the infinite realm. Perhaps when Jesus said, "the Kingdom of God is within," he had been referring to this dynamic."

Tarnoff's eyes widened. Now he understood. *This knowledge would destroy the Brotherhood. Croft's empire would crumble! Croft wants to control this, keep it for himself. Perhaps he wants to use this technology to set himself up as the Second Coming of Christ. This changes everything. It changes the very fabric of the Brotherhood's doctrines of belief. No wonder Croft wouldn't share this with me.*

He cursored down the article looking for anything else that would help him, and then he found it:

> *"... In a universe with a feedback-loop, consciousness is echoed back to the observer as physical manifestation. In normal time, this loop can be so long that the observer does not equate something that manifests in his field with the causative action. A device that opens a portal to the energy field in the vacuum would reflect the consciousness back onto the observer instantaneously. Anyone attempting to access this energy field must be initiated to control negative thoughts while in the presence of the field. The field can be deadly to those not trained to control their negative emotions."*

CHAPTER 37

John Croft assembled a squad of a hundred men to storm Alex's lab. It was a bit of overkill, but he wasn't going to take any chances. He had everything he needed in place. From months of surveillance, he knew how to operate the device. He didn't need Harmon or Stewart anymore, and his men had orders to shoot them on sight.

He felt absolutely giddy. With this device he would be the most powerful man on Earth. Even immortality was within his grasp. Nothing could stop him now. He watched Sydney through Alex's eyes as she prepared to start up the device. Croft ordered his men to take their places surrounding the building, and in the stairways and elevators.

They blocked off the entrances, and no one was allowed in or out. There was no escape for anyone in the building now. Soon Harmon and Stewart would be silenced, and the world would not learn how he derived his power. He would be like God, able to heal, raise the dead, split the seas, make matter out of the vacuum, and even travel the stars. He would be worshipped! The only thing left to do would be to eliminate anyone who knew about the device. It was a small price to pay for the new world that was about to unfold. *All great changes require sacrifice,* he thought to himself smugly.

"Lock and load, and wait for my mark," he barked into his vidphone. The men drew their guns and waited for the order to break down the door.

Ian Long, Croft's lead man in the operation, awaited the order to move in. Croft had ordered him to kill everyone in the lab. This kind of slaughter seemed unnecessary, but it was part of the job. He had a sworn duty to carry out the orders of the Grand Master of the Brotherhood, and it wasn't his place to question why. It was always hard to go home to his wife and two young daughters after an operation like this one. He didn't like killing anyone. But he knew it was for the greater good. He didn't know what these people he was about to take out had done, but they were obviously heretics and needed to be eliminated. If people had to die to create God's rule on Earth, then so be it. He was a trained professional. He would do his job.

John Croft sat in the control van outside the physics building. Brandon Tarnoff sat next to him drinking a cup of coffee and watching the operation. The street was littered with squad cars and a maze of blue strobes lighting up the grey morning. There were no sirens. This operation had to catch Harmon and Stewart by surprise. It was 6:20 a.m. and few people were in the building, but the swat teams were ordered to go door to door to evacuate those remaining. Once all the people were cleared out, he could send in his men.

Croft and Tarnoff watched the scene in the lab as Alex began spinning the plasma. Watching through the chip in Alex's optic nerve and listening from the chip in his ear canal, it was as if they were positioned inside his head. They could see and hear everything.

"This is it. They've set the frequency. It's starting to run," said Tarnoff.

"Okay, let's go," ordered Croft.

Tarnoff signaled to the officer sitting at a control station in the back of the van.

"Mitchell, take over the main monitor. We're going in."

"Yes, sir." Mitchell got up and took Tarnoff's position in front of the monitor.

"Good luck sir."

"Yes, yes," said Croft as he stepped out of the van.

Croft and Tarnoff headed for the building entrance when Croft stopped in his tracks.

"Wait a minute. I need to get something out of the van." Croft turned and walked around the back of the large white vehicle and opened the double doors.

"Sir? Is there something I can do?" asked Mitchell.

"Yes, as a matter of fact there is." Croft pulled a gun with a silencer attached out of his vest pocket and fired a shot into Mitchell's forehead. "You can die."

"Did you get what you were looking for?" asked Tarnoff as Croft walked back towards him.

"Yes, let's go."

The two men walked briskly to the basement entrance where Brian Sheppard's was located. The twenty men who were to lead the attack were gathered, guns drawn. Croft nodded at his man Long. This was the signal that they were good to go. Croft positioned himself in the middle of the men, back a few rows as they made their way down the staircase to the basement lab and down the long corridor of storage room doors.

"Tarnoff, you go in with Long." Croft looked behind him, but Tarnoff wasn't there. "What the hell?" He grabbed the man next to him, a skinny kid, probably no more than nineteen years old. The Brotherhood liked to get them young and malleable.

"You. What's your name?"

"Garrett, sir. Garrett Whipple."

Go find Tarnoff and kill him. He's a traitor."

"Sir?"

"Do it," shouted Croft shoving him out of formation.

"Yes, sir!" He clicked his heals together, as was the Brotherhood custom, saluted and turned back to carry out his order.

Croft had planned to eliminate Tarnoff in the lab along with Harmon and Stewart, but he couldn't stop the operation to look for him now. He'd just have to kill the kid too. *'Just a little bit more collateral damage,'* he thought. This was his moment ... the manifestation of his destiny. The power of the ancient Sun Gods would soon be his! The world would be united under his leadership, and he would become omnipotent.

Garrett Whipple rushed back up the stairs. He had just seen Tarnoff a minute ago. He couldn't be far. He pushed open the door and saw Tarnoff walking towards the van.

"Sir?"

Tarnoff kept walking. Whipple cocked his gun.

"Sir!" He took his gun in both hands and took aim, about to pull the trigger when Tarnoff turned and faced him.

"Do you really want to be a cold blooded murderer?"

Garrett's mouth dropped open and his eyes bulged. "The Grand Master has ordered your execution!"

"The Grand Master is mad," answered Tarnoff. "Put your gun down, son. You don't want to do this."

Garrett stood motionless, the color draining from his face,

his finger still on the trigger. His heart was racing and his eyes blinked wildly. He reaffirmed his aim.

"Son," said Tarnoff again. "Murder is not the Christian way."

Garret let out a deep breath and stopped. He dropped his arms to his side and lowered his head.

"I wouldn't go back if I were you," warned Tarnoff. "Croft won't want a witness to my murder, so he'll kill you too." Garrett looked stunned as Tarnoff's words registered.

"Go home to your family, son. Don't be a part of this atrocity."

Garret turned around and ran away.

Tarnoff walked slowly towards the van. He pulled his gun out of his underarm holster, not knowing if the order to kill him had been given to Mitchell as well. As he neared the van, every nerve in his body was on high alert. He kept his gun drawn and slowly approached the vehicle. He listened by the door, but heard nothing. He pulled the latch and swung the door open quickly, ready to shoot, when Mitchell's lifeless body fell over on him.

"Mitchell?" He pulled the body off him and let it fall to the ground. Mitchell's lifeless eyes stared vacantly up at him. Tarnoff peered into the van cautiously. Every muscle was ready for action, but the van was empty. At the control panel, the scene inside the lab was unfolding.

Tarnoff stood staring at the sight in stunned silence. *The feedback-loop,* he thought in quiet satisfaction.

CHAPTER 38

Alex and Sydney no longer needed the safety wall. This time they wanted to be directly in the field. They entered the containment room.

"Are you sure we'll be okay in here?" Sydney said, hesitating to enter the claustrophobic vault.

"Hurry, Sydney. I hear them coming. We don't have any choice now. We can't let ourselves and the resonance chamber get captured," whispered Alex as he bolted the heavy door behind them and entered the codes into the control panel to pulse the magnetic field.

"If this doesn't work, we're dead," said Sydney shooting Alex a look of surrender.

"Keep your thoughts positive. Remember the feedback-loop." Alex closed his eyes and called out. "I AM that I AM calling on the indwelling of my mighty I AM presence. As we open this portal to the sacred realm, I ask protection and safe journey. We now transcend time and space in pristine alignment with the LAW OF ONE. SO BE IT, SO IT IS, anchor, lock, and seal. I AM." He turned to Sydney and said, "Now visualize the light like we learned in Tibet."

Alex took a deep breath and gave her a determined look. "Ready?"

"As ready as I'll ever be," she replied bracing herself.

Alex flipped the switch and the chamber began to spin. The whir intensified as the plasma spun faster and faster towards the optimum speed of one million rpm. The room began to fill with bright white light when the thrashing sound came from the door of the lab.

Sydney felt Alex's hand grasp hers as they stood in silent prayer.

Ian Long banged on the titanium door of the containment room. "Open up, police!" he shouted, waving over his men. "Break down this door!"

A deafening rumble filled the room as the spin of the plasma increased. Rays of bright opalescent light radiated in long plumes from the resonance chamber, enveloping Sydney and Alex as the ramming sound reverberated against the vault door.

"How much longer?" gasped Sydney her eyes darting from Alex to the door, trying to abate the fear rising in her gut.

"Keep positive. Do not go into fear! 800,000 rpm, 835,000," shouted Alex staring at the control panel as if his sheer will could get it to accelerate faster.

Sydney held her breath as the bolts on the door began to give way.

"900,000 rpm, 950,000 rpm."

The door began to buckle and the room started shaking as the plasma spun past 975,000 rpm.

The light streaming out of the resonance chamber was now creating a vortex. Alex saw the door bending from the pressure of the ramming.

"985,000, 986,000," shouted Alex above the din.

"Alex, now!" shrieked Sydney.

The door flung open and Long and his men stormed in. Sydney and Alex recoiled, holding each other as the door burst open and a horde of men dressed in OEB uniforms rushed in with weapons raised. The white light filled the room and the sound of the resonator muffled the shouts of the men. Ian Long drew his gun, and aimed it at Alex's forehead and pulled the trigger.

Sydney gasped, her heart raced, and she could hardly breathe. The lab had turned into a tunnel of white light. There were no Brotherhood agents surrounding her. She could not see anything in the blinding light and felt as if she were hurtling through a vortex in space.

Before she could question what was happening, she found herself standing in what looked like a plaza of a crystalline city. The vortex she had travelled in surrounded the plaza, and now began to dissipate into a faint wisp of white vapor.

Beneath her feet were hexagonal crystals forming a flooring of varying pastel shades. The hexagons looked like translucent honeycombed tubes that extended to infinity vertically below her. In front of her were three pillars that appeared to be made of sheer light. Behind the pillars lay a lush garden filled with plants in colorful hues she had never seen in nature before. Beyond the garden, she could see a pyramid made of gleaming white stone with a long, wide opalescent staircase extending from a tall set of ornately carved golden doors.

Sydney heard a whooshing sound and looked over to find Alex materializing beside her. "Alex! You're alive! Oh my God, I thought you were dead!" Tears of relief poured down her face as she scanned his forehead for the bullet wound, but there wasn't even a scratch. "How can this be? I saw him shoot you point blank."

"The last thing I saw was the bullet stop in mid air right in front of my eyes, and then turn back on the gunman. The scene was horrific. Everyone had been killed, and then Croft came in with his men."

"But how?"

Suddenly a man materialized in front of them, dressed in a long, sky blue robe with white trim and a white bib neckline. He was seven feet tall with long blonde hair and handsome, even features. He appeared to be Nordic and about thirty-five years old. Belying his appearance, he seemed like a man of far greater years with a look of great intelligence in his intense blue eyes. As he came closer, Sydney could see that he was not quite human. His eyes were much larger than normal, and he had extremely high cheekbones and six fingers. He wore a very tall gold and jeweled headpiece that seemed to conform to an elongated skull.

He held his hand up in greeting. "I am Arcadia of the Galactic Federation. Welcome, we have been expecting you." A bright glow seemed to surround the Being giving him an almost angelic appearance. Sydney noticed that his lips were not moving, and realized she was hearing him in her head. He motioned for them to follow him and smiled.

"Where are we?" asked Sydney looking around, dazed by the brightness of the light.

"Are we on another planet?" she realized they could no longer be on Earth. "You are not on a planet. You are on my spaceship."

"A spaceship? It looks like we are outside. There's sunlight," said Sydney looking up at the blue sky bewildered.

"This ship is larger than your planet. We have built an artificial atmosphere to create perfect environmental conditions, so it appears much like being on the surface of a planet. But we can travel wherever we wish."

Sydney's eyes widened in disbelief. A myriad of questions rushed through her consciousness. Arcadia smiled, and she heard the words, "Patience, all your questions will be answered shortly. Come with me."

Tarnoff stared transfixed as the scene in the lab unfolded on the screen in front of him. The bullet headed straight for Dr. Harmon's forehead had stopped in midair. It then made a u-turn and plunged straight through the forehead of Ian Long. The men started shooting wildly at the two scientists whose forms had begun to evaporate into white funnels of light. But the bullets turned back on the men in a hailstorm that rained death upon the attackers. Blood and bone fragments spattered against the walls, and the cries and moans of the shocked and dying men filled the room.

Croft shouted into his vidphone, "Long! What's going on in there?"

There was no response. He turned to Jack Maple, his second-in-command who was trying to reach his men inside the lab on his communicator.

"Send in the rest of the men," roared Croft.

"But sir, I don't know what's going on in there. Long isn't answering his phone, and I can't get Mitchell in the surveillance van either, so we're essentially blind!"

"I don't care!" barked Croft. "Send in everything we've got."

Arcadia led Alex and Sydney out of the plaza into the garden. The path was surrounded by lush vegetation that, upon closer inspection, was solid but rather made of undulating light. In the distance, Sydney could make out what appeared to be a city of towering crystal buildings, sparkling in the sunlight and radiating long rays of light in every direction. They followed Arcadia to the Pyramid that was emitting a vortex of light from its apex. Steps made of milky-white quartz crystal led up to the fifty-foot-high golden doors. Arcadia held up his hand and the doors opened.

They entered a cavernous room surrounded by golden statues that stood twenty feet high and were lit from below, casting an ethereal glow across the floor. They looked like standing Buddha's with their eyes closed and their hands in prayer pose. The statues extended in a seemingly endless sea of rows as if guarding the sacred sanctuary. The sound of a low humming tone filled the air, and Sydney was overcome with a deep sense of calm. Arcadia stopped and turned to them.

"Humanity is at an evolutionary transition point. You are about to evolve to a higher level of being. You both have an important role to play in how the destiny of humankind unfolds. There may be cataclysms depending on the level of humanity's consciousness."

Sydney swallowed hard at these words, and a feeling of apprehension shot through her. "Cataclysm and consciousness? What do you mean?" she asked, shocked at Arcadia's words.

"Your sun is rotating around the galactic arm and is moving into position to align with the galactic center. In addition, the Earth's axis is tilting toward the great black hole.

This unique alignment that happens approximately every 25,600 years could create seismic and tidal disturbances as the magnetic fields of the Earth begin to shift. There could be massive extinctions on your planet in the near future."

"Massive extinctions?" exclaimed Sydney, feeling panic welling in her chest.

Alex reached over for her hand and held it tightly. He had a knowing look on his face as if he had foreknowledge of what was being revealed to them.

"Yes. It may very well be a time of great loss and great sorrow," continued Arcadia. "There may be tidal waves over a thousand feet high that will submerge the coasts all over the Earth. The planet may experience Earthquakes, extreme tornadoes and hurricanes reaching destructive levels never seen before, abrupt temperature changes and more. If it happens, it will continue over a five-week period. All of the coastal cities on the Earth will be destroyed."

"Eighty percent of the population on Earth lives near the coast!" Sydney gasped. "It's the Apocalypse after all!"

"In a sense, yes," replied Arcadia

"But you keep saying if. What do you mean?" asked Sydney.

"The collective consciousness on your planet will play a part. The more people realize their power and use their thoughts to create a positive reality, the more it will manifest. If they descend into fear, the worst will happen."

Sydney stood in shocked silence at his words.

"In the worst case scenario, only those who have attained higher consciousness will survive."

"That's awful!" cried Sydney.

"Not necessarily," answered Arcadia. "Even in the case of a great purging, a whole new level of civilization for humanity will be rebuilt, like a phoenix rising from the ashes."

"But why would you let so many people die?" cried Sydney, tears streaming down her face. "Certainly you have the power to help us!"

"Remember," answered Arcadia. "Death is but a

transition. Everything is eternal and infinite. Nothing dies. This transition is part of the great plan and will bring about a new age for mankind."

Sydney found little comfort in his assurances and struggled to accept what Arcadia was saying. She could not comprehend how so much death, could possibly be sanctioned by a higher intelligence.

"Once you realize the greater plan and how the universe works, tragedies turn into blessings and death becomes a doorway. And there is still time for humanity to raise its vibration and avoid the Earth changes," Arcadia said placing his hand on her shoulder and smiling reassuringly.

Sydney did not return his smile. "How in the world are we going to do that?" she asked.

She couldn't conceive of things changing enough to avert the calamity. "All people ever hear is doom and gloom blaring twenty-four hours a day from every news source around the world! Our minds are filled with fear. Almost every television show and movie is laden with fighting and death. You can't help witnessing a murder just by flipping through the channels for even a minute!" She looked at Arcadia intently. Her distress contorted her delicate features.

"Yes, this is true and it needs to change. Many people are waking up around the world to the understanding that their thoughts are creating reality. When the number of like- minded people hits a critical mass, the new consciousness will spread through the population," said Arcadia. "You and Alex are to play a large role in this awakening."

"What if not enough people wake up?" asked Sydney.

"That's where your technology will be critical, as you will need to build levitating cities to get the chosen people off the surface of the Earth during the change."

"But who will be chosen to survive and based on what criteria? Is Source or the Galactic Federation judging us?" asked Sydney.

"Life, no matter how it is lived, is but an experience," replied Arcadia smiling as if he knew exactly where Sydney was

338

going with this question. "There is no judgment of good or bad."

"So who are the chosen ones?" asked Sydney

"Those who are listening to their inner guidance are being directed to move to the appointed places," answered Arcadia.

"You mean you have been in communication with others?" asked Sydney.

"We are in communication with everyone, but only a few listen. Those are the chosen ones. Follow me," said Arcadia.

Arcadia led them across the cavernous room to an elaborate golden altar. A ceremonial fire burned in a pit in the center, filling the air with the soothing scent of sage. The Altar was covered with an ornately embroidered red silk cloth, bordered with long black tassels and crystal beads that sparkled from the light of the fire. On top of the silk cloth lay three large scrolls positioned between two golden candelabras. Arcadia bowed as he approached the Altar. He took a lighting stick from an urn and kindled the ten candles on each of the candelabras.

"The technology of God is the ability of a species to interact directly with Source to manifest anything it desires," said Arcadia.

"What do you mean?" asked Sydney. "How does someone use the technology we have invented to do this?"

"It's all about consciousness. When you use the technology to open a portal and come in direct contact with the Field, the feedback-loop is immediate and thoughts manifest instantly. Without the technology, it may take days, weeks, years, or even lifetimes for thoughts to manifest. In that time, other thoughts interfere, and so people don't see the cause and effect so readily."

"You mean with our technology we will be able to manifest things we think about?" asked Sydney, incredulous.

"It's a little more complicated than that, but in a sense, yes," said Arcadia.

"Our technology will help to save humanity!" Sydney gasped as she realized the enormity of the task before them.

"It will change everything," said Alex. "Our civilization won't even be recognizable!"

Arcadia nodded in agreement. "With manifestation technology, humans will no longer have to toil to survive. Existence will become peaceful and non-competitive as you learn to create through the vacuum. Instead of seeing the world as a place where there is a lack of resources, you will come to see the universe as the place of unlimited abundance that it is. Competition for resources will become a thing of the past."

"Did Jesus use this kind of technology to accomplish His miracles?" asked Sydney.

"No. He didn't need it. Humans don't need technology to interact with the Field, as all beings are born with that innate ability. Within the boundary condition of your bodies is the potential of infinite information," said Arcadia. "It is possible to manifest anything out of the vacuum, and is how your great masters were able to perform seemingly impossible acts."

"It must be how Jesus had been able to walk on water!" Sydney said as the realization hit her that this feat had been a gravitational effect of the vacuum.

"As the infinity is much like a hologram where all points contain the whole, all time, past, present, and future, exists at all points," added Alex.

"Yes, that's the ability to access what so many have called the Akashic records," said Arcadia. "But this takes much study and discipline. Using technology is the only way an entire civilization can interact with the vacuum. However, controlling your thoughts is the key, as you learned during your initiation in Tibet. With the technology comes the realization that consciousness is everything. It is hard to escape the connectedness of all things, and the role of consciousness, once you have unlocked the secret of creation. A great awakening comes with the technology, as this is where science and spirituality converge as one discipline. When people are exposed directly to the vacuum energy, it will be obvious that the Field lines up to reflect conscious intention. That's why you needed to study with the monks to learn how to control your thoughts.

"So this must be why positive thoughts, affirmations, and prayer work!" It was all starting to make sense to Sydney.

Arcadia continued: "People have always been creating their reality in this way. But most of the time they are doing it in an unconscious manner – and so getting unwanted results."

"But sir, we can't send the men in there with no intel," protested Maple. "No one is answering. Something is wrong in there!"

Croft glared at him, pulled out his gun and shot him point blank in the forehead. The men crowded in the stairwell stood in shocked silence as Maple's body tumbled down the stairs.

"Follow me men!" Croft charged down the stairs, kicking Maple's lifeless corpse aside, and rushed towards the lab. The men filtered past the body, casting furtive glances at each other. Sean Harris stopped and turned around.

"Where are you going?" asked the Brotherhood agent next to him, grabbing his arm. Sean pulled his arm away angrily.

"I'm not doing this. Croft just killed Maple in cold blood. I'm not following that murderer anymore!"

"You'll be court marshaled!" yelled the man as Sean rushed back up the stairway.

CHAPTER 39

Arcadia led Alex and Sydney out of the cavernous room of statues. They passed through a doorway and descended a long staircase that led to another, even larger space. Sydney held her breath as she stood staring in disbelief. For a moment, she was frozen, unable to breathe. Before her was what appeared to be a thin-as-air plasma screen that stretched as far as the eye could see. It contained billions of small, swirling lights against a pitch-black background.

Arcadia looked back at them and smiled, his deep blue eyes reflecting the sparkle of the galaxies encased in the projected image. Alex approached the wall of black sky and held out his arm. It passed through the image causing it to expand out into a three-dimensional hologram. Arcadia reached out and touched on one of the swirling pools of light. The space around them readjusted, magnifying the area. He then touched it repeatedly, each time magnifying a smaller and smaller region of the galaxy until they recognized a solar system with a tiny blue marble.

As Arcadia touched the blue sphere, it magnified again. The tiny blue dot expanded until they could see it was the Earth. Arcadia swung his hand through it and the Earth expanded like an endless reflection between two mirrors engulfing the entire space around them.

Now they could see landmasses and then cities. Then they found themselves standing in the middle of an urban center with monolithic buildings surrounding them. It was a great city and the people had brilliant glows around them. Some flew through the air without the apparent assistance of any technology.

In the center of the city was an enormous pyramid, at least five hundred feet high, smooth as glass and made of a white gleaming stone. It had a brilliant vortex of golden light emitting from its apex.

"They've got my energy device in there, don't they?" asked Alex pointing to the pyramid.

Arcadia smiled and nodded in agreement, his brilliant blue eyes glistening in the sunlight.

"Where are we?" asked Sydney.

"The question is not only where we are, but when we are." said Arcadia "This is your future. This is the future of Earth and humankind."

"It's beautiful," said Sydney twirling around to take in the scene. She looked up and saw a spherical ship hovering above and then taking off silently, so fast it seemed to disappear.

"With Source energy, the gravitational field is completely malleable. The people of Earth can travel through space at the blink of an eye; and with just a small crystal on their person, can fly through the air at will," said Arcadia.

There were lush gardens that surrounded the plaza in which every plant bore some sort of fruit or vegetable, twice the size of any Sydney had ever seen before. People stopped and picked the food directly from the vines and ate as they continued on their way.

"Every plant and tree in the city is edible. People no longer have lawns, they have gardens, and all food is grown locally," said Arcadia picking two bright red fruits off a tree and handing them to Alex and Sydney. Sydney bit into it and swooned.

"It tastes like a cross between an apple and pear. It's lovely."

"There is no lack of food or natural resources as all can be pulled directly from the Field," said Arcadia. "There no longer is hunger or poverty. As no money is needed anymore, people have been freed from the slavery of having to trade their time and life to make money to survive. All is provided."

"What do they do?" asked Sydney. "Don't they get

bored?"

"No longer shackled to jobs they dislike, people are free to pursue their passions, be it art, music, study, exploration and such. Humanity is the newest member of the Galactic Federation, and people are busy meeting the other species and learning about their cultures. It is a time of great excitement with no lack of things to do."

Sydney noticed the temperature was perfect, about seventy-two degrees with a soft breeze. People were dressed in brightly colored light fabrics that swayed as they walked. Everyone looked beautiful and young, with long, lean bodies. They seemed serene and most were with companions, engaged in conversation.

"There are only young people here," said Sydney, looking around. "Where are the older people?"

"The Field has rejuvenating properties. People now live to be well beyond a thousand years old, so there are no old people yet."

"What is that sound?" asked Alex noticing an unusual humming.

"You mean that low din in the background?" asked Sydney.

"You are hearing other people's thoughts. With a little practice you will learn to tune out what you don't want to hear."

"People are telepathic in this time?" Sydney was clearly shocked.

"Humans are interacting more closely with the Field where thoughts travel, and so can hear each other as you have heard me in your minds."

"Wow, I bet that changes life!" said Alex.

"Indeed," said Arcadia. He waved his hand and they now stood outside the hologram and the scene appeared like a program on a gargantuan television screen. Arcadia turned and faced Alex. "Now is the time of ascension and you must bring it about."

"Me? Ascension? I'm no second coming of Christ!" Alex protested. "Don't tell me all that mumbo jumbo the OEB has been espousing is true!"

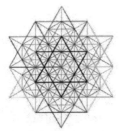

Tarnoff watched as John Croft rushed wild eyed into the lab, his men following behind him. A bright whirlwind still engulfed the lab. The bodies of Long and his men lay strewn across the room, their blood covering the floor like a thin red carpet. Croft burst through the door, his face crimson with anger and horror. The veins in his forehead bulged as if they would burst. Tarnoff stared in silence as he witnessed the man who had ordered his execution start to bubble as if he was boiling from within. Huge sores appeared all over Croft's face and hands, and Tarnoff had to pull off his headset, unable to stand Croft's screams of agony as his body burst into flames and crumpled to the floor. What came next took his breath away as a vortex of white light surrounded the eyes through which he was viewing the scene.

Arcadia laughed. "No, no, ascension is much more literal than that. Your religious beliefs are very amusing. Humanity had been given the truth long ago, but has distorted it and drenched it with so much dogma, tradition, and mythology that you have lost the true meaning of the message. In every religion on Earth, the truth has been obfuscated and used for political purposes to control the masses, instead of for true enlightenment."

"Are we so hopelessly pathetic that we can never understand?" asked Sydney.

"Oh, not at all. Human Beings are designed to understand. Your brain and pineal gland are the receptors to universal forces. You have everything you need within you. The only problem is that your culture has cut-off the path to enlightenment. You are constantly bombarded with outside stimuli like your television and radio, and are no longer taught to look within. No one takes time to listen to the infinite realm that lies within the confines of your consciousness.

"Your traditions retain some of the knowledge, but you no longer know how to interpret the information. Many of your religions have told you that you are powerless and must look to an outside authority and beg for the mercy of an angry and vengeful God. You have been robbed of your birthright – that you have everything you need within you – to be one with the forces of creation."

Sydney and Alex exchanged incredulous looks.

"What you have discovered is, in essence, the technology of God," said Arcadia. "The vacuum is the Source, the One, the ubiquitous and omniscient conscious energy field that connects and permeates all things. The only way to travel the stars is through the vacuum. To be in the vacuum is to be in the presence of Source. Now you have the technology for ascension, which is the *literal* ability to get off the planet and travel to other solar systems and galaxies. It is not only a technological advancement; it is a spiritual one as well. Only through understanding the forces of creation, and by understanding that the underlying conscious energy field is what causes gravity, can a species leave the surface of their planet."

"Of Course!" exclaimed Alex. "We're opening up a controlled black hole to harness antigravity."

"Yes, when a civilization understands the true nature of gravity and how to use anti-gravity, it can travel the stars through the Field."

"You mean going through a wormhole?" asked Sydney.

"Yes. When you open up an event horizon to the Field …"

"By opening a controlled black hole?" interjected Alex.

"Exactly," continued Arcadia. "You are entering the infinity. One can travel to various places in the universe by going from black hole to black hole. So for instance, ships leaving the Earth travel through the black hole in the center of the Earth and then to the largest black hole in the solar system which is in the middle of the sun and then on to other suns."

Sydney turned to Alex. "Maybe that's why they called ancient aliens Sun Gods ... they literally came out of the sun!"

"Yes, the Sun Gods of your mythologies were all from the Galactic Federation," said Arcadia. "So you see, the understanding of how to travel the universe comes with the understanding of the nature of the infinite, conscious energy density field in the contracted side of the universe."

"The black hole," said Alex.

"As you have discovered, everything in the material universe is just a different sized black hole leading to the infinite density of the vacuum and connecting all things through it. Matter is like vortices in a lake, embedded in the Field, made of the same stuff as the Field, and inseparable from it. When matter takes on a dynamic in the Field, like a vortex or a wave, it can be seen as something individual. But in essence, it is not something apart from the whole. When a civilization finally advances to this understanding, it evolves to a new level of technology and spiritual consciousness."

"So the Rapture is not people going to heaven, but rather people going into space?" asked Sydney.

"Exactly," replied Arcadia.

"So you don't have to believe in Jesus to go up," she said with a wry intonation.

"There's actually some truth to the idea of the good being able to ascend, but it has been misinterpreted because of the dogma." Arcadia sighed, as a master does when a pet has yet again soiled the rug. "The idea that the faithful will be the only

348

ones able to ascend is based on some reality but once again, it has been distorted."

"How so?" asked Alex.

"The Field is reflective in nature. What one feeds the Field, one gets back."

"The feedback-loop," said Sydney.

"Exactly. When you travel on a ship powered by Source energy, the feedback-loop is immediate. So if you are hostile or have negative intent, it will come back on you instantly. Thus, it's true in a sense, only those with loving intent can be in the presence of the Field, and can get on the ships that will lift you off the planet, allowing you to ascend!"

Sydney's head seemed to expand with this new understanding. Alex caught the look in her face and squeezed her hand.

Arcadia continued: "It has absolutely nothing to do with any of the dogmas attached to any of your religions. You see the real meaning of the word sin is separation from Source, and has nothing to do with being good or bad. When you are aligned with Source, all is good. This is what you have learned. All is infinite and eternal. Every atom that was ever created is still in existence. Matter changes form, but does not disappear or die. So you see, there is no need to be '*saved.*' What you need to do is to resonate with the Field. Ascension is far less mystical but no less profound a change, and is absolutely essential for the long-term survival of your species."

"Will the Galactic Federation be coming with ships to get us off the planet if the Earth changes come?" asked Alex.

"We will assist, but you have to build the ships on your own. The resonance chamber you built opens the Field and creates the anti-gravitational effects that can lift huge ships off the planet for the five weeks until the Earth changes settle down. Areas on the planet that are at least two thousand feet above sea level will not be affected. But much of your civilization will be inundated by the coming tidal waves.

We will give you dimensions for the levitating cities. You will need to organize the chosen communities so that they can build their vessels, and distribute the charged crystals to them."

Cities!" exclaimed Alex. "How big will the resonance chambers need to be?"

"You have the chamber already. You know how to build them. It is done. You now only have to expose bigger crystals to the field it produces, and disseminate them to these populations."

"How large are the crystals?" asked Sydney.

"About the size of a football. It doesn't take much to generate a field large enough to lift a city. With anti-gravitational propulsion, size and weight are not a significant factor."

"Of course," said Alex shaking his head.

"How will we find the chosen people?" asked Sydney.

"Those who are listening to the call have gone to either safe places or to the appointed areas on the Earth where the ships will be waiting."

"How will we do all of this now that the Brotherhood has found us?" asked Alex.

"Things are about to change. The Grand Master of the Brotherhood is dead. You will be getting help from a very unexpected source. Remember that the technology must be free for all," said Arcadia. "As people become exposed to the field, the truth about the nature of creation will become apparent. All of the dogma of your religions will be exposed as tools for controlling the population. The Brotherhood will no longer stand as it has with its politically controlling ideology. However, the basis of most religions will be verified by this new knowledge. With an accurate understanding of how the universe works, religious strife will be a thing of the past."

"I don't know ... won't it be chaos?" asked Alex shaking his head.

"Perhaps for a while," replied Arcadia. "Those who listen to their inner guidance will be helped through the difficult times."

"We can get some people off the planet," said Alex. "But what about saving all the animals and plant life?"

"There are warehouses where the DNA of many animals, plants and insects and others life forms of your planet are stored. These structures have been built to survive the Earth changes.

Others have been guided to do this for decades. Now it is your task to save the people."

Sydney's nerve endings fired as she heard Arcadia's next words. "You have ushered in the new age for humanity – you are the Noah's of the modern age – and you too Brandon Tarnoff," he said looking directly into Alex's eyes.

Tarnoff almost fell over in his seat realizing Arcadia was aware he had been observing them. He had just witnessed something that seemed more like a scene out of a science fiction movie rather than a surveillance feed. He sat frozen, unable to move, not knowing what to think or do. Then a beam of light came through the ceiling of the van and surrounded him like a small tornado. He felt himself being hurled through a vortex. When the whirlwind dissipated, he found himself standing with Alex and Sydney in front of Arcadia. In shock, his hands frantically felt his body as if he were making sure all his body parts were still there. He had just experienced being disassembled atom by atom and put back together, and panic was still ripping down his spine.

"You're fine," said Arcadia reassuringly.

"Brandon Tarnoff!" exclaimed Alex in shock. "He's with Croft! He is second in command of the Brotherhood! Why have you brought *him* here?" Alex's face was red with fury at the sight of Tarnoff.

"He is here to help you," answered Arcadia trying to reassure Alex.

Tarnoff looked around as if in a daze. "You knew I was watching all along?" Tarnoff asked Arcadia, stunned by the scene around him.

"Watching? How was he watching?" interrupted Alex in bewilderment.

"We had a device implanted in your eye and ear," said Tarnoff shaking his head apologetically.

Alex grasped at his eyes and ears. "You did what?"

"You mean you've been watching everything?" asked Sydney, her expression betraying her mortification at the invasion of their private moments.

"I'm sorry," said Tarnoff. "We can remove it when we get back. John Croft is dead. I am the new leader of the OEB. Things will be different now. My eyes have been opened. The Brotherhood is an abomination. I am deeply sorry." Then he looked at Sydney, his eyes filled with compassion.

"Your friend's daughter, Beth ... Croft ordered her execution.

Sydney gasped in horror.

"No, no!" he interjected. "It didn't happen. She's okay. I had her identity changed and set her up at Oregon State University."

Sydney let out a sigh of relief. "Oh thank God. Thank you. Bless you. Does she know Brian is dead?"

"Yes, I'm sorry."

Sydney grabbed Alex's hand. "She must be so frightened, so alone. We'll have to watch out for her."

Alex nodded. "Of course," he said squeezing her hand reassuringly.

"When Croft ordered her murder, I saw him for the monster that he was. I knew I could no longer follow him. Since then I have read much about your work and have come to understand that many things will have to change," said Tarnoff.

"And change they will," said Arcadia. "You are now the most powerful man in America ... perhaps the world. You can do much good. That is why I have brought you here. Humanity is on the dawn of a new age. You have the political influence, and Alex and Sydney have the technology to bring it about. Humanity is about to join its space brethren as a star-faring civilization and undergo a shift in consciousness. The economic, political, and religious structures of the world need to shift as well."

"New consciousness?" Tarnoff asked. Alex and Sydney also looked surprised at these words.

"The galactic center is the largest black hole in the galaxy, and thus it is the largest portal to the infinite field. The Earth is moving into direct alignment with this portal."

"The event horizon," interjected Alex.

"Exactly," said Arcadia. "The same alignment that can cause the turbulent Earth changes is also bombarding the Earth with high energy particles emanating directly from the Source Field, and are changing and upgrading DNA and consciousness."

"Changing consciousness?" Sydney was incredulous.

"Think about it," said Alex. "One's consciousness would have to be altered coming into more direct contact with the Field."

"But DNA too?" asked Sydney.

"Yes, human DNA is going through an upgrade or an evolutionary leap as it does every time the solar system is in this alignment. The new upgraded bodies will be available for reincarnating souls, and those reborn on Earth will experience a completely new level of existence – one where humans can fulfill their potential and become the God-like beings they were meant to be."

Sydney, Alex and Brandon exchanged puzzled stares.

"This is the great secret that has been hidden from humanity since before your known civilizations," said Arcadia. "It has been obfuscated, shrouded behind barriers of religious dogma and political oppression. The knowledge has been handed down through the ages, known only to a select few in secret societies who have used it for personal gain and control. These bonds are about to be broken. Humanity's birthright is about to be revealed to all.

"Humans are made of God, are inseparable from God, and are God, with all the abilities to manifest reality and to transcend death itself. You are about to awaken from thousands of years of darkness. A new dawn is beginning and the evolutionary leap is upon you. Mankind is about to be transformed like a caterpillar metamorphosing into a butterfly. You have deciphered the knowledge. You now have the technology of God!"

Alex, Sydney, and Brandon stood spellbound as Arcadia's words resonated through the cavernous room.

"You now must go back," said Arcadia. "Together you will transform the world. The future is in your capable hands."

They looked at each other in knowing recognition of the mission before them. Arcadia asked them to join hands and stand in the middle of the sanctuary. A vortex of light surrounded Alex, Sydney, and Brandon, and transported them back to Earth to fulfill their destiny.

THE END

INFINITIES
BY
ALEYA ANNATON

The nocturnal sky with its luminous points of light
Spinning infinitely in the blackness of night
What is this wondrous universe of ours?
With billions of galaxies, each with billions of stars?

I fly up to the moon and out past Mars
Past Jupiter and Pluto, then on to the stars
Past Orion's Belt and the Pleiades
Beyond the Milky Way to the galaxies

The Earth has long since vanished from my view
The sun has withered to a drop of morning dew
And our galaxy has become a distant speck of light
Now fading completely from my sight

With each leap in scale my heart stands still
To fathom how the infinitely large, withers to nil
As galactic clusters become a small dim light
There is still no end in sight

I fall back to Earth to where I stand
And start another journey into my hand
Through the pores of my skin,
To the cells below and the atoms within

Each dot grows as I descend in scale
Revealing another world as I pierce the veil
Smaller and smaller without end
To eternity I descend

Infinitely large, infinitely small
We will never find an end to it all
For creation is not found in the tiniest part
It is the structure that is at matter's heart

So seek not the end of size
Nor the universe's birth or demise
For where all creation must reside
Is in how the space divides!

The ancient symbols hold the key
To the sacred geometry
Two pyramids within a ring
Can divide to create everything

Infinite fractals with infinite spin
Create the shape of Yang and Yin
David's star is a pyramid up and down
Where the conscious feedback-loop is found

Sixty-four tetrahedrons form the greatest stability
And match the I Chings' grid of reality
What the ancients knew so long ago
Was how matter ebbed and flowed

All the universe is on a spinning keel
From the tiniest particles to a galactic wheel
What force could play such a role?
If not the gravitational pull of a dynamic black hole?

A black hole at the center of all that spins
Is where matter ends and soul begins
Moving infinitely between the two
A double torus in an infinite loop

From the quiescent potential of pure energy
To the manifestation of material reality
We are tied to the Source from every atom and cell
Constantly moving in and out of the creative well

The key to heaven's door
Need not be hidden any more
The hole is the whole, is the Holy place
With omniscient energy to embrace

With each breath I expel
I see the transparency of this mortal shell
Dare we not forget where we trod
For everywhere is the face of God

FUNDAMENTAL PHYSICS TERMS GLOSSARY

ANGULAR MOMENTUM
    Standard Definition: With respect to a reference point (closed system), a measure of the extent and direction to which an object rotates about the reference point.
    Holofractographic theory: Within an open system, the relationship of two points experiencing consecutive presence in which the entities undo and redo themselves (pulsing in and out of the vacuum) in such a way to appear as rotating around one another.

AFFINE CONNECTION
    An affine connection is a geometrical object on a smooth manifold, which connects nearby tangent spaces. In the presence of singularity, the affine connection becomes undefined since it loses continuity and differentiability in the standard approach.

BLACK HOLE-WHITE HOLE – BLACK/WHITE WHOLE
Standard Definition:
    Black Hole: An astrophysical object with a gravitational field so strong that nothing, not even light, can escape it.
    White Hole: An astrophysical body that is the time reversal of a black hole. A black hole acts as a point mass that attracts and absorbs matter. A white hole acts as a point mass that repels or ejects matter.

HolofractographicTheory:
    Black/WhiteWhole: Terminology describing the same object as above (black hole), however, in this

case, due to the torsional and coriolis effects generated by a space-time torque as defined in the Haramein-Rauscher solution, the surface event horizon is no longer smooth. This generates wave interactions of a holographic and fractal nature, resulting in the emission of information from the surroundings of the black hole (the white hole portion) which we experience as the radiation of electromagnetic fields.

BOSON
Subatomic particles having integer spin that transmit forces.

CHARGE
Standard Definition: An intrinsic property of matter responsible for all electric phenomena,, in particular for the force of the electromagnetic interaction, occurring in two forms arbitrarily designated negative and positive. **Holofractographic Theory:** An effect resulting from a slight polarization of the vacuum energy at the surface event horizon of black/white wholes (at all scales) generating the electromagnetic field.

CORIOLIS EFFECT
In physics, the coriolis effect is an apparent deflection of moving objects when they are viewed from a rotating reference frame. The coriolis force is proportional to the speed of rotation and the centrifugal force is proportional to its square. The coriolis force acts in a direction perpendicular to the rotation axis and to the velocity of the body in the rotating frame, and is proportional to the object's speed in the rotating frame. On Earth the coriolis effect deflects moving bodies to the right in the northern hemisphere and to the left in the southern hemisphere.

COMOLOGY
The study of the total Universe and humanity's relationship to it.

CURVATURE
The amount by which a geometric object such as space-time deviates from being flat.

ELECTROMAGNETIC RADIATION
Described as a self-propagating wave in space with electric and magnetic components. Examples include light, radio and microwaves.

ELECTRON CLOUD
Electrons around the atomic nuclei.

ERGOSPHERE
The ergosphere is a region located outside a rotating black hole that typically contains large amounts of plasma and dust. The ergosphere is ellipsoidal in shape and is situated so that at the poles of a rotating black hole, it touches the event horizon and stretches out to a distance that is equal to the radius of the event horizon. Within the ergosphere, space-time is dragged along in the direction of the rotation of the black hole. This process is known as the Lense-Thirring effect or frame dragging.

EUCLIDIAN FLAT SPACE
Standard Definition: A mathematical space in which two parallel lines never meet.
Holofractographic Theory: No such space exists as every point is curved to infinity (no flat space).

EVENT HORIZON
Standard Definition: In general relativity, a boundary in space-time surrounding a black hole with respect to an outside observer beyond which events cannot affect the observer.

Holofractographic Theory: In general relativity with the Haramein-Rauscher solution, the boundary surrounding a black hole which divides the collapsing function (black hole) and the expanding function (white hole) of space-time.

FIBONACCI SERIES

A sequence of numbers beginning with 0 and 1 where each subsequent number is the sum of the previous two. For example, O, 1+1= 2, 2+1= 3, 3+2=5, 5+3=8, 8+5=13, etc.. Note that the ratio between two consecutive numbers approaches the phi ratio (1.618) but never reaches it, each division missing the absolute phi sequentially above (larger number) and below. For example, 3 divided by 2 is 1.5 (just under phi) and 5 divided by 3 is 1.666 (just over phi). Each consecutive division comes closer to approximating phi but never reaches it. These ratios are typical of one's found in nature everywhere, from the coil of a snail shell, the branching patterns of a tree or the nervous system of a human body.

FIELD EQUATION

An equation in a physical theory that describes how a fundamental force or a combination of such forces interacts with matter.

FRACTAL

A shape that is recursively constructed or self-similar, i.e. a shape that appears similar at all scales of magnification and is referred to as infinitely complex.

FRAME DRAGGING

Albert Einstein's theory of general relativity Predicts that rotating bodies drag space-time around themselves in a phenomenon referred to as frame dragging. It is also known as the Lense-Thirring effect.

FUNDAMENTAL FORCES
Standard Definition: The four fundamental forces of nature, namely: electromagnetism, gravity, the weak force (radioactivity), and the nuclear strong force (proton/neutron interaction).
Holofractographic Theory: The two fundamental forces of nature, namely gravitation and electromagnetic radiation.

GENERAL RELATIVITY
The Theory of Gravitation developed by Einstein that unites Special Relativity and the classical Newtonian view of gravity where the curvature or deformation in space-time is due to mass energy producing the gravitational effect.

GLUEON
Standard Definition: Subatomic particles that mediate interactions (the strong force) between quarks.
Holofractographic Theory: Replaced by the gravitational component of atomic and subatomic interacting black holes.

GRAND UNIFICATION THEORY (GUT)
Any theory in physics that unifies these fundamental gauge symmetries: hypercharge, the weak force, and quantum chromo dynamics.

GRAVITATIONAL FIELD
A field generated by massive objects that determines the magnitude and direction of gravitation experienced by other massive objects.

GRAVITY
A property by which all objects attract each other.

GYROSCOPIC EFFECT
The gyroscopic effect can be best explained as the principle of

behavior of a gyroscope. According to the equation that describes gyroscope behavior, a torque on the gyroscope applied perpendicular to its axis of rotation and also perpendicular to its angular momentum causes it to rotate about an axis perpendicular to both the torque and the angular momentum. This rotational motion is referred to as precession.

HARMONIC SCALE

A set of harmonic waves, that are component frequencies of a signal which are integer multiples of a fundamental frequency.

HOLOIMAGER

A fictional communication device that displays a real-time holographic image.

HYPERDIMENSIONAL

Standard Definition: Any dimensions above 3-D.
Holofractographic Theory: All dimensions present in each point.

ISOTROPY – ISOTROPIC

Isotropy is uniformity in all directions.

LINEAR GEOMETRY

A structure of points and lines possessing the characteristics of having at least two lines, with every line incident with at least two points, and for any given pair of points, there is exactly one line incident.

MANIFOLD

In mathematics, more specifically in differential geometry and topology, a manifold is a mathematical space that on a small enough scale resembles the Euclidean space of a certain dimension, called the dimension of the manifold.

METRIC

A system of parameters of periodic or Quantitative assessment of a process to be measured, as in space-time metric.

NONLINEAR TIME

The radial structure of time recursively replicating to infinity in all directions (expansion and contraction) from any point in the Holofractographic Universe. This function is the result of the observable nonlinear mechanical behavior of orbiting bodies (angular momentum) in an infinite fractal Universe. For instance, an atom is embedded in the rotation of the Earth, the Earth is embedded in the rotation of our galaxy, and so onto infinity or, in the other direction, to infinitely small.

PHI RATIO

The "golden ratio," denoted by 1.618 expresses the relationship that the sum of two quantities is to the larger quantity as the larger quantity is to the smaller. The total length of A+B is to the length of the longer segment A as the length of A is to the shorter segment B.

PLANCK DENSITY

Standard Definition: Generally given as 10^{93} gm/cm^3. It can be calculated by stacking little Planck volumes a cubic centimeter of space. Take a Planck length (see Planck length) and cube it, you will get 4.22×10^{99} per cm^3. Now divide a cm^3 by that number so you can get how many Planck volumes there are in a cm3 and you will get 2.37×10^{98}. Then multiply it by the Planck mass 2.18×10^{-5} gm (which is the mass of each Planck length) and you will obtain a density of 5.166×10^{93} gm per cm^3. This is commonly given as well as an approximation 10^{94} gm/cm^3.

Holofractographic Theory: Fundamental constant of the natural world resulting from the fractalization of the structure of space-time. In this view, this fundamental density is infinite and defines the boundary of our experience due to our scale relationship to it.

PLANCK LENGTH

Standard Definition: A fundamental constant of nature commonly expressed as 1.66 x 10 -33cm. Current standard theory suggests it is the smallest distance or size about which anything can be known.

Holofractographic Theory: Fundamental constant of the natural world resulting from the fractalization of the structure of space-time. In this view, this fundamental distance has infinite discreteness.   But defines the boundary of our experience due to our scale relationship to it.

PLASMA

A fourth state of matter. An ionized gas, usually considered to be a distinct phase of matter in contrast to solids, liquids, and gases because of its unique properties.

PLATONIC SOLIDS

The five geometric convex regular polyhedron shapes: tetrahedron (4), hexahedron or cube (6), octahedron (8), dodecahedron (12), icosahedron (20).

POLARIZATION

Standard Definition: The property of electromagnetic waves described by the specific direction of their transverse electric field.

Holofractographic Theory: The change in polarity between one level of a fractal event horizon and another (coined nonlinear polarity); for instance, the change of polarity between the electron shell (negative charge) and its nucleus (positive charge).

PRECESSION

A periodic change in the direction of the axis of a rotating object, such as a gyroscope.

QUANTA

Standard Definition: The smallest indivisible entity of energy in quantum theory.

Holofractographic Theory: A change in energy states resulting from the discreteness of the fractal structure of space-time.

QUANTUM THEORY

A term that may be used to refer to several related types of theories which make use of quanta or discrete units of energy as in quantum electrodynamics.

QUANTUM VACUUM

According to present-day understanding of what is called the vacuum state or the quantum vacuum, the vacuum is not truly empty but instead contains fleeting electromagnetic waves and particles that pop into and out of existence and its energy is related to the zero-point energy and the Planck density.

QUARK

Standard Definition: A fermion in the Standard Model which has half-integer spin which make up protons (3), neutrons (3), and mesons (2).

Holofractographic Theory: Singularity structure at the center of the black hole proton.

QUASAR

(Quasi-stellar radio source) An astronomical source of high electromagnetic energy, which shows a very high red shift i.e. quasars are the most distant objects in the Universe and generally are extremely large.

RELATIVITY

The theory of relativity, or simply relativity, generally refers to two theories of Albert Einstein: special relativity and general relativity.

RENORMALIZATION

A collection of techniques used to produce finite mathematical relationships or approximate relationships between observable quantities, when the assumption that the parameters of the theory are finite breaks down, giving the result that many observables are infinite.

RESONANCE

In physics, resonance is the tendency of a system to oscillate at larger amplitude as some frequencies than at others. These are known as the system's resonant frequencies (or resonance frequencies). At these frequencies, even small periodic driving forces can produce large amplitude vibrations, because the system stores vibrational energy. When damping is small, the resonant frequency is approximately equal to the natural frequency of the system, which is the frequency of free vibrations. Resonant systems can be used to generate vibrations of a specific frequency (i.e. musical instruments). Or pick out specific frequencies from a complex vibration containing many frequencies. For example, in an auditorium filled with tuning forks of different frequencies, if one is struck, all other tuning forks of the same frequency in the auditorium will resonate sympathetically (sympathetic resonance). Resonance was discovered by Galileo Galilei with his investigations of pendulums and musical strings beginning in 1602.

SCALAR

A measure of energy that has no associated vector (direction).

SCHWARZSCHILD RADIUS

In 1916, Karl Schwarzschild obtained an exact solution to

Einstein's field equations for the gravitational field outside a non-rotating, spherically symmetric body. The term is used in physics and astronomy, especially in the theory of gravitation, and general relativity. The Schwarzschild radius (sometimes historically referred to as the gravitational radius) is a characteristic radius associated with every quantity of mass. It is the radius of a sphere in space, containing a correspondingly sufficient amount of mass (and therefore, reaches a certain density), then the force of gravity from the contained mass would be so great that no known force or degeneracy pressure could stop the mass from continuing to collapse in volume into a point of infinite density – a gravitational singularity (colloquially referred to as a black hole).

SHEARING
The deformation of a material substance in which parallel internal surfaces slide past one another.

SINE WAVE
A continuous curved sinusoidal waveform consisting of peaks and troughs.

SINGULARITY
An infinity occurring in an astrophysical model, involving infinite curvature in the space-time continuum, associated with models of black holes, white holes and worm holes.

SPACE-TIME
A mathematical model that combines three dimensional space and one-dimensional time into a single construct called the space-time continuum, in which time plays the role of the 4th dimension.

SPACE-TIME GRID
A coordinate grid in space-time that is the set of curves obtained if three out of four coordinate functions are related to a constant.

SPACE-TIME MANIFOLD

A four-dimensional pseudo-Riemannian (non-Euclidian geometry) manifold and a phase space in classical mechanics that are used to model space-time in general relativity.

SPECIAL RELATIVITY

Einstein's theory of light which posits all frames of reference in uniform motion to be relative, i.e. there is no absolute frame of reference. Therefore, all frames of reference will always measure the speed of light to be the same.

STANDARD MODEL

A theory in particle physics which describes the strong, weak and electromagnetic forces.

STRING THEORY

A model whose building blocks are one-dimensional extended objects (strings) rather than the zero-dimensional points (particles), which is the basis of the Standard Model. New mathematical and physical ideas are required to mesh together its very different mathematical formulations, one of which is the 11-dimensional M-theory, which requires space-time to have eleven dimensions, as opposed to the usual three spatial dimensions and the fourth dimension of time.

THEORETICAL PHYSICS

Employs mathematical models and abstractions of physics to explain physical experiments.

TOPOLOGY

The branch of geometry that studies the continuity (topological equivalence) of geometrical figures when they are stretched or bent - but not broken.

TORQUE

A rotational force, e.g., the force applied to a lever, multiplied by its distance from the lever's fulcrum.

TORSION
Twisting, wrenching or distortion of a body or manifold segment by exertion of forces along a longitudinal axis.

TORUS
A donut-shaped surface of revolution generated by revolving a circle in three-dimensional space about an axis coplanar with the circle, which does not touch the circle. The fundamental topological geometry associated with all microscopic and macroscopic objects in the Haramein-Rauscher Solution.

TRANSDUCER
A device that converts one form of energy into another.

UNCERTAINTY PRINCIPLE
States that one cannot measure conjugate (simultaneous) quantum quantities such as position and momentum with arbitrary precision.

VACUUM
Standard Definition: Space that is empty of matter.
Holofractographic Theory: Contracted space that is infinitely dense.

VECTOR EQUILIBRIUM/ CUBOCTAHEDRON
The only possible geometry in equilibrium in all vectorial directions (other than the sphere) due to the fact that the length of the radiating vectors and the edge vectors are equal.

WAVEFORM
The shape and form of a signal, such as waves moving across the surface of water, acoustic pressure waves or electromagnetic waves.

Made in the USA
Middletown, DE
30 October 2018